## Praise for The Sentinel Trilogy

*"If you love action and mystery then this is for you"* –
Guardian Children's Books

*"Unsettling and entertaining... A very tasty trilogy"* – SciFi Now

*"Sentinel sets a dark, gritty tone. The action is fast and violent, the monsters, including a seductive vampiress, are memorable"* – The Sun

*"Solidly entertaining"* – Starburst

*"Not for the faint-hearted"* – The Book Bag

*"This is one of those books that I started and couldn't stop until it was finished. It has hints of Rowling, Clare, and even Whedon, but still stands on its own. Take a gamble on this one, lovers of YA; I promise you won't be disappointed"* – MiniMac Reviews

*"A sort of Buffy meets Shadowhunters meets Morse! I liked this a lot"* –
Elizabeth Corr, co-author of The Witch's Kiss Trilogy

*"I wish there had been more books like this around when I was a teen. I would have devoured them all, one after another"* – The Eloquent Page

# SPLINTER

First published in 2018 by
Peridot Press
12 Deben Mill Business Centre, Melton,
Woodbridge, Suffolk IP12 1BL

ISBN: 978-1-911382-85-0

Set and designed by Theoria Design
www.theoriadesign.com

Visit: www.thesentineltrilogy.com
Follow: @SentinelTrilogy
Like: facebook.com/SentinelTrilogy

JOSHUA WINNING

EVEN
GODS DIE...

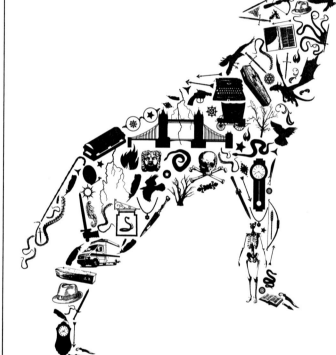

# SPLINTER

BOOK THREE OF THE SENTINEL TRILOGY

## BOOKS BY JOSHUA WINNING

**The Sentinel Trilogy**
Sentinel
Ruins
Splinter

**Sentinel Novellas**
Witchpin

**Also by Joshua Winning**
Vicious Rumer
Camp Carnage

# THE STORY SO FAR

After discovering he was a Sentinel, Nicholas Hallow used his special abilities as a Sensitive to fight Malika, who had schemed to return the Dark Prophets to the world. With the help of his friends Dawn, Merlyn, and Rae, Nicholas succeeded in closing the gateway opened by Malika and her evil cohort, Laurent. But unbeknownst to Nicholas, Malika had secretly delivered three pods that, one day soon, will hatch the Dark Prophets.

Steadfast hero Sam Wilkins also survived an encounter with Malika, but at a price. During a battle in an abandoned school, his friend Liberty Rayne was killed. Isabel Hallow transferred her soul from the body of a cat into that of an old headmistress, while former safehouse landlady Aileen came out of the battle relatively unscathed, but desperate to find her granddaughter Dawn.

Meanwhile, at Hallow House, Jessica Bell seemed to have lost her mind. The woman who served as a guide to the Sentinels was falling apart, and appeared to have killed her bodyguard, Lash. She was discovered by Esus, an emissary of the Trinity, who feared the Sentinels were about to crumble from the inside...

# A BRIEF GLOSSARY OF TERMS

The Trinity
God-like figures revered by the Sentinels. Centuries ago, they retired after defeating the Dark Prophets, but they're prophesied to return when the world needs them most.

Vaktarin
Translating from the old tongue as "guardian", the Vaktarin is a powerful, benevolent priestess who guides the Sentinels.

Esus
An ancient creature who served the Trinity, Esus is formidable and unpredictable. Nobody has ever seen his face, which is hidden behind a silver mask.

Sentinels
Guards. Detectives. Killers. Sentinels are the agents of the Trinity. They're stationed all over the world and it's their job to watch for signs of emergent evil and protect the innocent.

Hunters
Elite Sentinels, Hunters are prize fighters who track demons.

Sensitives
A select few Sentinels who are born with psychic abilities.

Demonologists
Experts in all things monster.

The Dark Prophets
The most feared demons in existence, they spread chaos and destruction. They were banished to the demon planes by the Trinity during the Great Battle.

Malika
A vicious manipulator who is believed to be unkillable, and who can control the weak-minded. She was the Familiar of the demon Diltraa.

Diltraa
A demon that succeeded in breaching Hallow House but was killed by Esus.

Harvesters
Savage and skilled in battle, they're experts at infiltration and disguise, and use a weaponised gauntlet, which is rumoured to turn Sentinels evil.

# PROLOGUE

1 DECEMBER, 1992

MUSIC THROBBED THROUGH THE NIGHTCLUB AND she felt it in her blood, hot and alive. Red lights strobed, making twitching puppets of the figures on the dance floor. Speakers thumped a mind-numbing Christmas classic. Her stomach grumbled and the woman's gaze slipped over the revellers, hunger prickling into irritation.

"Boring, boring," she murmured.

She'd find somewhere else. Somewhere quieter. Somewhere people's thoughts weren't being smashed apart by a moronic beat. As she turned toward the exit, though, her body went rigid. Her cat-like eyes glimmered at a couple of young men nursing beers at the bar. They were identical in every way. Hair gelled up. Woolly jumpers. Eyes a little too far apart. Something about them made the hunger worse.

"Let me guess, you're Rudolph," she said as she leaned into the bar beside them.

The two men stopped talking.

The guy in the reindeer jumper nodded at her question.

"Red's my favourite," she purred.

"I can tell. What's your name?"

"Stacey."

"What's your real name?"

She turned the full power of her gaze on them and knew she had them.

It didn't take her long to get them outside. They stood shivering in the alley behind the club, just the three of them, their eyes all over her body, the short red skirt and leather jacket she'd picked for exactly that reason.

"Aren't you cold?" they asked, their teeth chattering.

"No."

He dragged on a cigarette. His brother finished his beer and tossed it, showing off. She liked it.

"You're not from 'round here are you?" they asked.

Even their voices were the same.

"You don't have an accent but you're… different."

"Unlike you," she said, baring her teeth, and they grinned back, crinkling in the same places. Where was the join? Where was the place where one twin started and the other stopped?

The hunger multiplied inside until it was all she could feel.

In the cold of the alley, she unwrapped their bodies like Christmas gifts. They didn't make a sound. Oozing red. Steam filling the air.

They were the same after all. Inside and out.

Nobody was like her. She peered at the blood pooling on the cobbles, seeing her tentacle-like hair reflected, her eyes, her icy skin, and wondered where she started and everything else stopped.

★

Present Day

Malika observed the still waters of the swimming pool. They were grimy and the surface rippled with oil. She caught her reflection, trapped suddenly by the memory of the nightclub, then shook it off. That was decades ago. She had been bored. Searching. Now, years later, she had finally found what she needed. The thing that gave her purpose.

Three objects rested in the pool's soupy depths. They resembled leathery boulders. Veiny and faintly pulsing. If she listened, she could hear them clicking, a sound like scrabbling insects.

It was difficult to listen, though, with somebody howling and squirming in her grasp. The cries bounced around the atrium, splitting apart the foggy gloom and threatening to shatter the glass ceiling.

"Scream all you like," Malika told the man. "It only excites them."

He was in his forties. From the look of him, he had been living off vermin and drain water for weeks. They had found him picking through the bins at the back of the leisure centre and she could discern his bones through the tatty jacket and trousers. But he would do. The Dark Prophets were hungry and they were not picky.

"What are you doing?" the man shrieked. "What's happening?"

"Listen and you'll hear them," she hissed, twisting an arm behind his back and forcing his face close to the water. "Whatever questions you have shall be answered by them."

The terror in his eyes was invigorating. Her marble grin bounced back at her from the boggy pool water, and it appeared to unnerve him even more. Malika's insides quivered with pleasure as he squirmed, though he was too weak to free himself.

"You should feel honoured," she whispered. "Your sacrifice will nourish the Dark Prophets. Make them strong. Bring them to us all the sooner."

"S-s-sacrifice?"

She opened his throat with her nails and seized the scruff of his jacket, suspending him over the water so that every precious drop of his blood splashed into the pool. He gurgled and thrashed for a while before going limp, and Malika tossed him into the water to be devoured.

"Yessss," she purred, watching as the blood swirled and then moved as if drawn by a magnetic current toward the pods. They convulsed and clicked as they consumed the dark liquid, and the atrium trembled, then grew still.

Malika's smile faltered. The ripples in the pool had split her into three. For a moment, she was mesmerised by the fractured image, lost in thought. Digging her nails into her palms, she shoved away the past, watching as her mirror image shuddered back into one.

"Soon Hallow House will crumble," she murmured. "And with it the world."

# CHAPTER ONE
## Running

NICHOLAS HALLOW SKIDDED TO A STOP just before the tentacles latched onto his face. He cartwheeled sideways to duck out of the way as they thrashed at him from the wall, viper-thin and barbed. Crouching low, he squeezed an axe in his palm and grimaced at the sight of the creature, which clung to a shop sign above his head. The demon was the size of a basketball and, somewhere in the centre of the flailing mass of tentacles, it emitted a whistling screech of irritation at having missed its target.

"Do you even have a mouth?" Nicholas panted.

The screech echoed through the derelict shopping centre and he shuddered as things in the walls gibbered back. The Lion Yard had once been a bustling retail outlet filled with shops and cafés. Now, like most of Cambridge, it was abandoned. Overgrown with deadly plants and overrun with monsters. Nobody shopped here anymore because nobody shopped in Cambridge at all. The city was half-empty. Maybe more than half. Like Bury St Edmunds, it had been consumed by some kind of evil that Nicholas still hadn't uncovered.

Backing away from the shop, Nicholas fixed his gaze on the krypist demon that had latched onto its awning. His right forearm itched. It was still in a plaster cast, a souvenir from his run-in with the flying demons that had plucked him from the ground and then thrown him back at it. Dawn had started complaining about the cast's smell but Nicholas wasn't ready to cut it off. He had grown attached to it. And what if his arm wasn't fully healed? He couldn't exactly check into the hospital for a replacement. The hospital was worse than the Lion Yard.

As more demonic shrieks convulsed through the shopping centre, Nicholas flashed a nervous glance at the escalator he had just chased the demon up. Then he peered over the side of the walkway, eyeing the boarded-up shop windows on the level below. He sensed the demons as shadowy smudges. He was getting better at using his powers to isolate them, but they moved so fast sometimes it was impossible to keep up. He had no idea how many were targeting him.

Above him, the krypist mewled and thrashed its barbed tentacles, preparing to attack. Although it didn't have any eyes, Nicholas could tell it knew exactly where he was crouched. What was it waiting for?

*Rae. Where are you?*

He boomeranged the thought through the Lion Yard. A little trick he had learnt.

*Busy.*

Rae's voice rang in his head and he cursed. What use was being able to communicate psychically when Rae always made it so difficult? He could sense her a few shops away. She always appeared on his radar as an angry red cluster of sparks, like a firework. He wondered if she could sense him, too. He'd never asked.

*Gee, thanks*, he thought at Rae, and then he yelped as the krypist hurled itself at him, a tangled ball of thorny tentacles. He swung the axe, but before the blade came near the creature, something coiled around his ankle and yanked Nicholas's legs out from under him. A second bogey.

His chin cracked against the floor and through the pain he felt a wriggling mass clamber onto his back. Why hadn't he sensed it sneaking up on him? Today's extermination must have taken it out of him.

Ignoring his throbbing jaw, Nicholas heaved himself up, attempting to free his arms as the krypist's tentacles wound about his torso. It hugged his makeshift armour and his ribs creaked agonisingly as the breath was crushed from his lungs. He threw up an arm but the monster's barbs sank into his plaster cast, and then tore free.

Howling, Nicholas rolled onto his back, crushing the krypist beneath him. It squealed and thrashed and Nicholas thrust the axe over his shoulder, hearing the squelch as it hit its mark. The tentacles released him and his chest inflated with air. Before he could gasp more than a single breath, the second kryptist flew at him and Nicholas rolled out of the way just in time, wrenching his axe from the floor and burying it in the monster. It belched purple blood all over him and then lay still.

"Gross, *gross, gross.*" Nicholas clambered to his feet, crumpling his nose at the blood smeared across his armour. Then he stopped and marvelled at his freed forearm. The demon had torn his cast clean off. He inspected the pale flesh of his arm. Aside from appearing a little withered and grubby, it seemed okay. He flexed and watched the muscles quiver.

"Thank god," said a female voice. "I thought I was going to have to cut that thing off in your sleep."

Nicholas grinned as Dawn clomped up the escalator. She was dressed in the same makeshift armour as him – a chest plate strapped over her purple hoody, and knee and elbow pads. A week ago they had raided one of the sports outlets and it was the best thing they had done since arriving in Cambridge.

"It feels… weird," he said, flexing his fingers as she approached. "I think I might–"

"If you say anything about putting that thing back on, I'm leaving you to the krypists."

He stuck out his bottom lip and she gave him a stare that said she meant it. Between the three of them, Dawn had changed the most. She had been overweight and shy when he met her, hiding behind her violet hair. In the month since they had left Bury St Edmunds, though, she had become thinner, harder; perpetually battle ready. He supposed shy people had nothing to be shy about when all the people were gone.

"Get what you were looking for?" he asked.

She held up a couple of books. "Not even close. For some reason, the library insisted on stocking *fiction.* Nowhere near enough occult stuff."

He shook his head. "You can't get the libraries these days."

"I got one for you." She handed him a book.

*The Idiots' Guide To Surviving The Apocalypse.*

"Funny," he said.

"Thought it might be useful."

"Weirdly, you might be right."

They still hadn't figure out exactly what was going on in Cambridge.

All they knew was that demons were everywhere, and more were arriving every day. Nicholas had no idea why, or where they were coming from, unless it was something Malika and Laurent had done. The red-haired witch and her perfectly manicured ally were in service to the Dark Prophets. They had tried to raise them in the ruins of the Abbey Gardens, but they had failed. Nicholas and his friends had stopped them, but that didn't seem to have made much difference. The world was crumbling around them, and Nicholas was determined to find out why.

"Where's Rae?" Dawn asked.

Twenty feet away, a shop window exploded and spat a figure to the floor. A dark-skinned girl leapt up just as a third krypist launched itself through the window, a snarled bundle of thorny limbs. Rae gestured with her hands and the demon detonated mid-air, splattering a halo of blood and mucus all over her.

"Nice," Nicholas said.

Rae wiped her face, flicking gooey strands to the floor.

"You okay?" he asked.

She shot him a look, as if assessing whether or not he really meant it. "Fine."

*One day I'll teach you some non-monosyllables.*

He had thought it at her before he realised what he was doing, and Rae's stare scorched the air between them.

"Sorry," he said.

"What happened?" asked Dawn. She seemed to notice the look he and Rae were giving each other. "Guys, you promised. When I'm around, use your indoor voices."

"Sorry." He was apologising a lot lately. For not having a decent place to live. For what happened in Bury. For the evil that was polluting Cambridgeshire. But when it came to the way he and Rae could communicate, he got it. Dawn couldn't hear them, so it was like they were whispering behind their hands. Sometimes it was just easier than speaking aloud, though.

Dawn checked her watch. "We should get back. It'll be dark soon."

"You mean darker," said Nicholas.

"Right."

"You sure you got everything you could from the library? I don't want to come back here any time soon."

"I'm good," she said, bundling the books into her backpack.

"Then let's get the hell out of here."

Hoisting the axe over his shoulder, Nicholas led the way down the escalator and past the gutted shops of the Lion Yard, all of them caked in leaves and mould and dried blood. He sensed the monsters in the dark but nothing emerged to challenge them. Anxiously, Nicholas ran a hand over his scalp. He had shaved off his curls and the short bristles felt velvety against his palm.

They were all changing. He supposed it was adapt or die when you were staring down the end of the world.

As they made their way towards the exit, he rubbed his shoulder. For a second he had felt a weight there, as if Isabel was perched by his ear, the way she used to. The black cat was dead, though. He had seen it in the ruins of the school in Bury. He didn't know if that meant Isabel was gone too. She was a powerful witch who had already survived death more than once. He dared to hope she was somehow alive, but in a world turned upside-down, that hope felt small and naive.

"You okay?" Dawn asked.

He found her gaze and nodded. She was good at sensing his moods, even though she had no special powers beyond an intimidating intelligence. Perhaps he wore melancholy too obviously. Before he could say anything, they had reached the gates that led out onto St Andrews Street.

He peered through, scanning for bogies.

Above the buildings, sickly green clouds thickened in the sky. The sun was a gauzy outline struggling to penetrate them and the street was deathly quiet. Most of the buildings on St Andrews Street were deserted. Some bore scorch marks, others had been half demolished by whatever demons happened to be passing through. The whole city had fallen into ruin and Nicholas often wondered where everybody had actually gone. North, maybe? Perhaps the servants of the Dark Prophets hadn't made it up there yet.

He sensed nothing beyond the usual. Sometimes he caught the patter of a heartbeat and saw the muscle flutter in his mind. Other times he felt the sharpness of a fang or smelled rotting breath. Most disturbing were the occasions he sensed the hunger of the things prowling the darkness and his own belly grumbled in response. Were he and the monsters all that different? They were all fighting for survival.

"Clear," he said, shoving the gate and prowling out into the street, his axe clenched in his fists. Rae and Dawn followed close at his back. They had only been in Cambridge for a few weeks and Nicholas could hardly remember what the city had been like before. A month ago, he had watched Bury St Edmunds burn, spewing demons from the hell-pit in the Abbey Gardens. They had spread quickly, devouring the surrounding towns. It had reached Cambridge before Nicholas and the girls had. The city had already been torn apart when they arrived.

Nicholas had wanted to yell and scream at the sight of it, but he forced the impulse down, burying it. He didn't want to upset the others.

Cambridge had fallen. Those who hadn't died had fled. Corpses had littered the streets, propped up in bus shelters and hidden in basements, and the whole city stank. Dawn suggested burning the corpses left out in the open, and although Nicholas had balked at the thought, they had dragged the bodies into a heap on Jesus Green and torched the lot. If nothing else, it would stop them being corrupted by demons.

"Wait." Nicholas held up a hand, tensing. He could swear he had heard something, maybe claws on tarmac, but it had been days since they had come across another living person. He pushed his mind into the air, scanning the area, but there were no bogies in this street nor the next.

He cast the girls a glance over his shoulder. They didn't seem to have heard anything, so they carried on down Hobson Street and were soon at The King Street Run.

"Home sweet pub," Nicholas murmured as they skirted around the side of the abandoned building. They went in the back like thieves. The front was still boarded up and nothing had tried to break in during the five days they had holed up there.

They squeezed through the toilet window. Once they were inside, Rae set to work covering it up with a plank of wood. She was good at finding places to crash. A perk of growing up on the streets, he supposed, and the pub was her best find yet – cosier than the draughty greenhouse and the stinky caravan they had sheltered in on their way to Cambridge. When they first reached the city, they had been forced to hole up in a rusty tin bucket of an ambulance.

Nicholas made his way into the dim bar, sighing with relief as he struggled out of his armour.

"Door one, good," he said, dropping the chest-plate onto the bar and checking the place over to make sure none of the boards on the doors or windows had come loose. "Door two, good. Window one, excellent." The faces in the yellowing photos behind the bar seemed to follow him as he went. A sign by the toilets told him it was curry night. Still. He'd kill for a curry, but the pub's basement had flooded at some point, destroying most of the food stocked there.

Satisfied their little holiday home was secure, he collapsed onto a sofa that smelled of beer, stretching out on his back and examining his newly-freed forearm.

"I could murder a milkshake," he murmured, kneading the pale flesh. No pain jagged through the newly formed bone. He had healed. Nicholas sniffed. He had seen plenty of magic in the past few months, but none of it beat the human body's ability to put itself back together.

At the bar, Dawn hopped onto a stool and flipped through one of the books she had taken from the library.

"I've been dreaming about Big Macs for weeks," she said.

"Remember fry-ups? And ketchup?" His stomach gurgled.

"Here." Rae tossed something at him as she joined them. Nicholas caught the bag of crisps and stared at Rae in surprise.

"Where'd you get these?"

"Back there."

He assumed she meant the Lion Yard. He watched Rae drop a second packet onto the bar beside Dawn and then go to study the chalkboard above the fireplace.

"Where's yours?" he asked, his mouth filling with saliva as he clutched the bag. They hadn't eaten since that morning, and that had only been half a rotten bagel. His stomach cramped with sudden craving. He was hungry all the time. Especially when they had been hunting. Sensing bit into his energy as if he were an apple. It burned more calories than running for his life.

"Ate them," said Rae.

Nicholas couldn't tell if she was lying. Even with their strange, Trinity-forged connection, she was almost impossible to read. If she really had already eaten, good for her. If not, he would make sure she got a bigger portion from the tin of beans they were saving for dinner. He tore open the pack.

"Wan' some?" he asked through a mouthful.

She shook her head and Nicholas was too hungry to insist.

"Whadooo lookun ah?" he asked.

Rae gave him an unimpressed glare and he forced down the hunk of crisps he had been rolling around his mouth.

"What you looking at?" he repeated, propping himself up on the sofa.

She nodded at the chalkboard. Dawn had scrawled all over it. In the *Specials* column she had made a list:

*Elvis Presley.*
*Creepy well.*
*Malika.*
*Laurent.*
*D. Prophets.*

A shopping list of evil. Or potential evil. Nicholas had been trying for weeks to decipher the visions that kept filling his head. The one of Elvis Presley was the weirdest. All he saw was the rock star's quiff and sparkly glasses. Then there was the well, but they hadn't found a well anywhere on their travels and the riddle was starting to grate. He had no idea how either related to their quest.

In the *Cocktail Club* section of the board were the words:

*Trinity.*
*Jessica.*
*Esus.*

A shopping list of good. Jessica was the Vaktarin, a sort-of queen to the Sentinels, although the Sentinels didn't really have a monarchy. She was more of a protector or a figurehead. Somebody to turn to when the world went to hell. Like now, for instance.

Nicholas grimaced at the thought of Esus, the phantom who could transform into a raven. He only ever had biting words for Nicholas.

And then there was the Trinity…

"Ready for another go?" he asked Rae.

She nodded and Nicholas hopped up, picking crumbs out of his T-shirt and nibbling them. You couldn't waste anything these days.

They sat facing each other before the cold hearth, their crossed legs almost touching. Rae was intimidating this close. Her dark eyes gleamed at him and no matter how hard he tried to return her stare, he always blinked first.

He sensed Dawn half-watching them from the counter.

"I really think it'll work this time," he said.

"Mhmm," said Rae.

She was good at limiting his expectations.

"Same deal?" he asked.

"You're the psychic one."

"And you're the crabby one."

"Ladies," said Dawn. "What if you tried not bickering?"

Nicholas shrugged and took Rae's outstretched hands. She always felt hot, like she was running a fever, and he tried not to think about how she could incinerate him in seconds if she wanted to. All the books said she was his protector. He was the mind; she was the muscle. They were supposed to be a pair, chosen by the Trinity as their champions, so why did they always seem to rub each other up the wrong way?

"Thekla. Athania. Norlath."

He recited the names of the Trinity, the ancient gods he was supposed to resurrect.

"Show us. Show us the way."

His vision dimmed. The pub blurred and disappeared. He felt the silvery connection between him and Rae, like a silkworm's thread. Then, in the gloom of the spirit plane, something emerged.

*The well nestles in shadow but he has no idea where it is. A garden? A park? The darkness weaves around the well like a physical thing, obscuring it.*

*Elvis Presley's sunglasses gleam through the fog. The pearly white grin and the unmistakable chin.*

"Same old, same old," muttered Nicholas, the familiar images trying his patience. "It's like a bad TV rerun. Give us something new."

*You feel that?* asked Rae, her voice in his head.

*Feel?*

That was meant to be his thing. He felt, she flamed. Had Rae sensed something he hadn't? He released a slow breath, attempting to curb his irritation at the lack of new information, and imagined his muscles growing lighter, becoming only breath, until all he heard was the wave of air entering and leaving his nostrils.

*There. A prick of light in the dark. The light flickers and as he strains toward it, it glimmers gold.*

*"Show me," he says, and the light flashes so brightly he's blinded.*

*There. Three figures pull away from the light, separating into solid beings. Their hair is white as sand, their skin the burnished copper of long summers. Nicholas finds himself bathed in the light of bright blue eyes. The Trinity glimmer in silver and gold armour and they wear benevolent expressions as they stand before him.*

*"You must find a way," says the woman at their centre. Her hands are tattooed and her energy spits the way Rae's does.*

*"Athania," says Nicholas. "Tell me how to bring you back. Please."*

*"You will find a way," says Athania's brother, Thekla. He has a musician's posture, his fingers long, his voice tuneful.*

*"How?" asks Nicholas. "Tell me how!"*

*Norlath's head is wreathed in flowers. She smells of earth and spring and her smile conjures a warmth like sunlight.*

*"The well?" Nicholas adds. "Where is it? Why do I keep seeing it?"*

*"It's not them," says Rae and he doesn't understand. Then his gaze drifts back to the Trinity, who are still watching him, but then he realises they don't see him. Not really.*

*"You have to help us," he pleads.*

"CEASE THIS!"

The shout shattered the vision and as Nicholas found himself jolted back into his body, something struck him in the chest with such force that he tumbled backwards. Tucking into a roll, he landed on his knees, his head spinning as he stared at the floorboards, his eyes still fuzzy with the light of the Trinity.

Dark robes trailed the floor before him and he blinked up into a silver mask.

"Esus," he choked.

The phantom's energy sputtered like dying embers and Nicholas's temples throbbed.

"What the hell was that?" he demanded, rising to face the figure. It was shrouded in dark robes, the oval of its silver mask shining at him and, in the centre of the mask, onyx-black eyes needled him. "Do you know–"

Esus raised a black glove. "Listen."

Nicholas frowned, straining over the blood thundering in his ears.

"I don't–" he began, but then he caught it. A soft scrabbling at the pub door. Claws. He sensed coarse fur and six legs.

"Demon," he whispered.

At the bar, Dawn seized a baseball bat and hopped to her feet. Rae crept to the door, her hands already shimmering with heat, and then the doorframe shuddered as the demon hurled itself against it.

Rae threw a questioning glance at Nicholas.

*Not yet*, he thought, and she turned to watch the door again. It shook violently and the scrabbling became desperate. The creature snorted and mewled, throwing its full weight against the door, which appeared ready to buckle. But then abruptly, with a whine, the demon gave up. Perhaps its energy was spent. Nicholas sensed its hunger; it hollowed his own gut. Then he felt its retreat as it disappeared into the next street.

Silence settled over the pub.

"What–" Nicholas began, facing Esus.

"Power," snarled the phantom. "The Dark Prophets' servants are drawn to it. You have been careless."

"Careless? We were doing what we're supposed to! And it worked! The Trinity were right there. We–"

"Almost made dinner of your own flesh."

Nicholas chewed the inside of his cheek, sensing Esus's indignation. It merged with his own and the emotional overload caused black spots to swim in front of his eyes. Frustration and anger and annoyance scalded his insides and he desperately wanted to lash out, find some way to purge the feelings from his body.

"Breathe."

Dawn was at his side. He hadn't even noticed her crossing the bar, but suddenly she was beside him, touching Nicholas's arm and shooting Esus a nervous glance.

"Nicholas, breathe," she said softly.

"Tantrums will accomplish nothing," uttered Esus, and Nicholas nearly hurled himself at the phantom. Only Dawn's reassuring touch stopped him and he screwed up the emotions multiplying like wasps in his chest, forcing them down away from his mouth, which threatened to unleash a torrent of stinging words.

"The Trinity," he managed to say. "They were right here. We saw them."

"Weren't them," muttered Rae, standing a little apart from the group.

"No," growled Esus. "The Trinity are gone."

"They were there," Nicholas insisted. "We saw them. We–"

"You saw a memory," rumbled Esus. "An imprint of their energy."

"But..." Nicholas trailed off, remembering what he had seen. The Trinity had been so close he had glimpsed the blue fire in their eyes. They had looked so real. And he could feel them. But then he recalled their blank stares. The way they had spoken. It was like a video recording. He had been attempting to interact with an echo.

"They do not hold the answer, but you do."

Esus barely moved. Not for the first time, Nicholas wondered what lay under the phantom's mask. Perhaps he could glimpse it if he really tried. He realised he'd rather not know.

"Easy for you to say," Nicholas snarled. "It's all we've been doing for a month, and then just when we get close, you come charging in and ruin it."

"You must find a way to raise them that doesn't involve overblown demonstrations of your power. It is too dangerous."

"But that's exactly..." Nicholas snorted angrily. Now Esus was accusing him of showboating. He chewed his tongue. "That's what we were trying to do. What else do you suggest?"

"I am merely a messenger," said Esus. "It is you who must discover the means to resurrect the Trinity."

"Gee, that's great. Don't kill the messenger, right?" Nicholas jerked his arm away from Dawn, stomping across the bar. He couldn't look at the phantom anymore. All Esus ever did was prick him with insults until he felt like a worn-out voodoo doll.

"If you're so perfect," he said from the door. "Why don't you fix this mess yourself?"

He barged into the back of the pub and trampled upstairs. In the drab room he had been using as a bedroom, he paced back and forth, clenching and unclenching his fists. The frustration was boiling lava in his stomach and he bit back hot tears.

Why had the Trinity chosen him if he couldn't do what they wanted?

He was useless. A waste of space. Like always.

He heard Dawn uttering a few soothing words to Esus, and then the floorboards rattled as the phantom departed.

Simmering with loathing, most of it for himself, Nicholas seized the windowsill and forced down a few deep breaths. As his heart rate calmed, a familiar tingling sensation spread through his abdomen. He peered out the window, seeing Midsummer Common over the rooftops of the next street. It was a sprawling patch of scorched earth that had once been a park. The red polls had long since fled but he could just about glimpse his old house at the edge of the Common.

Home.

His real home.

He hadn't been back since arriving in Cambridge, but in the days they had holed up in the King Street Run, the same prickling sensation kept pulling him towards it.

At first, he'd dismissed it as melancholy, but the feeling had only intensified and he was beginning to think it wasn't a feeling at all, but a sign. His nails dug into the windowsill. He couldn't go back there. If Harvesters were hunting him and Rae, that was the first place they would go.

The thought of another night in the pub made him shudder, though, and he wanted nothing more than to race for his house. Maybe he'd bump into his old neighbour Tabatha on the way, the one who'd looked after him before all this insanity. Maybe he'd find Anita and

Max waiting for him. Maybe he'd curl up in his bed and wake up to find it had all been a nightmare.

His heart thudded in his chest at the thought. He was still getting used to the fact that they weren't his real parents. Anita and Max had raised him, but only a few weeks ago, Nicholas had discovered Anita was actually his sister. Anita chose to raise Nicholas with her new husband, Max. They had moved to Cambridge. Created a life away from the Sentinel community. But it hadn't done them any good. Anita and Max were killed in the train wreck orchestrated by Malika, and Nicholas had lost his sister and brother-in-law.

Nicholas's biological parents died in Orville the night Nicholas was born. He kept seeing the village in his dreams. Its creepy Christmas-town streets and the ghosts who wandered them. It felt inevitable that he would return there before all of this was over. The urge to return to Orville was almost as strong as the urge to return to his home on the Common.

*Get a grip*, Nicholas thought. He had to be strong. Even though sometimes all he wanted to do was sleep the apocalypse away.

He couldn't do that, though. What would happen to Rae and Dawn?

As he stared across the Common at the three-storey building that had once been his home, a plan formulated in his mind and his jaw set with determination.

"I'm coming," he told the house.

# CHAPTER TWO
## THE VOICE IN THE DARK

THE NEXT MORNING WAS BITTERLY COLD. Nicholas awoke to his breath hanging in the air, like it had been watching him sleep, and he lay there for a moment, replaying his dreams in the dark. He had glimpsed three glowing pods and the cremated remains of the Tortor, the faceless monster that Laurent had unleashed on Bury St Edmunds. And there had been Laurent himself. In his dream, Nicholas watched as Laurent clutched his throat, blood welling between his fingers.

Nicholas couldn't tell if it was a premonition or just wishful thinking. Was Nicholas going to kill Laurent?

Knowing he couldn't put off getting out of the warm bundle of his bed, Nicholas slipped into the freezing air and tugged on his jeans and hoody. In the dim bathroom, he washed his face and ran a hand over the bristles of his hair, and then went downstairs.

He found Rae was already up, flicking tiny flames at bar mats in a game he didn't understand. She slept so little she might be a nocturnal creature. On the rare occasions he caught her sleeping, she frowned through angry dreams and sometimes muttered about "twigs", whatever that meant.

Nicholas grabbed a stool down the bar from her and flipped through Dawn's books, ignoring his gurgling stomach. When Dawn was up, they'd think about food, and then he'd broach the topic that he knew was going to lead to an argument.

He distracted himself with the book, turning page after page, all of them familiar after weeks of scrutiny. This was one of the books

Dawn had salvaged from her personal collection before they left Bury, and it contained vital information about the Sentinels. He paused on an artist's sketch of the Trinity, which was surprisingly close to how they had appeared in his and Rae's vision. He re-read their legend, how the Trinity were ancient gods forged from the world's soil to keep Ginnungap, the end of the world, at bay. Esus was their messenger and general, a wild thing they had tamed for battle. They created a Sentinel army and, when the Dark Prophets challenged their rule, the Trinity banished the Prophets to a hell dimension.

Depending on the book, the Dark Prophets always looked different. Sometimes they were dragons. Sometimes they were a three-headed monster like a Hydra. Occasionally they looked like men with flaming orange eyes. Nobody seemed to know anything concrete about them, other than that they were the opposite of the Trinity. Old gods twisted by a desire for chaos. Demons served the Prophets in the hope that, one day, the Prophets would succeed in unravelling the fabric of the universe so that chaos ruled.

Nicholas contemplated what was happening to Cambridge and realised a kind of chaos already was seeping into the world. He shivered, an anxious knot creaking between his shoulder blades. He couldn't let it happen. He'd do anything he could to stop the Prophets returning.

He glanced up from a drawing of the Prophets as Dawn came into the bar, her purple hair sticking out in different directions. Knowing it was now or never, Nicholas jumped off his stool.

"I'm going to the house," he announced.

"House?" asked Dawn, yawning.

"My house. Or what's left of it."

Dawn shook her head. "Sorry, I must still be asleep. For a second I thought you said something completely insane."

"He did," mumbled Rae. She was still slouched against the bar surrounded by smoking beer mats.

Nicholas ignored their grim expressions.

"I mean it. I'm going to the house," he said.

"Are you nuts?" Rae hissed.

"I thought we agreed–" Dawn began.

Nicholas raised a hand. "We did. But I'm un-agreeing."

"That krypist did something to him," said Rae. "Sucked his brains out."

"I keep getting this… feeling," Nicholas said. "Like I need to go back there. And what are we even doing here? In Cambridge, I mean. Esus told us to come and find something that would help with the whole 'raise the Trinity' thing, but we've been here a week and there's nothing. No books, no people, just a big mess. Except for this feeling I have about my old house."

"That's called nostalgia," said Dawn gently. "I get it all the time about Gran–"

"No, it's more than that." He dug his fingers into his chest. "The feeling, it's right here, the way it is when I'm sensing something. Look, I know it's nuts, but it's morning, which means not as many nasties. I have to see."

"See what?"

"If I'm right. That there's something waiting for me there. Or if I am just nuts. In which case you should probably find a new leader."

"Leader?" sneered Rae.

Dawn looked like she was going to argue, then she bit her lip. "If you have to."

"Idiots," Rae muttered.

Nicholas glared at her. She was always so quick to tell him how useless he was, and even though that's how he felt half the time, he didn't need her reminding him every ten seconds. She acted like she knew everything, but she was as imperfect as anybody else. And she was hiding things from them.

"Why do you keep thinking about twigs?" he asked pointedly.

Rae's expression drew into a shocked scowl and he knew he had found a soft spot.

"Come on," he pushed. "You think about it all the time. You talk about twigs in your sleep. And sometimes that word jumps out of your head like it's been trying to get free for years."

A rattling sound filled the bar. The glasses on the shelves were juddering as if they were afraid. Rae's annoyance was affecting the pub like a miniature earthquake and Nicholas felt a twinge of satisfaction that he was pissing her off.

"If it's important, we have a right to know–" he began.

"You have no right!"

He had never heard Rae shout and the sound made the hairs on his neck bristle. Glasses leapt off the shelves and smashed on the floor.

*I'll look for myself,* he thought at her, feeling the resentment steaming off her. The air grew hotter by the second, rippling around Rae.

*Back the hell off,* she thought at him.

*Make me.*

"Guys, this isn't helping anybody," Dawn said, going to stand between them.

The glasses stopped rattling and the temperature in the room dropped back to its usual tomb-like chill. Ignoring Rae, Nicholas lumbered over to the sofa and began pulling on his armour, aware that, begrudgingly, Dawn was doing the same. Rae idled by the bar. He wouldn't have done what he had threatened, looked in her head, but she didn't need to know that. He had just wanted to show her that she couldn't tell people what to do all the time. Yes, she'd had it rough growing up, but that didn't give her an excuse to act superior.

"I'm going," said Nicholas, strapping on his kneepads. "Stay here if you want."

"Like I have a choice," said Rae.

They ventured outside, Dawn wearing a nervous frown, and Rae's expression blank, but he could still feel her annoyance. He was glad they weren't making him do this alone. The pull became stronger as they approached Midsummer Common and Nicholas had to stop himself breaking into a run; it would only attract the wrong kind of attention. His stomach ached with hunger and he realised they'd forgotten about food. He supposed they'd think about that if they survived the house.

Together, they skirted the park and hurried along in the shadow of the terraced houses. He wondered what had happened to his neighbours and decided he'd rather not know. Then suddenly they were outside his old house and, staring up at it, a strange calm washed over him.

Home. He was home.

Except it wasn't home anymore. The downstairs windows had been smashed and the front door was open, creaking in the wind. Harvesters. Had to be. Nicholas pushed his mind inside, searching every room, but he came up with nothing. Either he was too tired and hungry to uncover them or the house really was abandoned.

Fighting the sudden urge to turn around and walk in the opposite direction, to preserve his memories of how things used to be, Nicholas mounted the steps and went inside.

The hall was filthy. Graffiti scarred the walls and beer bottles littered the floor. Whoever had been here had shown it the sort of respect rock stars reserve for hotel rooms.

"Nice place," whispered Dawn.

"I'll put the kettle on," he murmured.

Rae pushed past him and went into the lounge. She was good at scoping places out. Nicholas had spent time honing his abilities and so had she. Dawn closed the front door behind them.

"I don't have to tell you Rae's right. This is a pretty stupid idea," she said under her breath.

"Fully aware of that, thanks."

"So what are we looking for?"

"Just give me a moment."

Nicholas closed his eyes and searched for the tugging sensation that had been drawing him to the house ever since they had arrived in Cambridge. There, a rope-like wrench at his chest. He grabbed it with his mind and felt forward, following its lead.

*"Nicholassss…"*

The whisper shivered around him and he remembered the first time he'd heard it. It had started the day Anita and Max died. He'd thought he was losing his mind. Sentinels and demons weren't part of his vocabulary until the moment the whispers led him to the hidden study in his parents' bedroom.

And now there was that same whisper, still calling to him as if no time had passed at all.

"Upstairs," he murmured, already climbing. His parents' bedroom door hung off its hinges and outrage stabbed between his ribs. Whoever had done this was long gone, though, so he crushed the anger in his fist and went into the room, ignoring the overturned furniture, not wanting to see his sister's possessions treated like this. He felt Dawn's eyes on him but he couldn't look at her, instead going straight to the far wall.

The photo of him as a baby still hung there.

"You were cute," Dawn said dryly.

"Were?"

Nicholas took the frame and tossed it onto the bed.

*"Nicholasssss…"*

The whisper pushed through the wall and there, in the spot where the photo had hung, was an alcove with a handle. He tugged the lever and stepped back. A rumbling of cogs vibrated in his chest and the wall-door popped open.

Nicholas followed the tugging sensation inside, the rasping voice filling his ears, although he knew Dawn couldn't hear it.

Whoever had trashed his house hadn't found the study. Nobody had been back in here since he had first found it in the wake of his sister's death. Dawn came in after him and uttered a soft "oh" at the books lining the left-hand wall. She wandered to them in a daze, running her fingers over the dusty spines in a respectful caress. Nicholas found himself drawn to the desk in the corner.

*"Nicholasssss…"*

Driven forward, Nicholas seized the desk and wrenched it across the floor. His weaker arm twinged but he ignored it, staring at the trapdoor he'd uncovered where the desk had stood.

There. That's where the voice wanted him to go; that's where the invisible rope led. A hidden room within a hidden room. His sister was full of surprises.

"What the–" Dawn uttered. All the furniture dragging had interrupted her excitement over the books.

Nicholas pulled open the trapdoor and peered into darkness. A step ladder led down into an unlit space, but he couldn't sense what was down there. The voice had stopped. The tugging sensation had evaporated. The whisper had done its job.

"You're going down there?" asked Dawn. At his stare, she added, "Right, stupid question."

"See if there's anything useful," Nicholas said, nodding at the shelves. "If I'm not back in five minutes, don't come looking for me."

Dawn eyed the trapdoor nervously but there was no point getting skittish. Nicholas swung his legs through the hole in the floor and began to climb down.

All he could hear was the quickening of his pulse in his temples. Strange smells – wax and old books and wet fur – made his head spin as his feet found the floor. For a moment, he was reminded of the oblituss, the dark tomb beneath the Abbey Gardens, and he had to force himself to let go of the ladder. This wasn't the oblituss. The faceless man wasn't going to emerge from the shadows and undo his sanity with a touch. His parents wouldn't have kept anything dangerous down here, he was sure of it. Then again, he'd never known Anita and Max were Sentinels. How much could he really assume about them?

Nicholas fumbled along the wall. If he could just find a light. He was sure it was a small space from the sound of his breath. Maybe little more than a cubby.

As he stumbled forward, his hands found a cord. A bare bulb clicked above his head, its fuzzy light settling over a bizarre collection of objects. Shelves, crates, broken lamps and intricate brass sculptures of what had to be the Milky Way.

"Heck, took you long enough, kid."

Nicholas froze. The voice had spoken just over his shoulder. A man's voice. Brassy and American. He turned around in the space, almost knocking over a stack of yellowed newspapers, but all he saw were shelves and inanimate objects.

"A guy could go nuts down here on his own."

"Who is that?" Nicholas demanded. The voice was familiar. He had heard it before, but he couldn't place where.

"Jeeze, don't lose your head, bub. Down here."

Nicholas moved towards the voice, spotting an old suitcase that had belonged to his grandfather. Beside it, on a low shelf, an object struck a dancing pose, its white flares, unmistakable quiff and glittery sunglasses moulded from plastic. Crouching, Nicholas crept closer to the figurine.

"Ya got me," said Elvis.

Nicholas blinked. Of course he knew the voice. He had heard it a hundred times coming out of the radio or on television. It was unmistakable, twanging like guitar strings, and it was coming out of the statue, which remained motionless and appeared just as Nicholas had seen in his visions.

"You're… you're not *Elvis*," Nicholas uttered.

"Not so bright, huh?" said Elvis. Only his mouth moved. His plastic hips remained motionless mid-thrust. "I get it; you're starstruck. Not every day you get a private audience with the king of rock 'n' roll."

Nicholas almost laughed. "But you're not *the* Elvis…"

"Kid, ya got eyes?"

"Of course. Alright. So what was your biggest hit?"

"Man, are you writing a book? I can't remember half those biscuits I baked. Geeze, your folks were never this difficult."

Nicholas's smile fell. "You knew my parents… Or, y'know, Anita and Max."

"Good folk. Shame to see 'em go like that, but now there's you, bub."

Nicholas frowned. "What are you? Really?"

"Aside from the obvious? Look, kid, most people don't ask so many questions when they meet me."

"I find that hard to believe."

"Funny; figured you'd recognise another emissary of the Trinity, being one yourself."

"How…" Nicholas stopped, suddenly excited, even if a plastic figurine of Elvis was the last thing he'd been expecting. Heck, Isabel had possessed a cat. Why not a talking statue?

Nicholas swallowed, trying to keep his excitement under control. "You're an emissary... Like a messenger? For the Trinity?"

"Gee, I thought you'd never ask. That's me, kid. Hey, you notice the world's going to hell quicker'n a bent-eight?"

"It's sort of hard not to."

"The Dark Prophets have that effect. They're infecting the whole lot. They got this world sicker'n a lizard in a Tequila bottle. You ever tried Tequila?"

Nicholas ignored the question; his entire body had gone rigid. "The Prophets? They're doing this?"

"Now don't tell me you didn't know?" Nicholas wasn't sure if he had imagined Elvis' eyebrows momentarily rising above his sunglasses. "They're back, bubba. Crossed the great divide and we've got you to thank for it."

Nicholas realised he'd clenched his hands into fists. Laurent had tried to raise the Prophets, but Nicholas and his friends had stopped him. True, monstrous things had clawed their way through the gateway before that, but they had closed the portal, prevented Laurent from releasing the Dark Prophets from their hellpit. But this figurine was saying they had failed.

"What did *I* do?" he demanded.

"Brace yourself, kid, cos this ain't pretty. The faceless goon, the one who set that town to burning? He was the real conduit, bub. When you and your lady friend performed your mojo – that was impressive, by the by – you sparked the Tortor up good, warmed up the eggs in his undercarriage, got 'em sizzling. He birthed 'em right there in the ruins. The Prophets are back and you don't wanna be around when they hatch."

The dreams. The glowing pods. The Tortor's cremated remains. Nicholas felt sick. He couldn't believe it. Had everything he'd dreamt been true? The image of Laurent's throat gushing blood leapt to the front of his mind.

"Laurent... he's dead," Nicholas murmured.

"Oh boy, he's deader'n a doornail. Deader'n JFK and Marilyn combined, may they rest in peace."

A shiver trickled down Nicholas's spine. "How?"

"Killed by that flame-haired sister of Satan."

"Malika." That didn't make any sense, either. Malika and Laurent had been working together. They had joined forces in the Abbey Gardens; Nicholas had seen it for himself. Why would she turn on Laurent? Trust probably wasn't a top priority when you were evil.

"She's the key to this, bubba. She's the key to all of it."

Nicholas scrutinised the statue. "How do you know so much?"

"Oracles sorta know things. It's our deal."

"You see things? The future?"

"When the music of the universe sings to ol' Elvis. Seen plenty of weird shit over the years, but nothing weirder'n the shit you're carrying around in that karmic suitcase of yours, kid."

Nicholas didn't know what to say. He glanced around the cubby hole and leaned in closer. "Did you talk to Anita and Max?"

"Sure, gave 'em my breakfast order every morning. Cuppa joe and a doughnut. Sorry, kid, bad joke. The sad truth is they couldn't hear Elvis. Most people can't. Coulda saved them a whole lotta trouble."

"You tried to warn them?"

"Told them a hundred times about the train," said Elvis. "But they couldn't hear worth a damn."

Nicholas doubted anything would have stopped his parents from boarding the train they died on. They had been determined and fearless.

He took a breath, knowing he had to focus on the important things.

"Malika," he said. "How's she the key?"

"She's nurturing the Prophets, boy-o. That makes her pretty darn important. Key player, you could say."

"So to stop the Prophets, I have to stop her."

"Bingo."

"How do I do that?"

"You're not gonna like it."

Nicholas thought of the Drujblade, the mystical knife Malika had stolen from him. He'd have no problem plunging it into her heart given half the chance, and not just because she'd killed his family.

"Try me," he said.

"You met her maker," said Elvis. "The demon she served. Or pretended to, for a while."

"Diltraa." Nicholas remembered horns, bone-white eyes and a rasping voice like skeletal fingers clawing glass.

"The one and only."

"Diltraa's dead," said Nicholas. Esus had killed the demon after it broke into Hallow House.

"Not dead," said Elvis. "Banished to the demon plane. You destroyed its corporeal form, kid, but a demon's essence is never truly toast."

Nicholas's jaw started ticking and he eyed the statue nervously.

"Just tell me what I have to do."

"Only thing that can stop the wench is her maker," said Elvis. "You gotta raise the demon, use it to end her."

*Sure, why not*, Nicholas thought. *Raising a demon should be way easier than raising the Trinity. Maybe I'll get a two-for-one deal.*

"Now I know I've gone crazy," he said. "Even if I could raise the demon, there's no way I could convince it to kill her."

"That's on you, bub. I don't have the answer, but I can push you in the right direction. Ever heard of the Skurkwife?"

Nicholas resisted rolling his eyes. "Don't make me ask."

"That's all I got, kid. Skurkwife. No idea what or who it is; believe me, I'd tell you. I'm jonesin' to know. All I know for sure is that the Skurkwife's gonna help you slay Satan's sister."

"What about the Trinity?"

Nicholas imagined he saw the statue shiver.

"That's on you, too, bubba. What, you think oracles know everything?"

"But if Diltraa's the only one who can kill Malika, what am I doing trying to raise the Trinity?" he asked.

"Think the Dark Prophets are just gonna roll over'n play dead? Ha! Malika's on you, bub. The Dark Prophets are on the Trinity."

Nicholas squinted at the figurine. He was sure it had moved. It seemed to be growing lighter, as if illuminated from within.

"The end's coming, kid." The statue was teetering on the shelf, hopping as if on a hotplate, and the light was burning brighter with every second. "You gonna look the other way? Turn that head?"

Nicholas fumbled back.

"What's happening?" he demanded.

"You wanna get outta here, Nick. Delivered my goods, seems I'm done."

The figurine bucked on the spot, the white light almost blinding as it shot through the glittery sunglasses.

Elvis' voice rose above a dull hum. "Get going. They're coming for you bubba. Like, NOW."

Nicholas glanced up through the trapdoor but he couldn't hear anything over the shuddering in the air. Where were Dawn and Rae? He'd left them for too long. Throwing himself at the ladder, he cast a final look back at the Elvis figurine, which had become a blazing pyre of white light.

"The Skurkwife!" he yelled over the din. "Where is she?"

"Right here in Cambridge!" Elvis hollered back. "That's all I got. Seeya kid!"

Cracks forked through the statue and Nicholas clambered up the ladder, hurling himself through the trapdoor just as an explosion rocked the bunker and a tongue of white fire lashed up into the study. Nicholas rolled across the floor, crashing into the desk.

He lay panting, his ears ringing, everything the Elvis figurine had said whirling in his head.

Dawn appeared over him. "What the hell was that?"

"Would you believe me if I said 'oracle'?" Nicholas got up from the floor. He eyed the bunker, but there was no sound. The whispers had stopped and he couldn't hear Elvis, either. The oracle was gone. But Elvis had said something was coming for them.

"Where's Rae?" he asked.

Dawn jabbed a book at the study door. "Patrolling upstairs. What—"

"We have to get out of here."

"But… you spoke to an oracle? What did it say?"

"I'll tell you when we get out of here. Something's coming for us. Now."

"Okay, let me just put this back."

Dawn went to the bookcase and began replacing a slim volume she must have been studying. Nicholas noticed the way her gaze lingered on the shelves.

"Take them," he said. "Any of them." At her surprised glance, he added, "Go on, quickly!"

Dawn grinned and seized a handful of the grubby volumes. Despite himself, Nicholas smiled. It was good to see her happy. He took a satchel from the desk and Dawn filled it.

"You sure they wouldn't mind?" she asked.

"You can put them back when this is all over."

He stopped himself adding: *Assuming we survive.*

Back in his parents' bedroom, he closed the secret door behind them, hanging the frame on the wall. On the landing, they bumped into Rae as she came down the stairs from the second floor.

"Have fun snooping?" he asked.

"Your room always that messy?" she replied.

"Only when I have guests."

He sensed the movement before he saw it.

"Watch out–" Rae began, but a shrieking figure was already bowling toward them from the stairs, a cricket bat raised. A blast of heat rushed past Nicholas's ear and the cricket bat splintered into a thousand pieces. Rae's aim was improving. The temperature on the landing rose the way it always did when Rae warmed up, but Nicholas threw his arms towards the ceiling.

"Wait!" he yelled.

The figure who had been wielding the cricket bat froze, shooting him a disbelieving stare through her tangled blonde hair.

"Nicholas?" she uttered.

"Tabatha," he breathed. The woman seemed to forget the inexplicably ruined cricket bat, panting as they regarded each other. A look he couldn't read flickered across her face, then she reached out and crushed him to her.

"It's you," she said. "I didn't recognise you. Your hair… What did you do to your hair?"

Nicholas returned the hug. "You're still here."

When she released him, he was unsettled by how different Tabatha appeared. His old neighbour had lost weight and there was a hard light in her eyes that hadn't been there before. She wore a thick jumper and combat trousers, her hair straining to escape a baseball cap.

Rae cleared her throat.

"Yeah, guys," Nicholas said. "This is Tabatha. She lives next-door." Raising an eyebrow at her, he added, "You still live next-door?"

Tabatha nodded. "Last one on the common. Everybody else got out when the… when things started to get bad."

Nicholas wondered what she'd seen. Demons were all over Cambridge and, unlike his parents, she wasn't a Sentinel. Tabatha was as normal as they came. Had she been fending off demons? More than likely she'd shut herself in her house, living off kitchen scraps and waiting for the end of the world to die down.

"What are you doing here?" Tabatha asked. "I thought you were with your godmother."

"That didn't work out." Nicholas shrugged.

"Where's Sam?"

"Not here, but he's okay." A lie. In reality, he had no idea how Sam was, but it looked like Tabatha could do with a few lies. "You really shouldn't be here. Cambridge… it's not safe anymore."

"I know. I'm all packed and ready to leave. I was about to go when I heard noises in here. Like somebody set off an explosion. The whole street's been ransacked and I couldn't let them get away with it anymore."

"So you thought you'd play a round of cricket with whoever was looting the place?"

"Except it was you." Tabatha put a hand to his cheek and he could tell she wanted to say something, maybe about how tired or beaten up or underfed he appeared, but then she dropped her hand and blinked away whatever she was thinking.

"I'm going to my sister-in-law's in Norfolk," she said. "It… whatever it is, it hasn't reached there yet. There are boats to France. You should come. There's plenty of room."

For a moment, he was tempted. The thought of leaving Cambridge, letting somebody else clean up the mess, was appealing. But if what the Elvis oracle had said was true, this was his mess; it was his fault the Dark Prophets were back, spreading their sickness, buckling the world one town at a time. It was up to him to find a cure.

"Thanks," he said. "We'll be okay."

Tabatha nodded, glancing down; she was still holding the charred cricket bat handle. "Yes, I believe you."

Nicholas frowned. Something was wrong. A razor red pain sliced into his mind and, knowing what it meant, he sent his mind hurtling through the house.

"We're not alone," he said. Dawn and Rae were at his side in a second, Dawn peering down the stairs to the front hall, Rae braced and staring up at the second floor.

"Can you tell what it is?" Rae asked.

"Bogey, not sure what kind. Downstairs."

"Did I mention this was a bad idea?" Dawn murmured.

"Maybe a few thousand times."

"Nicholas?" Tabatha asked.

"Just stay behind us," he told her. "Come on, the stairs."

Together, they moved for the stairs. If they could get to the front door, they could get Tabatha to safety, then go back for whatever was hunting them.

"Quickly," he said, taking the steps two at a time, Tabatha behind him, Dawn and Rae taking up the rear. As he neared the bottom, though, a massive shape appeared, blocking the front door. The man's head nearly grazed the ceiling and he wore battle-scarred armour painted with an insignia of a three-headed monster, his greasy hair falling into an equally scarred face.

Nicholas swore, stopping at the foot of the stairs, shielding the others.

"Harvester," Dawn hissed.

A growl rumbled up through the Harvester's chest and he raised a hand, twitching his fingers at them. Blades glinted on each of his fingers.

"Nice, where'd you get those?" Nicholas asked.

"Yeah, those things look mean," Rae added.

"Guys, this isn't helping," Dawn said.

"STOP. TALKING."

The Harvester bellowed as he charged at them. Nicholas grabbed the wall and the banister rail, rocking up to boot the Harvester in the chest. The man barely registered the attack and Nicholas thudded to the hall floor. It was like kicking a solid iron shield.

"Get back," Rae told the others, putting Dawn and Tabatha behind her on the stairs. The air shimmered with heat and a fiery explosion left her palms, barrelling into the Harvester's chest. The man staggered back, appearing momentarily confused. Then he roared, hurtling towards her.

Sparks flashed in Rae's eyes as she hopped down the steps into the front hall, but the Harvester lashed out with his finger-talons, breaking her concentration. She ducked just in time to avoid the glittering blades, but then the Harvester buried his fist in her jaw. She slumped into the wall by the kitchen, dazed.

Back on his feet, Nicholas leapt onto the Harvester's back, yanking his hair and shoving his hands into his face, blinding him. Bellowing, the Harvester staggered back and Nicholas leapt free just in time to avoid being crushed against the wall.

"Anybody got any ideas?" he shouted, grabbing the Harvester's legs. Wielding her bat, Dawn rushed down the stairs to help, but the Harvester booted her away and she tumbled down the hall, landing in a heap by the kitchen door. Miraculously, she'd managed to hold onto the bat.

Another Harvester emerged from the kitchen. A woman with a tattooed face and a blood-red hood. She raised a hand, onto which a metal contraption like a glove had been strapped. A gauntlet. Nicholas had seen other Harvesters wearing them. They blasted electrical currents that paralysed and killed. This Harvester had her gauntlet pointed at Dawn.

"Look out!" Nicholas yelled.

Dawn swung her baseball bat and the Harvester caught it in her hand. Grunting, Dawn butted the bat into the woman's face and she staggered backwards into the kitchen.

As Nicholas grappled with the male Harvester, the huge man delivered a blow to Nicholas's chest that felt like it had burst one of his lungs. Gasping for air, Nicholas caught the glint of steel as the Harvester's claws slashed for his throat.

"Nicholas!" Dawn yelled, raising her bat again and charging the male Harvester. At her cry, the man pivoted with a speed that Nicholas hadn't expected given his size. He grabbed Dawn's arm and nearly lifted her off the floor.

Tabatha helped Nicholas to his feet as Rae attempted to wrestle Dawn free of the Harvester.

"The door," Nicholas wheezed at Tabatha. "Get out. Now."

Tabatha's face was drawn tight with worry.

"We'll be right behind you," he added, and Tabatha clenched her jaw, sizing up the male Harvester. He practically filled half of the cramped hall, and perhaps knowing this wasn't a fight she could help with, Tabatha hurried outside.

As Dawn beat her free hand against the Harvester's armoured chest, the man cackled, his talons flashing. Rae's hands shimmered with heat as she threw a punch that made the Harvester's jaw sizzle and, shrieking, he hefted an elbow into Rae, knocking her aside. Nicholas caught her, and then nearly dropped her again because her skin was unbearably hot.

"Together," Nicholas told her. They'd been practising combining their powers ever since they had taken down the Tortor. Rae focussed on the Harvester and the temperature in the hall rocketed. Paint cracked away from the door frames and the wallpaper bubbled. Nicholas created hands in his mind, cupped them around the molten ball of energy Rae was summoning, keeping it under control as it threatened to destroy everything.

"Dawn, now!"

Still caught in the Harvester's grip, Dawn slugged the man between the eyes and the Harvester dropped her. As Dawn scooted back into the dining room, Nicholas released the charge.

The Harvester turned just in time to see the fireball hurtling towards him. A blinding flash of light tore through him and Nicholas threw his hands in front of his face as a wave of heat gusted at him. When he lowered his hands, all that remained of the Harvester was ash and the glittering finger talons, which thudded to the floorboards.

Nicholas released a deep breath, still buzzing from the exertion.

"Dawn?" he called.

"I'm alive." Her voice came from the dining room.

Relieved, Nicholas massaged the chest-plate of his armour, his ribs sore from where the Harvester had pummelled him. He frowned. There had been two Harvesters. "What happened to the other one?" he asked as Dawn emerged back into the hall, looking shaken but otherwise okay. She pointed at the kitchen door.

Together, all three of them approached, finding the female Harvester out cold on the floor, an ugly welt rising on her forehead where Dawn had struck her.

"Remind me never to get between you and a baseball bat," Nicholas told Dawn. He moved towards the unconscious woman, but Dawn grabbed his arm.

"What are you doing?"

"The gauntlet," he said, nodding at the metal contraption on the Harvester's hand.

Dawn shook her head. "Don't. Those things are dangerous."

"Could be useful," Nicholas reasoned.

"They kill people. And put a demon inside. Those things have

**44**

corrupted Sentinels. We don't want to mess with anything made by a Harvester."

Nicholas hesitated, eyeing the gauntlet, and realised she was right. It was too risky, even if gauntlets were unbelievably powerful. He frowned, noticing a tattoo on the Harvester's upper arm. It was the same image of a three-headed creature that had been painted on the male Harvester's armour.

"What's that?" he asked.

"Never seen it before."

"Me either," said Rae.

Nicholas shivered. "I'm thinking Prophets."

"Must be the new look," Dawn said. "I'm thinking it's time we get the hell out of here."

"I can't convince you to stay for a cuppa?" Nicholas deadpanned. As they went back into the hall, he threw a worried glance at the front door, suddenly fearful that other Harvesters might be lying in wait outside. He rushed to the door and released a relieved breath when he discovered Tabatha shivering on the pavement.

"You okay?" he asked as he approached her, Dawn and Rae behind him.

"I should be asking you that," Tabatha said. She was ashen-faced and gazing at him like he was a stranger rather than somebody she'd lived next-door to for years.

"You need to leave now," Nicholas said.

"My ride's already waiting." Tabatha gestured across Midsummer Common where a transit van sat, its headlights off. Whoever was driving had some common sense.

"Go," Nicholas said. "I'll wait until you're inside."

Tabatha squeezed his hand and she seemed to want to say something again, but then she turned and hurried away across the Common. The three of them stood and watched, ready to charge if more Harvesters emerged from the shadows, but none did. Tabatha clambered into the van and the door slid shut behind her. Barely making a sound, the vehicle trundled off down the road, and disappeared around a corner.

"She seems nice," Dawn murmured.

"She is," Nicholas said. A strange feeling had lodged in his throat.

His old life really was over. His home was destroyed and even Tabatha had gone. Now it was just him and his friends against the rest of the world.

"God, I wish Sam was here," he muttered.

# CHAPTER THREE
## DAMAGED

BLADES CLASHED AND SHADOWS TUMBLED. As Samuel Wilkins made his way between the fighting figures, he tried to remember when he'd last slept. His scratchy eyelids told him it had been a while, maybe even twenty-four hours, though he had no idea where the day had gone. Watching the sparring Sentinels made him yearn for the single bed he'd claimed at Hallow House, even though the springs dug in and made him dream of burrowing parasites. He'd grab a few hours soon, after he'd assessed the camp.

All around him, tents huddled between the trees. Over their peaked roofs, he spied Hallow House. The old mansion's windows appraised the encampment the way a general might. In one of them, a pale figure stared out and Sam grew uneasy.

"Nuisance things, shoo, begone!"

Beside him, a wiry elderly woman flapped a hand at a mob of cats. Isabel Hallow had been a woman for a month now, but Sam still imagined a black cat whenever he heard her voice. He watched as she hissed and stamped at the felines that had been following them. They scattered in different directions and melted into the night.

Isabel caught Sam smiling. "Blasted things. Where were we?" She hoisted herself upright using a knotted staff. Wrapped in an afghan embroidered with gemstones, her grey hair coiled up to reveal her neck, she looked nothing like her old self, but Sam had finally grown accustomed to her new appearance.

"Inventory," he said. "Ten thousand arrows, five hundred bows…"

"Yes, yes." Isabel tutted. "And a hundred useless felines with nothing better to do than pester my shadow."

"You might find a use for them at some point."

"I'll fashion myself a winter coat."

Sam chuckled, then caught himself. Laughing felt wrong at a time like this. His friend Liberty was dead. Bury St Edmunds was a festering ruin. Nicholas was nowhere to be found, and Jessica… He glanced up at the house again, but the figure had vanished from the window.

"The camp grows by the day," said Isabel as they ambled between the tents. Some housed families who had fled their homes, while others held racks of weaponry. One was being used by Sensitives who were attempting to intercept information about the opposition. A sea of canopies rolled out into the countryside, huddling beneath leaden clouds. "We cannot provide for everybody for much longer. We must send for supplies."

"We'll send Hunters to the nearest town," Sam said. "One of them has a van, I think."

He noticed one of the cats was still following them. It was the bravest of the lot; a tufty grey bully with only one eye. By the size of it, Sam guessed it was a male. Isabel ignored it, or at least pretended to, and it crept silently along in their wake.

"Even so, provisions will only become exhausted again. And still we delay." Isabel's hooded gaze flickered up at Hallow House and Sam knew she was thinking the same thing he was.

"Esus will come," he said. "We cannot strike until we know what we're up against."

"We know already," Isabel spat, and Sam imagined her hackles rising. Just because she wasn't a cat anymore didn't mean she was any less feline. "The Prophets are back–"

"According to rumour," Sam interjected.

"Old man, there is no smoke without fire."

"It could all be part of Malika's game plan. Spread fear and hysteria along with the rumours."

"Have you not eyes?" The old woman gestured at the swollen sky. "The Prophets' lecherous grip on the world tightens. Their sickness spreads more rapidly than a medieval plague. We must amass the Sentinels and strike before it's too late."

"Strike where, though? We have no idea where Malika and her army are based, nor what sort of arsenal she has at her disposal."

Isabel fell silent, though he sensed her simmering frustration. And she was right. How much longer could they wait before striking? The camp was growing irritable. Sentinels worked off their nervous energy by training, but training sessions were quickly developing into real fights. Tension was fraying decade-old bonds. Many Sentinels had lost their homes, their families. They wanted to fight. They were dogs straining at their leads, mouths foaming at the stink of danger.

Only one person could unleash them.

Sam eyed Hallow House as they emerged from the camp and stood before the crumbling mansion. Isabel struck the earth with her staff and tutted, her voice like rustling grass.

"The camp's number strengthens by the day and, by the day, so she weakens."

Sam didn't know what to say so he went up the steps to the front door. He paused as rooks scattered into the air from a nearby tree, but Esus wasn't among them, so he went inside, Isabel close by him. The main hall bustled with Sentinels, all of them high ranking, but even they were not immune to gossip. Hushed chatter bubbled between them.

"Did you hear about the collision in Newcastle?"

"...snakes, she said. Falling from the sky like rain..."

"...fire in the swimming pool. No water, just a sea of fire. They were all cooked alive..."

A few of the Sentinels paused and flashed curious glances as Isabel passed. She still made them nervous weeks after her arrival. In their first few days at Hallow House, when Isabel, Sam and Aileen had journeyed from Bury St Edmunds, Isabel had wasted no time ordering the camp and seeing that everybody knew their place. She was a born leader, and although she had been the *Vaktarin* five-hundred years ago, it wasn't she they wanted.

Sam wound his weary way upstairs. Most of the house was off limits to even the highest-ranking Sentinels, but Isabel had led him up here numerous times. Not because he had endeared himself to her but because he knew Nicholas, and Nicholas was who really mattered.

Still, Sam had seen parts of Hallow House he never knew existed, discovering areas that fed his keen interest. Tonight, though, his interest was blunted, his bones weary with worry.

Isabel's staff beat a steady rhythm down the length of a narrow corridor and they burrowed deeper into the belly of the house. Here, lamps cast a dim haze that made Sam's eyelids scratchier still. He'd check on *her*, then snatch a few hours' sleep. He might even be spared the dreams tonight, he was so tired.

Isabel stopped at an unremarkable door and tilted her head, listening. Sam caught the sound of a voice within.

"Go away. Leave me be."

He recognised Jessica's voice, but who was she talking to?

Without knocking, Isabel went inside and Sam followed. Jessica stood at the centre of the parlour, a ghostly figure in a silver dress, her golden hair curling about her shoulders. Her eyes widened as they entered, and Sam gazed at the dark room, seeking whoever Jessica had been talking to. There was nobody else here. The fire had long since cooled in the hearth and a gloomy shroud had settled over the collection of antique furniture.

"You are back," Jessica said. Her voice wavered slightly and she looked unsettled, as if she had forgotten she wasn't alone in the house.

"Have you eaten?" Isabel asked. Sam pressed the door closed and hovered by an armchair, noting a dark shadow as it hopped on to the windowsill. The bully cat had followed them upstairs. Isabel didn't appear to mind.

"I was just…" Jessica stared down at her hands. "There was somebody…" Her gaze roved to the window. "The moon cannot see us."

Sam followed her line of vision. Unnatural black clouds churned above the camp. He hadn't seen the moon in weeks. Or the sun, for that matter. The demonic infestation had blocked out the sky, obliterating all celestial light so that every day felt stifled and half dead.

Was it the moon Jessica had been speaking to before they had interrupted her? Sam eyed the parlour uneasily, hoping that some invisible thing hadn't found its way into the house.

"The moon is blind. It's crying. Oh, can you hear it?"

Sam shuddered at Jessica's words. Sometimes she appeared almost lucid. He could see that old steel in her jaw. Other times she was like this, drifting like a sleepwalker. She was a shadow of the leader she had once been. Unpredictable and often unintelligible.

"*Vaktarin*," he said, using her old name. "We must–"

Isabel raised a silencing hand.

"Ginnungap approaches," she said. "First the snow, then the heat. Now this festering gloom. What is your plan? Simply watch as the Prophets destroy the world piece by piece?"

A low hiss caused the hairs on Sam's arms to prickle. Jessica had approached the one-eyed cat and her hand hovered above its ears as it crouched on the windowsill.

"Pyraemon," Isabel snapped. "Down."

Sam almost snorted with surprise. Isabel had named the creature. Miserably, it slipped to the floor and disappeared behind a chair. Jessica moved as if to follow it, but Isabel stood in her way, striking the floor with her staff.

"Enough. This is pitiful. We cannot continue in this manner. We need you, do you hear me? You are the hope they cling to. Have you seen the tents? All of them waiting? They gather for you. For *your* guidance. I will not beg but…"

The old woman trailed off. Jessica wasn't listening. Her gaze had drifted to the other side of the room.

"Stay back," she said.

Sam stared at the corner, but it was empty. What could Jessica see?

"No," Jessica said. "No, don't… They mustn't know."

"Is there somebody–" Sam began.

"This is useless," interrupted Isabel. "Her mind is no longer her own. She sees phantoms where none linger."

"Are you sure? What if there's something in here with us?"

"I would sense it."

"Get *out*!" Jessica screamed, and her fingers went up to tangle in her golden hair. "Get out, *get out*!" The breath caught in her throat and she stared right through Isabel. "You wouldn't dare. You wouldn't."

Sam squeezed his aching knuckles together. He wished there was something he could do. This wasn't the Jessica he knew, but he had no power. No words that might stitch her sanity back together.

"Make her stop, make her stop." There were tears in Jessica's eyes and she resembled a child gripped by a nightmare.

"What is she seeing?" Sam asked.

Isabel strode forward and took Jessica's arm. She murmured something as she brought the tip of her staff to Jessica's shoulder. The grill rattled in the fireplace and a faint vibration travelled through the staff. Jessica's veins glowed where the wood touched her skin.

The crying ceased immediately and Jessica's hand snapped around Isabel's arm. She surveyed the room with fresh urgency.

"She was here, wasn't she?"

Isabel released the staff. "There is only myself and Mr Wilkins."

"But I saw—" She sounded more like her old self now. She peered into Isabel's face, her brow crinkled. "What's happening? What day is it?"

"Don't worry yourself with that."

"The boy went to Bury. He found the girl. Where are they?"

"Jessica, please. Calm. Breathe."

Sam clutched the back of the armchair.

A dim look of horror crossed Jessica's face. "Malika. We must stop her!"

Isabel's back straightened and she entwined her fingers with Jessica's. "Yes, yes, we know," she said.

"It must be me." Jessica bit her lip. "I…"

"Leave it to us," Isabel said. "We shall see to it that—"

"No! No. You mustn't."

The leather armchair creaked as Sam's grip tightened. He didn't know what Jessica was talking about but the way she spoke made his spine tingle. The women remained locked together by the window, their faces inches apart. Then Jessica's expression changed. She blinked, appearing confused, and cast a blank look at Sam. She released her grip on Isabel.

"Where's Lash?"

Sam released a slow breath. The moment had passed. Jessica's mind had retreated once more. She didn't remember that she'd killed her bodyguard. Esus had found her cradling his severed head; the result of one of her fevers. She had not been violent since, but Sam dreaded to think what she would be capable of if she snapped again. As the Vaktarin, she possessed unimaginable power.

He noticed Isabel was attempting to get back to her feet and hurried over, helping her up. He expected her to shove him away, but he found himself staring into a face white with worry.

"The Sentinels demand a leader," Isabel whispered. "We cannot keep her from them for much longer."

He shook his head. "But we can't let her out like this." He peered through the window at the encampment. They had all come here, to the font of Sentinel power, only to find it emitting little more than a trickle.

"Let us hope Esus returns bearing agreeable news," Isabel murmured.

Sam couldn't help thinking that was unlikely.

"What did she mean?" he asked. "About the red witch?"

"I do not know. There may have been some truth in her words. Or she may simply have been…"

Isabel didn't have to complete the thought. Jessica had rambled before, some of it about her mother and father, most of it incomprehensible. This had felt different, though. She'd seemed to know what she was talking about.

"Go, rest." Isabel released Sam's hand. "I will see what I can uncover."

"What about you?" he asked.

"I slept my fill when I was dead."

After parting ways with Isabel, Sam took his time climbing the stairs to the second floor. He lingered by a high window, gazing out over the pleated rows of tents. Beyond them, a vague glow drew his eye. Orville. The town Nicholas and Rae were born in. The town Sam had lived in with his wife all those years ago, until Judith died and Sam moved to Cambridge to be near Nicholas's adoptive parents.

The glow churned up regret and longing.

Judith. Anita. Max. Richard. Liberty.

They formed a clothes line of ghosts before him. Grieving one person means grieving everyone you've ever lost. The clothes line was getting longer and one day he'd be on it, but not before he'd seen Malika and the Prophets destroyed. He'd live for that, then happily join his wife.

Sam rubbed his face, stifling a yawn as he reached the landing. He'd kill for one of Liberty's sleeping potions. Just to escape for more than a few hours would be bliss. He found himself remembering Liberty as he'd first met her; a young girl who first flourished into an angry teen, then a kind and formidable young woman. She'd had a way about her that he missed. He wondered how her mother and daughter were faring. He hoped they had survived the onset of Ginnungap.

"Look at you," a voice said softly. "You could store a week's shopping in the bags under those eyes."

Aileen stood in a doorway, her pink robe straining around her plump figure, her silver hair secured in a net.

"Don't fret, I'm off now," Sam assured her.

"Four hours, you'll get. That's all you'll allow yourself. Don't think I haven't noticed."

Sam fumbled with his pocket watch, if only for a distraction, and clicked his tongue.

"It's two am. What are you doing up?" he asked.

"Same as you. Counting my worry lines."

"Ha. I find at least ten new ones every day."

"I could've told you that." Aileen hugged herself, studying his face. It had been weeks since that night in Bury when the safehouse landlady confessed her feelings for him, and she hadn't mentioned it since. But Sam found cups of tea around him whenever he most needed them, and his poky room always smelled sweet when he returned to it after a long day.

Aileen's lips pressed into a line. "Any word from them?"

"No. Nothing." There had been no sign of Nicholas or Dawn, Aileen's granddaughter, since they fought Malika in Bury. Sam thought about them every minute of the day, praying to whichever gods would listen that they were okay.

"No news is good news, I suppose," the landlady murmured. "What do you suppose they're up to?"

"If I know Nicholas, and I have since he was a sprog, he'll be trying to finish what we started."

"Dangerous out there now, though. Dawn used to be so outdoorsy, but then Cambodia happened and I couldn't drag her out of her room if she was cuffed to me."

"They'll look after each other." Sam wasn't sure who he was trying to reassure. In the space of two months, Nicholas had lost his adoptive parents, discovered he had supernatural abilities, and faced half a demonology's worth of monsters. He'd had to grow up quickly and Sam admired how he'd coped – but now was the real test.

Aileen's eyes flashed conspiratorially in the dark. "Here, I have something that'll help us nod off." She disappeared into her room and Sam went to the door. By a cabinet, Aileen beckoned him inside.

"Close it," she hissed, and Sam obeyed, stepping into the cosy bedroom. Soft snores rose out of a four-poster bed and sleeping figures filled a couple of camp beds against the wall. Space was getting tight – the Sentinel army was wriggling into every corner of Hallow House, waiting for battle.

"Don't wake the others, they'll only want some." In the dark, the landlady clinked two glasses down on a bureau and poured honey-coloured liquid from a bottle. She handed Sam a glass, which he lifted to his nose.

"Brandy," he marvelled. "Where–"

Aileen put a finger to her lips and raised her own glass. "To Dawn."

"And Nicholas."

"And a better tomorrow."

"And–"

"Alright, no need to go on. Cheers, duck."

The glasses rang and Sam sipped, tangy warmth flooding his mouth, then spreading down into his belly. Aileen ushered him over to the window seat.

"I've been thinking about the Trials a lot lately, don't ask me why," she murmured softly. "How old were you when you went through them?"

"Fourteen. A week after my fourteenth birthday, in fact."

"Huh, typical."

"Feels like centuries ago."

Every Sentinel went through them. The Trials revealed a Sentinel's true nature. You had to fight your way out of an underground labyrinth. How you did it – if you succeeded at all, and many didn't – revealed whether you were a Hunter, a Sensitive or a Demonologist. Most became the latter, although a select few, like their friend Benjamin Nale, became elite Hunters tasked with most of the grunt work.

"Dawn never had her Trial," Aileen said, refilling their glasses. "She was always off round the world with John and her mother. Suppose that was trial enough."

"And now Nicholas is getting his very own real-world version."

"We all are."

Sam sighed, swilling his brandy. "I'm worried, Aileen."

"What's to worry about?" The landlady's face remained expressionless for a moment, then she clucked softly. "Apart from the apocalypse, missing teenagers and the rumours about, well, you know…"

"Rumours?"

Aileen checked the sleeping figures and leaned in closer. "The Vaktarin. They say she's dead."

"Dead?"

"Nobody's seen her in weeks. And Lash… him neither. Now, I'm not one for idle gossip – though there was plenty of it in the safehouse – but you'd think at a time like this, with everything going to the pits, she'd be around with at least a few words of encouragement." Sam wasn't surprised. Sentinels were born detectives. They'd be idiots not to have noticed Jessica's absence.

He sipped his brandy and found his glass was empty again.

"She's not well. Going crazy, actually." A croaking laugh burst from his throat. Suddenly everything seemed so funny. "She's more cracked than a dropped egg. Her brain's scrambled."

Aileen giggled. "Could be worse; she could be evil."

Sam hooted louder.

"Shhhhhh." Aileen grabbed his hand. "The others." Then she giggled again and tossed her glass back.

"How different things could have been," Sam murmured.

"You know what I regret? Not having more fun. Those days of running around the country hunting monsters… they were over far too soon."

"I know what you mean."

"Oh pish! You've never stopped! I'll never forget finding you on the doorstep dripping wet, like you'd taken a shower fully clothed."

She was talking about that day a month ago when Sam had nearly drowned in Ipswich. He'd been visiting the fake psychic, Solomon, on the barge when Malika's forces attacked, submerging the whole thing – and its owner with it.

"Solomon," Sam murmured, recalling the strange little vole-like man. He peered into his glass, feeling suddenly soberer, tasting the murky water as the barge sank, and something floated to the surface of his mind. "Names," he said.

"Names, dear?" asked Aileen.

"It's the only thing Solomon said that made a jot of sense. He said that names have power."

Aileen topped up their glasses again. "I don't know anything about that. Tuh... We all spent so much time worrying and fighting, I really do wish I'd had more fun. I always wanted to try abseiling. I think I'd have been good at it."

Sam sighed. Whatever Solomon had said about names, he hadn't explained what he'd meant. He'd ask Isabel about it when he next saw her. For now, he was content to sit in the dark with Aileen and embrace the warm numbness of a night cap.

"If we make it out of this, we're going abseiling," he said, finishing his drink.

"Oh, toffee." Aileen glanced at him. "You mean it?"

"I do."

"Cheers to that."

They clinked their empty glasses.

★

Malika listened to the music of bones snapping and a gleeful shiver prickled the nape of her neck. The Prophets were always hungry, and when she fed them, they devoured their prey with the eagerness of a carnivorous newborn. In the mottled light of the atrium, Malika contemplated what destruction they might wreak when they finally came of age. Already they had transformed the atrium into a toxic tomb thick with spiny weeds. The air was so putrid in here that few Harvesters dared enter. Their skin blistered in minutes.

They were weak. She was immune.

The sound of crunching and sucking ceased and she sensed the Prophets' satisfaction. It would be fleeting. She gazed down into the swimming pool, the water now the yellow-green of bile, black mould floating on its surface.

At the centre, the pods had doubled in size. Veins pulsed and their whistling demands were not dulled by the water they rested in.

*Mooooore*, they hissed, their voices scratching the inside of her skull.

"You shall have more," she promised. "Soon."

They were tiring of her scraps. They needed pure energy. Something to nourish them to their full potential.

"Soon," she whispered.

"My liege." A man's voice spoke nearby. Malika turned to see a Harvester standing by the door, already sweating at the lack of breathable air. On his armour, he bore the three-headed insignia of the Prophets.

"They are ready," the Harvester said.

She nodded and her crimson dress trailed across the tiled floor. She went out into the leisure centre's corridor, following the Harvester until they reached another door, and a set of concrete steps that led into the car park beneath the building. It was large and low-ceilinged, devoid of vehicles.

"Where are my babies?" she asked, her voice echoing off concrete pillars.

Near the exit, three muscle-bound Harvesters in sleeve-less black shirts strained to keep hold of a number of leashes. Attached at the collar, six slavering beasts gouged at the concrete floor, panting and growling as they attempted to get across the garage. The svartulfs were almost canine in shape and size, with six legs and ghost-white skin through which a mosaic of purple veins spread. Their fangs dripped black spittle and their eyes were electric blue.

At the sound of Malika's voice, the monsters whined and their leashes snapped tight as they tried to reach her.

"There," Malika cooed, going to them. She kneeled before them and the svartulfs snapped at her hands, missing her fingers by centimetres.

Malika ran a palm over the ridged spine of one of the creatures and it whined loudly.

"Yes, you're ready, aren't you?" she purred. "The babies don't like being locked up, do they? They like to sniff out and destroy. Will you do that for me? Will you lead the first charge?"

They gnashed their teeth, flicking black slobber, and Malika rose to her feet.

"Send them," she instructed. "Now."

At the garage door, a Harvester hit a switch that sent the doors rattling up into the ceiling. The muscular Harvesters detaining the svartulfs reached down and unclipped the leashes from the collars.

Instantly, the svartulfs darted forward. They moved with deadly silence, rippling through the garage doors and out into the night, merging with the darkness of the city.

"Go," Malika called after them. "Tell them we'll be there soon."

# CHAPTER FOUR
## Breaking In

"So the Dark Prophets are back."

"Mmhmm."

Dawn was perched at the bar in the King Street Run, which she was using as a desk. Books were piled up before her, most of them the ones she'd salvaged from Anita's study. Nicholas was glad they were being put to good use. Dawn was reading by the light of a torch they had nabbed from a camping shop. It was the only light in the whole pub.

Sitting a few barstools down from her, Nicholas dug a fork into a tin of baked beans they'd scavenged from a corner shop, knowing he had to eat, even though his stomach seemed to have shrivelled into a stone.

"They're back," he said. "That's why everything's gone crazy like this. Bury and Cambridge full of demons. The lack of sun. The Dark Prophets are here and they're already turning everything upside down."

He shuddered at the memory of the dream he'd been having of the pulsing pods. The Tortor had given birth to the Prophets, and it was only a matter of time before they hatched. He eyed Rae at the end of the bar. She was deep in thought examining some singed beer mats.

"They're still incubating," he said. The word sent snakes oozing through his abdomen and he stared at the gloopy contents of the tin.

"Incubating?" Dawn asked.

"They're cute little monster eggs at the moment. At least, that's what I've been seeing. Malika's nursing them. Helping them grow."

"And soon they'll hatch." He could swear Dawn's face had turned a little bit green. She sat up straighter. "So we have to make sure they never hatch. Get the Trinity up and running before the Prophets come to power. Did the emissary say anything about where Malika is? How long we've got before she brings reality crashing down?"

"No."

"Shit," Dawn breathed. "Also... shit."

"I know."

Rae shoved away from the bar and went to the boarded-up window. She peered through the tiny gaps in the wood like a badger guarding its set. He didn't have the heart to tell her that the Prophets were only here because of something they had done. She was angst-ridden enough without being told she was partly to blame for the apocalypse.

"He did say something else, though," Nicholas said. He set aside the beans, its contents uncomfortably heavy in his belly. "Have you ever heard of the Skurkwife?"

"Skurk..." Dawn tapped her chin with a pen. "Not sure. I'll check."

"Apparently it'll help. Anything with the word 'wife' in its name has got to be warm and cuddly, right?" He imagined an old lady knitting, or brewing healing tea, or baking charmed pastries. His thoughts always seemed to return to food these days. There was only so long he could keep going on baked beans and crisps.

"If we want to take down Malika, and thereby the Prophets, the Skurkwife will help us," he continued. "Somehow. That bit was sort of fuzzy. But you know how Malika laughs in the face of bullets and sharp objects? Well, there's one thing that can definitely kill her."

"I'm not sure I want to ask," said Dawn.

"Diltraa."

"Now I'm glad I didn't ask."

Nicholas smirked, and then grew serious. "Diltraa's the only thing that can kill her, because the demon's the one that made her. Or something. Sorry, fuzzy."

"Uh, isn't that going to be a slightly enormous problem?" said Dawn.

"Yeah, considering Esus sent Diltraa back to the demon wastelands months ago. And the demon, by its very nature, is evil, so it would probably only help Malika if we *did* figure out how to bring it back. But Elvis..." He stopped, nearly laughing at how crazy it all sounded.

"The psychic hunk of plastic that *looked* like Elvis… It said we have to find a way to bring Diltraa back. And then convince it to kill Malika."

Dawn looked like she wasn't sure if she wanted to laugh or bang her head against the bar. Instead, she started leafing through a book.

"Let's just do one impossible thing at a time," she said. "Skurkwife… Skurkwife…"

"Rae?" Nicholas asked. "That name ring any bells?"

Rae was still peering through a gap in the boarded-up window. She wasn't good at sitting still and even worse at chit-chat. She turned her dark eyes on him, obviously having missed the entire conversation.

"Skurk… Ever heard of it?" he asked again.

"No."

If she was still brooding after their fight earlier, he couldn't tell. She was always like this. When they had first met, he had seen into her mind, glimpsing razor-sharp slices of what she had been through – how crummy her life had been growing up, isolated from the world of the Sentinels and wrestling with a power she couldn't control.

"Anything out there?" He went to her side and squinted through one of the rifts in the wood.

"Nothing."

That was strange. Things usually came out in the dark. Maybe it was too early. Or maybe the demons were done with Cambridge and had moved on to the next town. Nicholas wondered how far the infestation had spread. Tabatha said she was going to France. Was it just here in Britain so far? How long before it learned to swim?

There were more pressing questions for now.

"How much longer do you think we can stay here?" he asked.

Rae shrugged. "Another day. The pub stink is covering us but that'll change."

Nicholas resisted asking how she was. How she *really* was. Rae gave away so little. He knew if he started prodding she'd curl up like a porcupine. The whole "twig" thing hadn't exactly gone well. It would take longer than a month to earn her trust. The fact that she'd saved his life a handful of times was the only proof he had that she cared, but it was enough. For now.

"Big Harvester, huh?" He grinned, wiggling his fingers at her to emulate the talons the Harvester had worn.

"Ugly, too," Rae said.

"He seemed to like Dawn."

"Huh?" Dawn was still lost in her research.

Nicholas smiled at Rae and, for the tiniest moment, everything felt somewhere near to okay between them. Rae blinked and returned to the window, and the moment was lost.

"What is she? The Skurk thing?" she asked.

"No idea, but she's here in Cambridge at least."

He really hoped the Skurkwife was as cosy as he'd imagined. Now, images of warty witches swam in his mind, but they weren't premonitions. He had no idea who the Skurkwife was or how she could help him defeat Malika.

"The Trinity..." he thought out loud, wandering to his favourite beer-stained sofa and flopping onto it. "They'll fix everything, right? When we figure out how to bring them back?"

"That's the idea," Dawn said.

"We raise them and they kill the Prophets, cos they're warriors. They'll win easily. They did it before."

"Hopefully." Dawn was still scanning pages, hunching closer to the books the more she looked.

"Good," Nicholas said. More quietly, he murmured, "Then what happens? When the Trinity have defeated the Prophets? Everybody bows down to the Trinity and a new world order? What happens to the Sentinels?"

Dawn slammed a book shut with a sigh. "I don't know. And there's nothing useful in this one, either; it's the only book I have on weapons and artefacts. I mean, we're assuming the Skurkwife is a person, but it could be an object for all we know." She stared forlornly at an old laptop resting on the bar. She had found it on one of their reconnaissance missions and had been trying to fix it up.

"I miss the Internet," she muttered.

Nicholas thought fondly of Dawn tapping away at her computer in her purple bedroom back home. She had helped him figure out what Laurent was up to. Severing her ties with the world wide web was like severing an arm.

"What would you need to get online?" he asked.

"Power supply mainly, and an internet connection. But if there's no wireless, I'd need to plug in manually."

"There's a telecom building a few streets away. Would that work?"

Dawn looked nervous and excited at the same time. "If it's still operational, which is unlikely…"

Nicholas nodded at Rae. "You up for it?"

"Now?"

"You sleepy?"

"We shouldn't go out at night."

Nicholas couldn't argue with that but the thought of doing something, chasing a lead, made him twitch with excitement. He was sick of wasting time. They finally had something they could work with. How many lives would waiting another day cost? The longer they waited, the more the swarming evil spread. Elvis's warning about the Prophets echoed in his head.

*"I don't wanna be around when they hatch."*

What if they hatched tonight?

"We don't have a choice," he said. "We'll be careful. Stick to the safe zones."

"There aren't any safe zones."

"Then we'll stick to the unsafe zones and arm ourselves to the eyeballs. Look, we don't have any choice. More of those things are turning up every day. Soon it won't matter if it's day or night. They'll be everywhere all the time. And then what? We hide underground? Dig a hole and bury ourselves? We may as well be dead."

Rae's jaw was clenched and she looked like she wanted to yell at him again, but then the fight left her and she glanced away.

"Fine. It's your funeral."

Ten minutes later, they gathered outside the back of the pub clutching whatever pointy things they could find. Rae was a walking weapon anyway, and Dawn's backpack was stuffed with hunting knives and aerosol cans and any other makeshift weapons they had uncovered over the past month.

Nicholas hugged his axe as he peered down the street. The quiet was unnerving and he felt the night's hungry eyes watching him. Whatever was out there, it was getting better at hiding. All they could do was move fast, keep their ears and eyes open. The humid air gusted in his face, putrid as a dog's breath, and he scrunched up his nose.

"Okay," he whispered. "Go."

They stuck together as they hurried down the street, close enough that Nicholas could hear Dawn breathing. He threw his mind ahead like a boomerang, picking up a handful of bogies, and steered them away into a small street. The telecom building was only a few streets away, but it might as well be a whole town away if something spotted them.

Rae shot a glance skyward and they ducked into a doorway as a winged shape swooped through the darkness. Its wingspan was enormous, hooked claws at each tip, and its livid green eyes blazed. Whatever it was, it didn't see them, and they hurried on.

Nicholas wondered how many more Harvesters were in town. Were they searching for him or had they just got lucky at his house? The Harvesters had united under Malika's rule and it was clear she wanted Nicholas dead. Had she despatched her forces to kill him? He realised it made little difference either way. They couldn't afford another run-in with Harvesters, though. Not when there was so much at stake.

Their best bet was getting online, researching the Skurkwife and tracking her down. They knew she was in Cambridge at least. He didn't allow himself to think about how difficult it might be to find her. One problem at a time. First the internet. Then the Skurkwife. Then whatever came after that. Hopefully something other than their deaths.

*Orville*, he thought, though he couldn't explain why. It was where he and Rae had both been born. It was within a stone's throw of Hallow House. And although it had been over a month since he'd set foot in the sinister village, he could feel it in him, behind his eyes, under his skin, and part of him yearned to go back. What if there was something in Orville that could help them convince Diltraa to destroy Malika?

Focussing on the current, more imminent peril, Nicholas traipsed past an alleyway of blinking red eyes. He spotted bent telegraph poles rising above the rooftops. It wasn't far off now.

"Why's it so quiet?" Dawn hissed.

Rae threw her a *shut-up* look.

"They're watching us," Nicholas whispered back.

"Think they're afraid of us?"

Nicholas almost laughed, but then a new thought struck him. Perhaps enough of the demons had seen Rae in action to know she wasn't worth messing with. Perhaps they could even sense her power. Those fiery red sparks that lit up Nicholas's radar.

"They're afraid of Rae," he said.

They rounded a corner and found themselves outside a run-down brick building with boarded-up windows. A filthy sign over the door read: COMLINK – Connecting people the world over. Nicholas hoped that was still true.

The front entrance was barricaded with broken up bits of table and Nicholas didn't want to risk getting Rae to blow it open, so they skirted round the side, finding another door. Planks of wood criss-crossed it.

"Think you can do it quietly?" he asked Rae.

She nodded, already stepping up and placing a hand on the wood. Heat waves rolled around her, and the scent of burning filled the alley. The wood blackened and charred and eventually dropped to the ground in pieces. Nicholas wondered what it felt like to have that much power. Did it make Rae feel indestructible? Or out of control? He watched her do the same with the door handle, and finally they could get in.

It was pitch dark on the other side. Clumsily, Nicholas unzipped Dawn's backpack and retrieved the camping torch, slipping a beam of light into their surroundings. It illuminated a small kitchen. Dirty dishes were piled in the sink and Nicholas heard something he'd not heard in a while. The fridge humming. The building had power.

Another block of light entered the room as Rae opened the fridge.

"Food," she murmured. "Fresh."

Nicholas felt breathless. "Somebody's living here."

"Maybe we should go—" Dawn began.

"We're here now." Rae shut the fridge.

Nicholas nodded. "We go quietly. And carefully. If they're using the fridge, they probably only have two legs and two arms, tops."

He was about to scan the building when a shape darted past the doorway and Nicholas tensed. Nobody hurtled inside, though. The figure had just dashed past in the hall. Nicholas had barely got more than a glimpse, but it had seemed human. Rae was at the door in an instant.

"No, wait." Nicholas scrabbled to her side and peered into a hallway. Killing demons was one thing but what if Rae accidentally blew up a person? "Let me look."

He closed his eyes and reached through the building, sensing hazy barriers like walls and doors, and indistinct shapes a few floors above them. It felt like people, but he couldn't be sure if they were Harvesters or just regular refugees of the apocalypse, holed up against the end of the world.

Opening his eyes again, he flashed the torch at the wall. A sign pointed the way to toilets and offices.

"Come on," he said, heading down the hall. At the foot of a staircase, a sign listed the various parts of the building.

"What are we looking for?" he asked.

Dawn scanned the list and jabbed a finger at SERVER HUB. It was on the third floor.

"There's somebody up there," Nicholas hissed. "I can't tell how many."

"Some*body*," Dawn said, "rather than some*thing*."

He nodded. They blinked at each other and seemed to agree it was worth the risk.

"Eyes open," Nicholas whispered as they made their way up, listening. He attempted not to throttle the banister rail as he went. If there were Harvesters up here, they'd have a fight on their hands any second.

They climbed past the first floor, then the second. When they reached the third, Nicholas threw his thoughts down a gloomy corridor. Something blipped on his radar just as a figure darted out of a doorway. Before he had time to react, the figure kicked Nicholas's feet from under him and he tasted carpet. He heard Rae grunting and a flash of orange lit the darkness.

"No," Nicholas grumbled, attempting to get up. "They're people."

Something dug him in the back and wrenched his arms behind him. Jags of pain ran down his arms and he almost chewed the carpet in annoyance.

He heard Dawn's voice – "Rae, don't kill him!" – and Rae panting. Then he was dragged to his feet and he saw that both girls had their arms pinned behind them by shapes that weren't much taller than them. The shadowy figures wore hoodies and Nicholas couldn't see their faces, but he was sure they were the same age as him.

"Happy?" Rae grunted, straining against her captor. She looked mad as a pit bull who didn't want to go back indoors.

"They're kids," Nicholas said, squinting at the dark figures.

"Shut it," one of them said.

"Yeah, shut your mouth," hissed the other in Nicholas's ear.

"Don't do it, Rae," Nicholas warned. He could tell from her expression that she was considering blowing them all to pieces. He spoke to her without moving his mouth.

*Let's see what they want.*

*You're an idiot.* Rae's thoughts were sharper than her voice.

*I don't have a problem with that.*

"Move."

Nicholas was shoved down the corridor. He hoped they weren't making a huge mistake, but he couldn't let Rae kill people, especially not teenagers, and Dawn didn't have Rae's kind of firepower to defend herself with. She might not survive a fight.

Maybe he could talk their captors round. Convince them to give them access to the server, then go on their merry way. He had no idea how the end of the world had affected the strangers, though. Food was running low. What if they'd acquired a taste for human flesh? Nicholas realised that if it came to that, he really would have to let Rae do her worst.

A door opened and Nicholas was elbowed inside. The girls were shoved in after him and he stopped short as he peered around the room. In the not-too-distant past, it had been an office. Candles flickered on metal shelves and the windows had been blacked out with paint. All the desks had been pushed against the walls.

In the corner of the room, a figure in a rock-band T-shirt and tatty jeans glanced up from a glowing computer screen and a jolt of recognition travelled through Nicholas. He'd know that puckish face anywhere.

"Merlyn," he said.

"Nicholas?"

Nicholas struggled in his captor's grip but the hooded teenager held firm.

Merlyn hopped up out of his bean bag chair, setting his laptop on a desk. Nicholas wasn't sure if it was just the candlelight playing tricks, but the other teenager looked different. Less gangly. As he strode toward them, Merlyn's feet bare on the linoleum floor, his shoulders were drawn back and his face had lost its puppy fat, whittling out sharp cheekbones. His sandy blond hair was shoulder-length and he had a tattoo of a dripping bite mark on his neck.

"You live here?" Nicholas asked. The last time he'd seen Merlyn, they had been in Bury St Edmunds. Merlyn had gone with Sam to fight Malika. But then Sam and the others had vanished, and Merlyn with them. That was a month ago and Nicholas hadn't heard from any of them since, but he had thought about Merlyn often.

"Not sure you'd call it living." Merlyn didn't smile as he drew closer. Nicholas frowned. Had something changed? Was Merlyn no longer an ally? "These guys aren't exactly big on housekeeping."

Merlyn held Nicholas's gaze a moment, then his mouth twisted into a snarl and he threw his arms around his neck. For a moment, Nicholas thought he was attacking him, but then he felt the warmth in the hug and realised Merlyn was laughing. He found his hands were free and he hugged back as Merlyn cackled.

"I thought you were dead," he said, pushing Nicholas away so he could look at him, and then flicking a glance at the girls. "All of you."

"We've come close a few times," said Dawn, rearranging her backpack as she and Rae were released. Their three captors removed their hoods and Nicholas saw how young they really were. Maybe fifteen or sixteen. But their gaze was suspicious and they stayed close by, obviously still distrustful of the newcomers.

"Looks like it," Merlyn laughed.

Rae turned and shoved the figure who had been pinning her hands. "Touch me again," she spat.

"Rae," Nicholas warned.

She didn't back down and, after a second, the guy strolled off to a set of monitors by the door. Nicholas saw him glancing at Rae out of the corner of his eye and didn't blame him.

"What the hell are you doing here?" Merlyn asked, going to a glass-fronted fridge. "Looking for me? I'm touched, really I am."

"Yeah, no, we just had to get out of Bury," said Nicholas.

Merlyn shut the fridge. "Whew, yeah, tell me about it. Talk about firing up the barbecue." He tossed something at Nicholas, who caught an ice-cold can of cola. He grinned.

"Figure you've not seen one of those in a while." Merlyn tossed cans to Rae and Dawn. Dawn only just managed not to drop hers.

Nicholas couldn't help downing the whole thing in one go. The shops in Cambridge had been bare for weeks and they had been surviving on lukewarm pub water. This was pure luxury. He realised Merlyn was shooting him one of his heavy-lidded stares and wiped his mouth.

"So you live here?" Nicholas asked.

"For the past week; we just arrived in town." Merlyn fell back into his bean bag, sighing as he raised his hands over his head. Nicholas couldn't help noticing his once weedy arms were bigger, more muscular.

"After what happened at that school," Merlyn continued, "we split up. Sam, Isabel and Aileen went to Hallow House. I teamed up with these rats and made my way to Cambridge. It's freakin' mental out there in the countryside. Figured it'd be better here, but it's worse. There are more of them and everyone's either dead or gone. Lost a couple of rats in the first day."

Nicholas cast a distracted glance at the other figures in the room. Two girls, two boys, all of them teenagers, probably from Bury or the surrounding villages. They were pretending to be preoccupied with their laptops, but they were clearly curious about him, Rae and Dawn. Nicholas was too full of questions to pay them much attention, though.

"Sam and the others, they're okay?" he asked.

Merlyn paused in the middle of scratching his armpit. "Well, yeah. But you know about Liberty, right?"

Something twanged in Nicholas's chest like a plucked piano wire. "What about her?"

"Crap." Merlyn dropped his hands. "Well, uh, yeah… she didn't make it. The witch got her."

*The witch. Malika.*

Nicholas felt hot with shock. All his visions of Laurent and glowing pods, and not once had he seen Liberty dead. She couldn't be. She was the most powerful Sensitive he had ever met. How had Malika overpowered her? He tried not to imagine it; Malika wouldn't have let Liberty go easily. They would have fought. A weary kind of grief washed through him. Didn't Liberty have a daughter?

"But… Nan, I mean Aileen," Dawn said softly behind him. "She's okay?"

Merlyn nodded slowly. "Was last I saw her."

"And Isabel?" Nicholas asked, remembering his vision of the dead black cat.

"Ha. You wouldn't believe me if I told you." When nobody said anything, Merlyn added, "She's had a makeover. Lost the fur."

"Meaning?"

"She's human. Performed some sort of *Freaky Friday* mojo and got herself a new body. Well, an old body. But it sort of works, I suppose. She's super ancient, right?"

"You're saying she's human again." Nicholas had forgotten how slippery Merlyn could be. Dawn and Rae were both quiet and to the point. Talking to Merlyn was like sifting sand from one hand to the other and losing most of it in the process.

"Yeah, human," Merlyn said, "but as catty as ever."

Nicholas couldn't help smiling.

"This place." Dawn's eyes were drawn to Merlyn's laptop, which emitted a ghoulish glow. "It's got power?"

Merlyn nodded.

"And the internet?"

"That what you're after? Need to update your Twitter?" Merlyn winked at her.

"Among other things." Dawn was already removing her laptop from her backpack. "You mind?"

Merlyn gestured lazily. "By all means. Not sure you'll like what you see, though. I'd take a thousand selfies over the pictures people are uploading these days."

"So the internet's still on," said Nicholas, watching Dawn plug into the mains by the window and sit observing the power light blink. It must feel like Christmas morning to her.

"A basic version of it," said Merlyn. "Loads of servers were destroyed when towns were invaded, and more go down every day, but some are still juiced. Ones in America and Australia."

"So it's just us at the moment?" Nicholas said. "That's overrun."

"It's most concentrated here, but there are reports in—"

"France. Denmark. Iceland." Dawn had loaded up her laptop and was blinking into it, her face pale.

Merlyn sat up in the beanbag. "How'd you get on so quickly?"

Dawn smiled coyly and raised a hand. "Dawn. Hacker."

"Just don't do anything stupid. Some people say Harvesters are using the web to track down Sentinel stragglers. Like they even have the IQ."

Nicholas went to peer over Dawn's shoulder as she scrolled through webpages. Headlines leapt out at him, each worse than the one before.

*NIGHT-TIME ATTACKS ON THE RISE.*

*GOVERNMENT DENIES CHEMICAL WARFARE.*

*GOVERNMENT ANNOUNCES STATE OF EMERGENCY.*

The pictures were grainy, dark, and caught on cameraphones. Horned shadows looming on hilltops. Pits of corpses and dead foxes and incinerated trees.

"This is—"

Dawn stopped on an image that stunned Nicholas into silence. Big Ben's Elizabeth Tower torn in half, the clock face pummelled into the ground. The Houses of Parliament choking with flames.

"They reached London," Nicholas murmured.

"The papers closed up pretty soon after that," said Merlyn. "Now any updates come through news feeds. Everybody's a journalist."

"Everybody's a soldier," said Nicholas. "Wait, what's that?"

He leaned in as Dawn clicked on a video. On-screen, a female news reporter stared stonily into the camera clutching a microphone. Behind her, Tower Bridge was deserted.

*"We can confirm they've made it in to the London sewers. It's still unclear just what the creatures are, but we're receiving numerous eye-witness reports that suggest this isn't one species of animal but, in fact, a number of different species. The only clear information we have is that all are deadly and if—"*

The reporter's eyes darted to the left, then somebody screamed and the camera hit the ground. Shrieks distorted the video's sound and blood splattered the ground.

"That's enough," Nicholas said and Dawn closed the video. Nicholas paced away, rubbing the back of his neck. Seeing it was worse than suspecting it. England was falling apart. The sight of the ruined Houses of Parliament sent worms slithering through his gut. He felt tiny in the face of the invasion's enormity.

"The conspiracy theorists had a field day," Merlyn said. "Then they realised this was for real and shut down their webpages. Paranoid they were next, I guess."

"We have to get to Hallow House," Nicholas said. "Find the others. Figure out a way to stop this."

*Then Orville*, he thought. He was connected to that place whether he liked it or not, and he had a funny feeling that he hadn't yet uncovered all its secrets. He had to go back and see if his newly developed powers picked up on anything he'd missed before.

*First the Skurkwife*, he reminded himself. *Then Orville. Then take out Malika once and for all. Easy-peasy gimme a squeezy.*

Merlyn pondered the floor. "We're heading north. Figured we should help any stragglers before the Harvesters get 'em. But we can point you in the right direction. You really set on Hallow House? 'Cos we could do with back up."

Nicholas realised he had been hoping the opposite; that Merlyn would join them. He was so calm in the face of danger. He would be good to have around in the middle of all this madness. And then there was the feeling Nicholas got whenever Merlyn was nearby. A warmth in his belly that made him feel like everything was going to be okay.

*Stop being an idiot*, he told himself. *You barely even know him.*

"Sorry," he said, and he meant it.

"I suppose you've survived this far," said Merlyn.

Funny how he had a way of making everything seem less impossible. Nicholas glanced at Dawn. He was about to ask if she had found anything on the Skurkwife when he noticed her expression. The grim line of her mouth.

"Dawn? You alright?"

She didn't seem to hear him.

"Dawn?"

Her gaze snapped up from the screen and Nicholas's stomach dropped.

"What is it?" he asked.

"Oxford," she said softly. "I was tracking the trajectory of the Prophets' forces. They've gone from Bury to Cambridge. If they keep following that course, next it'll be Oxford." She blinked. "Mum's there."

Dawn's mother. She had been in a psychiatric hospital for the past year, ever since Dawn's dad was killed by Laurent in Cambodia. Dawn hadn't mentioned her in weeks, but Nicholas wondered if it had secretly been bothering her. If she'd been worrying about her mother and her grandmother. Whereas she now knew Aileen was safe, she couldn't say the same about her mother.

"What do you want to do?" he asked gently.

"I think... I need to go. At least try to get her out."

It was exactly what he had hoped she wouldn't say. He knew how she felt, though. If it were his parents, or Sam or Isabel, he would do the same in a heartbeat.

"Okay," he said, and she looked both relieved and scared. "How long will it take to get there?"

"By foot? Two days if we only sleep a few hours."

"We'll need supplies," Nicholas said. "More camping gear, any food we can get our hands on."

"You'll come?" Dawn's eyes were glassy.

"No," said Rae. She was leaning against a threadbare sofa, her arms crossed. One of Merlyn's gang members flinched when she spoke.

"We have to try–" Nicholas began.

"No," Rae repeated. "You stay here, find the Skurkwife."

"But–"

"We go, me and Dawn. Get her mum if we can. Meet you at Hallow House. It's the only way."

"We can't split up." He had been sent to find Rae. According to all the Sentinel jabber, they could defeat the Dark Prophets together by raising the Trinity. If they separated, they might as well just give up on the whole damn thing.

*You're going to let her go alone? 'Cos there's no way she's not going.*

Rae's voice was a blunt instrument in his head. He stared her down.

*We can't split up,* he thought at her.

*It's a couple of days. Gives you time to find the Skurkwife and head to the house.*

*Anything could happen in a few days. If you die, we're dead. We have to figure out how to do this together.*

*Gee, so caring.*

"Uh, guys?" Merlyn said. "Did somebody say Skurkwife?"

Nicholas snapped free from Rae's glare. "Yeah. Wait... you've heard of it?" he asked.

"Skurk?" Merlyn let out a breath. "Messy stuff. What do you want with her?"

For a moment, Nicholas forgot his irritation. "She's going to help us take down Malika." He hoped. "You know who she is?"

Merlyn nodded slowly. "You sure you want to get into that? Chaos Priests are tricky. They'll twist your words, find half-meanings and part-truths. You ask them the wrong thing and you end up with your tongue cut out, or you give them a funny look, they blind you."

"Chaos Priests?" Dawn asked.

"That's what the Skurkwife is."

A leaden weight fell on Nicholas's shoulders. He had read about Chaos Priests in *The Sentinel Chronicles*. They were rare, almost extinct. Some claimed they had been around since the time of the Trinity and the Dark Prophets. Back in the day they were called '*dy-wytches*', and Merlyn was right. They were tricksters. Deadly and unpredictable. Their allegiance was hardly ever clear and they were almost never worth the risk – but only almost.

"You know where the Skurkwife is?" Nicholas asked. Merlyn nodded again, his sombre expression causing Nicholas's unease to fizzle and crack. He couldn't let grim fairy tales get in his way, though. If this was what it took, at least he could say he died trying.

"Not sure you're going to like it," Merlyn said.

"You'll tell me where to find it?"

"Better. I'll take you." Merlyn began pacing.

"But you're going north," said Nicholas.

"The north can wait. Things just got interesting right here."

*So we're going.* Rae's voice needled in his mind again.

Nicholas's gaze passed from Rae to Dawn. The thought of them traipsing through the countryside together set his teeth on edge. If they came across something big, or a group of big things…

*You owe her,* Rae's voice said, and Nicholas gritted his teeth, then exhaled slowly. She was right. Dawn had never asked him for anything. She had helped them reach Cambridge, never complaining, going along with anything he said. He blinked and looked away.

Rae was right, but the thought of them going off without him hurt. Like he was losing his family all over again.

"We go now," Rae said to Dawn.

"Uh, what just happened?" asked Merlyn.

"They do that." Dawn sighed, closing her computer and getting up off the floor. She slipped the laptop into her backpack and went to Nicholas's side. "We'll be careful."

He could see the determination in her eyes. The gratitude that he wouldn't try to stop her. Finally, he said, "Don't let her push you around."

Dawn hugged him.

"I hope you find her," he whispered in her ear.

"Be safe." She let him go and turned to Merlyn. "Thanks for the juice."

"Pleasure."

"Two days to Oxford, then a day to Hallow House from there," Dawn said.

Nicholas nodded. "See you in three days, then." He just hoped it was that straight forward.

# CHAPTER FIVE
## LASHING TAILS

WHEN THE GIRLS HAD GONE, NICHOLAS distracted himself by asking Merlyn to fill him in on everything he knew. They left Merlyn's gang in the computer hub and wandered through the office's murky corridors, patrolling for bogies. Every now and then, Merlyn checked a window, making sure the boards weren't coming away from the frames, then he sent his torch beam ahead to separate the shadows.

"So you've not been back," Nicholas said, squeezing his axe. "To Bury, I mean."

"Nothing there now." Merlyn's voice was tight, and Nicholas wondered if his parents had escaped before the town fell. He didn't ask. When Anita and Max died, the sympathetic stares at the funeral had almost crushed him.

"Besides, who wants to be in Bury when you can live it up in Cambridge?" Merlyn hopped up and down on the spot as if he was in a night club, throwing the light around.

Nicholas laughed. "I think we have different ideas of fun."

"Come on, nothing wrong with a few more battle scars. Mine were starting to look pathetic next to the rats back there. Kit's missing two toes and Gen has a hole in her head."

"And that makes them better fighters?"

"Makes them slower to get to the food when we find it." Merlyn winked. "But c'mon, we're in the middle of the freakin' apocalypse! Or, Ginnungap. That's what the old timers call it. But yeah, apocalypse, yo!" He slapped Nicholas on the back. "That's exciting, right?"

"That's one way of describing it." His back felt hot where Merlyn's hand had been. And Merlyn *would* think the apocalypse was exciting without Esus breathing down his neck making him feel guilty for not figuring out how to resurrect the Trinity.

As they wandered down a narrow corridor filled with gloomy offices, he asked, "How come you know about the Skurkwife?"

"Impressed? I don't know if you noticed, but I'm sort of a nerd. I like knowing things. S'pose it's 'cos I got put in the 'demonologist' category when I went through the Trials."

"Trials?"

Merlyn turned to him, open-mouthed. "Are you for real? Rite of passage? Every Sentinel goes through them? Usually when they turn sixteen?"

"I just turned sixteen a month ago."

"Right when the shit hit the fan. Huh." Merlyn shrugged. "I guess you got to skip the theory and went straight for the practical." He looked him up and down, and Nicholas blushed, feeling suddenly aware of himself. "You're too puny to be a Hunter, although you're bigger than you were before. Not *fatter*, just bigger. Got the soldier hair, too. It suits you. But you're too clever for hacking at demons. Maybe you're a demonologist, too."

A combination of anxiety and pleasure wriggled through Nicholas. He didn't like Merlyn scrutinising him, but he sort of enjoyed the attention, particularly the compliment about his hair.

"Don't worry," said Merlyn. "I didn't want to be a demonologist, either. Fighting is way more fun than books."

They entered a stairwell and climbed to the next floor. It was equally barren up here, and now that Merlyn wasn't focussing entirely on him, Nicholas began to wonder what sort of Sentinel the Trials would have showed him to be. A Sensitive, probably. He would have found out how to hone his abilities properly, maybe been trained by another Sensitive, rather than learning on the fly.

"Liberty," he murmured.

"Huh?"

Nicholas shook his head. "I just can't believe… Liberty."

Merlyn released a slow breath. "Right."

"You were there? When she…"

Merlyn nodded. Morbid curiosity bit at Nicholas and although he wanted to know what had happened, Merlyn's sombre expression prevented him from asking. He kicked himself for bringing up the subject.

"The sooner that witch is dead, the sooner we can all forget her," Merlyn said. He flashed a warm grin at Nicholas. "Speaking of, I haven't forgotten what we said before. About getting drunk and listening to AC/DC."

*He remembered.* On the nights he couldn't sleep, Nicholas often replayed his conversation with Merlyn from a month ago. They had been traipsing through the Abbey Gardens, facing certain death, and Merlyn had suggested they hang out properly some time. The idea still fizzed excitedly through Nicholas, but he couldn't let Merlyn see that. He'd think Nicholas was clingy and besides, Nicholas wasn't sure what all the feelings that Merlyn stirred up meant.

"Cool," he said. "But… Skurkwife…"

"Right, right, right. Stop changing the subject, will you? Yeah, the Skurkwife is nasty business. You sure you want to meet her?"

"I'm less sure by the minute."

*Especially*, he thought, *as she's supposed to help me bring back Diltraa.*

"You're on some kind of mission," said Merlyn. It clearly wasn't a question.

Nicholas nodded.

"Sheesh, I thought you were serious *before*. You're making Rasputin look like Robin Williams." Merlyn took on a dangerous expression and poked Nicholas in the ribs. "Funny bone's around here somewhere." Nicholas tried to dodge out of the way, but Merlyn kept jabbing him, and Nicholas dropped his axe. "That not it? How about that? No? Wait, maybe it's this one."

Merlyn caught him in the armpit and Nicholas squirmed, laughter erupting from his mouth.

"Got it!" hooted Merlyn. He dug his fingers in until Nicholas found the strength to shove him off. He wiped tears from his cheeks and found Merlyn grinning back, his eyes glinting in the gloom. For a moment they stared at each other and Nicholas's cheeks burned as his heart hammered.

A scratching sound came through the darkness.

Merlyn swung the torch beam down the corridor.

"You hear that?" he whispered.

Nicholas nodded. The beam lit up a pair of elevator doors and, in a flash, an image slipped into Nicholas's mind. Scuttling, furry shapes.

"Something's in there," he said, not smiling anymore.

"Had to happen eventually." Merlyn paced towards the silver doors and ran his fingers down them lightly. He pressed an ear to them.

"Hear that?" he whispered again.

Retrieving his axe from the floor, Nicholas touched one of the doors and saw them. Dozens of rodent-like creatures scrabbling over one another in the dark, silent and determined, scaling the elevator shaft. It was like they'd waited for Rae to leave before attacking.

"They can smell us," he said. "Fifty of them, at least. Small but... they've not eaten in a while."

Merlyn's teeth shone. "Damn, you're not a demonologist. You're a Sensitive! Why didn't you say?" His grin slipped at the sound of claws scraping metal. "How much time you reckon we have?"

"Fifteen seconds, maybe ten."

Merlyn dragged him away from the elevator as the tinny scrabbling sound erupted into an ear-splitting din. The metal doors shrieked under an assault of dozens of needle-like claws.

"Fifteen seconds my arse," Merlyn yelled, racing down the corridor. "We have to get the others out."

Nicholas hurried after him, but then glanced over his shoulder and watched as the elevator doors were shredded like paper, depositing a writhing mass of bodies to the floor. Beady eyes quickly found them and the horde surged through the dark.

Nicholas stopped. Firming his feet on the floor, he clutched the axe in both hands, ready to confront them.

"What are you doing?" Merlyn asked from the stairwell.

"They're too quick. I'll hold them off, you warn the others." He was already pushing his mind into the thrashing mass of fur and teeth. If he could find their weakness, he could use it against them.

"Don't be an idiot," Merlyn said, grabbing his arm.

Nicholas shrugged it off and swung the axe as the creatures spilled towards them. The contact vibrated up the wooden handle and black blood splattered the wall.

"We never did get our second training session." Merlyn smirked, drawing a concealed dagger and slashing it in front of him. Amid the chaos, Nicholas remembered them sparring together in Aileen's back garden. Merlyn had a way of releasing the valve on all the tension he'd scrunched into his shoulders.

Pain burst in his neck and Nicholas grabbed a twitching, sinewy thing that had buried fangs in him. He twisted and crushed it in his grip until it let go, then he hurled it into the writhing mass of monsters at their feet. There were so many of them, he couldn't isolate any of their thoughts. All he felt was their amassed hunger, monstrous all by itself.

"Down!" Merlyn yelled, and Nicholas saw they were scrabbling up the walls, pooling above their heads and spilling into the stairwell.

"They'll reach the others before we do," Nicholas panted.

"They have their fight, we have ours." Merlyn skewered a furry shape and its squeal caused every hair on Nicholas's neck to bristle.

"You know a way out?" Nicholas's eyes were drawn to the shredded lift doors. They had climbed three floors to reach Merlyn's den. The creatures were going in the other direction. Could they scale back down the inside of the elevator shaft?

"Plenty." Merlyn grunted as he kicked more of the creatures, seizing one that was clawing up his leg. "What the hell are these things?"

"Pissed off," Nicholas said, and Merlyn laughed, flinging the creature into the wall.

"Last one out of here's monster munch!" He turned and raced back the way they had come. Nicholas gave chase. Only Merlyn could turn a demon infestation into a game of 'it'. He broke into the stairwell.

Merlyn was already charging down the steps. "GUYS, RUN!" he yelled as he went, and Nicholas hoped the gang could hear. Hoped they weren't already bleeding out somewhere. He tried to send his mind through the building, but his heart was pounding and he couldn't think clearly enough. It was like flicking a leaf into a gale. His powers skated into the air before floating dizzily to the floor.

He peered up at the other floors as he descended. Feverish scuttling sounds came at him and he glimpsed little lashing tails. They really were hungry – and angry with it. He knew that feeling.

"Keep up!" Merlyn's voice echoed up through the stairwell and Nicholas sped after him. Finally, they reached the ground floor and he followed Merlyn, who kept going, not looking back, trusting that Nicholas was behind him.

"We can't go outside," Nicholas shouted. There were more outside. Bigger and meaner.

"Only option."

Nicholas followed Merlyn into a stock room. Merlyn slammed the door after him and Nicholas threw his weight against it. They both pressed back as the creatures scratched and squealed on the other side.

"Man, I've never seen so many," Merlyn panted.

"Way. Out?" Nicholas clenched his teeth, digging his shoulder into the door.

"Back there." Merlyn jerked his head at a fire exit tucked behind rows of free-standing shelves. It was at least fifty feet away. Nicholas wasn't sure they could make it in time, not with the creatures tearing at their wooden shield.

"You go," Merlyn said, fixing his gaze on Nicholas.

"Don't be a hero."

"You love it."

"I'd love it if we both got out of here alive."

Merlyn grew serious. "So go."

"No." Nicholas took a breath and sunk into himself. He searched for the speck of light in the busy darkness of his mind, the part that helped him do things other people couldn't.

"What are—"

"Go," Nicholas said. At Merlyn's stubborn glare, he added, "Get the door. I'll be right behind you."

Merlyn seemed torn, but maybe he saw something different in Nicholas, something he hadn't expected, because he nodded and then began counting.

"Three… two… one!"

Together, they sprang back from the door. Everything seemed to slow down. Nicholas heard Merlyn's footsteps ringing as he raced across the floor and Nicholas edged backwards, watching the door as it splintered apart. The speck of light in his mind pulsed and he imagined turning it over in his hands, warming his palms with it.

The door burst apart, spitting splinters, and Nicholas gulped as the thronging mass of rodent demons poured inside. They surged towards him and he attempted to stem the panic in his mind, instead looking for their weakness. It was there somewhere. He just had to find it. His body trembled with the exertion and sweat trickled down his temples.

*There*, he thought, sensing a bend in their will.

*We're not the enemy*, he thought at them. *You are.*

The change occurred instantly. The creatures stopped in their tracks, appearing dazed, then they turned on each other. The swarm turned inwards, the vermin chewing and clawing at one another. Squeals rent the air as the demons tore at each other, and the stink of metal reached Nicholas's nostrils.

"I did it," he murmured in disbelief. Sweat trickled down to his chin and he watched with horror and fascination as the demons devoured each other.

"Hey, hero… now!"

Snapping out of it, he ran.

Merlyn was holding open the exit, already outside, grinning and waving with his free hand. Nicholas barrelled out, crashing into him. They toppled into an alleyway, tumbling to the ground. The door slammed behind them and Nicholas found his face was so close to Merlyn's that he could see the specks of black in his green eyes.

"That was quite something," Merlyn panted.

"Uh-huh."

"They went nuts."

"I…" Nicholas didn't know what to say. He was practically on top of Merlyn and their limbs were all tangled up. "I lost my axe."

Merlyn laughed and Nicholas blinked free from his gaze. He got to his feet, helping Merlyn up.

"We'll get you another one," Merlyn said. "An early Christmas present."

How did Merlyn always remain so cool and collected? Suddenly aware that they were outside, Nicholas glanced around the alley. Above them, the sky was almost black. Then he sensed something and turned to find a pair of red eyes gleaming at him.

The demon was perched atop a bin. Stag-like antlers forked from a flat skull and its muscular back expanded with each monstrous breath. It was almost as big as Nicholas.

"Can we get a break?" he breathed, before quickly adding, "RUN!"

"Great," Merlyn muttered.

They broke for the main street and the demon pursued them, emitting hideous shrieks. Nicholas had no idea where they were going as they darted over the cobbles, slipping in and out of little alleyways, attempting to confuse their pursuer.

"Any ideas?" Merlyn asked.

The pub. Midsummer Common. With a sinking feeling, Nicholas realised both were in the opposite direction and he wasn't sure he had the energy to turn and fight his way through the demon.

With a start, he sensed more things emerging from the dark, joining the hunt. He decided not to tell Merlyn and wished Rae hadn't left. All this time, she'd been protecting him simply by being around. Now that she was gone, hunting season had begun.

"This way," Nicholas said, a desperate thought occurring to him. They turned down another street, and another, the sound of claws striking the pavement at their backs. Nicholas didn't need to look over his shoulder to see the demons closing in. He sensed them as angry white smudges on his radar. The whole area was swarming with them.

"I think… I need to stop…"

Merlyn had slowed down and was clasping at his chest, wheezing.

"Asthma," he gasped.

"Just hold on," said Nicholas. "It's down here. Just hold on."

They kept going and, finally, Nicholas saw the opening to the street he was aiming for. Without thinking, he grabbed Merlyn's hand and spurred him on to the street corner. And there it was, exactly where he remembered it being. A rusted, clapped-out ambulance parked at an angle by the kerb.

"Inside," he said, tearing open the back doors and bundling Merlyn in. Hopping in after him, he looked back at the street and caught sight of enormous drool-dripping fangs as he slammed the doors shut.

Merlyn was on the floor, his head between his knees. Nicholas stood waiting for the inevitable.

The ambulance shook as the demons attacked it from the outside. They screeched and tore at the vehicle, and just when Nicholas thought they might never stop, the demons finally gave up. The old rust bucket was sturdier than it appeared.

Silence fell.

Nicholas went to sit at Merlyn's side on the floor. His breathing had evened out and he wasn't wheezing anymore.

"You alright?" he asked.

Merlyn nodded and, for the first time Nicholas could remember, he seemed embarrassed.

"Nice find," Merlyn said.

"Yeah. Same thing happened last week. We got caught out in the dark and only just found this thing in time. Thought it might come in handy again." He peered around the inside of the ambulance. A bed was pushed against one wall and medical equipment was suspended on hooks on each side.

"Guess we found a bed for the night," Merlyn said, crawling up onto the mattress. He scooted to one side. "Plenty of room for two."

Nicholas eyed the tiny bed and although he wanted nothing more than to climb up onto it, something stopped him.

"You rest. I'll keep an eye out for a bit, make sure they've really gone."

Merlyn was already asleep.

# CHAPTER SIX
## In The Pentagon Room

SAM WATCHED UNEASILY AS ISABEL MURMURED in Jessica's ear. They stood before twin doors that led out onto a balcony at the front of Hallow House and, outside, a trickle of voices filled the morning air. The Sentinels were waiting.

"Are you sure this is a good idea?" he asked Isabel as she stepped away from Jessica. The cat, Pyraemon, sat under a table against the wall. Sam swore he could hear it grumbling to itself, although what it had to grumble about, he couldn't be sure.

"We have no alternative," was Isabel's clipped response.

He couldn't argue, but he eyed Jessica apprehensively. Isabel had fixed her hair into a plait that wound about her head. She almost resembled her old self, apart from the way she stood twisting her fingers together. The feathered dress she wore appeared too large.

Isabel turned to a woman who towered over the small congregation at the balcony doors.

"You have swept the area?" she asked.

"The area is secure." General Hudson wore a steely expression to match her armour. She was old-school, her features sharp as a fox's, her manner polite but unbending. In the face of Ginnungap, the highest-ranking Sentinels had formed their own army, and General Hudson was its leader. Sam was glad. He had accompanied her around the camp an hour ago, checking in with the officers stationed at the fields surrounding the house, and nothing escaped her attention. From the sentry at the border who clearly hadn't eaten enough for a few days and was almost dead on his feet, to the way the forest bordering the camp was withering without sunlight, she saw everything.

Despite that, Sam was starting to feel the same anxiety that permeated the camp. They were waiting, all of them, for an attack. Nobody had uncovered Malika's base, and each time hunting parties were dispatched, fewer Sentinels returned. It made sense to consolidate at Hallow House and wait for the fight to come to them, but the waiting was wearing Sam down.

"Then it is time," Isabel said. "Five minutes and it will be done. That is all we can hope for."

Sam realised he was holding his breath, and he released it slowly, his insides juddering at what was about to happen. It was madness to let Jessica address the Sentinels. She could barely talk with one person, let alone a crowd.

"Now," Isabel said, squeezing Jessica's shoulder.

A pair of Sentinel officers opened the balcony doors and stepped through. Unknotting her fingers, Jessica followed them outside and Sam watched as she moved to the front of the balcony, placing her hands on the stone support. Gasps rippled through the crowd below. Hundreds, Sam guessed. It had been weeks since the Sentinels had seen Jessica and they had all gathered eagerly to catch a sight of the Vaktarin.

"It warms my heart to see you here today."

Her voice was firm and clear.

"I must apologise for my absence. There has been much to attend to and, regretfully, I have been kept apart from you all."

Sam's heart beat a shocked rhythm. He hadn't heard Jessica speak so coherently in weeks. Had Isabel done something to her? Perhaps she had found a way to piece Jessica's sanity back together, even temporarily. In an instant, he forgot the hopeless creature Jessica had become and was filled with delight.

"I am sure you all understand the gravity of the situation," Jessica said. "The world is dying. The Dark Prophets have returned and they are seeking to claim the world for themselves."

The crowd hummed anxiously. Rumours about the Prophets and Ginnungap had been passed from tent to tent like a hot coal for weeks, but having them confirmed was different.

"We cannot let that happen. This is the fight we were born for. The reason we exist. As long as one Sentinel lives, the Prophets shall never have dominium over the world. *Our* world."

Still awestruck, Sam searched for Isabel, and found her tucked behind the doorway, out of sight, clutching her staff. He frowned, seeing that the woman's eyes were closed and her lips twitched, although no sound came out. Under its table, the cat's eyes were fixed on her.

"The fight will come here, that much we know," said Jessica, but her words left Sam suddenly cold. He watched Isabel uncertainly. Every time Jessica spoke, the old woman's mouth quivered.

"We shall triumph. You have prepared. You are ready. Fight for your families, your loved ones, yourselves. Now go. Spend the day training, working together. The Prophets *will* fall."

The crowd cheered and Jessica swivelled away, stepping back into the hall. The balcony doors closed behind her and Sam found himself face to face with her. He searched for any sign of recognition, desperate to disprove his suspicions, but Jessica's expression was blank again.

Isabel put an arm around Jessica's shoulder.

"You did very well," she said. Jessica didn't appear to hear her, and Sam felt suddenly angry. Isabel had tricked the Sentinels. Somehow, she had spoken through Jessica. It was a grand charade, and the crowd had lapped up the entire thing.

"I trust everything is in order."

Isabel was addressing General Hudson. Already they were pacing down the hall. Sam nearly tripped over Pyraemon as he followed and the cat hissed at him, scuttling alongside the wall with its matted tail dragging behind it.

"We have a safe room prepared," Hudson said. "For the Vaktarin, in the event of an attack. My finest officers are patrolling the perimeters dawn to dusk, or what's left of it in this weather. So much as a demon's little toe enters the camp, we'll know about it."

"Good, good."

They reached a flight of stairs that led through the back corridors of the house. Sam had no idea where Isabel was going but he determined to follow her and find out what she was up to.

Isabel remained motionless at the top of the stairs, holding on to Jessica. She looked up at the General. "Was there anything else?"

Hudson appeared embarrassed. Perhaps she, too, was curious about where Isabel was headed at this late hour, especially with Jessica in her present state.

"No, ma'am," she said.

"Thank you, General. Your efforts, great as they are, have not gone unnoticed."

Hudson nodded and turned, her junior officers following at her heels. Sam wondered if he was about to be dismissed as well, but then he found Isabel's eyes glinting at him. He couldn't tell what she was thinking, if she suspected that he knew what she had just done; deceived every Sentinel who was protecting this house.

Before he could say anything, Isabel uttered, "Follow me," and swept Jessica down the stairs and into a warren of corridors. Chasing after them, Sam found himself drawn deeper and deeper into Hallow House, until they reached a dank, unlit corridor that made him think of the Hammer horror films he'd watched as a youngster.

"Never seen this part of the house before," he murmured. Pyraemon slinked behind them, appearing somehow sinister in the gloom. Sam wanted to ask Isabel about what Solomon had said about names, but he could tell she would brush him off. She was rigid with determination about something.

Isabel stopped at a door, releasing her hold on Jessica to examine it. "Whatever is happening to her, the answers lie here, I am sure of it." Sam shivered with anticipation as the old woman produced a key. The door creaked as she went inside, tugging Jessica along with her as if she were a stray balloon, and Sam ventured after them.

The first thing he saw was a skeleton sitting in a chair. It was festooned in jewellery and dressed as if it were attending a glamorous dinner.

"What the devil," Sam breathed, but the skeleton was by far the least unusual thing about the room. "Five walls," he murmured. The room was pentagon-shaped. The ceiling was half caved-in and a glittering dust lay over the table at the centre of the room. It was laid with ceremonial instruments, including a shallow bowl, and even if he had been a green young Sentinel, he would understand this was a hallowed space.

What did Isabel think she would uncover here? Ahead of Jessica's speech, he had found the old woman meditating in the library. She had sat crossed-legged on the floor, her staff resting before her, and as she chanted, the staff had levitated, pulsing with light. Sam had no idea what she was doing, but the library books had trembled along with his insides.

In the pentagon-shaped room, Jessica giggled as she poked the skeleton in the eye socket.

"Isabel, look how big your eyes are," she said. "Oh!" The skull rocked loose and rolled to the floor.

Isabel was too busy appraising the room to notice. She touched the walls and finally stopped in the far corner, examining a dark patch on the floor.

"Jessica," she said. "Come here."

The woman obeyed and Isabel took her hand, then touched the tip of her staff to the base of Jessica's skull.

"Show us," she whispered.

White light blinded Sam for a moment, and when he blinked the room back into focus, he found it appeared much the same as it had seconds before. Something was off, though. He was seeing double. There were near-transparent shapes in the room. Two women seated at the table.

Where the skeleton rested, another woman also now sat, her hair black as feathers, her arms flashing with jewellery. Sam had seen paintings of her. It was Isabel Hallow as she had been in life, five-hundred years ago.

And sitting opposite her, transparent as a reflection on glass, was Jessica.

"This is the night I died," murmured Isabel.

Sam resisted rubbing his eyes. They were seeing the past? It was like a three-dimensional projection, flickering like old film. If it hadn't been playing right in front of him, he wouldn't have believed it. Perhaps that's what Isabel had been doing with the staff in the library. Imbuing it with magic that would enable her to see through time.

He watched as the projected version of Jessica rose from her chair and then danced, trance-like, towards the projected Isabel. Sam's abdomen spasmed with horror.

"No," he uttered. Past Jessica had her hands around the woman's throat and was crushing it. He watched as Past Isabel thrashed and struggled. The phantom projections were locked in silent battle for what felt like an eternity, Past Jessica's teeth clenched into a hideous expression. Finally, Past Isabel's eyes rolled up into her skull and she slumped back in her seat.

"She killed you…" Sam whispered.

The vision wasn't over.

Past Jessica blinked at her surroundings as if surfacing from a dream. She didn't seem to know what she had done. Her gaze fell on Past Isabel. She shook the dead woman. Her hands went into the air. She paced the room, her mouth opening and closing. She seemed to be shrieking, but no sound reached Sam's ears.

Something changed. Past Jessica beat her chest, tearing at her hair, screaming at the ceiling.

The room shook and Sam watched with horror as Past Jessica split in two. It was like watching cells divide under a microscope. Something tore its way out of Past Jessica's body. Another woman.

Past Jessica wobbled and seized the table, steadying herself. Then she turned to stare at the naked thing crouched in the corner. The thing she had birthed. The woman had wild red hair and Sam would recognise that face anywhere.

"Malika," he whispered.

She was trembling like a newborn. Eyes wide. Teeth bared. She hugged her knees, rocking back and forth. Past Jessica's mouth opened again, as if she was screaming, and then she staggered for the door, disappearing from the room.

The projection faded.

Sam felt frozen in place. He couldn't believe what he had seen.

Across the room from him, Isabel drew her staff away from Jessica's skull. The vision appeared to have aged the old woman a decade and there were dark bags under her eyes as she stared at Jessica, her mouth downturned.

"It tore her in two," she said. "When the demon Diltraa took control of her, it made her…"

She didn't need to finish the sentence. Sam's mind reeled. He felt both numb and nauseated. Jessica had killed Isabel. And Jessica and Malika were the same, but not... Malika was a part of Jessica, but how? He didn't understand what he had seen.

"Something happened when the demon released her," he murmured.

"It tore her in two," said Isabel, watching Jessica drift to a shelf and poke a decrepit candle. "Malika is half of Jessica and half of Diltraa. That at least explains her abilities, and the fact that she's so old. And Jessica..." She considered the other woman, who didn't appear to have been listening. They might as well have been discussing taxes or profit margins. "That is the reason for her current sorry state. She is weakening as Malika grows in strength."

A chill ran the length of Sam's spine.

Jessica was supposed to be the purest of all Sentinels. Their guardian and keeper. But all this time, she had harboured a secret so awful it would blast the fur off a cat. He knew about secrets. How they grew heavier the longer you carried them, growing from pebbles into boulders. Jessica's secret would drive anybody crazy.

"Is she still..." His voice was like gravel. "The demon, is it still in her?"

Isabel contemplated Jessica. "No, that at least is a small salve. The demon left her completely when Malika was created. But... They share a connection, even now, all these years later. Bound together. It is the only explanation for Jessica's loosening grip on reality."

"Malika is killing her."

"Malika is strengthening herself by draining away Jessica's power, the way a leech drains its host's blood." Isabel sounded so sure, as if she didn't find any of this particularly shocking, but her grey expression told Sam otherwise. She slammed her staff against the floorboards and Sam realised Isabel was just better at masking her emotions. It must be something to do with being born in the fifteen-hundreds.

"We must find a way to help her," Sam said. The more he thought about it, the sicker he felt. If they were connected, Malika could exploit Jessica. A horrible thought struck him. "The room the other day, when she was talking to somebody."

"She was seeing Malika."

"But... Malika wasn't here. Not really."

"I do not know." Isabel squeezed her staff. "If there is a way to sever the connection, I will find it. In the meantime, she must rest. I shall ask the Sensitives to see what they can do. There may be a way to protect her from Malika."

# CHAPTER SEVEN
## The Demon Inside

Nicholas came to with a start. He jerked upright, remembering claws and lashing tails, and he felt the swarm needling his flesh, but there was nothing on him except a sleeping bag. The relief crumpled as he blinked at his surroundings. Where had the sleeping bag come from? At first, he thought he was in a small cell, but then he saw the doors at the other end, and the medical equipment in the corner, and he remembered they were in the ambulance.

"You're up," he said to the figure at the other end.

Merlyn sat cross-legged on the floor. He glanced up from a book. "Sleeping beauty! Thought you'd never wake up."

Nicholas rubbed his face and stretched on the floor. He felt achey and fog-brained, and he worried it looked weird that he'd taken the floor over the bed. Did Merlyn think he was strange for not bunking with him? That was the normal thing to do, surely. Totally innocent. So why did the idea of sharing a bed with Merlyn make him feel so nervous? Like it would mean something more?

"How long was I out for?" he asked, deciding to ignore the questions rattling around his skull.

"Seven hours. You sleep like the dead."

"I haven't slept that long in months."

"Burned yourself out is my guess."

The telecomm building. The creatures. He had beat them by tapping into whatever it was that made him able to do things. It must have taken all of his energy.

He noticed a fresh bandage on Merlyn's neck. "You got bit."

"Still got ten fingers and toes, though." Merlyn wiggled his hands and feet. "Shame. I was hoping to beat Gin in the limb-loss stakes."

"The others, do you think they–"

Nicholas trailed off as Merlyn shook his head.

"Not seen 'em. If they got out, they're doing the smart thing and holing up somewhere like us. If not…"

Nicholas thought of Dawn and Rae. When Merlyn had passed out the previous night, Nicholas had attempted to reach Rae using their connection, but either the girls were already too far away or they were laying low, because Rae didn't answer.

At least Rae had her fire-power. If they stumbled into anything nasty, he was sure she could deal with it. But he had his limits and so did Rae. What if she burned out? Dawn would be defenceless.

"Here." Merlyn hopped up and handed him a silvery packet with a cap. "Glucose. There were a couple of packs in one of the boxes. It'll help."

"Cheers." Nicholas squeezed the contents into his mouth and immediately felt more awake. He noticed something in Merlyn's other hand. "What's that?"

Merlyn's eyebrows lifted in surprise and he held up a wooden carving of a fox. "Oh, it's Tails. Sort of my lucky charm."

"Somebody give it to you?"

"Dad carved it when I was a kid." He pocketed the fox and slapped a sheet of paper onto the floor beside Nicholas. It was a map of Cambridge. "While you were sleeping, I've been planning our route."

"To the Skurkwife?" Nicholas asked.

"No, to Disneyland."

Nicholas grinned. "Doubt there'd be any queues these days."

"Ha, if only." Merlyn jabbed the map. "We're here." He carved a line across the paper. "Skurk's here."

Nicholas leaned in to where Merlyn was pointing. "Seriously?"

"Yep."

"The Skurkwife's at King's College?"

"Ever been?" Merlyn asked. "Figured we'd kill two birds with one stone. Bit of saving the world, bit of sightseeing. The view's sweet up there."

"I went with school once." Nicholas grimaced. That life seemed so far away now – lost in a mist of monsters and secrets. He'd been bored during the trip to King's College. It was probably the last time he had been bored. There was always something to do now. Food to find. Creatures to kill. A warm, dry place to sleep.

"You can be the tour guide then," Merlyn said. "You ready for action?"

"Always. What's the time?" Nicholas realised he had no idea. He couldn't say what day it was, either. It all got so confused without a routine. Dawn would know. She was methodical like that. She'd probably scratched the days off on the pub counter.

"Ten."

"It's morning already?"

"Yeah. So we better get moving. They still come out less in the day."

"You noticed that, too."

Merlyn was already clambering over the seats into the front of the ambulance. Nicholas followed him, ignoring the fact that his legs seemed to have forgotten how to move properly. Fighting those things really had taken it out of him, but he couldn't let Merlyn know that. He had to keep going. He sank into the passenger seat and watched Merlyn fumble around under the steering wheel.

"You're not thinking what I think you're thinking."

Merlyn gave him the mischievous smile that gave Nicholas butterflies. "Quickest way there," he said.

"We can't drive."

"Why not?"

"Moving target? Way too obvious."

"It's worth the risk. Plus it's quicker and safer – this thing's like a tank." Merlyn wrenched the casing away to expose a knot of multicoloured wires.

"How do you know it'll even run?"

"Tank's full, did that while you got your rest." Merlyn's fingers worked the wires nimbly. "Everything under the hood looked good. No reason she won't purr for us." He retrieved a camping knife from his pocket and peeled one of the wires like an apple, revealing its gleaming underbelly. He tied two of the wires together and the ambulance rattled to life.

A siren howled above them, and Nicholas threw himself at the dashboard, flipping a switch. The siren fell silent.

Merlyn shot him a sheepish glance. "Oops."

"Oops?"

"Oops."

Nicholas searched through the windscreen for movement. The street remained quiet. "Let's make that our last 'oops'," he breathed.

"Can't promise it."

"You like making me nervous."

Merlyn slapped Nicholas's knee and laughed. "You're cute when you're nervous."

Nicholas felt his ears reddening and grabbed the map from the dashboard. "You know the way?"

Merlyn nodded as he clicked in his seatbelt. As they trundled down the rubbish-strewn street, Nicholas threw his mind around them, seeking out any hidden attackers. The ambulance's speedometer barely shivered past 20mph and Nicholas was surprised Merlyn was a decent driver. His knee felt hot where Merlyn had slapped it, and he found he couldn't stop wishing it was still resting there.

*Stop it*, he told himself. He couldn't get distracted. They had to be ready if something threw itself at the ambulance.

*Skurkwife. Diltraa. Malika dead. Trinity. Prophets dead.*

He repeated the mantra in his head, training his focus, imagining the way an archer sees nothing but the bullseye.

Memories of the attack at the telecoms building returned in suffocating waves. The scrabbling things that had spilled from the elevator. The way he had turned them into kamikazes. Pure instinct had kicked in. Then he'd raced from the building and collapsed in a heap on top of–

"Take a picture, it'll last longer."

"Sorry." Nicholas hadn't realised he was staring.

"What's going on?" It was crazy that Merlyn never sounded annoyed, not even a little bit. Nicholas felt like he could talk to him about anything.

"I… you…"

He couldn't say it.

"Are we playing some sort of vowel game? 'Cos I suck at those."

Nicholas realised there was no way of saying it without sounding like an idiot, so he might as well get it over with. "You haven't mentioned what happened. Last night. With the creatures."

"You mean the mojo? What's to mention?"

"I guess… you might have questions." Nicholas dug his nails into the seat. He shouldn't have said anything. He definitely sounded like an idiot.

"Sure, tons, but you don't want to talk about it so we won't."

"How did you kn—"

Of course Merlyn knew; he could always tell what he was thinking. Merlyn wasn't a Sensitive, though, and Nicholas should find it unnerving, but it was oddly comforting. Somebody understood him, even if he felt like he understood everything less and less.

They passed under the shadow of the Fitzwilliam Museum and as they crawled down King's Parade, he spotted spires stabbing at the sky. The crown of the King's College chapel rose above the surrounding wasteland and a warm ripple of hope spread through him. The college appeared untouched. A small miracle in a world that had given up on such things.

"Why is it at the college?" he asked.

"The Skurk? I guess… You know how leeches feed on people? Chaos Priests feed on knowledge. Centuries of research is stored here. It's a feast every day for something like the Skurkwife."

*Let's just hope it's not hungry for something else.*

Nicholas's jaw ached. He had been clenching it the whole way. Releasing it only caused the vein in his temple to tick. He had no idea what the Chaos Priest would be like, but she sounded formidable.

At the college gates, Merlyn bumped the ambulance over the kerb and steered through the archway, entering the college grounds.

"Keep off the grass my arse," he said as they ploughed onto a square of parched earth that must once have been a lawn. Nicholas noticed that the sign had survived and he whooped when Merlyn mowed it down.

"Ten points!"

"Come on, fifty at least," Merlyn said. "You know how long that sign's been there?"

"Nope."

"Ha, me neither."

Nicholas peered up at the chapel spires, a million insects scuttling in his belly. He hoped the Skurkwife had the answers he so desperately needed. If it turned out to be another bust, he'd have split from the girls for nothing.

Merlyn drew the ambulance to a stop beside the fountain at the centre of the lawn. He was uncharacteristically quiet as he unknotted the wires beneath the wheel and shoved the plastic panel back in place. Scanning the brown lawns for anything with legs, Nicholas popped the door and got out.

"Not even a little bit of sun," Merlyn murmured as he came around the side of the vehicle.

"Something tells me we won't see it again until this is all over."

"Better get going, then."

Nicholas retrieved his backpack from the ambulance and wished he hadn't lost his axe. The hunting knife attached to his belt was no substitute, but it would do for now. He'd kill to have the Drujblade back.

Merlyn stood studying the building opposite the chapel. Wilkins' Building was three storeys high, its windows grand, while dozens of chimneys reached up from the battlements. Merlyn ran his hands over the sandstone.

"You know the way in?" Nicholas asked.

Merlyn pointed up, grinning.

"We climb?"

Merlyn nodded. "Door's too strong to break down. Plus, climbing's fun."

"I had a feeling this wasn't going to be easy."

"Nothing worth doing is. Wow, sometimes I surprise myself with my wiseness."

"Wisdom," Nicholas corrected him.

"Yeah, that."

Nicholas stepped forward as Merlyn reached up to grab a narrow ledge that ran around one of the windows. Knitting his fingers together to form a stirrup, Nicholas took Merlyn's foot and hoisted the other teen up. When Merlyn had found his footing, he reached down and, kicking at the wall, Nicholas hauled himself onto the ledge.

"Easy peasy," Merlyn breathed. "Now we just have to reach that top window." Nicholas didn't dare look up. 'Window' meant high. If he looked up, the enormity of the task would paralyse him. Nicholas's appetite for high places had soured after his run-in with the swooping demons in Bury.

Ignoring the twinge of unease in his gut, he focused on Merlyn, who was appraising the building like a mathematician faced with an equation. On anybody else, his optimism would become irritating, but Nicholas found himself swept up in its tide. He watched admiringly as Merlyn seized a ridge and began to scale the building.

Steeling himself, Nicholas followed, and together they clawed their way up the side of the college. The muscles in Nicholas's weak arm ticked from the exertion, but he ignored it, digging his boots into crevices and feeling his way up the wall. Statues and guttering became footholds and he stuck close to Merlyn, copying where he put his weight. He'd seen photos of the 'night climbers', students who scaled the college buildings using their bare hands, and Nicholas pretended he was one of them – though he'd never seen one weighed down with daggers.

The wind picked up the higher they climbed, wrenching at him then crushing him into the hard stone. His eyes watered. A month ago, he would never have made it off the ground. A month of demon hunting had toughened him up, though. His body had changed and he felt the strength in his muscles.

As the college's scorched lawns fell further away, though, Nicholas found his concentration slipping. He clung to the wall, now at the first floor, his fingers numb with cold. Merlyn was speaking but the wind kept snatching his words away and Nicholas wasn't sure how much longer he could grasp the clefts in the building.

"Here!"

Nicholas glanced up to see Merlyn leaning out of a window. They were only a few feet from the college battlements. How had they climbed so quickly? Just above the window, the chimneys skewered the clouds, which looked even darker up close.

"How'd you get in there?" Nicholas asked, but the wind must have swallowed the question as Merlyn didn't seem to hear. Instead, he stared off across the city. Nicholas seized the window frame and used a final burst of energy to haul himself inside. He only just got his boots under himself in time to prevent his skull cracking against the stone floor. Merlyn was still standing in the window. He hadn't said a word.

"What's wrong?" Nicholas asked.

He moved to Merlyn's side and the hairs on his arms bristled. Beyond the spires of the chapel, the city lay below them, a scorched pit of broken houses as far as he could see. He'd known it was bad, that the emissaries of the Dark Prophets had destroyed everything they could hook their talons into, but seeing it laid out like this stirred a deep ache in his chest. He'd grown up here. This was home. It was where his sister had raised him as her own, and now it was a blackened quarry of sharp edges and smashed lives.

"Man," Merlyn breathed. "That's some view."

Nicholas barely heard him. He couldn't tear his eyes away. This was what they were up against. If he didn't stop Malika and the Prophets, this was what the whole world would become.

"Let's go," he said, shoving away from the window. Retrieving his dagger, he squeezed it until his palm hurt. Nerves wouldn't serve him now. Whatever the Chaos Priest turned out to be, he wouldn't let her get the better of him.

"This way." Merlyn began down the wood-panelled hall, sweeping a torch ahead of them. The scent of ash and old books mingled. They dipped into poky rooms, one leading to the next, and Nicholas's head grazed the ceiling. Finally, they stepped into an alcove and Merlyn touched an old door, then pushed it open.

Squeezing the dagger, Nicholas followed him inside.

The study was neat and deserted. Desk piled high with papers. A painting of a saint. A globe resting by a bookcase. Nicholas imagined it had been cosy once. Now it was somehow old-fashioned and naïve; it had been hermetically sealed off from the madness outside.

There was nobody here, though. No professor. No Skurkwife.

Nicholas raised a questioning eyebrow at Merlyn, who casually strolled up to the bookcase and slid out a volume. He tossed it to the floor, then retrieved a bottle from his bag, dousing the book with liquid. The stink of petrol singed Nicholas's nostrils.

"What are you doing?"

"Only way to draw it out," Merlyn said. He stuck a hand in his pocket and took out a lighter. "Ready?"

Nicholas nodded, wondering how this could possibly summon the Skurk. Merlyn flipped the lighter, then dropped it. The book burst into flame, black smoke choking up to the ceiling.

*"Desecration!"*

A strangled voice filled the room.

*"Thieving, stinking, destructive fools!"*

Nicholas couldn't tell where the voice was coming from, but as he stared into the smoke, he saw a shape forming. He tensed as a shrouded outline emerged. The figure extended bony fingers, becoming more solid by the second, until it hunched before them, cloaked and hooded, strings of lank hair obscuring its face.

*"Debts will be paid! Punishments will be dealt!"*

"Alright, alright," Merlyn said, "you can stop with the theatrics. You're not impressing anybody."

The figure wheezed as it bent down to scratch the charred remains of the book with one of its three hands. Smoke caressed the figure's spindly form, clinging to it the way mist hangs over water.

*"Gone gone gone. Gone forever."*

Nicholas cleared his throat. "We need to talk to you."

The figure's head snapped up and the hair parted. Nicholas's insides hardened in disgust as he glimpsed its skull-like face. Noseless. Lipless. Empty eye sockets like broken egg shells. It was more dead than alive, and though he couldn't tell if it was male or female, the sharp shoulders hinted the Chaos Priest had once been a woman.

*"Speak. None speak to the Skurkwife. None who value their tongue."*

"I was told you could help us." The creature was hideous, but Nicholas had encountered plenty of hideous things in the past months. It would take more than a shroud and an ugly face to intimidate him.

*"Skurkwife helps nobody. Skurkwife observes. Spins shadows. Learns."*

"Pretty soon you'll have nobody left to learn from. Have you been outside lately? The world's dying one town at a time. Cambridge will be gone in weeks, maybe less. The Dark Prophets are coming." Nicholas watched the Chaos Priest's barbed fingers closely, trying not to wonder why it only had three arms. "You've learnt something we need to know. You have to help us."

*"Idiot. Fool. The child knows nothing. Leave. Leave now."*

"It doesn't know who you are, Nick." Merlyn winked at him. "Maybe you should show it what you can do."

Of course. This thing had a mind like anything else they'd ever encountered. Nicholas could read it, push his thoughts into that rotting skull and extract what they needed.

The Skurkwife observed him through greasy strings of hair and Nicholas sharpened his focus, imagining a hand stretching for the Chaos Priest's cranium and roving inside.

A scream tore from the Skurk's throat and it flew at him in a ragged whirl of fabric. The connection severed, Nicholas staggered back as bony fingers plunged for his neck, but then the Skurk came to a halt, its hollow eye sockets gaping at him. He shuddered but stood his ground.

*"Power there. Yes, power."*

Slowly, the Skurk's head tilted from one side to the other, as if it were considering how to peel off his skin in one piece.

*"Different, isn't he? Different as copper and tin. War and sun."*

"Who you calling different?" Merlyn asked.

Nicholas took a step toward the Skurkwife. He'd had it with riddles and people dancing around the truth. It wasn't the first time something had noticed Nicholas wasn't a normal teenager. When Malika had observed it in the upturned bus all those weeks ago, Nicholas had been scared. Not any more.

"You're right, I am different. I was chosen by the Trinity to fight the Dark Prophets. Only they forgot to leave a note, so I've been chasing around in circles like a three-legged cat trying to figure it out. I've been all over town searching for the answer and then your name came up." He jabbed the dagger at the thing. "You look like a maggot farm but apparently you're my last hope, so I'm not going anywhere until you give me what I need."

The Skurk's gurgling breath filled the silence, black smoke guttering from its lipless mouth, but Nicholas wouldn't back down.

*"Mettle, he has. Mettle and metal. There is sense in his words. The world crumbles. Soon there will be nothing left. No towns. No Skurk."*

"Right. No Skurk. Nothing. So you'll help us?"

*"Raise the Trinity. That is his desire."*

"Yes. And…" He took a breath, not wanting to acknowledge what the Elvis figurine had said but knowing it might be important. "Diltraa. We need the demon to stop Malika."

*"Yes."* The Skurk rubbed its skeletal fingers together. *"He desires destruction. Revenge. And there is another… The tall man. Beware him."*

"Who's it talking about now?" Merlyn asked.

The last thread of Nicholas's patience snapped. He pounced on the Skurk, ignoring the stinking plumes of smoke scattering around him, feeling only bone and papery flesh as he seized the Chaos Priest by the neck.

"Start talking sense or we'll burn this entire library to the ground."

*"Savage!"*

The Skurk gnashed its jaw, fingers tugging at Nicholas's hands, but he wouldn't let go, even though they were cold as stone.

*"The tall man undid everything. He lay the pieces."*

Tall man? Nicholas racked his brains. Laurent had been tall, but Laurent was dead. One of the Harvesters, perhaps? Jessica's bodyguard Lash?

*"He hid, but he returned. Him and the wolf."*

It was as if he had been punched in the stomach.

"Nale," Nicholas murmured. The Skurkwife was talking about Benjamin Nale. That was impossible, though. Nale was a Sentinel, an elite Hunter. He had helped them fight Laurent. He wouldn't hurt them unless…

Had he been turned?

Nicholas glanced at Merlyn, whose face was pale, and though his knuckles ached, he squeezed the Skurk tighter.

"What about Nale? What do you know?"

*"Only that he is a piece of the puzzle."*

Nicholas stared into the creature's empty eye sockets, searching for more, but there didn't seem to be any more. The creature was toying with them. Grunting, Nicholas released the Skurkwife. He couldn't bear the feel of it any more.

"Diltraa," he said, trying to focus on what they had come here for. Nale would have to wait. "Will the demon help? Will it kill Malika?"

The Skurk swayed, steepling its fingers.

*"The boy must convince it."*

"Boy? Me? How do I do that?"

*"The demon can return... through the boy."*

Nicholas's head began to spin. He couldn't keep up with the little seeds of information the Skurkwife kept scattering. Why couldn't anybody just give him a straight answer?

*"Yesss,"* the creature hissed. *"Through the boy, Diltraa can return."*

"No," Merlyn said, stepping forward. "You can't."

"What's it talking about?" Nicholas asked.

"It means you."

"But–"

*"Blood. The demon's blood exists within him. The battle. The boy fought and the demon blood mingled with his."*

Nicholas's hand went absent-mindedly to his side where the Drujblade had hung before Malika took it from him. He'd used it to fight Diltraa, and the demon had bled sticky black blood all over him. He remembered being able to taste it. Had he swallowed some of it? Was a part of the demon still inside him?

"How?" he asked, ignoring the trembling in his knees.

*"Skurkwife can do it. Skurkwife can raise the demon. Inside the boy. Stop Malika. Tides might turn. Might not. Skurkwife wants to know."*

Nicholas felt sick. The Skurkwife would bring Diltraa back inside him? He tried to imagine what that meant. Would it be like the Sentinels who were turned into Harvesters? Would he lose himself to the demon? Or would he only acquire Diltraa's power?

He looked at Merlyn, whose face was drawn tight, his sandy hair in his eyes. Merlyn shook his head, his gaze pleading.

"What'll happen?" Nicholas asked the monster. "To me?"

*"Unpredictable."*

"Will it... Diltraa... Will it be able to, you know, control me or anything?"

*"Unpredictable."*

Merlyn's hand closed around his arm. "Nick, don't do this."

But Nicholas knew there was no other way. Somebody once said that when you'd exhausted all the logical options, it was time for the crazy ones. He'd tried them all. He'd failed to raise the Trinity. Rae and Dawn were gone. Esus was flying around the country rallying troupes... He'd seen Bury and Cambridge fall. If this was what it took to stop Malika, he didn't have a choice.

Nicholas ignored Merlyn. "Let's just... Just do it."

"No!" Merlyn cried.

Nicholas closed his hand over Merlyn's. "Trust me."

"We'll find another way. You don't have to do this."

"I do."

"Don't be an idiot. You have no idea what'll happen if you let it raise the demon." His grip tightened. "You'll die."

Nicholas smiled. "We're all going that way anyway. At least the Skurk's giving us a shot. If we can stop her, we can stop all of this."

Merlyn's mouth opened and closed. Nicholas gave him a reassuring squeeze.

"It's okay. Just... promise not to go anywhere. Even if I grow horns."

Merlyn seemed to want to say something but then he simply closed his mouth. Nicholas wanted to hug him, feel his warmth, believe it was all going to work out okay, but he resisted. If he did that, he'd never go through with it.

He turned to the Skurkwife. "Do it."

*"As you wish."*

The Chaos Priest raised its three hands, spreading its fleshless fingers, and planted them on Nicholas's temples. He closed his eyes as the monster drew him close, its freezing touch winding a chill into his bones. Gurgling whispers filled the study and he felt the Skurk corkscrewing in his head, searching, tugging at the stuff that made him.

Where was the grain that could be used to summon Diltraa? Every cell in Nicholas's body resisted this demonic intrusion, but he forced the impulse away, dismantling the barriers Liberty had taught him to create. He imagined his mind splitting open, the protective walls coming away like an orange peel.

*"There."* The Skurk's voice echoed in his skull.

Nicholas felt something shift and then razors tore at the inside of his skull. He opened his mouth to scream and black smoke flurried from the Skurk's maw, pushing into his throat. He couldn't breathe. In his mind's eye, he saw a pulsing red ember illuminating the dark, then two eyes blinked open.

The Skurk released him. For a moment, Nicholas's body didn't feel like his own. He stumbled back, unsure of his feet, his arms flailing, then somebody caught him. Merlyn helped him up and Nicholas found himself clinging to the tattooed teenager.

The Skurkwife's voice rattled at them.

*"It is a man's own mind, not his enemy or foe, that lures him to evil ways."*

The Skurk shuddered into a pulsing mass of smoke, becoming little more than a blurred outline, before fading to shadow. They were alone in the study once more.

"You okay?" Merlyn asked.

"I…" Nicholas found his strength returning. He let go of Merlyn and shoved his hands into his close-cropped hair.

"No horns," Merlyn said.

"Maybe it didn't work. I don't feel any different."

"I hope it didn't work. Let's just get out of here."

Nicholas had expected more pain, more fireworks, more *something*, but he didn't feel any different. Except… The hope he'd felt earlier had vanished, as if a candle snuffer had been dropped over it. In its place, an unfamiliar sensation buzzed. He tried to focus on it, but it kept moving around as if purposefully evading him. Was that the demon? Was Diltraa waiting in there?

Shaking off a shudder, Nicholas headed for the door. "Yeah, let's go."

He felt Merlyn's hand on his back and, for the first time, a ripple of annoyance caressed his insides.

# CHAPTER EIGHT
## AN END OF THINGS

THE RUMOUR OF BATTLE BEGAN AT DAWN. Sam awoke to the wail of a horn and he was up out of bed immediately, his joints creaking as he hurried to the window and stared out over the rows of tents. Smoke eddied between them and Sentinels emerged bleary-eyed, sniffing the air before darting back into the darkened canopies.

Sam didn't bother straightening his crumpled attire – he'd slept in his shirt and trousers again – as he turned from the window, pulling on his shoes and seizing his satchel from the floor. Speeding into the hallway, he shouldered the bag and pushed his hand inside, checking the inventory by touch. Gun. Knife. Poison parcels.

His mind cartwheeled ahead of him, imagining what the sounding of the horn meant, and he checked himself. Took a breath.

*Could be anything*, he reasoned. *A false alarm or a training exercise.*

He arrived at the main hall just as General Hudson barrelled through the front door. The Hunter was grim-faced, her armour smeared purple. Sam went to her.

"What news?" he asked.

"Scavenger demon. Big."

Other Sentinels pooled around them and Hudson gave swift orders, sending them off to rouse the ranks.

"Calm and quiet, lads," she cautioned, though half of them were women. "Let's not lose our heads just yet."

Sam peered up at the general. "A scavenger you said. Show me."

Hudson nodded and Sam followed her out into the camp. Her lieutenants flanked her, their knuckles tight around blades, their young faces set with determination.

Murmurs trickled between the tents and Sam heard the clink of weaponry as the Sentinels assembled. He quick-stepped to match Hudson's pace, not speaking. There was nothing to say until he'd seen what the general had. They passed row after row and Sam was shocked by how much the camp had grown in just a few days. He'd never seen so many Sentinels in one place.

Finally, they emerged onto the outer rim of the encampment. By a mist-wreathed field, Sam spotted sentries standing over a shape. They divided to let Hudson through and Sam followed.

He stared down at the dead thing, a muscular six-legged creature like a hairless wolf, purple veins forking through its fish-pale flesh. It was studded with arrows and its throat had been cut.

"Found it sniffing around the borders," Hudson said.

"A scout." Sam squinted at the horizon. A low fog caressed the tree-line. This demon had been despatched to sniff out the area and report back.

"It's her. Has to be."

"The witch?" Hudson said.

"She'd attack here?" asked one of the younger-looking Sentinels.

"Of course," Sam replied. "She's unafraid of us, no matter our number. Now that she has Them at her back, she will be feeling more confident than ever."

The Sentinel paled.

Sam looked to Hudson. "I'll speak with Isabel, find out what the Sensitives know."

"And I'll station my best fighters around the encampment," the general said. "Sam, stay with her. She'll need your protection."

"Don't let her hear you say that."

He made his way back into the camp, heading for the Sensitives' tent. Even without speaking to them he knew this was what they had been waiting for. Malika was making her move. The Sensitives should be able to confirm specifics, though. The size of her army, how close they were, how long they had.

He swept open the tent and spotted Isabel, wrapped in a purple and gold kaftan, at the centre of a group of Sensitives. She turned to meet his gaze as he entered.

"There isn't much time," she said, leaning into her staff. Pyraemon, the cat, sat at her feet with its fur puffed up against the morning chill.

"How many?"

"Theo? Tell us what you saw."

A boy of about eighteen wiped blood from the corner of his eye. "I only saw a little before she blocked me," he said steadily. "They're obscured by an unnatural fog, but I glimpsed hundreds. She's leading a mongrel army; each creature is different to the one beside it."

"And the Prophets?" Sam asked.

"I didn't see them but that doesn't mean they aren't with her."

"Could you tell the distance?"

"They'll be here within the hour."

Sam sucked in his cheeks. They had less time than he'd feared. He patted the boy's shoulder in thanks, thinking of Nicholas, and one of the other Sensitives handed Theo a tissue for his eye.

"Hudson's crew is protecting the borders," Sam told Isabel.

"They'll need us, too," Theo said.

Isabel nodded, touching the teen's arm. "Pair each Sensitive with a guard at the border, then weave a net. A strong one. Go."

Theo bowed and led the Sensitives away.

"Where is Jessica?" Sam asked when they were alone.

"In the Pentagon Room. She refused to leave. Slept there last night."

"So she's—"

"No change."

Isabel started for the exit but before she could sweep the fabric aside, a muscular shape burst into the tent. It landed on six sinewy legs and crouched, snarling, its purple lips peeled past yellow fangs. Another of Malika's scouts.

"Back!" Sam yelled, but it was too late. The creature flew at Isabel, knocking her to the ground. It lunged for her neck. Before it could snap its jaws around her flesh, Sam buried his boot in the monster's ribs.

The scavenger barely registered the assault, but it turned its slime-dripping muzzle on Sam, rippling across the ground toward him. Sam drew his gun from his satchel and aimed it at the creature.

Before he could fire, a furry shape emitted a strangled shriek, and Pyraemon threw itself at the monster. The cat raked its claws across the demon's muzzle and the creature brayed, but it couldn't reach the cat, which scuttled down its spine, clawing and biting as it went.

"Begone vermin!"

Isabel was back on her feet. She thrust her staff at the creature and the air rippled. Sam watched with a mixture of horror and relief as the scavenger erupted in mid-air. Its skin shrank back and it turned inside out, flopping to the ground in an oozing pile of guts.

Pyraemon only just leapt to safety in time. The cat peered at the mess with satisfaction.

"Filth," Isabel muttered, taking Sam's hand and helping him up.

"You'll have to teach me that trick," Sam said. He eyed the steaming heap. "Another scout. Hudson killed one at the border. This one must have slipped through."

"There will be more. Come, we must ready Jessica." Isabel was already striding for the exit, throwing the canvas aside and heading for the house.

Sam went after her and was jostled by Sentinels who were racing in the opposite direction, towards the centre of the camp, tugging on protective gear and fastening weapons as they went. Hudson would give her orders. Perhaps deliver a stirring speech about overcoming great odds. Remind them this was what they'd been waiting for. But nobody knew about Jessica and Malika. Their terrible link.

"Have you found a way to break their connection?" he asked, out of breath.

"There is no way," said Isabel. "It is unbreakable."

So they were alone against Malika.

Shouldering into the tide of Sentinels, Sam followed Isabel to Hallow House and they headed inside, pushing their way into the packed main hall. Some Sentinels remembered to bow as Isabel passed but most of them were too buzzing with adrenaline, jostling to get outside and fight. The leash was loosening.

"This is where it gets real," bellowed another of the generals, from the staircase. A congregation of Sentinels had formed below him.

"Remember your stations and stick to them. This ship is ours and it ain't going down today or any other."

Ignoring the congregation, Isabel stalked towards one of the back corridors, striking the floor with her staff as she went. Somehow, Pyraemon had kept up with her and was dodging between the Sentinels to follow.

"We're taking her to the safe room, yes?" Sam asked.

"That was the advice of the generals, but if this truly is a Prophet ambush, the hour has come for the Vaktarin to fulfil her duty."

"In what sense?"

"She must gather her strength and fight."

"But… she's so…" He couldn't bring himself to finish the sentence. The darkness of the corridor suddenly felt smothering and Sam hoped the Sentinels weren't pegging their hopes on Jessica to win the battle. Her link with Malika was killing her. She would be no use in battle. Worse, she would be a liability.

"She is the Vaktarin," Isabel snapped, "imbued with a drop of the Trinity's hallowed power and entrusted to safeguard this hamlet. Her mind falters but there is yet power within. She will defend this stronghold until her last breath." She paused and added sombrely, "Even if it is the last thing she does."

Sam shuddered. How could Isabel talk about Jessica like that? Did she mean so little to her? They were practically family, both from another time, another world, but Isabel was dismissing her death as if she were little more than collateral in the fight against the Prophets.

"Cease gawping at me." Isabel struck the floor. "It is what she agreed to all those years ago. What *I* agreed to. She understood the terms. She knew this day would come. I'm surprised it took this long."

Sam kept his mouth shut, though his mind darted in a hundred directions. What would happen if Jessica died? Would another Vaktarin take her place the way Jessica had replaced Isabel? It had been five centuries since her calling. Who could possibly inherit the title?

The question was too huge to contemplate, especially now, and Sam was relieved when they reached the Pentagon Room and he could ignore it.

He watched as Isabel produced a key. She'd locked Jessica in. His anxiety doubling, Sam stood by as the old woman opened the door and slipped into the room. He peered in, his sight adjusting to the dark. Jessica was pacing, murmuring something under her breath, appearing to count on one hand, then curling her hands into frustrated fists. He strained to hear her.

"She was here she was here she was here," Jessica whispered. "And so was I and so was I and so…"

More nonsense.

"Jessica," Isabel said. "Come."

She spoke as if commanding a dog, Sam thought. Dutifully, Jessica drifted to the other woman, peering into her face. She raised a hand and twisted fingers through Isabel's white hair.

"Ash and snow and chalk," Jessica breathed.

"Come with me," Isabel said, ignoring Jessica's words. "Now."

She took the woman's arm and drew her roughly back into the corridor.

"You, man, go ahead and clear the way," Isabel ordered.

Sam nodded and hurried down the corridor ahead of them, his unease expanding like a balloon in his chest. There was no way Jessica could fight. She was a ghost now. A child. Isabel was mad to think differently but he couldn't interfere. She'd shoot him down or dismiss him entirely, and he had to stay with Jessica; she had offered him sanctuary more than once over the years and he wouldn't abandon her at her weakest ebb. Isabel would soon discover that her plan, whatever it was, would not work, and then she'd need him.

"Sorry, chap, to one side if you would," he asked an elderly Sentinel at the end of the corridor.

"Is it one of them devils?" the Sentinel asked, his eyebrows bunching together as he peered over Sam's shoulder. Sam thought of Richard and his father. It had been months since then.

"Not yet," Sam said, and the Sentinel looked surprised when Isabel and Jessica emerged from the darkness.

"Trinity bless you," he whispered hoarsely, bowing his head.

"And you, son of Norlath," Isabel said as she passed. She pushed Jessica through the main hall and up the stairs, bending into her staff, jaw clenched. Just what was she doing? Sam had half expected her to cast Jessica out into the camp.

Swiftly, he went after them.

At the landing, the two women finally stopped at a set of double doors. Isabel nudged her staff at them and they flew open. A clamour of yells and monstrous squeals pushed inside.

"They have arrived already," Sam breathed.

Through the doors, he glimpsed a balcony and, beyond it, the camp. Figures charged for the fields at the edge of the encampment, which had transformed into a seething arena of thrashing figures. The camp's borders hadn't yet been breached but Sam wasn't sure how long they'd hold – he hoped the Sensitives had raised a protective barrier in time. His eyesight wasn't what it used to be, but he could tell there were as many Harvesters toiling in the fields as Sentinels. They clashed blades and livid blue light flickered as the Harvesters' gauntlets wreaked their terrible evil.

Sam found he wasn't breathing. He should be out there, not a party to Isabel's cruel parade. He was needed. Every man and woman was needed now.

Isabel held Jessica steady before the open doors.

"Listen!" she said over the din of battle. "Remember all those years hence! Steel yourself! The Trinity call you!" She pushed the staff between them. "Take it! Drain it of the power I have imbued it with! Remember! Do what you must!"

Jessica's eyes were emotionless marbles, her face blank, but somehow she seemed to understand Isabel's words. Her fingers crept around the staff and for a moment she held it the way an infant might an alien artefact.

Then, as Sam watched, the staff vibrated in her grip. Jessica's spine straightened, and pin-pricks of golden light stirred in her pupils. Her knuckles tightened, her cheeks flushing pink and her lips firming into a line. She bent to peer beyond the balcony with renewed interest. Whatever Isabel had done to the staff, it appeared to have revived her.

When she spoke, Jessica's voice was unbending as steel.

"All who stand against us shall perish."

Isabel grinned as she spread her arms wide, and Jessica turned on her heel, wind tangling in her hair as she stepped through onto the balcony.

Mouth agape, Sam watched as she thrust the staff aloft, stirring the air so that the clouds churned.

"My goddess," he murmured, and found Isabel shooting him a look of triumph.

"Oh he of little faith."

Sam couldn't speak. He recalled Isabel in the library, muttering incantations over the staff. She had appeared so tired for so long, and now he understood why. She had been sacrificing her own power; pouring it into the staff. All for this moment, when Jessica would need it the most.

Even if he tried to speak, Sam's voice would be drowned out because, at that moment, a sound boomed across the battlefield and lightning blasted from the sky. On the horizon, beyond the fields, enormous shadows loomed. A dozen creatures, all twice the height of a double-decker bus, tore trees aside and beat and bruised the landscape as they bore down on the battlefield. They thumped along on their knuckles, their backs solid muscle, their heads snout-like and swivelling with a single cycloptic eye.

"Daikaiju," Sam whispered. Ancient monsters he'd only ever seen in textbooks.

The Sentinels' steel flashed and sang and the bravest mounted the first of the Daikaiju, digging blades into its hide. Most were thrown aside and stomped on and the Daikaiju emitted a bone-splitting roar.

Above the warring figures, the sky spewed winged monstrosities that mewled as they dove into the thronging mass. The Sentinels were being attacked from all sides, hemmed in and forced back toward the camp. They fought to stand their ground, but the forces they faced were terrible.

Observing it all from her lofty perch, Jessica raised her free hand, clenching it into a fist, then bringing it down. At the camp's furthest border, the earth shuddered as if pounded by an immense force, and a sucking hole appeared. Two of the Daikaiju were dragged into the earth's belly, followed by smaller demons. Harvesters grappled with the shifting earth and were swallowed whole while Sentinels hooted, immune to the power tormenting their enemy.

"Yes!" Isabel hooted. "Show them! Show them the power of the Sentinels!"

Jessica raked the air with her fingers and lightning burst from the heavens, sending Harvesters flying.

But Sam glimpsed something she hadn't and the breath snagged in his throat.

One of the enormous Daikaijus had made it across the field to the camp's border, its back studded with arrows. It bowled towards the first row of tents, but it stopped suddenly as veins of green light crackled through the air. It tried again and again but it could go no further.

The Sensitives' net was holding. The Prophets' forces couldn't enter.

Enraged, the monster beat its fists against the invisible barrier, sending shockwaves of green light crackling upwards.

"None shall pass!" Jessica hollered, raising a hand. Lightning flashed from the sky and struck the beast. Shrieking, it jerked and twitched as the lightning ravaged it. Finally, it toppled and, as it collapsed in a steaming heap, the house shook under Sam's shoes.

He had never imagined the Vaktarin could command such power. He watched as Jessica thrust the staff at an enormous oak tree, which strained against its roots, then toppled to the ground, pulverising a pack of creatures. She sent her gaze skyward and emitted a guttural shriek.

For a moment, there was nothing. Then the air filled with zipping black specks that darted in their hundreds across the fields.

"Birds," Sam uttered. They clawed at Harvesters' faces, digging their beaks into eye sockets. The Sentinels went untouched and each took advantage of this new attack, sliding blades into the pelts of six-legged creatures and felling howling Harvesters.

Emboldened by their leader's assault, more Sentinels turned on the Daikaiju, loosing arrows and hacking at their legs. One was set ablaze and became a gyrating funnel of flame.

Sam's hand ached from gripping his knife. The tide was turning. Tentacled monsters were hacked limb from limb and the Harvesters were tiring. Even the Daikaiju were suffering – now only eight stood, blood-stained and exhausted.

"Is this the full might of the Prophets?" Jessica bellowed, her voice booming over the tents and out into the battlefield beyond the protective barrier.

*The Prophets*, Sam thought. It was their evil that polluted the land, but where were they? If this was the battle to end them all, where were the masters of all evil?

A sudden hush fell. Sentinels and Harvesters alike turned to peer at the trees at the far edge of the field. It was as if they'd heard something. Sam strained to listen, but he heard only the wind.

Then a figure slipped from the forest. Sam squinted, his eyesight failing him, but he could tell it was a woman, her dress ice white, her hair flame-red, and though his vision was poor, he knew who it was.

"And so she comes," Isabel murmured, knotting together her fingers.

For a moment, Malika stood motionless, assessing the misty battlefield. Then she raised a gleaming sickle and howled, dashing into the field, her white dress a flickering flame. Sentinels rushed to meet her, but she was swifter and deadlier than any of them. She danced between their blades and her own curved weapon flashed. Blood spurted into the air.

"It's no good," Sam murmured. "More. We need more fighters."

*We need the Trinity*, he thought, but he knew that was impossible until Nicholas and Rae arrived. Where were they? What if they were too late?

Unable to wait any longer, he turned and hurried down the landing, taking the stairs as swiftly as his old bones allowed. In the entrance hall, the second wave of Sentinels waited, eyes burning with battle fever. They'd heard everything taking place outside and were desperate to join the fight.

"Now!" he yelled at the general at the front. "We're needed now!"

The man shook his head. "Hudson will give the order."

"The witch is here!" Sam reasoned. "If we don't stop her she'll take the house."

"Sorry, Wilkins, I've been ordered to await Hudson's command."

Sam held the general's gaze a moment and, knowing it was futile, ran for the door, staggering out into the camp. He had no plan. He was driven by pure instinct. He had to find a way to protect the house, bring Malika down. His knees complained as he half ran, half shambled between the tents, heading for the field.

Before he could clear them, though, the air changed. It vibrated painfully in his ears, like a helicopter's whomping blades, and the earth trembled. Around him, the pegs holding the tents in place pinged from the ground and they collapsed in a wave. The camp levelled in a sickening rush.

Standing at its centre, Sam now had a clear view of the battlefield. Green veins of light crackled and died at the camp's edge and there, a figure stepped forward.

Sam didn't move. He couldn't – his insides were spasming in horror. Malika's dress was no longer white. The fabric was soaked in blood, turning it a glistening crimson. Blood ran in rivulets down her face and her sickle was caked in torn flesh.

She had undone the Sensitives' protective barrier.

"Still standing, old man," she hissed as she approached.

A wall of Harvesters and demons pressed behind her and, beyond them, loomed the remaining Daikaiju.

"You'll die this day," Sam told her. "None shall take the Sentinel stronghold."

Malika's lips twisted with amusement. "The fool cannot see what is before his very eyes. It is already done. The stronghold is breached. There's nowhere left to hide."

Sam's hand went for his satchel and Malika wagged a finger at him.

"Oh, not this time," she said. "Now it's your turn to scream."

She pounced, knocking him to the ground. The breath huffed from his lungs and Sam gasped as Malika raised the sickle, blood between her teeth as she grinned.

"Stop!"

The red witch faltered. She glanced past Sam, toward the house, and her grin widened.

"Don't tell me you care for this shrivelled old mummy," she spat.

"Leave him. Take me."

It was Jessica. She had abandoned the safety of Hallow House.

Sam struggled under Malika's weight. If he could reach his gun or his dagger, he could stop her. Buy them some time. He didn't get the chance, though. Malika grunted as something knocked her off him and he rolled out of the way, pushing himself up from the ground.

Somebody helped him to his feet and he looked up at the general from the front hall, whose face was grim. Beside them, Isabel watched and Sam saw that the second wave of Sentinels had gathered at their backs, forming a barrier in front of the house.

All eyes were on the two women at the centre of the camp. Sam realised Jessica had struck Malika with the staff. The red witch was already back up and the two women faced each other, one sticky with blood, the other faintly glowing.

"Finally," Malika hissed, "we are together again." She laughed. "You look weary. What could possibly be the cause?"

"Leech all the power you like from me," Jessica said, plucking a knife from the ground. "You will never be whole. You will never have dominion over the Sentinels."

Sam frowned as Jessica raised the knife, and his mouth gaped as she plunged the blade towards her own belly.

"NO!" Isabel shrieked. She hurtled forward and seized Jessica's arm, deflecting the blade before it could do any damage.

"Stop this!" she said.

"It is the only way." Jessica attempted to free her arm. "I have always known it, but I was afraid. Please. You must let me finish it."

"This is not the way," Isabel pleaded. "Killing her will not stop the Prophets. You cannot leave us yet."

"Look out!" yelled one of the Sentinels.

Sam grimaced as Malika flew at Jessica and, at that moment, the stillness that had settled over the battlefield split apart. Sentinels surged forward to clash with Malika's army and chaos erupted around Sam. Sentinels and Harvesters clashed, while monsters tore at any available limb, devouring the half-dead as they lay wounded.

Amid the war cries, Malika and Jessica wrestled each other for the knife. Isabel was thrust aside, and Sam caught her before she could fall. Steadying herself, Isabel attempted to lunge for the two women, but he held her back.

"We cannot *all* die," he grunted.

"We must stop this insanity!" the old woman yelled.

Malika buried a fist in Jessica's face but the Vaktarin barely registered it. She twisted out of the red witch's grip, a flicker of triumph playing on her lips before she plunged the knife into her own stomach.

Malika howled, writhing into the earth in agony.

"No!" Isabel broke free from Sam's grasp and lurched forward, wrapping her arms around Jessica. Weakened, the other woman leant into her mentor.

"Do it," she murmured. "Finish it."

"Shhh." Isabel pulled the dagger free and tossed it aside, pressing a hand over the wound. "Inside. We must retreat."

Malika writhed in the mud, her own hands digging into a twin wound in her gut, attempting to stem the flow of blood. None came to her aid; her Harvesters were too busy hacking at Sentinels, and for a moment Sam glimpsed the loneliness of evil. He felt a tiny twinge of pity in his chest, but then he remembered what Malika was, what she had done, and he dismissed her as she attempted to get to her feet, then collapsed back into the mud.

He squinted around them and spotted Hudson trading blows with a Harvester. The general drove her sword through the figure's chest and shoved it aside.

"Hudson!" he called. The general's head snapped in his direction and she understood without him having to speak. Sheathing her sword, she hurried over and took Jessica into her arms, scooping her off the ground.

"Inside," Isabel urged. "Now."

The general turned and pushed through the crowd, Jessica's head bobbing into her shoulder. Hudson mounted the front stairs and charged inside. Sam and Isabel went after them. He drew his pistol and shot anything with tentacles or fangs.

In the entrance hall, the walls were blood-stained and gouged to pieces. The Prophets' forces had made their way inside. The protection Jessica had gifted the house for five centuries was spent, and Hallow House was vulnerable. Anything could get inside now.

Hudson booted a scavenger demon aside as she headed for the stairs, stomping on its skull as she went.

"Where are you going?" Isabel demanded sharply.

The general looked confused. "The safe room."

Isabel shook her head. "No such thing, not now. The garden is the only safe space."

The floor shuddered and Sam watched in horror as the front doors were smashed inward. An enormous fist burst inside along with the unmistakable stench of a Daikaiju.

"The house will be torn apart," he uttered hoarsely.

"This way!" Isabel urged, hurrying for the corridor that led into the bowels of the building, but Sam stopped abruptly as he glimpsed a portly figure hurrying down the main stairs.

"Aileen!" he exclaimed. The former landlady was covered in dust and blood, wielding a crossbow.

"They've reached the first floor, dear," Aileen puffed. "Held them off as long as I could."

A six-legged svartulf came tearing after her and Aileen spun to fire at it. She hit the creature right between the eyes and Sam almost whooped. Then he noticed a single grumpy eye staring at him from Aileen's back, and he almost chortled in surprise.

"What's he doing in there?" he asked. Pyraemon was stuffed into a bag slung across Aileen's back. The ugly cat's fluffy head stuck out the top and his pinched face appeared more cross than ever.

"Oh, him. Found him upstairs." Aileen shrugged. "He was fighting off something with too many eyes to count. Nearly joined the big cat-scratcher in the sky. He squashed himself into my bag after I'd rescued him, must be tired. Doesn't he remind you of Rudy?"

Sam recalled Aileen's cat at the safehouse.

"Perhaps," he said. "Follow us." Sam clasped her free hand and, together, they plunged into the corridor, seeing Hudson and Isabel ahead. Other Sentinels charged after them, shooting back at whatever gave chase, and Sam was grateful for their protection, though he knew it couldn't last much longer. They were heading deeper and deeper into Hallow House. From here there would be no escape. What was Isabel planning now? He'd already misjudged her once today, but this felt like an even more desperate move.

"Is she alright?" Aileen asked. Sam knew she meant Jessica and he couldn't answer. He was still piecing together what he'd seen. Jessica had weakened Malika by harming herself. Was that the only way to stop the red witch? By killing Jessica? He grimaced at the thought, not wanting to believe it.

At the end of the corridor, two doors stood open and they hurried into a garden. Once, it must have been magnificent, but now the plants were dying. Blackened trees slumped into the earth and the ground was littered with mulched petals.

"My, my, I had no idea this existed," Aileen said.

"Me neither." Sam didn't have time to take it all in. He could already hear Malika's army approaching. He slammed the doors behind the last of the Sentinels.

"Barricade it," Hudson ordered the other fighters, setting Jessica down against a tree. The Vaktarin was barely conscious, her dress stained at the belly, her complexion ashen.

The Sentinels set about destroying a bench and using it to board up the doorway. Hudson approached Sam and Aileen. "You up to a fight?"

"I've seen more battles than you've had cold dinners," Sam said, brandishing a dagger that he had kept in his satchel.

"I don't doubt it."

Sam noticed that Isabel had gone off into the garden, her wiry form almost disappearing amid the withered foliage.

"Wait here," he told them, hurrying after her. He found Isabel seeking something out in a small clearing.

"What are you doing?"

"The chamber," she said, leaning into her staff to bend down and smooth the earth away.

"Chamber?"

"Below the garden. There is an opening here. We must find it."

"Below? You mean underground?"

"Yes, yes."

"That's risky."

Isabel pushed aside clumps of earth, making a small hollow in the ground. "It is the only sanctuary now."

"But, down," Sam reasoned. "We can't go down."

"We must. The chamber will protect her."

"If we go down, we'll be trapped."

A sound like stone against glass came from above and Sam's gaze snapped skyward. Up past the tops of the emaciated trees, the garden's firmament was under attack. Winged things hurled themselves at the glass and Sam watched in horror at the fine cracks already appearing.

"We can't go down," he said again. "They have already breached the house. If they breach the gardens and then the entrance to the chamber, we're done for."

Isabel paused, cocking her head at him like an unsettled cat and Sam saw that Pyraemon was still nestled in Aileen's bag. The cat's eye darted about at the demons.

"What do you suggest?" Isabel asked.

"If we fight, we fight here in the open. Take Jessica, weave whatever charms you can, just keep them away from her."

The old woman regarded him a moment longer, her expression conflicted. She must know he was right, but she was too proud a creature to take orders. On this occasion, though, her instincts to protect Jessica won out.

Above, one of the winged monsters had made a hole in the firmament. It scrabbled and bellowed, pushing its way inside.

"BREACH!" Sam yelled. "Above!"

At the doors, the Sentinels' heads swivelled skyward. The winged creature strained through the hole in the glass and finally burst into the garden, spreading huge sail-like wings and diving swifter than any bird Sam had ever seen. It plucked Hudson off her feet. She thrashed her legs as she was dragged up and the monster clawed at her neck. Red rain fell.

"Jessica!"

Isabel scrambled back through the garden, going to kneel at Jessica's side. She was pale as parchment, clutching her stomach. Isabel touched her temples and, as Sam joined them, he saw her hand shaking from exertion. Finally, the Vaktarin's eyes struggled open.

"Isabel," she murmured. "Is it done? Is she dead?"

Sam eyed the firmament. More creatures were shoving through the hole in the glass roof.

"Fan out," he commanded the other Sentinels, whose eyes were filled with the pain of watching Hudson die. "Weaver, Grieves, May, guard the entrance. Everybody else split up, cover as much ground as you can."

He looked down at the two women by the tree.

"We must fall back," he told them.

"You did well," the old woman was saying to Jessica. "But we must get away from–"

The garden doors splintered apart.

Raising his arm against needling shards of wood, Sam watched as a dozen tentacles lashed through the ragged opening. He plunged forward, slashing the tentacles with his dagger while his other hand fumbled with the catch on the satchel. Panic rising in his throat, he felt inside and finally gripped what he sought. Withdrawing a white parcel, he hurled it into the centre of the thrashing limbs.

The creature emitted a piercing shriek and the stench of sizzling flesh filled Sam's nostrils. The tentacles flopped lifelessly to the earth, but he heard other things scrabbling around in the hall outside.

"Fall back," he said, seeing that Jessica was on her feet, leaning in to Isabel. Aileen was braced before them protectively, her crossbow aimed at the door. Together, the four of them moved deeper into the garden. Already, the other Sentinels were battling the winged monsters that had breached the firmament.

Sam kept his eyes up, watching the swooping creatures target the other Sentinels, cackling whenever they tasted blood. Aileen shot one of them and reloaded her bow, aiming for another.

An almighty crash sounded behind them, and Sam chanced a glance over his shoulder. Where the doorway had been, a Daikaiju had demolished the entire wall. Its single red eye swept the garden and stopped as it reached Sam and the others.

"Isabel," he said, wondering if she could do anything to hold it back, but he remembered her trembling hand. Aiding Jessica was draining her. She looked fit to collapse.

"They're uglier than the drawings," Aileen commented, and Sam felt a swell of affection for her. She was a Sentinel to the core.

"Keep going," he said. "I'll hold it off."

"Admirable, dear, really," Aileen said. "But where you fight, I fight. Remember?"

Sam caught her eye and smiled.

"Aye, I remember." He gestured to Isabel and Jessica. "Go. We'll do what we can."

"Brave until the end," Isabel said. "May the Trinity ever watch over you."

"From you, madam, that is quite a gesture."

Sam and Aileen watched as the two women staggered further into the withered heart of the garden, then they turned to confront the Daikaiju. Even at a hundred yards away, it was colossal, its muscular forearms the size of tree trunks. It beat the earth, preparing to charge.

"Plan, dear?" Aileen ventured.

"Stab it in the soft bits generally works."

"Right you are."

Aileen placed her crossbow on the ground and drew the sword from her back, stabbing it into the earth and then retrieving the bow. Sam removed the last of the white parcels from his satchel. A few well-aimed blows should bring the thing down. As long as it didn't paste them with its granite fists first.

The Daikaiju leered down at them, its meaty breath blasting into them and Aileen pulled a face.

"No wonder they were banished. What a pong."

"Quite."

As if it had understood them, the demon bellowed so loudly the remaining glass panels in the firmament exploded. Lethal shards rained down. Sam threw his satchel over their heads, wincing as the shrapnel lanced his flesh.

The ground shook as the Daikaiju charged.

Not wasting a breath, Aileen loosed half a dozen arrows at it. They bounced off the demon's tough flesh and it kept coming. A massive fist swung at them and Sam ducked just in time. Aileen was more agile than she appeared, scooting back, then seizing her sword from the earth and landing a well-placed lunge. The demon screamed as a massive finger was lopped free.

"Ha!" Sam hooted. "One down."

"Let's not keep score, dear!"

Enraged, the Daikaiju went for them again.

"The eye!" Sam shouted, dodging another blow that sent him tumbling.

"What?" Aileen slashed with the sword, missing the monster's hoof by inches.

Sam struggled back to his feet. "I need to get the eye."

"Nasty. I like it."

An idea struck him and Sam looked sidelong at Aileen.

"How's your aim today?"

"Never better."

"Good. Load her up."

Sam watched as Aileen stowed her sword and slotted an arrow into the crossbow, then he wrapped one of the white packages around the arrowhead.

"When you're ready," Sam said, grunting as the Daikaiju's claws flashed at him again. "Meaning now!"

Aileen fired.

The arrow seemed to fly in slow-motion. It sailed through the air before plunging into the demon's red eye. White powder exploded and the Daikaiju clawed at its face, its screams so loud Sam worried his eardrums would burst.

As the package did its horrible work, Sam and Aileen scurried back, anticipating the inevitable. Seconds later, the demon crashed to the ground right where they had been standing. The remnants of its eye foamed and its huge limbs twitched, then went still.

"I believe I should start calling you David," Sam panted at the former landlady.

"It has a certain ring, dear."

A new excited gibbering filled the atrium as a dozen svartulfs flew into the garden.

Fatigue washed through Sam. It was never-ending. Malika's army was indomitable. They'd keep coming until every one of the Sentinels was dead.

"Oh my," Aileen uttered.

"Yes," Sam said. "I just hope Isabel and Jessica found their way to safety."

"Not much safety round these parts now."

"No."

Sam didn't want to think about it. The svartulfs rippled between the trees, their electric blue eyes flashing in their direction, and Sam braced himself for a fresh attack.

"It's been fun, dear."

Aileen's hand was in his.

"Like the good old days," Sam said.

"To the death, eh?"

"And whatever's after."

The svartulfs surrounded them, forming a ring of bared fangs and twitching viper tails.

Sam and Aileen stood back-to-back, blades drawn.

The first of the demons pounced, but its jaw slammed into the ground and it yowled angrily, unable to move. Sam squinted past it and saw a furry shape had the demon by the tail. It looked like a dog.

Growling, the dog dragged the demon back. Strong jaws snapped around the demon's throat and it sagged lifelessly to the ground.

"Is that who I think it is?" Aileen murmured.

"Zeus!" Sam exclaimed.

As one, the svartulfs turned on the grey wolfhound, but they were no match for the dog's swift and ferocious dance. Sam watched as it tore at the demons and, all around the garden, new figures emerged from amid the parched foliage.

"Reinforcements," Sam said.

A tall, broad man clomped towards them. A bushy beard concealed the lower half of his face and his eyes were quick and bright.

"Well blow me," Sam uttered.

"Nale," Aileen cried.

Benjamin Nale clubbed a svartulf aside as it pounced at him. His club was stuffed with bent nails and the svartulf didn't appear to know what had hit it. It sagged lifelessly to the ground and the Hunter stood before Sam and Aileen, panting.

"Come." His voice was so low it vibrated in Sam's chest.

"Where'd you come from?" he asked.

Nale used his club to point back at the far side of the atrium, where a fresh hole had been rent in the firmament at ground level. He had busted his way inside. Jessica and Isabel were already limping towards the opening.

"Well I never," Aileen said.

"Hurry."

Nale led them through the garden. They fought off more demons as they went, though there were fewer now that reinforcements had arrived. A dozen other Sentinels roared as they tackled the demon horde, loosing arrows and driving their blades into the monsters until the ground was slick with black blood.

At the opening, Isabel and Jessica were delaying.

"We can't leave," the old woman was saying.

"The house has fallen," Nale reasoned.

"We cannot abandon it," Isabel said, but as she gazed around the atrium, then at Jessica, her expression darkened. She peered at Sam and he nodded, though he wished he didn't agree with Nale. Finally, Isabel said, "Take her," and Nale helped Jessica through the hole in the firmament.

"Go," Isabel told Sam, and he and Aileen squeezed through the hole, standing back as Isabel stepped through. She paused, moving out of the way to allow the remaining Sentinels to barrel outside. As the demons gave chase, Isabel stepped up, touching the broken glass around the hole in the firmament, murmuring under her breath. The air rippled and then she turned to face Sam.

"That'll hold them for a while," she said. Black bags were under her eyes and Sam could tell she had given more of herself than any of them.

Aileen stepped forward and gave Isabel her arm. The old woman would normally have dismissed the gesture, but she took it silently, her staff clasped in her other hand, taking stumbling steps away from the atrium.

The air was charred by battle. Sam had never been on this side of Hallow House, and he found that it was almost entirely surrounded by forest. A way had been cleared through the trees. An escape route, perhaps, should the need arise. He wondered if Hudson had planned the route and alerted Nale.

A ragtag gang of Sentinels hurried down the makeshift road. They were all broken in their own ways, some covered in demon blood, others seemingly held together by hastily applied bandages. Only a dozen or so in total. Was this all that was left of the Sentinels?

Sam went after them, Aileen and Isabel at his side.

Ahead, Nale helped Jessica into what resembled an old carnival wagon. It rested beside a decrepit old caravan and a minibus that had seen better days. So this was the cavalry. Nale's little army. That must be where he'd been all these months. Assembling his own infantry.

"Inside," Nale said as they reached the wagon.

Aileen helped Isabel up the steps and they disappeared into the wagon. Sam stepped up, then paused to stare back. He felt his sanity slipping. Hallow House was ablaze, half destroyed, ash and black smoke belching into the sky.

"Trinity spare us," he murmured, then he clambered into the wagon and slammed the door.

# CHAPTER NINE
## Esus

Rae stood at the street corner watching people mill about. She frowned. It had been over a month since she had been anywhere resembling a functioning town, but Oxford seemed to have evaded the Dark Prophets' poisonous reach. The sight of so many people, two dozen at least, going about their lives as if nothing had happened was a shock. Although leaden clouds hung above the mottled yellow-stone buildings, everybody appeared to be getting on with things as usual.

"It's like they have no idea," said Dawn.

They had to know, though. There were reports all over the internet. Perhaps the internet had busted here, too, and nobody knew about the demonic energy polluting the rest of the UK.

Rae snuck a look at Dawn and could tell she was nervous. They had traipsed all the way here, barely sleeping, crossing fields strewn with corpses and strange eggs that stank when they crushed them. The landscape was changing as demonic creatures bedded in, destroying the balance. They were top of the food chain now. She'd seen no birds. No wildlife. Only shadows in the trees and slimy burrows so big they could fit a wild cat.

At first, Dawn had attempted to make small talk. She had been practically mute when they first met, but ever since the apocalypse kicked in, she had grown more talkative. Maybe her desire to fix the world had short-circuited her shyness. As they trudged through the countryside, she filled the silences and Rae quietly fumed, because silences didn't always need to be filled. The closer they drew to Oxford, though, the quieter Dawn had become, and Rae knew her thoughts were occupied with her mother.

She wasn't any good at comforting words, so she had done what she could. She forced Dawn to sleep, keeping watch as things gibbered and shrieked in the night. She foraged for food and shelter. She incinerated anything that moved. For years, she had clung to a set of rules, but the rules had changed with the world. Except for the last one. *Don't let the monsters see you.*

As Dawn became preoccupied with her thoughts, Rae became lost in her own. The voice in her head wouldn't shut up. Sometimes when she blew up a demon, the voice fell quiet for a bit, but it always came back. Sneering at everything she did. Spinning prophecies of doom.

"Who's Twig?" Dawn asked on the second day as they traipsed down a country road. "It's a name, right?"

Rae's fists curled and she hated Dawn for asking. Why did everybody always have to poke their noses where they didn't belong?

"Sorry." Dawn's cheeks were pink. "I didn't mean… It's just, you talk about them in your sleep and I thought maybe…"

They wandered in silence but Rae's head buzzed. Just the mention of Twig caused painful memories to crash around inside her skull. She saw him with the dirty blanket drawn up to his nose. Then she saw him dead. His face half-buried in debris. The shop had blown up because of her. Because she lost her temper when that gang invaded her hiding place.

"Uh, Rae?"

Dawn was staring at the ground. Rae smelled burning and saw that where she had been walking, the earth was black and smoking. The girls regarded each other and then Rae slumped on, adjusting her rucksack, which was hot against her back. Dawn hurried along beside her and Rae felt her eyes heavy on her. Maybe she was worried she'd explode.

"He was my friend, okay?" Rae said, unable to take Dawn's stares any longer.

"Okay."

Rae felt the words multiplying in the back of her throat and she squeezed her knuckles. "He died in Bury."

"I'm sure…" Dawn closed her mouth. "I'm sorry… I'm sorry your friend is dead."

"Don't need pity."

"Just because… That's not what I meant."

They turned onto another road, following Dawn's map.

"He was good at stealing. Kept us alive. Stuff he found… I'd be dead too if it wasn't for him."

"You were on the streets."

Rae nodded.

"That explains why you're always able to find shelter." Dawn smiled, and Rae didn't know what to make of it. She always felt like she was under a microscope. Something to be studied. The things she could do, she'd probably be locked in a government lab if she wasn't so good at hiding. She pushed the image away.

"Your mum a nut?" she asked.

"Sort of."

"I'm sorry."

"I don't need your pity." Dawn smiled again, sadly, and Rae found herself smiling back.

After a few more miles, they had arrived in Oxford. They were out of water and Rae could tell Dawn was exhausted, but she was determined, too.

"It's this way," Dawn said, and they wandered into the city. Now that they were closer, Rae saw that most of the shops were boarded up. Some had been looted. There were no monsters, though.

"Waiting for night, maybe," she murmured. She found herself wishing Nicholas was here, but only because he could sense the enemy.

They kept going, cutting a path through the streets. Dawn picked up the pace and her breathing quickened. Rae kept watch as they went, feeling like a tourist, as if they'd travelled into the past. The demons must have moved north. They hadn't yet spread across England's belly.

Finally, they stood before an old house that bore a hospice sign.

"This it?" she asked, and Dawn nodded, taking the steps and pushing her way into the white reception area. Rae followed, balking at the smell of bleach, and watched Dawn go to an unmanned front desk.

"Nobody's here," she said, looking confused.

"Lunch break?"

Undeterred, Dawn shoved open a set of double doors and Rae went after her, up a staircase, unease squirming through her as they went down one empty corridor after another. In the distance, she heard somebody yelling. They went up another set of stairs and came to a door marked 'SUNBEAM WARD'.

Dawn punched the keypad a few times, but the door wouldn't open.

"My turn." Rae pooled heat into her palms and blew the door apart.

"Thanks." Dawn hurried through the singed doorway and into an antiseptic corridor that was lined with more doors. The nurse's station was deserted, and Rae began to wonder what had happened to the staff. They couldn't have abandoned the hospice.

"She's got to be here," Dawn muttered. "Got to be."

As she hurried ahead, Rae paced from door to door, finding empty bedrooms and a room with a TV playing static. As she returned to the corridor, she saw that Dawn had stopped in a doorway. Rae came up behind her and glanced over her shoulder.

In the room, a woman stood by the window. She was rake-thin and Rae imagined she could see right through her, but then she realised it was just the way the light caught her white dressing gown.

Dawn stood still just inside the door and Rae felt the tension in the air. Then Dawn took a few furtive steps into the room and, when the woman looked at her, her pupils so big and black they were almost inhuman, Dawn froze.

"Mum?" she said.

★

Nicholas awoke to the sound of Merlyn's voice in his ear.

"It's just a dream. You're fine. You're fine."

He had a vague sense of being gently rocked. Where were they? What was going on? His tongue was fat in his mouth and a sticky heat coursed through him, as if he'd been wrestling a monster. Or a nightmare. Yes, a nightmare. There had been flames and bone-white eyes and a voice like claws dragging steel.

"Are you back?" Merlyn asked. His arms were around Nicholas, his face so close he could smell the sleep on him. They were squashed on to the bed in the back of the ambulance, the sleeping bag discarded, a pillow on the floor.

"What happened?" Nicholas asked.

"Nightmare, I'm guessing."

Merlyn's embrace slackened but he didn't let go. His customary grin was pinched.

"The Skurk really did a number on you. Are you alright?"

Nicholas wiped sweat from his forehead.

"I'm fine."

But the nightmare was trapped in his chest. He tried to shake the feeling of dread the way a dog shakes off water. They had left King's College and driven to the outskirts of Cambridge, parking in a copse that gave them cover from the roads. He hadn't felt any different after the Skurkwife's magic. He'd expected something – if not horns, then a sick feeling; cramps or a crashing headache. The lack of symptoms was more disturbing than what he'd let the Skurkwife do.

Maybe the Skurk hadn't succeeded. Maybe Diltraa really was banished forever. But the dreams… The images were jumbled, like a deck of cards thrown in the air, and he was left with a marrow-deep sense of unease. Maybe the demon was just inside him waiting.

"Want to talk about it?"

Merlyn's rough fingers grazed his inner arm.

"Later. We should get going."

He had to move. If he didn't, he'd lie here all day and what would that accomplish? He couldn't be selfish. If the Skurk's trick *had* worked, Diltraa was somewhere inside him now and he was the only one who could vanquish Malika.

"Yeah. Hallow House," Merlyn said. He eased up out of the embrace. Nicholas ignored the strange sense of longing knitting together his insides.

No. No distractions.

Hopping off the bed, he went to one of the wire racks, casting around for the remaining bottles of water.

"You sure you know the way from here?" he asked. "To the house?"

Merlyn didn't reply.

"Merl?"

"Uh, Nick…"

Nicholas felt the air change. It thickened and charged the way it did before a storm. Sombrely, he turned, knowing what to search for. There, in the corner of the ambulance, darkness pooled as if attempting to conceal the figure that had materialised. Its silver mask was a shining oval in a web of shadows.

"Took your time," Nicholas said.

Esus stood still as a statue.

"You are difficult to find."

"Yeah, you know, trying to get through the apocalypse and all that."

Malevolent energy lashed from the corner, but Nicholas wouldn't be intimidated. He raised the protective barrier around his mind. Whenever Esus showed up, the emissary's white-hot energy pierced his skull like a sizzling poker. Not anymore.

"This is no time for game-playing."

"Who's playing?" Nicholas asked.

"Yeah, there's no game if there's no rules or something," Merlyn murmured. His voice was smaller than usual but Nicholas appreciated the support.

"Where are the others? The girl?"

"On their way to Hallow House," Nicholas said. Esus didn't need to know they'd taken a detour.

"Alone?"

"They've got each other."

"You separated. Why?"

"Made sense at the time," Nicholas said. "They'll be fine. Rae's not going to let anything happen to them."

"You possess the optimism of a fool."

"Gee, thanks."

Nicholas unscrewed a bottle and gulped down some water, smacking his lips dramatically. "What are you doing here? Come to check up on me?"

"You're making this more difficult than it needs to be, Hallow."

Nicholas tossed the other bottle to Merlyn, who fumbled as he caught it, then tentatively drank, his eyes not leaving Esus.

"You want to talk difficult? How about backpacking from Bury to Cambridge on your orders, only to find we're catch of the day?"

"The answers are here. If you have been unable to find them—"

"Oh, I found them." Nicholas crushed his bottle.

"What have you found?"

"You first. Why are you here? Something happened, right?" Maybe the nightmares had been a premonition. Maybe they were nothing to do with Diltraa.

For a moment, Esus remained motionless. Then the figure lunged for Nicholas and, before he could raise his arms in defence, a gloved finger dug into Nicholas's temple.

"See," Esus hissed.

Sights and sounds exploded through the antechambers of Nicholas's mind.

*A camp rests outside Hallow House. Esus flies above, watching as armoured Sentinels clash with six-legged monsters. Trees blaze. Screams distort like amp feedback.*

*A figure in white dances between the fighters. She hacks the air and tosses her red curls. When she reaches the camp, she's drenched with blood.*

Images flashed before Nicholas's eyes.

*Jessica confronts Malika. An enormous demon barrels into the house, tearing it apart. Hallow House ablaze.*

Nicholas fell away, released from Esus's grip. He grabbed the bedside and lowered himself onto the mattress. He stared at the floor, seeing the destruction over and over. The house. The bodies.

His ears rang and a hand pressed into his shoulder. Merlyn. What would Merlyn say if he saw what had happened to the Sentinels and their stronghold?

"When?" Nicholas asked, still catching his breath.

"Yesterday."

"How many?"

"How many—"

"How many dead?" Nicholas demanded.

"Hundreds."

"What's going on?" Merlyn asked.

Nicholas couldn't meet his eye. "Hallow House is gone."

"That's… that's not possible."

*"It has fallen to the enemy."* Esus had retreated to the shadows. *"Malika and the Prophets have seized control of the house. Many perished, but not all."*

"Sam?" Nicholas asked. "Isabel?"

*"They live. As does the Vaktarin."*

Nicholas closed his eyes, relief stemming the flood of panic. At least they were okay. For now.

"If the house is gone…" Merlyn murmured.

"It doesn't change anything."

"But–"

"We still go." Nicholas shrugged Merlyn's hand from his shoulder. "They need us and if we're going to fight, we fight there. It's where Malika is."

He noticed Esus staring at him and he felt the phantom's volatile energy needling his mind.

*"You are changed. What have you done?"*

Nicholas stood to face the phantom. "Exactly what you told me to do. I found a way to stop Malika." He felt Esus probing at his mind, pecking at it the way birds crack snails against stones. Nicholas let him see what the Skurk had done, and the phantom's presence withdrew sharply from his mind.

*"No,"* Esus uttered.

Anger stirred in Nicholas's chest. "This is what you wanted!" After everything he'd done, Esus was still disappointed.

*"Not this. You fool."*

"You told me to come here. You told me–"

*"To pervert your power? To make an ally of the darkness? You have doomed us all, but none more than yourself."*

"She said it was the only way," Nicholas argued. "The Skurk; the one your stupid Elvis emissary sent me to find. She wasn't exactly overflowing with suggestions. Just this one."

He felt Esus's energy shift again. The malevolence dissolved into melancholy. Nicholas tensed, surprised. What was happening? He'd done as Esus asked. He'd found a way to stop Malika. The price was high, but it was worth it. Wasn't it?

The space shrank between them as Esus glided forward. The figure raised its gloved hands once more, pressing a quivering finger to Nicholas's temple.

*"Esus,"* the phantom whispered.

Before Nicholas's eyes, the ambulance melted away and the years unravelled in head-spinning colours. Nicholas thought he'd vomit if he had a body, but he didn't anymore. His mind was all that existed, racing back in time and finally settling on a searing image.

*The land is raw and barren. An echoing wasteland ravaged by a braying wind.*

*A youngster in his late teens scrabbles on all fours through orange dirt. Lightning claws the sky and he clutches a knife carved from rock. He's hunting.*

*"This is where I grew into a man."* Esus's voice is thick with something. Regret, maybe. Or longing.

*A heartbeat hammers nearby and the youngster charges, plunges the blade, dipping his fist in a sticky hotness.*

*The beast is dead. The youngster crows at the clouds, then drags the meat to a cave. Two figures huddle, one small, one lean. A child and a young woman.*

Somewhere in Nicholas's mind he knew he was seeing Esus's history. His family. This was a primal time when gods and monsters prowled the earth.

The scene bled like a ruined watercolour. Nicholas found himself somewhere new.

*A hulking tentacled beast tears a tree from the earth, hurling it into the sky. The young man ushers the woman and child behind him, waving the blade at the monster.*

*A tentacle lashes around the woman's waist, plucks her from safety. Its maw gapes wide and crunches the woman, devouring her screams. Another tentacle lashes and the child is caught.*

*The man flees.*

Darkness fell and Esus's voice filled it.

*"I was weak. I could not do it alone."*

A new image bloomed in Nicholas's mind.

*The man stands naked in a cave of flickering firelight. He smears bloody symbols on his skin and paces around a circle of stones. His chant bounces with the shadows and a shuddering shape forms within the circle. A feathered, scaly thing with huge, rustling wings.*

Nicholas felt the weight of Esus's shame like a pocket of rocks.

*The man speaks but the words are not English. The demon squeals, then the head dips in subjugation and the man steps into the circle. Twin howls rent the air as the winged thing rears up and the two merge. Bones snap and reform, skin tears and repairs itself, black feathers ooze blood.*

*When it is over, the man lies alone in the circle of stones, his eyes raven black.*

"*I was changed forever. Powerful but corrupted. Even nature shrank from me.*"

Images flickered behind Nicholas's eyelids.

*A raven perches in a rocky crevice watching a pride of creatures. When they near, it swoops, becomes the man. He slays the entire pride, then consumes them hungrily with his bare hands.*

*Later, three figures pursue him on horseback. Two women and a man, their skin like copper, their hair white flame. The Trinity.*

*They capture him. Feed him. He snarls and fights and then learns speech, begins to understand their ways.*

*They put him in clothes. He grows wise in their presence but the wild thing inside him is never tamed for long. He flies to ports, to forests, to mountains, enlisting Sentinels, slaying creatures and devouring their entrails.*

"*The curse has grown heavier with every decade.*"

Nicholas gasped and broke free from the vision. He must have lashed out because Esus was sent tumbling across the ambulance. As Nicholas gripped the side of the vehicle for support, his gut heaving, he heard the phantom crash into the back doors, knocking them open. Then Merlyn gasped.

Pulling himself together, Nicholas looked down to where Esus had landed in a heap of dark fabric.

The silver mask lay on the floor beside him.

As the phantom dragged itself up, Nicholas glimpsed something in the dark of his hood. Bare bone, red-raw flesh and matted feathers, a nightmare countenance that made his arm hair prickle and rise.

Hissing, Esus swept up the mask and refitted it as Nicholas tried to forget what he'd glimpsed. He picked over what he'd been shown.

Esus as a primitive man hunting the wastelands thousands of years ago. He'd been weak, but the demon had made him strong. It was why the Trinity recruited him as their guardian.

Esus had meant to scare him by showing Nicholas what he'd condemned himself to by agreeing to resurrect Diltraa, but Nicholas felt resolve hardening in his chest. The demon had made Esus strong, and it would make Nicholas strong, too.

"You did what you had to," he said. "To survive."

"It was a different time," Esus rasped. "What you have done…"

"May save the world, or at least some of it. I had no choice."

"The thing inside you will kill you."

"I'm not going to let that happen," Merlyn said.

"You will be unable to stop it."

"Just watch me."

Esus straightened to his full height, his darkness filling the corner. "Ignorant children. You cannot comprehend the terror that will envelop you."

"I guess we'll find that out for ourselves," Merlyn said. Nicholas had never seen anybody stand up to Esus. That probably made Merlyn stupider than the average Sentinel, but it also made Nicholas like him even more.

The phantom seemed to have run out of fight. Nicholas was glad. There was nothing more to say. What was done was done.

"Orville," he said. His dreams kept taking him back there. Hallow House had fallen but Orville was where it had all started. The town was harbouring something, he knew it. That's where they had to go. "We're going to Orville. It's only a few days' drive. By the time we get there, Sam and the others will have a plan to take back the house and I'll be able to find out what Orville's hiding."

"Go, then. I am needed elsewhere. See what you can accomplish in Orville. Perhaps you will make it there alive. May the Trinity bless you."

The shadows gathered around the phantom, which became a raven that darted through the open door, swooping up into the leaden sky.

"Hear that? The Trinity bless us, even though you're a monster now." Merlyn punched his arm playfully and Nicholas gave him a lopsided smile. He couldn't hold the smile for long, though. The things Esus had shown him kept flickering before him. Hallow House destroyed. Malika exultant and blood-soaked. Esus's tortured past. The thought of becoming like Esus leeched at his resolve, but he knew he'd done the right thing.

"Try not to worry," Merlyn said softly, his fingers brushing Nicholas's.

Nicholas nodded, pushing his hand into Merlyn's. It felt so natural.

"You still have that lucky fox carving?" he asked.

Merlyn's eyes flashed. "Tails? Safe and sound."

"Good. We need all the luck we can get our hands on." He squeezed Merlyn's hand and peered around the inside of the ambulance. "Let's get on the road. Is this thing ready?"

"As ready as she'll ever be. I'm thinking of calling her Barbara."

"You can call her anything you like as long as she gets us to Orville."

"Barbara it is. Babs if she gets us there early."

They checked the ambulance over one last time, securing as much as they could in the back, then they strapped into the front seats and Merlyn kicked the vehicle into gear.

"Know any good road songs?"

Nicholas put on a thinking face, then beat a rhythm against the floor with his boot. "'Highway to Hell'," he suggested, and they began to sing at the top of their lungs as the ambulance jolted to life.

★

"There," Malika sighed, stepping forward to contemplate her work.

Nervous eyes watched her in the dark of the tomb. They were deep underground, below Hallow House. The craggy rock walls were decorated with Sentinel legends, the stories of the Trinity, and the Harvesters were uneasy being confined in a space so charged with nurturing energy.

But this was the reason Malika had taken the house. For what the tomb contained.

She pressed her hands to the cold glass of a transparent coffin. Three of them rested in the centre of the hallowed space. Once, a long time ago, the Trinity had slept here, submerged in the sacred water, patiently waiting to return.

They had long since departed, though. Where to, Malika didn't know or care to know. All she needed was the water.

The pods had already been transferred into the glass coffins, and she sensed the Prophets' hunger being sated. The water frothed and foamed around the leathery objects, which throbbed as they devoured the power stored there.

As the tomb trembled, the Harvesters raised anxious eyes to the rocky ceiling, and Malika beamed.

# CHAPTER TEN
## Bad Dreams

"Dawn?"

The woman by the window frowned, her dark gaze going from Dawn to Rae and back again. Even from the door, Rae found her unsettling. She was too pale, even her lips, and the white dressing gown barely concealed her bird-like frame.

"It's me, Mum," Dawn said, moving slowly past a small bed to join the woman. Rae thought it looked more like a cell than a place to get better, but she'd never seen a hospice before. Maybe they were all like this; their walls the same off-white as the sink and single wooden chair. The mirror was blotchy with age.

"You look different," said Dawn's mother. "Is it really you?"

Dawn wrapped her arms around her. "It's me. It's me, Mum."

The woman stared blankly at Rae as Dawn hugged her. Perhaps she was in shock. Or perhaps she was as good at hiding her emotions as Rae. Wishing the woman would stop blinking at her, Rae shrugged off a chill.

Releasing her mother, Dawn stared at her, and Rae saw she was trembling. She tried not to think about her own mothers. Four women had fostered her, most of them kind in a smothering sort of way. She hadn't known her real mum and she didn't care. There was no point trying to imagine somebody she'd never meet.

"Are you okay?" Dawn asked her mother. "Here, why don't you sit down?"

They perched on the bed and Dawn's mum stared at the wall. She seemed to be distracted by the shadows. Rae couldn't tell what was wrong with her. Apart from her alarmingly slight figure, she appeared physically well, and she didn't look mad. Not in the way some of the people were that she'd met on the streets.

Dawn took her mother's hand. "Mum, are you alright? Have they treated you okay? When was the last time you saw a nurse? Or ate?"

"I don't… what time is it? You were here yesterday, too. The days start to blur together."

"I haven't been for a while," Dawn said softly. "I'm sorry. But we're going. You want to go, don't you? We're here to get you out."

"Out?"

"Away. It's not safe anymore."

"Where's Mum?"

"Gran's fine. We're going to her. Would you like that?"

Dawn's mother peered at her and Rae wondered what sort of drugs she was on to make her pupils so large. Then Dawn's mum smiled.

"Dawn. Where did you come from? Is it time for the TV show I like?" She frowned. "What was it called?"

Dawn squeezed her hand. "We're going away, Mum."

"Will John be there?"

The expression on Dawn's face sent a shiver down Rae's spine.

"Let's just get you dressed," said Dawn.

"I want John." The woman began scratching her thigh. She shot up from the bed and began stumbling towards Rae in the doorway. "Where is he? He was here yesterday. He should be here. He should be—"

"Mum!" Dawn took the woman's arms and held her still. "Dad's gone. He's gone. It's just us now."

Her mother's eyes filled with tears and Dawn stared past her at Rae. "See if there are any clothes?"

Rae went to the modest wardrobe that was built into the wall. A few garments were folded on shelves. She took them to the bed, eyeing Dawn's mum and wishing Nicholas was here. He could fix her head from the inside out. Or at least try to.

"Thanks," said Dawn. "Mum, let's get dressed. It's a bit of a walk."

But her mother was peering at the wardrobe. "There's something…" she mumbled, her brow furrowed, and then she was detaching herself from Dawn, moving quickly to the wardrobe and sticking her head inside.

"Mum, what–" Dawn began, but then her mother lifted a plank of wood, revealing a dark recess in the bottom of the closet. The woman grunted as she reached inside and drew out an object.

"The nurses don't know about it," she said, blowing dust off it. "They'd have confiscated it, like Gran's neckerchief."

She passed the object to Dawn. Rae grimaced at the sight of it. It was an ancient book that had been torn in half. All that remained were the front cover and a few inches of yellow, water-damaged pages. It stank of mildew and rot.

"What is it?" asked Dawn.

"Spells," said her mother. "Good ones."

Rae bit her tongue. The book looked useless. The floor shuddered as Dawn examined it. The shuddering travelled up the walls and shook the lights, and Rae saw that darkness had fallen outside.

"Dammit," she muttered. "Wait here."

Leaving Dawn with her mother, Rae hurried into the corridor. The floor juddered again, and she'd been in enough buildings to know they were the tremors that came after a detonation. Someone was blowing something up.

Rae hurried across the corridor into an open communal area with sofas and board games. At the far side, ceiling-high windows stared out at Oxford. Breathlessly, Rae went to the window and saw buildings on fire. A winged shape wheeled above the city dropping projectiles. The building trembled around her as a shop in the next street erupted in a shower of flame and debris. Rae stumbled backwards as the winged shape flew on, disappearing above the hospice.

"Incoming!" she yelled, racing for Dawn's mother's room, but then she heard the crash of something smashing through the roof, and she was lifted off her feet as a blast tore through the building.

She landed with such force that the air was crushed from her lungs. Stunned, she lay crumpled in the remnants of the communal room, marvelling at the drifting embers. For once the destruction wasn't her doing. Then all she saw was black.

She came to with a gasp, drawing a painful breath and spluttering. Her chest ached, and she had no idea where she was, but then she remembered the flying monster and its deadly payload. The windows were smashed and the walls were on fire, but the building was old and it would take more than a single projectile to level it.

"Dawn?" Rae wheezed, coughing. Her limbs jerked to life and she clawed herself upright, spotting the corridor through the caved-in ceiling. *Go*, she told herself, and suddenly she was up, staggering across the ruptured floor, crossing the corridor and into Dawn's mother's room.

It took her a second to figure out what had happened, the room had changed so much. The far wall was missing and hot air whipped inside. An ash-covered figure crouched by a warped metal frame and Rae stumbled towards it, recognising the rucksack on Dawn's back.

"Dawn," she croaked, and then stopped short.

Another figure was on the floor. Dawn's mother lay under the metal frame, and Rae realised the bed had twisted up under the impact of the blast. A piece of it had speared the woman's side. Rae glimpsed bone and sightless eyes and gritted her teeth.

"We have to go," she said.

Dawn was pressing her mother's hand to her forehead. In the distance, Rae heard other buildings exploding and hoped more demons or Harvesters weren't on their way.

"Dawn," she said, and Dawn placed her mother's hand on her stomach, and then stood. Her face was tear-stained and Rae never knew what to say, so she hugged her. Dawn shook for a moment and then drew back.

"Let's go," she said.

★

Night had fallen, and Nicholas could see his reflection in the ambulance window. The square jaw and dark eyes could belong to another person, they were so alien to who he used to be. With his cropped hair, he almost looked like a soldier. He hoped that meant monsters would think twice about attacking them.

The ambulance trundled along a country lane. They had driven for hours, only stopping for toilet breaks and so Merlyn could stretch his legs. The countryside was unnervingly quiet.

"They like the cities, always have," Merlyn had said. "More game."

That seemed to be true. They barely saw anything hunting in the fields. At one point, they spotted orange flames dancing on the horizon. Another town swallowed by the Prophets. They stuck to the B-roads, lights off, but Nicholas's fingers ached from clawing at his seat.

He peered over at Merlyn and wondered what he was thinking. If he was worried or scared. If he felt the same way about Nicholas that Nicholas was beginning to feel about him. He'd liked waking up in Merlyn's arms, even if it had been from a nightmare. And the memory of Merlyn's hand in his filled his stomach with a warm fluttering sensation.

He couldn't bring himself to say anything, though. It should feel so insignificant in the middle of the apocalypse. Except, to Nicholas, it was anything but insignificant. He'd never felt this way about anybody.

Nicholas noticed that Merlyn's eyes were beginning to droop.

"Think it's time we slept."

Merlyn blinked and suppressed a yawn. "Sleep's for the sleepy."

"Really."

"I'm fine, I'm awake."

"Yeah, I completely believe you but, look, there's a farm or something up there. It'll give us cover. If you drive any more, you'll be in the back of this thing instead of up front."

"You'd make a good nurse."

"Trust me, I wouldn't."

Merlyn yawned. "I suppose a cat nap couldn't hurt."

Whenever Nicholas thought of cats, he thought of Isabel. A weird sort of yearning stirred up his guts and he hoped she was okay. The sight of Hallow House in ruin returned to him and he wondered what sort of damage Isabel, Sam and the others had suffered.

They pulled off the road and parked behind a barn. In the dark, they swept the farm's out buildings. Whoever had lived here was long gone and the countryside was quiet. A few hours' sleep would revive them and they'd hit the road again before sunrise.

Nicholas didn't like the look of the house – too obvious if anybody came by, Harvester or otherwise. They'd spent two days in the ambulance and they were accustomed to it. It was his and Merlyn's.

When they returned to the vehicle, Merlyn crawled into the back and, by the time Nicholas had checked that the windows and doors were secure, the other teenager was face down on the bed, his dirty blond hair messy against the pillow. Nicholas eased himself onto the mattress next to him, resisting the urge to stare at Merlyn's drowsy face.

"Night, demon boy," Merlyn murmured.

"Night."

For a while, Nicholas lay listening to his soft snores, his mind spider-walking back over the past few days.

Of all the things Esus had showed him, the image of the Trinity kept filling his head. He'd felt what Esus felt in their presence all those centuries ago. It was like standing too close to a fire, except the heat was invigorating, life-giving. They smelled of turned earth and fresh rain; breathing in the Trinity was like breathing in the air after a storm. Their eyes were dark inkwells that soothed his anxious mind. They saw so much. He wondered if, like Esus, they'd look on him with disappointment. They'd chosen him, and he was nobody.

Before long, Nicholas slipped into an uneasy sleep. His dreams bound him in wire. He was in a wood, the trees crowded so close together there was no room to breathe. Between the trunks, he glimpsed a crouched, sinewy form.

He tried to run but the figure flicked its wrist and a paralysing dart pricked Nicholas's skin. He collapsed, feeling nothing, not even the hard earth beneath him.

The monster burbled with wicked laughter as it wriggled onto him. He'd heard that sound before. He knew the monster. He had to get away. He dug his heels into the earth, but it crumbled beneath him and he was trapped. The monster's eyes flashed fire, and a sudden hunger stirred in Nicholas's belly. His stomach rolled and – not thinking, only feeling – he buried his teeth into the demon's neck, chewing and tearing the flesh.

The demon shrieked with pleasure and a pumping hotness filled Nicholas's mouth.

"Nick! Can you hear me!"

He came to with a start. Immediately, he gagged. He tasted metal and the coppery stench of death stuck in his throat.

He was crouching in the dirt. Before him, a bloody tangle of organs and hair spilled from a matted carcass, and his hands were slippery. They were halfway to his mouth and his stomach was still grumbling.

He choked and spat out a hunk of meat.

"Are you awake?"

Merlyn was beside him, his face grey.

Nicholas began to shake uncontrollably. It was freezing and he was covered in blood. He stared at his hands, his arms dark up to the elbows. The animal he was crouched over had probably been a sheep, it was about the right size, but it had been gored beyond recognition.

"What... What–"

The words wouldn't come. He couldn't comprehend what he'd done. They were in a field, the ambulance a few hundred feet away, its doors flung open.

"Shhh, you're fine."

"I... What did I–"

Merlyn's hand squeezed his shoulder. "Nothing. You didn't do anything."

Nicholas shrugged him away, staggering to his feet. He couldn't breathe. His gaze was drawn back to the shredded sheep and he could still taste it. Something inside him had enjoyed tearing at it.

Diltraa. The demon had whispered in his ear, though he couldn't remember what it had said. Only that somehow he'd come outside and killed an animal with his bare hands.

"Stay away from me," he warned Merlyn.

The other teenager moved forward, but Nicholas threw his hands out in front of him.

"Stay back! It's not safe."

"It is now. You're okay."

Nicholas trembled, wanting to vomit. Why was he so cold? Merlyn came closer and Nicholas tried to push him away, but Merlyn grabbed hold of his arms. He was so close Nicholas could see the vein throbbing in his throat, right by the tattooed bite marks.

"That thing's in me," Nicholas said. "I can feel it. Oh god... What have I done?"

"Let's just clean you up. You'll be okay. You'll feel–"

"NO! You have to go. You have to get away."

"I'm not going any–"

"NOW! Get away from me!"

Before Nicholas knew what was happening, Merlyn had pressed his mouth to his. The panic burst like a poppyhead. His mind abruptly ceased its see-sawing. A cool calm swelled through him and Nicholas kissed him back, not thinking anymore, not remembering why he'd been upset or that the world was ending. He just wanted this. A new kind of hunger stirred.

When Merlyn pulled away, his mouth was smeared red.

"We're in this together. You and me."

Nicholas nodded, still feeling Merlyn's lips, tasting blood and him.

"Come on."

Merlyn put an arm around him and they trudged back to the ambulance. The sky was already beginning to turn a lighter shade of its usual sickly grey and Nicholas knew he wouldn't sleep again. For about the hundredth time in the past two days, Merlyn seemed to read his mind.

"Lucky I got those fifty winks," he said when they were back at the ambulance. "I feel fresh as a daisy. Or at least a daisy that hasn't showered in a while and is desperate for a piss. Back in a sec."

He left Nicholas to clean himself up. Relieved that he could do it in private, Nicholas went through the drawers in the back of the cabinet and found a box of medical salves. The cotton wool came away grimy with gore and he shoved it to the bottom of the small bin. Shame wriggled through him; shame at what he'd done to the sheep.

"What's that?" he asked, thinking Merlyn had returned. But Nicholas was alone in the ambulance. For a moment, he thought he'd heard a voice.

"You say something?" Merlyn asked as he appeared at the doors.

"No. Nothing."

"Okay. Well this thing isn't going to drive itself. Ready?"

Nicholas nodded. He must've imagined the voice.

They drove for a couple of hours. Merlyn cracked a few jokes but quickly realised Nicholas wasn't in the mood. He felt bad. He wanted to joke with Merlyn, make him laugh, but he'd forgotten how to be light and silly. He worried that Diltraa had killed that part of him.

The countryside had gone wild in the months since Bury St Edmunds fell. Trees obstructed the road and Merlyn had to manoeuvre carefully around them. Sometimes there were bodies. Nicholas forced himself not to look at them. Not just because they were hideous, but because if he glimpsed the torn flesh, he thought of the sheep and a horrible delight prickled the nape of his neck.

*You're in there,* he thought at Diltraa. *I know you are. This isn't me. It's you.*

Diltraa didn't respond and Nicholas didn't want it to. If the demon was inside him, he had to push it down as far as he could; stop it from taking control.

"Woah, see that?" Merlyn asked suddenly.

For a second, Nicholas thought he might have finally started growing horns, but Merlyn wasn't looking at him. He was craning to peer through the windscreen. Nicholas did the same and swallowed hard.

In the distance, an unnatural fog thickened above the tree-line. Winged shapes wheeled through the air, darting around plumes of smoke.

"It's the house," he murmured, "must be. Malika's army must've set up camp outside Hallow House."

Merlyn's grip tightened about the steering wheel.

"Is there a long way round to Orville?" Nicholas asked.

"I'll take the next right we come across."

Nicholas eyed the smoke, remembering what Esus had showed him. He shuddered, wondering what Malika had done to the Sentinel stronghold. He was tempted to push his mind inside, take a peek, but he had a feeling she'd sense that. And what if he came up against the Prophets? He had a feeling they could kill him even from a distance if they got into his head.

They skirted away from the house, trundling into thick forest.

"Eyes open," Merlyn said.

"Affirmative."

"If Malika's army's any good, they'll have this whole area staked out. Orville, too. You know, we're pretty much heading into the first circle of hell."

"I know."

Fifteen minutes later, Merlyn drew the ambulance to a stop. "Best to go the rest of the way on foot."

They suited up in the back of the ambulance. As Nicholas pulled on his armour, he hoped Dawn and Rae were still going. He was sure he'd feel it if something had happened to them.

He packed his rucksack with the last of the water and checked his weaponry. A short blade and a pocket knife. Malika didn't stand a chance.

Outside the ambulance, Merlyn patted the vehicle.

"Good Barbara. We'll come back for you."

Nicholas stared at him.

"What? She's been good to us."

"Yeah. She has."

The forest was dark and quiet, and Nicholas couldn't see the sky as they walked. The trees had knitted themselves together as though they were trying to keep certain things out.

"You hear that?" Merlyn asked.

"What?"

"Nothing. Absolutely nothing. Forests are never this quiet."

"Try not to think about it."

Nicholas stopped and closed his eyes.

"Mojo?" Merlyn asked.

Nicholas nodded, pushing tentatively with his mind, imagining it as a whisper so quiet that even Malika couldn't hear it. He swept their surroundings. Orville was a twenty-minute walk west. He could still feel the creepy biscuit-tin village in his bones. The place Snelling had tricked him. The place that was alive with ghosts that didn't know they were ghosts.

He frowned.

"Bad juju?" Merlyn asked.

"I'm not sure."

Nicholas cast about the forest again. "There's somebody nearby."

"A bad somebody?"

"I'm trying–"

He sensed a large shape. And something with three legs. A Harvester and its pet demon? They were only fifty feet away, concealed by trees, and they were headed straight for them.

Nicholas's eyes snapped open. "Move. Quickly."

They ran in the opposite direction. Merlyn was faster, speeding ahead, and Nicholas could sense the Harvester gaining on them. He was running, too. Giving chase. His heartbeat filled Nicholas's hearing, and there was something else. Something scurrying through the undergrowth, gaining on him, and he remembered his nightmare. His concentration wavered and that was all it took for his boot to catch on something in the undergrowth. He yelped as he went down and, grunting, he rolled over just as the demon pounced on him.

Nicholas threw up his hands, his fingers tangling in thick fur.

A rough tongue scraped his cheek and the demon panted in his face, then barked.

He heard Merlyn laughing. "Hey, look who it is!"

As the panic subsided, Nicholas stared up into a furry muzzle. Not a demon at all.

"Zeus?" he said in disbelief. The dog licked his face again. "Ah, get off!"

Nicholas pushed himself into a sitting position and the wolfhound hopped back, then bounded up to Merlyn, who tussled with him. Nicholas noticed the dog was now missing a back leg. He'd had a full set a few months ago. It seemed the war was taking its toll on everybody.

"Nicholas."

He looked up as a mountainous figure approached. Benjamin Nale appeared even bigger than Nicholas remembered him, but that could just be because he was on the ground. The Hunter reached down and lifted Nicholas to his feet like he weighed no more than a toddler.

"Nale," Nicholas said, wiping the dog drool from his face. "What are you doing here?"

"Patrol."

He'd forgotten that Nale talked in short, sharp syllables.

"The house. Were you there?"

Nale nodded.

"What about the others? Are they okay? Sam and Isabel?"

"They're alive. Come."

Nicholas paused. The Skurk's warning repeated in his head.

*"Beware the tall man."*

It couldn't have meant Nale. As far as he could tell, Nale was as stoic and clear-eyed as ever. He hadn't been turned the way other Sentinels had. But Nicholas hesitated. He had to get to Orville; time was already running out. Was Nale trying to delay him?

The Hunter was already strolling back the way he'd come. "Zeus," he gruffed, and the dog's ears pricked up. It licked Merlyn's face one last time before galloping after Nale.

"Think they've got a surprise party for us?" Merlyn asked as he joined Nicholas.

"I hope not."

"What's wrong?"

"Don't you remember what the Skurk said? About Nale?"

"The warning? You think it was about him?"

"You know any other tall guys with wolfhounds?"

Merlyn looked torn.

"The others are with him, right?" he asked.

"That's what he said."

"Then we go with him, get reinforcements, keep an eye on Nale, watch for any evil ticks."

Nicholas knew he was right. Reinforcements would be very welcome and the thought of seeing Sam and Isabel made up his mind for him. He had to make sure they were alright. They were the nearest thing he had to family nowadays.

"Okay," he said. "Let's just make sure we take turns watching him."

"Affirmative."

"That's my line."

They went after Nale, making their way through the forest. Ten minutes later there was no sign of the others and uneasiness wound its way into Nicholas's shoulders. They went another two-hundred yards and Nicholas's heart started pounding. Just when he was about to suggest splitting, he spotted a rickety old wagon. It resembled something from a circus; so old it couldn't possibly be road-worthy. A little further on, a handful of people milled about a caravan and a minibus. Survivors of the attack on Hallow House, perhaps.

Nicholas watched as Nale leaned in through the wagon's open door. "Found something."

A voice came from within. "Something worth worrying about?"

Nicholas's stomach leapt. It was Sam's voice. As Nicholas hurried for the carriage, the old man appeared at the door. Their eyes locked and they regarded each other for a second, seeing the battle scars and the weariness, then Sam hobbled down the steps and gathered Nicholas into a hug.

"Lad," he said.

"Yeah."

Sam had lost weight; Nicholas could feel his shoulder blades through his shirt. He should be feeling something else; elation or relief at finally tracking down the old man, but it was like a cork had been jammed into wherever his emotions were stored. Maybe emotions were too big to feel sometimes. If he felt them, he'd fall apart.

"The boy's here?"

An elderly woman appeared in the doorway. She was wrapped in a floor-length kaftan, her silver hair scraped back from a high forehead. Nicholas balked. It looked like the headmistress from the school in Bury; the Harvester. But the sharp gaze and voice were unmistakably Isabel's.

She came down the steps as Sam released him. For a surreal second, it felt like Nicolas was visiting his grandparents at their holiday home.

"Look at you," the woman tutted, and surprised him by putting a warm hand to his cheek. "The boy is a man."

"Uh, what happened to the cat?" It was all he could think of to say.

Isabel withdrew her hand. "She had served her purpose." She reached for his arm and he thought she was attempting a hug, but then she squeezed the point where the broken bones had fused back together. "You've healed quickly. Good. All that hunting, no doubt."

"We've had our share," Merlyn said.

They all stared at him.

"Good to see you, lad." Sam winked at him.

"You too, Bogey."

"Bogey?"

"Don't ask," Nicholas said.

"Nicholas? Is that you?"

He turned towards the new voice and found Aileen emerging from the forest, her arms laden with chopped wood. She had survived the battle, too? He felt pleasantly surprised. This was turning into a real reunion.

"Where's Dawn? Is she with you?" the landlady asked.

"No, but she's okay. She's meeting us here. She said it'd take three days, so she'll get here today, if they haven't been held up."

"They?"

"She's with Rae."

Perhaps sensing his discomfort at being the centre of attention, Sam slapped Nicholas's back. "We have a lot to catch up on. Come on, lads, get inside and I'll sort you a hot brew. You must be freezing, all those cold nights in the wilderness."

"Oh, yeah, my toes double as ice-picks now," Merlyn joked. Nicholas found Isabel giving him a curious glare and hoped she hadn't noticed him blushing.

The wagon was surprisingly spacious. With its assortment of knick-knacks, weapons and home comforts, it looked like something out of a fairy tale.

"Take a seat," Sam pressed, lighting a travel stove on the counter.

Nicholas shrugged off his rucksack, balancing on a creaky chair at a small table. Merlyn joined him and Nicholas watched as Isabel went to a curtain at the far end of the room. She tweaked the edge and he glimpsed a sleeping space. Was somebody in there?

"Nice digs," Merlyn said as Nale settled into a bean bag that threatened to explode its contents.

"Nale's," Sam explained, placing a tin kettle on the stove.

"It's not bad as safehouses go," Aileen commented, filling a bucket with the firewood. "Or safe-wagons, anyway. Even got our own guard dog." She nodded at Zeus, who stood staring out of the door.

"We're lucky to have him." Sam beamed wearily at Nicholas. "He's earning his keep far better than that fleabag over there."

Nicholas followed Sam's gesture, spotting a fluffy shape curled up in the corner below some dangling puppets. It took him a moment to realise it was a cat, its fur was so mangy. For a second, he'd thought it was another of Nale's strange trinkets.

"You just leave Pyraemon alone," huffed Aileen.

"My, you're a sight for very sore eyes," said Sam, and Nicholas wondered if he'd used that phrase at the cat's expense; Pyraemon only seemed to have one eye. "Tell us everything. What happened in Bury?

Where did you get that kit? And how on earth did you find each other?"

Nicholas didn't know where to begin, so he told them about getting to Cambridge, the Elvis statue, finding Merlyn and the Skurk. At the bedside, Isabel sat up straighter at the mention of the decrepit soothsayer but said nothing. He didn't mention Diltraa or the Skurk's ceremony. He was still unsettled by Esus's reaction to that particular wrinkle, and he couldn't bear the thought of seeing the Sentinels' faces fill with fear and confusion at what he'd done.

By the time he reached the part where Nale found them in the woods, the tin kettle was whistling, and Sam poured their tea.

"My, my, you've had a time." The old man handed out tin mugs.

"You don't know the half of it," Merlyn breathed, his eyes shining at Nicholas over the rim of his mug.

"So Laurent's dead," Sam said, perching on a mushroom-shaped barstool. "That explains his absence on the battlefield."

"And you've not heard from Dawn since she left?" Aileen asked.

Nicholas shook his head. "But she's with Rae. They'll be alright."

Aileen didn't seem any less anxious.

"I saw," Nicholas said softly. "What happened here. The house. Malika. Esus showed me."

Sam's shoulders drooped. "Yes. There aren't many of us left. Malika has taken the house."

"What about Jessica?"

"She's resting," Isabel said. That answered who was in the bed behind the curtain.

"Is she…" Nicholas wasn't sure what he was asking. Injured? Dying?

Isabel got to her feet. "So you've learned nothing more about the Trinity. How to return them to us." She clearly didn't want to talk about Jessica. Nicholas struggled to look at the elderly woman as she wandered to the door, peering out at the forest. Could she sense what he'd done? The demon inside him? He felt he'd betrayed them somehow, but it was the only way to kill Malika.

"Orville," he said finally. "The answer's there, always has been. That's where we were headed when Nale found us. However the Trinity can be raised, the answer's there."

"It stands to reason; it is where you were born," Isabel said.

"You know what you're looking for, lad?" Sam asked.

Nicholas shook his head. "All I know is that I need to get into that village, poke around a bit. Something's waiting for me there. Has been for years."

Sam's gaze simmered beneath the brim of his fedora. "Whatever it is you can do with that mind of yours, you're more attune to your powers than the last time you were in the village. Are you ready for whatever you find?"

"It's not a case of being ready," Isabel snapped. "It's a case of not getting yourself killed. The village is overrun. Malika's forces have seized control of this entire area."

"Not this wagon," Nicholas pointed out. "Or the people in it."

"Not yet," Aileen breathed.

"Whatever you find, it must be enough to destroy both the Prophets and Malika," Isabel said. "Jessica cannot fight any longer. She is weakened beyond recovery."

Aileen sniffled. "Never thought I'd see the day…"

"She's… will she make it?" Nicholas asked.

Isabel met his gaze. "Malika has all-but destroyed her, mind and body. The responsibility falls to us now."

Nicholas nodded. It had been leading up to this, all of it. Discovering the truth about his parents, fighting Laurent, finding the Skurkwife. He peered around the wagon. "We're going to do this. I'm going to Orville, I'm finding out how to raise The Trinity, and they're going to destroy the Prophets before they hatch."

"And Malika?" Sam asked.

"When the time comes, I'll kill her myself."

Nobody blinked. He realised they believed him, and that both comforted and unnerved him. He just had to find a way to get Diltraa to work for him.

"So who fancies a little day trip?" Merlyn asked. "I've never been to this Orville place; it sounds like a hoot."

"We'll go, me and Nicholas," Sam said. "Aileen, Nale, you're okay to stay here? Somebody has to protect the survivors."

Nale hadn't said anything since entering the wagon. Nicholas didn't like the thought of him being left alone with Isabel and Jessica. He wanted the Hunter close; he could try to read him, find out what he was hiding, if anything.

"Nale and Zeus could be useful getting into Orville," Nicholas said.

Sam threw a questioning glance at the Hunter, who nodded. The dog turned its head at the sound of its name and seemed to pant in agreement.

"Alright," Sam said. "Merlyn, you alright to hold down the… well, wagon?"

Merlyn saluted. "Guess I'll live without seeing some Harvester-riddled village."

"Good. I'll introduce you to the others, you probably already know a few of them. Nicholas, you have supplies? Weapons?"

Nicholas nudged his rucksack with his boot. "Everything I own's in there."

"Now's the time, then. Merlyn, come with me and I'll give you a quick tour."

Sam got up and Merlyn followed, winking at Nicholas as he went out the door. Aileen began busying herself with inventory and Nale left the wagon with Zeus. Pyraemon squinted lazily at his surroundings, and then curled himself into an even tighter fluff-ball.

Nicholas found he was alone with Isabel. The old woman was back by the curtain, her features drawn. Her gaze pierced the gloom.

"Whatever it is you have done, I hope it was not in vain," she said sombrely.

"Me too," Nicholas said. So she knew. Perhaps not precisely what he'd done, but she could sense something different about him, the way dogs sense sickness. He had to speak to Jessica; she'd know if he was okay.

"Let me see her," he said.

Isabel hesitated and then withdrew from the bed, crossing the wagon and picking through shelves of herbs. Drawing a breath, Nicholas pushed aside the curtain and peered into the gloom beyond. Jessica lay back on a mound of pillows. She was so pale she looked translucent, and a pang of unease vibrated in Nicholas's chest. He swallowed and eased onto the edge of the mattress.

"Jessica," he whispered.

Her head moved towards him.

"Nicholas." Her voice was so light he wondered if he'd imagined it. A pallid hand reached for him and closed around his own.

"It's so good to see you again. You are my hope," she said.

Suddenly he didn't know what to say. He realised he had hoped she might reassure him, the way she had before, but the sight of her filled him with concern. She was the Guardian. Godmother to the Sentinels. She should be leading an army, not hiding behind a curtain.

"You'll get better," he said.

Her smile was slow and knowing. "There are beginnings and there are endings. It's funny how similar they can appear."

Her tone sent shivers up his back.

"We're fighting," he said. "We'll get the house back and we'll fight until they're all dead."

"Yes. Yes, I believe you. We won't all survive, but an end is in sight. And a beginning. We shall all be forced to choose."

"Choose?"

"That is the way. It shall always be."

She wasn't making any sense. Nicholas felt an irresistible urge to run. Get out of the wagon and run and never look back.

"Here," Jessica whispered. "Everything happens in its own time. It is time you knew everything." She reached up and touched his forehead. He felt warmth and something slipped into his mind as if she had pressed a scrap of paper into his palm.

Three words.

*Unseal, peel, reveal.*

"What is it for?" he asked.

"You shall find out soon enough. Go, do what you can."

Shaking, Nicholas grabbed his rucksack and went outside.

# CHAPTER ELEVEN
## SPECTRES

NALE WENT AHEAD WITH ZEUS. THE dog danced like a ghost between the trees, returning periodically to his owner before darting off again.

"He's just as fast with three legs," Nicholas said, kicking leaves as they made their way through the forest.

"He's had to be," said Sam. "A Hunter's dog is only useful if it can kill. It was either adapt or retire for old Zeus."

"Well I'm glad he's still around. And you."

Sam clucked. "It'll take more'n Ginnungap to take me down."

Nicholas swallowed. "I saw what happened to the house. Jessica's home. Esus showed me. And... I heard what happened in Bury. Liberty..."

He left her name hanging before them and felt the edge of grief like a dull blade. He didn't need to look at Sam to know that, when it came to Liberty's death, his emotions perfectly mirrored the old man's.

"There have been losses everywhere," Sam said.

"But Liberty—"

"Fought well. Her best. In the end, the witch was too much for her."

Sam tugged at his fedora and Nicholas struggled to find words for what he wanted to say. Talking about it made it more real. Brought it into sharp focus. He peered sidelong at Sam. This was the first time they'd been alone together since Bury St Edmunds, and memories flurried in his mind like feathers. He'd known Sam since he was a kid. Sam always told the best stories; the ones about monsters and heroes.

At the time, Nicholas had no idea the old man was using the stories to prepare him for this.

"She used to slip a little whisky into my hot chocolate at night." Sam's eyes twinkled at their surroundings. "After her father passed, I often stayed with her and her mother. We'd sneak whisky when Gloria wasn't looking." He chuckled and then sighed. "My, those days seem so long ago. Cambridge… Is it completely…"

"Trashed? Worse than Mick Jagger after a bender."

Sam's smile lifted the gloom. "You've been spending a lot of time with Merlyn, he's rubbing off on you."

Nicholas coughed and hoped the old man couldn't see him blushing. "I, uh, ran into somebody else in Cambridge, too, before we left," he said, changing the subject.

"Oh?"

"Remember Tabatha?"

Sam clucked. "Oh my, Miss Blittmore. Now there's a name I've not heard in a while. Was she… well, was she okay, given the current climate?"

"She hasn't changed much. A little grubbier maybe, but she asked about you. She was going to France with her sister. Or maybe her sister-in-law."

"Good egg, that one." Sam's face darkened. "I hope they made it across the Channel."

They walked quietly for a while, following Nale's square back through the woods. Nicholas sensed a strange tension between Sam and himself, like a sheet pulled tight, and he searched Sam's face for the answer.

"Nicholas, I owe you an apology," the old man said.

"What–"

"The way you found out the truth about your parents… It wasn't right." His voice was hoarse. "I should have told you long before then."

Nicholas stared at his boots. He'd never forget the day in Aileen's garden when Sam had explained the truth about Anita and Max. How she was really his sister, and although Max was her husband, he wasn't Nicholas's father. His biological parents had died in Orville the night he was born, they'd been destroyed by whatever power blasted into the world with him.

"It's alright," Nicholas said.

"They loved you, lad, more than you'll ever know."

"I know."

There was more. Nicholas felt it. The dull thrum of anxiety in Sam's brow.

"There's something else you're not telling me," he said, trying not to sound accusatory.

"You're right." Sam rubbed his forehead. "It's about Jessica. She's... not in great shape, lad."

"I know. But she'll recover, right?"

Sam shook his head slowly. "I don't think so. She's lived hundreds of years. That takes its toll. And... she's kept something from us. Something about Malika."

Nicholas's own brow began to throb. Even the mention of that name coursed heat into his fists.

"What about her?"

"It's... complicated."

Sam talked and, with growing unease, Nicholas listened. Sam talked about the night Isabel died. How Diltraa had taken control of Jessica's body. Used her to kill Isabel. And then the demon had torn free from Jessica, creating Malika.

Throughout Sam's tale, Nicholas became more and more aware of the shushing of the leaves beneath his boots, and he felt the information sinking into his skin, finding form.

"I know," he said finally.

"You–?"

"I saw it. Or at least some of it. When Malika broke into Hallow House the first time, I saw something from her past. She was in a room with five walls. Somehow... I think I've known it all along. That they were connected."

Now that Sam had told him, it all made sense. Jessica and Malika were different sides of the same blade. Separated only by the thinnest, sharpest line.

"Can we do something?" he asked. "Help her?"

"Not according to Isabel."

Nicholas chewed the inside of his cheek. Diltraa was the thing that connected Jessica and Malika. And now Diltraa was in him. The demon had made Jessica kill. It had already driven Nicholas to do the same with the sheep. What if it got out of control? What if Nicholas killed a person? Somebody he loved?

"Don't be too disheartened." Sam patted him on the back and Nicholas jumped. "There's still a chance we can fix this. Make things the way they were. Better."

His words bounced off Nicholas, unable to make him feel anything other than the stifling closeness of the unnatural air. It was impossible, what they had to do. They were being asked to do the impossible. And he had a demon in him, somewhere, changing him from the inside out. What if–

"Lad." Sam drew them to a stop. "Whatever happens, you have to know… Malika and the Prophets poison everything they touch. They'll do anything for power and you're stuck in the middle of their war against the Trinity. We all are. But it's different for you. The Trinity chose *you*; that's a blessing and a burden that would send the sanest Sentinel mad." He paused. "And I couldn't be prouder."

Nicholas stared back at the old man, noting the fresh seams in his wrinkled face, the weary light in his blue eyes. He wanted to say he believed him, but he didn't know what to think. It was all so complicated and trying to unpick the knotted events that had led to this made his head hurt.

"Apocalypses." Sam tutted. "They make everybody so earnest."

"Hey, just name another topic and I'm there." Nicholas paused, noticing that Sam's expression had changed. "Sam? What is it?"

"Hm? No, it's just… Names…" Sam patted his satchel, smacking his gums in thought. "Funny how things slip out of your head as quickly as they go in. Must be my age. But that barmy psychic I met on the narrow boat a while back was obsessed with names. He said they had power. I wonder if that's significant in some way." He shook his head. "Of course, this was a man who talked to his stuffed rabbit… Let's just get in and out of that infernal village as quickly as we can, eh? Aileen should have something marvellous cooking for our return."

Nicholas nodded and they continued on between the trees. He wasn't sure if he understood what Sam had meant about names having power but it was probably worth asking Dawn about when she turned up. He made a mental note to find out if she thought it was important.

They caught up with Nale and Zeus, who were waiting for them at the forest edge. Nicholas eyed the Hunter but Nale's expression was as unreadable as his thoughts. How did he do that? Nicholas could usually sense people's mood if he got close enough, but Nale was like a mirror reflecting back Nicholas's own thoughts and feelings.

"Not many guards," Nale grunted.

Nicholas and Sam peered round a tree and Nicholas's insides hardened at the sight of Orville. It resembled any other English village but that was part of its insidious charm. Anybody could stumble across it and fall for its cosy allure, unaware that they were being tricked.

At the mouth of the high street, five Harvesters clutched axes and sickles, prowling like hyenas with empty bellies. They all wore the Prophets' three-headed insignia on their chests.

"Hardly any of them. There's a chance Malika has underestimated the significance of the place," Sam murmured.

"I don't think she's that stupid," Nicholas said.

"No. Then let's make the most of this good fortune. Perhaps her army is yet to properly establish a foothold here."

"I only sense half a dozen of them in the village," Nicholas said, the Harvesters blipping in black smudges on his radar.

"Behind me," Nale said flatly, and before Nicholas could say anything more, the Hunter strode out from the forest's cover, heading straight for the Harvesters.

"The balls on this guy," Nicholas breathed, pressing into Sam's side as they hurried after the Hunter. The Harvesters spotted Nale immediately and snarled, whirling their weapons.

"Sentinel stragglers," one of them spat through her gap teeth.

"Here comes dinner," another grinned.

Nale bore down on them with alarming force, smashing the two Harvesters' heads together before they had a chance to thrust their blades at him. The wet sound of their skulls cracking made Nicholas wince.

Zeus rippled ahead, darting for a third Harvester and knocking him off his feet. The dog snapped efficiently at the guard's throat and the Harvester went limp. Losing a leg really hadn't slowed down the wolfhound one bit.

A hand grabbed Nicholas's shoulder and he whirled round to stare into the face of a one-eyed woman who wore a tacky gold eyepatch.

"Wow, ever heard of subtlety?" Nicholas asked, punching her good eye. The Harvester shrieked, half-blinded, and he punched her again, knocking her unconscious.

Sam tussled with a fifth attacker, digging his dagger into the Harvester's ribs, and then letting her collapse to the ground.

Quiet returned. The three Sentinels nodded at each other, regrouping and then hurrying for the cobbled high street.

It was quiet, aside from a few villagers in dated attire. They weren't alive, but they weren't phantoms, either. Nicholas's birth had blasted the souls of every villager out of their bodies, pinning them at a specific moment in time so that they wandered the streets in ghostly echoes, going about their business as if nothing had happened. They couldn't see the living, though, so he, Sam and Nale continued unhindered, Zeus sniffing the villagers in bewilderment and bouncing away from them in surprise.

Nicholas sent his mind through Orville, searching for the thing that would help him raise the Trinity. There was nothing out of the ordinary, though. Nothing lit up his internal radar and he was so intent on uncovering Orville's secret that he didn't realise where his feet had taken him until he was standing outside Rumours, the shop the Harvester known as Snelling had used to pose as a Sentinel.

Unease plucked his nerves like piano wires, but somehow this felt right; the magic shop was where Nicholas had to go. Not wasting a breath, he pushed the door and went inside.

Rumours was as Snelling had left it. Nicholas stalked between the glass cabinets and their ghoulish contents, ignoring the stuffed iguanas and shrivelled heads on pikes. He stopped at the centre of the shop floor, something prickling his mind.

"Here we are, then," a voice whispered.

Nicholas jumped. Sam was right behind him, while Nale and Zeus remained by the door. Nale closed it and watched through the square panes.

"You know this place?" Nicholas asked Sam.

The old man's eyes glistened in the gloom. "Oh aye. Came here all the time. I'm surprised you can't tell. This shop belonged to your parents. Your real parents."

Nicholas gave him a cynical stare, but Sam wouldn't joke about something like that. Half shaking his head in surprise, Nicholas looked around with renewed interest. Yes, he'd known it the moment he stepped inside. The shop recognised him. Its energies pulsed warmly around him, as if in welcome. He'd felt this way when he first visited Hallow House. Somehow it seemed like home.

Renewed hatred for Snelling burned through him. Had the Harvester known this was his parents' shop when he had posed as a Sentinel? Or was it just one of those weird coincidences he and Dawn didn't believe in?

Either way, he knew where he had to go.

"Upstairs," he told Sam, nodding at the curtain behind the counter. "Lead the way."

Reminding himself to breathe, Nicholas approached the curtain and pulled it aside. He'd been upstairs before; Snelling had made them tea in the lounge above the shop. Nicholas hadn't sensed anything then, though. No apparitions or dead family members. It was like he'd been asleep his whole life. Until his powers matured, he'd been numb to the world and everything it was trying to tell him.

He climbed the small staircase and went into the sitting room. The hairs on the back of Nicholas's neck shivered as a man and woman turned to look at him. They stood by the window, holding hands, and although Nicholas had never seen them before, he knew them instantly. His fingernails dug into the arm of a tatty sofa and a storm of emotions stirred in his chest.

"Judith," Sam breathed behind him, and Nicholas tore his eyes from the couple. A woman was sitting in an armchair in the corner. She seemed to be in her fifties and she was so absorbed by her book that she hadn't noticed Nicholas or Sam enter.

"Is that–" Nicholas managed to croak.

"Aye, that's her. That's my Judith." Sam sounded short of breath. "And… Alice and Daniel. I never thought I'd see them again."

Alice and Daniel. They were Nicholas's birth parents. Nicholas's gaze moved between the three figures. His parents and Sam's wife. They seemed so alive. They had all been dead for over a decade, but all were here, looking at him.

No, he was mistaken. Judith couldn't see him. She was staring right through him at the stairwell, her expression crinkled like she thought she'd heard something. After a second, she went back to her book.

But his parents… They gazed at him with unconcealed love. They knew him. It was as if they had been waiting for him all this time. He could go over and touch them, they were so real.

Finally regaining power over his body, he moved into the lounge. His parents' eyes followed him.

"How… how can they see me?" he murmured.

Sam came in after him. "I never understood spirits, but I'd hazard you share a connection. That's them alright, the way they looked before."

Nicholas couldn't believe it. His parents were right there and he resembled them both; a perfect fusion of the two. His mother had dark curly hair, like his before he shaved it all off, and her green eyes seemed so wise and knowing. He could see Anita in his father, too. The surly brow and bottom lip; the short brown hair and kind smile.

"Can I speak to them?"

He noticed his mother's mouth moving but no sound came.

Straining with both his ears and his abilities, Nicholas tried to catch what she was saying, but it was futile. Whatever words his mother had for him were echoing in another version of this room, in the spectral plane her spirit was tethered to. Another cruel joke at his expense.

"I think that's the limit of it, lad," Sam said softly. "Only so much we can ask for."

The old man stepped stiffly across the room and Nicholas heard the breath catching in his throat as he went to the phantom of his dead wife. She was engrossed in her book, checking her watch every few minutes as if expecting somebody. Maybe in this frozen moment she was expecting Sam.

Sam moved closer, putting his hand to Judith's hair but not touching it. She was oblivious as he caressed the air about her, perhaps pretending he could feel her. He leaned in and a cry parted his lips.

"Her perfume. I can smell it."

He straightened and backed away, wiping his eyes.

"No," he murmured. "It isn't real. She isn't here."

Nicholas put a hand to Sam's shoulder and Sam patted it. As he gazed at his parents, Nicholas felt a tug at the ball of grief he'd shoved into the closet of his mind. He'd almost forgotten about it.

There was so much he wanted to say… and nothing at all. He could study their faces for hours, attempt to learn every crease, every smile. He wanted to tell them that Anita and Max did well. They were good parents. They had raised him right and he had known the comfort of a happy home.

He trembled with emotion. It was almost too much. The air was charged with it. He was only just able to hold it at bay, but his vision was blurring with tears and he almost crumpled at his mother's feet. He wanted her to put her arms around him.

*I miss them so much,* he wanted to say. *Anita and Max. The life we could have had.*

He sniffed and straightened, puncturing the bubble of emotion that was trapping him. He had come here for a reason.

"There must be something here," he said, wrenching his gaze from his parents, whose tears mirrored his. "Something they left for me. But I can't–" Nicholas raised a hand and probed the flat with his mind. "I can't sense what it is."

As if they'd heard him, his parents moved away from the window. Nicholas jumped back, surprised by the sudden movement, but he relaxed when they walked to the door and gazed over their shoulders at him.

"They want us to follow them."

His parents melted into the darkness beyond the door and Nicholas chased after them, following their dark outlines down the stairs. Instead of heading back into the shop, though, they went to the back door and stood waiting.

Nicholas paused to peer through the curtain at Nale. He considered leaving him where he was, but he knew they'd need the Hunter if this went south. Nale may have secrets, but he was currently their most powerful ally.

"Hey," Nicholas said, and Nale's heavy gaze settled on him from across the shop. "This way."

Zeus peered up at his master and the Hunter clomped towards the back of the shop. Nicholas went to the back door and opened it, stepping aside so his parents could go through first. Then he hurried after them into an overgrown garden that was barely any bigger than the living room.

Which was when he saw it.

The well.

The hairs on his arms prickled. It was the same well from his vision. It rested towards the rear of the garden, its ancient bricks crawling with moss and vines, a creaking wooden eaves above it to shelter it from the rain.

His parents glowed faintly in the afternoon light, standing beside the well. Staring meaningfully at him, his mother pointed. *Here*, she seemed to be saying. *It's here, Nicholas.*

He edged closer, peering into the well's depths. He couldn't see the bottom, just a black circle like a tea stain. A splitting headache lanced through his skull and he pushed the heel of his palm into his forehead.

*The Trinity stand in an underground chamber.*

The image sizzled and faded. Nicholas blinked, bringing the garden back into focus. He peered down into the well again, wondering if it was a well at all. It was starting to feel like another Sentinel trick.

He shot Sam and Nale a glance as he bent to grab a stone, and then tossed it into the well.

It rattled all the way down and then fell silent.

"No splash," he said. "Either it's empty or it's dried up. We go down."

"No."

Nale's voice struck like a hammer blow and Nicholas faced him.

"We have to."

For the first time, the Hunter's expression shifted away from its usual blitheness. The hair on Nale's upper lip trembled as if he was attempting not to blurt something out.

"I know this place," Nicholas said. "The seeing glass showed it to me, and *they–*" he gestured at his parents, "–obviously know something about it. They wouldn't send me down there if it was dangerous."

"It is."

Nicholas clenched his fists. The time for pretending had passed. "What are you hiding, Nale?"

The Hunter said nothing. He offered no denial or explanation. His brown eyes shone at Nicholas and he couldn't tell if they held fear or pity.

"Wait, wait," Sam said huskily. "Liberty… She saw this, too. In your head, Nale; she found the image of a well. She said you were scared. You've been here before, haven't you?"

"What aren't you telling us?" Nicholas demanded.

The Hunter's whole body was rigid, like it was turning to stone, and he remained silent, though his glare was full with emotion. Unable to bear it any longer, Nicholas launched himself at the man. Perhaps it was Diltraa's constant thirst for violence inside him, but he was momentarily blind to Nale's size; he didn't care that the Hunter could crush his throat with his thumb and forefinger. He had to see what was in the man's head.

Nale hadn't anticipated the attack and Nicholas felt the demon in his chest swell at the promise of a fight. Diltraa's power flooded his fists and he battered Nale's ribs.

Zeus hopped back, barking wildly.

The Hunter attempted to shove Nicholas away, but Nicholas was too quick. He punched Nale in the gut, winding him, then bowled into him, knocking him to the ground.

"Show me," Nicholas ordered through gritted teeth, thrusting his hands at Nale's head.

At the contact, Zeus's yelps fell away and images flickered before Nicholas's eyes.

*Jessica stands in the chamber below Hallow House.*

*A fresh-faced young man with wild brown hair watches. He's built like a fortress and looks like a younger version of Nale.*

*The chamber shudders.*

*In the dark by the throne, three sets of purple eyes glint.*

*The Trinity are dragged from their watery coffins.*

*Two women and a man.*

*Lethargic, barely able to stand, they're lined up—*

The connection broke suddenly. Nicholas found himself sailing through the air. Nale had kicked him free and hurtled Nicholas across the garden. He crumpled against the side of the well, almost toppling over headfirst. Nicholas only just managed to catch himself, watching stones skitter down the shaft into darkness.

"Nicholas!" Sam yelled, hurrying to his side. "What's—"

Shakily, Nicholas found his feet, his legs weak with what he'd seen.

"You were there," he said, cutting off Sam and glaring at Nale. "With Jessica and the Trinity. They were awake. What was that? *When* was that?"

Nale clambered to his feet, Zeus sniffing him protectively, his tongue hanging out.

"What's going on?" Sam asked. "Nicholas, what did you see?"

"Nale?" Nicholas demanded. The young man in the vision had been unmistakably Nale, perhaps twenty years ago, but Nicholas couldn't tell. The Hunter's facial hair made it difficult to identify his age.

"Stop." The big man's voice rumbled. "You must stop."

"Tell me!"

Nale returned his furious stare and said nothing. Nicholas considered launching at the man again, but the element of surprise was lost.

"Then we go down," Nicholas said. It was clear Nale didn't want them to, and as much as Nicholas hated the idea of climbing down that dark shaft, it was a shot at answers. He wouldn't need Nale to tell him anything if he could see it for himself.

"Nale," Sam interrupted. "It's time you started talking."

The Hunter shook his head, his eyes wide. "Can't. Can't…"

"He's lost it," Nicholas said. He tested the rope hanging from the eaves above the well. It seemed sturdy enough. He could lower himself into the well, take a look around and get back up to the garden in less time than it would take to subdue Nale and get into his head. "I'm going down."

He tied the rope around his waist.

Nale appeared torn, his usual stoic poise having dissolved. He paced restlessly. Ignoring him, Nicholas swung his legs over the side of the well and Sam grabbed the winch's handle, stopping it from spinning and sending Nicholas plummeting to his death.

"Got it?" Nicholas asked, and the old man nodded.

Clasping the rope above his head, Nicholas made sure it was taut, then began to lower himself into the well. The damp smell of old stone filled his nostrils and the air cooled with every foot he dropped.

The black mouth at the bottom of the well slowly swallowed him and when Nicholas glanced up, the opening had shrunk to the size of a ten-pence piece, Sam peering over nervously. Nale wouldn't hurt him, would he? Nicholas was sure Sam could take care of himself if the Hunter suddenly lost it completely.

It was so quiet, Nicholas could only hear the blood in his ears. He sank lower and lower before the well shaft suddenly ended and he found himself dangling in an open space. He glimpsed the rough floor a few feet below and untied the rope, dropping to the ground.

The rope dangled above his head and Nicholas squinted through the darkness. It was so dark he could barely see, but from the light above, he could tell he was in a small rocky cave. At first, he thought there was nothing that remarkable about it, but as his sight adjusted to the gloom, he saw that one of the walls was different. Moving closer, he noticed that the rock had bubbled and calcified into tumour-like ridges. It resembled cooled lava. At some point, it seemed to have been intensely heated, then left to harden.

"What is this place?" he murmured.

He touched the strange wall and images poured into his mind.

*Jessica and a young Nale stand in the chamber below Hallow House.*

*By the throne, three sets of purple eyes flash.*

*Jessica weeps, clutching her breast.*

*Then nods.*

*And the young Nale takes his blade.*

*Hesitates for only a moment.*

*Standing before the two women and the man.*

*The Trinity.*

*One of the women says something.*

*Then he slits the Trinity's throats.*

The images flashed before him and Nicholas pieced them together, nausea squeezing his torso, the truth of what had happened at Hallow House hitting him like a truck.

"He killed them," he choked, unable to believe what he'd seen. It didn't make any sense. Why would a Sentinel kill the Trinity? They were the old gods, revered by all. And why *Nale*? In Bury, Nale had fought the monstrous emissaries of the Dark Prophets alongside the Sentinels; he didn't seem to have been corrupted. So why had he committed such an atrocious act? And why had Jessica permitted it?

Dizzy with what he'd seen, Nicholas realised the tugging sensation had returned in his stomach. It was pulling him towards the other side of the cave. Was there something else down here?

Attempting to focus, he held out his hand, imagining it grasping an invisible cord, and followed it to the cave wall. There were no markings. Nothing to tell him that there was anything extraordinary about the wall, except for the feeling in his stomach. Something was hidden here.

He touched the wall.

*Jessica crouches down, nursing the dead Trinity.*

*There is nobody else around.*

*The purple eyes have vanished.*

*It is only Jessica and the Trinity. The beings she was charged with protecting.*

*Then she unlatches something at their throats.*

*Three collars.*

*She places them in a sack.*

*Hides them in the wall.*

*Then retreats.*

Feeling woozy with everything that had crammed into his mind over the past few minutes, Nicholas assessed the wall and wondered how the hell he was supposed to retrieve what Jessica had hidden in there. Then he remembered what she had said in Nale's wagon. The words she slipped into his head.

*"Unseal, peel, reveal,"* he uttered.

Before him, the rock shuddered and glowed before erupting in a cloud of dust.

"You alright lad?"

Sam's voice echoed down the well.

"Fine," Nicholas called, distracted by what was revealed as the dust cloud cleared. An ancient bit of sacking lay amid the rubble and a high-pitched whining sound came from it.

Gritting his teeth, Nicholas seized the sack and, not wasting another breath, pulled it open to peek inside.

The noise ceased. Nicholas stared at the three collars. They looked exactly as they had in the vision. They shone with silver and what appeared to be bone, slender and looping. They resembled a shark's jaw, lined with runes and sharp ornamentation.

Jessica had removed them from the Trinity.

He was holding something that had belonged to the ancient gods.

Shaking with excitement, Nicholas then remembered what Nale had done and the excitement dulled into anger. He couldn't let him get away with it, and he couldn't leave the murderous Hunter with Sam another second.

Knotting the sack closed to protect the collars, he pushed it into his backpack. Then he seized hold of the rope and called up to Sam, who began winching him up. Nicholas scrabbled at the sides of the well, hauling himself up, and the more he climbed, the angrier he became. Nale had sacrificed the Trinity. He had committed an unthinkable crime. The worst possible crime a Sentinel could commit.

He was a traitor.

Finally, Nicholas found the lip of the well and grabbed it, hauling himself over the edge and collapsing to the ground.

"There you are, lad," Sam said, but Nicholas ignored him. He scrabbled to his feet and his gaze found Nale.

"You killed them," he spat.

He half expected Nale to retaliate, perhaps even hurl him into the well after all. But the Hunter wasn't angry. His head was hung in shame, his long brown hair concealing most of his bearded face, and Zeus pawed at his leg, whining.

"Killed who?" Sam asked. "Nicholas, what did you see?"

"The Trinity. That's why we're in this mess. Nale... He killed them."

Sam looked like he'd been told two plus two equals beetroot. "But... that's not possible," he wheezed. "What did you *see*?"

Nicholas could barely form the words. "Nale and Jessica waking up the Trinity. Then he cut their throats, let them bleed out. And Jessica just watched. She just watched them die."

The old man's face was chalk-white with disbelief as he stared at Nale. But the way the Hunter was slumped told him Nicholas wasn't mistaken. Nicholas was surprised Nale hadn't fled the moment he went into the well.

"Nale, you tell me what's going on, *now*," Sam told the Hunter. Nicholas had never heard him sound so cold.

Nale didn't move.

"NALE!" Sam bellowed, and Nicholas jumped.

The Hunter raised his head, his face tear-streaked.

"We had to," he said, and for the first time, Nicholas sensed the emotions roiling within the enormous man. The self-loathing and shame. Nicholas had smashed his way into Nale's head and his defences were ruined.

"The Prophets…" Nale gruffed. "They had found an opening into our world. In the cave below the well."

Nicholas thought of the purple eyes piercing the gloom. The deformed, tumour-like wall. It certainly seemed like something had tried to punch its way through.

"Jessica managed to hold them at bay, but her powers were weakening," Nale continued. "The only way to banish them and seal the opening was to unleash the Trinity's power."

"Unleash…? You killed them!" Nicholas shouted.

"It was the only way!" Nale roared. The sound echoed around the garden, tortured and desolate. At the back of the garden, Nicholas's birth parents stood holding each other's hands, their expressions grim.

"I don't understand. How?" Sam demanded. "How did they find a way in? And why was it the only way?"

"Ask her. The Vaktarin made the order."

"And you just did it? Without any hesitation?" Sam said.

Nale didn't reply. His darkest secret had been uncovered and he was broken.

"Oh, he hesitated," Nicholas said. "For about a second. Loyal to the end, right Nale? A true Sentinel." He paused. "That's why you went into hiding. Why nobody saw you for years."

"Why I had never heard of you," Sam added. "Nobody could know, could they? What you did."

Nicholas was trying to understand how this new information affected his mission to revive the Trinity. He couldn't tell if anything had really changed. The Trinity's earthly forms had been destroyed but Jessica still believed they could be returned. He felt the weight of the collars in his bag, heard their strange humming like something from a beehive, and wondered how they could help.

"She said something to you," Nicholas said with fresh urgency. "Before she died. Norlath, right? She's the one you killed first? She said something to you."

"She…" Nale rested a huge hand on Zeus's head, stilling the dog. "She said: '*He will find a way.*'"

*He.* Nicholas thought. *Did she mean me?*

"When was it?" he asked. "That night?"

"The night you were born." Nale's head nudged at Nicholas. "You and the girl."

*Of course it was.* Everything took him back to that night; the night that changed everything. He pulled together the scraps of information he had. It was all starting to make a horrible kind of sense. That was why the Trinity has allowed themselves to be killed; at the moment of their deaths, they had chosen him and Rae, two newborns, given them the powers to resurrect them when the time was right.

"There must be a reason for all of this," Sam said, rubbing his forehead. "Jessica wouldn't have done it for nothing. She committed an unforgivable act, sacrificed the old gods. That's so far beyond desperate I cannot… She must have known something."

"She did," Nicholas said. "She knew the Trinity had chosen me and Rae. That night… They died the night we were born. That's why this town is ruined. And…" He stopped. He couldn't tell Sam about the collars with Nale listening. Although he wanted to believe that Nale really was on their side, he couldn't get the image of what he'd done out of his head.

They fell into silence. Nicholas couldn't look at Nale. He'd played a part in something that had defined Nicholas's life; thrust a responsibility on him that nobody would ever ask for. If Nicholas's mother hadn't gone into labour that night, perhaps he would have been spared it, but Nale's actions had assured it.

"What's that?" Sam asked. He was staring over the rooftops at the sky, which was bleeding orange. It wouldn't be sunset for hours, though, and even then the sky would be the same depressing grey.

"Fire," Nale said.

"It's the forest," Sam murmured.

Nicholas's heart skipped. "The others." What if Malika had found Merlyn and the rest of the Sentinels in the forest? Had her army infiltrated their little camp?

Without saying a word, Sam, Nale, and Zeus hurried for the back door, disappearing into the shop. Nicholas went after them but paused to peer back at his parents. They were still by the well, their hands entwined. His mother was crying.

"I'm coming back," he said, "don't worry," though he didn't know how or when. Then he chased after the others, bowling through the shop and out into Orville. In the distance, he glimpsed trees aflame. Sam was right. The forest was burning down. Was this Malika's plan? Smoke the Sentinel survivors out and slaughter them at the forest edge?

Nale and the wolfhound charged ahead, and Nicholas watched them uncertainly, scared that the Hunter wasn't racing to save the Sentinels, but to finish them off for good. What if, all this time, he really was a Harvester?

His panic for the safety of the others overrode those doubts, though, and Nicholas ran alongside Sam down the high street. They jumped over the bodies of the Harvesters they had killed earlier and then plunged headfirst into the forest. It was choked with fire and ash and Nicholas couldn't remember where the wagon was, but Sam seemed to know, and Nicholas followed the old man into the blaze.

*Merlyn*, he thought, over and over again. He didn't know what he'd do if Merlyn was hurt or killed. An image of Merlyn's throat being cut leapt into his mind, but it wasn't a premonition. It couldn't be. If Merlyn was dead, he'd feel it, just like he'd feel it if Dawn and Rae were in trouble.

They raced between the trees, chasing after Nale and Zeus, and finally the wagon came into view, miraculously untouched by the fire that blazed around it. A figure ran to him and Nicholas's chest swelled when he saw it was Merlyn, his features pale with worry. They seized each other in an embrace.

"I made them wait," Merlyn said. Nicholas squeezed him back until his arms ached, wanting to choke up everything that had just happened; that he'd seen his parents, and found the collars, but then he noticed the wagon was alone in the glade. The minivan and the caravan had vanished.

"What's happening?" he asked, drawing back from Merlyn as Sam peered around in bewilderment.

"It's her, or at least her Harvesters. Has to be. Either they really hate trees, or this is them preparing a Sentinel barbecue."

"Where are the others?" Sam asked. "Aileen and—"

"Gone. I sort of made them. Told them I'd wait here for you with—"

At Merlyn's words, the door to the wagon banged opened and Isabel appeared.

"Where is she?" the old woman demanded.

"Where's who?" Nicholas asked.

"Jessica!" Isabel's face was gaunt. "Where is Jessica?"

# CHAPTER TWELVE
## HEART

"Jessica's missing?"

Nicholas had never felt more like he'd jumped from the frying pan into the fire. Jessica couldn't be missing. Not on top of everything else. He needed her now more than ever, especially after what he'd learnt in the well. The more he discovered, the more this was all about her. Malika. The Trinity. *My entire freaking existence.* It was all linked to Jessica.

"She was here," said Isabel, her fingers gripping the doorframe. "Now she's gone."

"You think somebody took her?" Nicholas asked. He threw a look behind him at the clearing, remembering that Nale had made it here before them. But the Hunter was still here and he seemed busy staking out the area, keeping eyes on the burning forest as Zeus sniffed the smoky air. Nale couldn't be responsible for Jessica's disappearance. Had a Harvester slipped into the wagon and dragged her out? She'd have struggled and made some sound, though. Isabel would have heard. The grim set of Isabel's jaw told him she hadn't heard a thing.

"Impossible." The woman's voice cracked. "I was with her. I turned my back for only a moment to heat some water. When I returned to her bedside, she was gone."

Nicholas considered the others. They were all sweating in the heat and they must all be thinking the same thing. Jessica had wandered off, perhaps followed one of her half-formed thoughts out the door, and she'd done so at exactly the worst possible time.

*Or perhaps*, a cynical voice in Nicholas's head reasoned, *Jessica knew what I would uncover and couldn't face the truth.* She had wanted him to find the collars, but surely she knew he'd find out what happened that night when she and Nale awoke the Trinity. Perhaps, like Nale, she was ashamed. Too ashamed to confront the truth of what she'd done.

Barefoot and still wrapped in her purple kaftan, Isabel stepped down from the wagon, her staff thudding against the steps. She crossed the clearing and seemed to be about to dive headfirst into the blazing forest in search of Jessica, but Nicholas stepped forward.

"Wait." He focussed on their surroundings, searching with his mind, but there was too much activity, or perhaps a little of Jessica's power was still protecting her. He couldn't pick her out from the choking heat all around them. And he couldn't leave her to the wolves, or risk Nale going after her. He'd have to find her the old-fashioned way.

He grabbed Merlyn's arm. "We'll look for Jessica. Isabel, you stay here in case she doubles back. She might just be confused. Sam, you go that way. Ten minutes tops, then we'll have to get out of here."

"Sounds like the best plan, given the circumstances," Sam said, eyeing the flames. His skin was already grubby from the smoke.

Isabel blinked uncertainly, then nodded. "Go. Find her. Please."

Nicholas hesitated as he considered Nale. The Hunter's brow was more brooding than ever, and Nicholas pitied him, and then grew angry at himself, remembering the spurt of blood as he killed the Trinity. As much as he hated the thought of leaving Nale alone with Isabel, he didn't have much of a choice.

"I'm sure Jessica will be fine," Nicholas said, hugging Isabel. She stiffened, and Nicholas drew her closer as she tried to pull free. "Keep an eye on Nale," he hissed in her ear.

Ignoring Isabel's questioning stare, Nicholas pushed Merlyn away from the wagon and they hurried into the forest. The heat was thick and smothering and he remembered Bury St Edmunds turning into an inferno around them. When this was over, he was going to move somewhere cold. Like Norway or Scotland.

"You think she's okay?" Merlyn asked as they raced between flaming tree trunks.

"Wish I could say yes."

"I miss anything with Sam and Nale?"

Nicholas rubbed sweat from his eyes. "Same answer."

"Had a feeling." Merlyn squeezed his hand. "You can tell me about it later."

"She didn't say anything? Jessica? Before she disappeared?"

"I was helping Aileen with inventory. It was just Isabel and the Vaktarin in the wagon. The first I heard about Jessica missing was when you did."

"This is bad."

"I'd say we're officially into the 'super bad' portion of the apocalypse."

With growing desperation, Nicholas frisbeed his thoughts around them, but nothing came back. No flicker of silver light that might be Jessica. Only the sound of heat-splitting wood and smoke. Their surroundings became more and more disorientating. Nicholas frowned. The direction they were running, it seemed like they were heading towards the side of the forest that faced Hallow House.

"She can't have gone back," he murmured. "Why would she go back to the house?"

"Seems like suicide."

Nicholas chewed the inside of his cheek. Had the final thread of Jessica's sanity frayed at last? Was this some foolish attempt at taking back the house; or had she forgotten it wasn't her house anymore? Maybe she was just trying to get home.

"Sam must have found her on the other side of the forest," he said. "There's no way she'd come this way."

At least, he hoped there wasn't. If Jessica had already reached the house, it was game over for her. He and Merlyn couldn't fight Malika's army alone, especially if the Dark Prophets had already hatched. That really would be suicide.

They slowed, sweat stinging Nicholas's eyes, and Merlyn's hand suddenly felt like a spider between his fingers. Nicholas yanked it free.

"You see something?" Merlyn asked.

"Just give me some space," Nicholas snapped.

Merlyn's ash-flecked face looked like it had been dealt a blow. He swallowed and blinked quickly at their surroundings, appearing to double his resolve to find Jessica.

Nicholas squeezed his knuckles. What had he said? He couldn't remember. A shiver of irritation travelled up his spine and he felt a sickly urge to run; to get away from Merlyn.

No, he didn't want that. He wanted Merlyn's hand in his again.

Nicholas turned his head. He'd heard something. The same something he'd heard in the ambulance. But the voice wasn't coming from anywhere in the forest. It was coming from within him.

Diltraa.

He felt the demon shifting somewhere in the pit of his mind. Unfurling claws and tweaking at his nerves.

Gritting his teeth, Nicholas pushed the monster down, imagining chains lashing its limbs and binding it to a finger of rock. He needed Diltraa but he wouldn't surrender to it. This was his body. *His life*, dammit. And now he'd hurt Merlyn's feelings. The monster wouldn't destroy that.

"Sorry—" Nicholas began, but then he glimpsed a shape slipping between the trees. A silvery dress reflected fire. It was Jessica. She was stalking away from them, a hand pressed to her wounded abdomen as she headed for the other side of the forest – straight for the fields that bordered Hallow House.

"There!" Nicholas pointed.

A shape hurtled from a tree to his right, knocking him to the forest floor. Nicholas somersaulted sideways and scrabbled to his feet, watching as Merlyn clashed with the Harvester that had barrelled from behind one of the trees. Metallic horns had been drilled into the man's bald head and his teeth flashed dirty gold.

"Get her!" Merlyn grunted, throwing up an arm to deflect the Harvester's blow, then burying his other fist in the Harvester's gut.

As Nicholas wavered, Merlyn yelled again. "Go!" And Nicholas knew this was his only chance. If he didn't hurry, he'd lose Jessica. "Get her before she runs off again!"

Nicholas nodded and raced ahead, chasing the flicker of silver fabric. He didn't shout in case other Harvesters were in the trees. The heat was unbearable against his skin, but he drove his boots into the charred earth, speeding up even though his legs felt ready to buckle.

There. She was just ahead. Nicholas sped faster. He was so close he could almost touch her if he stretched out a hand.

"Stop!" he hissed.

Jessica's golden hair flicked the air and her eyes shone at him in surprise.

"Nicholas."

Without a word he seized her arm and dragged her behind a tree, his ribs aching as he tried to catch his breath.

"What... what... are you doing?" he gasped.

"She is coming." Jessica's voice was calm.

"Who? The witch? We know that... We... have to get out of here. Get back... to the others."

"No, I'm not going back. She's coming for me and I won't allow anybody else to perish at her hands."

Jessica's gaze was level. She seemed to have regained some of her old self. Maybe Merlyn was right. This was suicide. She was sacrificing herself the way she'd sacrificed the Trinity. But what would that accomplish? They needed her. She'd waited five-hundred years for this.

Finally, Nicholas could breathe again. "But... I need you."

She smiled sadly, emotion flickering across her heart-shaped face.

"I have done everything the Trinity asked of me. My time is at an end. Soon a new Vaktarin will be called."

It was the most he'd heard her say since first meeting her all those months ago. She spoke with the clarity of somebody who knew her hour had come. Was that why she suddenly seemed so lucid?

"But the Trinity... They're dead. I saw what happened when you and Nale were in the chamber below the house..." He tried to find the right questions. Finally, he breathed, "Why did you do it?"

Jessica's hand was warm on his arm. "It is not up to us to understand the ways of the old gods. They are mysterious and unknowable. But understand this: nothing is ever truly dead. What you glimpsed of the past was one piece of a greater whole." Her eyelashes brushed her cheeks and then her eyes locked with his, her voice soft. "I had no choice, Nicholas. Two decades ago, the Prophets were a breath away from reclaiming our world. They would have devastated it just as they are now. Their mere existence poisons and corrupts everything around them. The only thing that could stop them was the Trinity's sacrifice. They died for us. And you will return them to us."

"But... how has nobody ever heard about how close the Prophets came to returning that night?"

"It was kept secret, of course." Jessica's lips hooked into a smile. "Like everything else about that night. Until you turned up on my doorstep almost sixteen years later, just as I knew you would."

"But... I don't know what I'm supposed to do."

Jessica's gaze was kind. "Listen to me, Nicholas. I don't have all the answers. Nobody does. The only thing I know for certain is this: you are emotion. You feel it all. That is your power. That is why you were raised oblivious to all of this: the Sentinels, the Prophets... It's all noise. How could anybody have any compassion for this world unless they had lived in it? Been a part of it? That is your gift."

"That doesn't tell me how to raise the Trinity."

"But it does. They gave you this gift for a reason. You have to trust that. When the time comes, you will know what to do."

Nicholas searched her face for more. Anything that wasn't a riddle or a cryptic non-reply.

"My time is over, child," Jessica said, and suddenly she sounded very old. She looked so young, but it was a mask that hid her true nature, and Nicholas remembered how ancient she really was. She may be the oldest person in the world, and now the world seemed to have become too much for her. "Malika has beaten me, taken everything from me, but she will not beat you. I see that as clearly as I see the kindness in your heart."

His hand thrust at her throat, pinning her against the tree.

"No!" Nicholas shouted.

His hand had moved on its own. Diltraa's fury boiled through him, blasting fire through his veins. Nicholas saw red and black and the pain of creation tore at every sinew in his body. He recalled what Sam had told him. Diltraa and Jessica were linked. The demon had used her to kill Isabel all those centuries ago.

As Jessica struggled in his grip, Nicholas found he couldn't release her. His fingers dug into the sinews of her throat and although he didn't know why, the window to Jessica's world opened before him. He found he could feel everything she did. The dizzy kaleidoscope of emotions whirled and changed before him, and within the emotion he saw her life. Her father. Her mother. Isabel. The love and the terror and the giddy ebb of days.

Nicholas's hand squeezed Jessica's throat tighter and the memories she and Diltraa shared flooded his consciousness. He saw her in the Pentagon Room. Her hands about Isabel's throat. And in the anguished moments when Jessica realised what she'd done, the pain tore her in two. The demon Diltraa split her body as it left it, and from the chaos Malika was born.

Everything Sam had said was true.

Diltraa. Jessica. Malika.

They formed a corrupt triad of their own.

Growling with effort, Nicholas wrenched his hand away and Jessica gasped, anguish crumpling her elfin features as she clutched her throat.

"I see it," she said thickly. "The demon is in you now."

The weight of her stare nearly forced him to his knees. Nicholas realised he had glimpsed Jessica's past and, in return, she had seen his. The cosmos always played fair. For a moment, he felt the same shame that must weigh on Nale. He had let the demon in. He had gone to terrible lengths to do the right thing. Nicholas felt Jessica's judgement and he couldn't escape her stare.

"How are you fighting it?" she whispered.

"I don't know." He breathed slowly, forcing Diltraa down, away from the surface so that it couldn't cause any more damage. "But it's the only way to stop Malika."

Her eyes widened with horror. "It will consume you. Tear you apart."

He shuddered at the memory of Malika's birth. "Not before I stop her."

"My, my," purred a voice. "Are we discovering new things?"

Malika had materialised as if from nowhere. She stood only a few paces to Nicholas's right, her snake-like hair as red as the flames, her dress the colour of blood. He didn't know if she'd been watching the whole thing, waiting for her moment, but her smile was that of a serpent whose prey was snared. She swept forward, her lips and fingernails black, and Nicholas glimpsed the Drujblade swinging at her waist.

He tried to pull himself together, placing himself between the two women. They were two halves of a twisted whole. Funny, he was part of that now. The Skurkwife had seen to that. But he wouldn't let Diltraa destroy him the way it had Jessica.

"I remember the last time we three were together," the witch said, swaying where she stood, her cat-like eyes mirroring the fire. "In the garden. It feels like decades ago, doesn't it?"

"You have become even more monstrous since then," Jessica said.

"And you even more pious, though perhaps a little saner. Did the medication finally kick in?"

"We all look sane next to you."

Malika tossed her curls back with laughter. "What a fascinating little family we are. I wonder what Jung would say. Am I your shadow aspect or are you mine?"

"You're the smart one," Jessica said. "You tell me."

"Oh now don't sell yourself short. You hid this one pretty well." She gestured at Nicholas. "It took me over a decade to find him. And that trick with the dagger; turning the blade on yourself to injure me. I didn't think you had the guts."

Nicholas had no idea what to do. Was Malika here to kill him? Or Jessica? Surely, if Malika attempted to hurt Jessica, she would be sentencing herself, too.

"It's a headache, no?" Malika said. She'd read his mind and he hadn't even felt it. "If the old shrew hadn't been training Jessica all those years ago, she never would have summoned Diltraa, and I'd still be a speck in the cosmos waiting to be born. Luckily, there's a loophole. Life would be so dreary without loopholes."

"Let the boy go," Jessica said.

Nicholas spotted movement behind Malika. Merlyn was ten feet away, peering from behind a tree. He'd caught up. Nicholas resisted the urge to gesture for him to get away; he didn't want to bring any attention to him.

"The boy stays," Malika said simply.

"Let him go and I'll do whatever you ask."

"No," Nicholas said.

"Nicholas, this is the way it has to be."

Malika's fingers caressed the Drujblade and Nicholas ignored Merlyn's shape as it dodged from one tree to the next, slinking closer, any sound of his movement lost in the crackle and spit of wood as the forest was eaten alive by fire.

"Ah, the heroes never understand sacrifice, unless they're the ones doing it." Malika paused. "Although… something's different about the man-child. What is it?"

Her catlike eyes flashed at him and Nicholas threw up the strongest barrier he could. If Malika knew her maker was present, she might try to draw the demon out; use it against them.

"The sapling's become an oak," Malika observed. "Keep your secrets for now, whelp. There's time. For you, at least."

Merlyn emerged from behind the nearest tree. He clutched a Harvester's sickle and crept up behind Malika. Nicholas watched the witch for any sign that she was aware of the Sentinel at her back, but her gaze rested on Jessica and the corner of her lip tugged into a snarl.

"I must say, I'm enjoying this little reunion."

Merlyn raised the sickle and prepared to plunge it into the witch's spine.

At that moment, Malika raised a hand as if to strike Jessica, but then her skirts fanned about her as she whirled about and seized hold of Merlyn's neck. Her other hand closed around his wrist, preventing the sickle from doing its worst.

Shock registered on Merlyn's face as Malika plucked him from the ground and tossed him against a tree. Nicholas heard a horrible crunch and Merlyn flopped to the forest floor.

Howling, Nicholas threw himself at Malika, lunging for the Drujblade. Laughing, Malika's claws flashed for his throat, but Nicholas dodged just in time and he somersaulted across the ground.

The witch tossed her curls at him. "Ah, yes, I remember now. Love. The boy's under your skin, and you his."

Nicholas thrust a psychic spear at her, aiming for her skull, and Malika's head snapped back as it struck her. She quickly regained her composure, though blood dribbled from one of her nostrils.

"Neat trick," she spat. "Liberty Rayne teach you that?"

He balked at the mention of the dead Sensitive, but Malika's taunts wouldn't distract him. Liberty wouldn't tolerate them so neither would he.

"Do you ever shut up?" he growled.

"Give me a reason."

Nicholas swept ash from the forest floor and threw it in Malika's face, then launched himself at her again. As she spat and swore, his hand snapped around the Drujblade at her hip, and the connection sent an electric tingle shooting up his arm.

Malika shrieked and smashed his jaw with her fist. Ignoring the pain, he refused to let go of the dagger, swinging at the witch with his free hand. The crack of contact made his knuckles scream as he caught her in the ribs and she snarled, kneeing him in the stomach.

Winded, Nicholas released the Drujblade and Malika dug a hand into his chest. His psychic barrier faltered and pain spasmed deep in his ribcage. It felt like she was crushing his heart.

"Let's get to the heart of the matter, shall we?" she hissed. "You think you can stop me. You know the sorry tale of my origins, but it doesn't matter where I came from. The scraps you cling to are nothing. What matters is that even now the Dark Prophets are preparing to hatch, and when they do, nothing will stop them destroying everything you prize."

Nicholas gasped for air, the pain cramping his chest almost unbearable. His gaze found Merlyn, still crumpled at the foot of a tree, and he couldn't tell if he was breathing.

Finally, Malika grunted and released him. Nicholas staggered back, retching, almost vomiting, and then Jessica rushed at the red witch. Shrieking words he didn't understand, the two women clashed against a backdrop of fire as the forest burned.

As he clutched his chest, Nicholas's heart shuddered. His limbs felt lethargic as he staggered over to Merlyn.

"Merl, can you hear me?"

He shook him, but Merlyn was out cold, blood smeared across one side of his face. Nicholas peered back over his shoulder, seeing that Jessica and Malika were locked together, equally matched in battle. Guilt wriggled through him. Jessica was fighting to save him; she seemed ready to die for him, but he couldn't let that happen.

"Stay down," Nicholas whispered at Merlyn, hoping he could hear him, then he straightened and summoned all the strength he had left.

He raised his hands, pouring all his hatred for Malika between his palms, forming a seething ball of psychic energy and preparing to hurl it at her.

As the energy between his palms reached critical mass, a pain like nothing he'd ever felt lanced through his skull. The energy in his hands dissolved and Nicholas grabbed his head. It felt like something was tearing him apart from the inside.

"Stop!" he cried, half-collapsing against a tree. He was being hollowed out, shredded with invisible claws. What was happening?

Through the haze of pain, he saw that Malika had managed to pin Jessica to the ground. The witch's fingers dug into Jessica's chest and Jessica seemed only half-conscious.

Shakily, Nicholas held out his hands and attempted to reform his psychic weapon. He screamed as fresh agony ripped through his skull. The demon. It had to be. Diltraa was preventing him from hurting Malika.

*STOP!* Nicholas bellowed in his mind. As he tried to unlatch the demon's claws from his skull, more figures charged from the trees, nearly a dozen of them, all Harvesters bearing weapons. They surrounded the clearing.

Sensing the newcomers, Malika glanced up from the forest floor. She was still crouched over Jessica, who appeared dazed and spent, her chest heaving and her eyes fixed on the flaming canopy above their heads.

Irritation furrowed Malika's brow, and then her expression smoothed. A delighted laugh spilled from her throat.

Gritting his teeth, Nicholas caught hold of a tree and saw that one of the Harvesters was shoving a figure forward.

"Sam," he breathed, crestfallen at the sight of the old man. Sam's hands were being forced behind his back and, as he struggled to get free, his captor booted his legs and Sam collapsed to his knees. One of the Harvesters flicked off Sam's fedora, and the hat bounced to the ground.

"Well, well." Malika rose, leaving Jessica where she lay. Her red dress rippled as she approached Sam. "You really are indestructible, Mr Wilkins."

"Found him in the woods," said the Harvester restraining him.

"He killed Mab," added another.

Malika traced the old man's jaw with a finger. "So keen to fight. Ha! The old dog has pluck even now, knowing he is beaten."

"The dark will never eclipse the light." Sam's voice was a craggy wheeze and guilt pulled at Nicholas's insides. He had sent Sam to search for Jessica, but Sam had found Harvesters instead. And he'd clearly taken a beating before being dragged here.

Malika stooped to Sam's level and wrenched his chin, pointing at Jessica, who lay motionless on the forest floor. Her voice was melted caramel. "Do you not see her? Even the fool must accede to what his own eyes show him."

The look of pain on Sam's face broke Nicholas's heart.

"Jessica," the old man murmured.

"Touching, really. Your love for her is almost as big as your fear for me. You believe she is a god." Malika shoved his chin as she released him. "Even gods die."

Sam's enraged howl filled the clearing and Nicholas's eyes widened as the old man wrestled free from the Harvester, throwing himself at Malika. The witch cried out in surprise and they tumbled together over the ashen ground. A couple of Harvesters leapt forward to help their leader, but Nicholas launched psychic darts at them that knocked them off their feet. The pain that followed felt like it had split his skull in two.

*Stop it*, Nicholas ordered Diltraa. *You're nothing. I'm in control. ME.*

The needling in his brain eased off and Nicholas saw that Malika had bested Sam. She had him up against a tree.

"You persist even when I have warned you," she hissed. "You insist on meddling and fighting. If you refuse to die, I must find another use for you." She held out her free hand and a female Harvester slithered forward, fixing something to Malika's forearm. When the Harvester drew back, Nicholas saw that the witch now wore a gauntlet. In a crackle of blue lightning, she could incinerate him, or hollow him out for a demon to take over his body.

She smiled and stepped back. "Sweet dreams."

"Sam!" Nicholas yelled, but even as he attempted to pitch himself at the Harvester, unbearable pain mangled the contents of Nicholas's skull and he found he was on his knees in the dirt, trying to tear out the thing in his head.

The clearing flashed with blue light and, wincing through the agony, Nicholas watched as Malika aimed the gauntlet at Sam and unleashed a devastating electrical blast. Blue energy flickered about the old man, who howled and fought to get free, but there was nothing he could do.

His eyes met Nicholas's.

"Find… a way, lad," he grunted.

Nicholas struggled on the ground, but his limbs wouldn't co-operate. Helplessly, he watched as Sam's eyes burned bright white and the old man heaved a final gasp before his legs gave up. He collapsed in a heap at the foot of the tree. Nicholas wanted to scream but he couldn't catch his breath. He couldn't do anything. His body wasn't his anymore and all he could feel was a spasming horror that forced his jaw shut so tightly he thought his teeth might crack.

Panting, Malika plucked the gauntlet from her hand and glided back to Jessica's slumped form. An icy chill slid down Nicholas's spine as he realised she wasn't finished. Malika crouched over the woman and Nicholas fought with everything he had left, but it was no use. His body had betrayed him. His fingers dug into the dirt, but it was as if he had already been buried and the earth was weighing him down.

Then the ground trembled beneath him and Nicholas heard a cry of triumph. Aghast, his gaze darted back to Malika, who got up silently from Jessica's prone form, her arm dripping blood as she raised a glistening fist.

It was done.

Jessica lay lifeless and pale as stone.

Horror crashing through him, Nicholas watched as Malika sniffed the organ in her hand and then tore at it with her teeth. A heart. Nicholas squeezed his eyes shut, the shock of what he was seeing causing his entire body to tremble.

Malika had won.

Everything took on a gliding quality, as if gravity had stopped working, and Nicholas felt as if the world was spinning out of control. He couldn't think or breathe. All the strength had left him, destroyed by Diltraa's internal assault, and he fought to retain consciousness, because if he passed out, the demon might seize control again the way it had when he awoke from the nightmare.

The next few moments skipped forward in a soupy delirium. Sam's body was hauled off by a Harvester.

Grunting, Nicholas dug his nails even deeper into the dirt, attempting to crawl for Merlyn, but then Merlyn was hoisted from the forest floor and borne off by another of Malika's servants.

Blackness closed in on him for a second, and when Nicholas came to again, he was still face-down in soil and ash. Malika swayed on the spot, devouring her victory whole, her face smeared crimson. Her hands were empty.

She turned to face him and her cat-like eyes were now black.

"It is done," she hissed.

Nicholas battled to stay awake, but lethargy assaulted him in waves and his eyelids were so heavy.

A white light burst into the clearing, so bright that Nicholas screwed up his face. He flinched. He imagined something prodding him, and then it seemed the earth had fallen away. He was drifting through the air.

No, he wasn't drifting. He was being carried. Nicholas opened his eyes and the light began to fade. He saw the forest and Isabel striding between the trees. The light flickered above her head.

Nicholas blearily stared up into the face of the man carrying him. "Nale…"

But he couldn't find any more words. Half delirious, he was bundled into the back of the wagon, then he felt it moving, and he collapsed into the bed that Jessica had once used, and he waited for the world to end.

# CHAPTER THIRTEEN
## ALL IS LOST

NICHOLAS WASN'T SURE HOW LONG THEY drove for. He kept seeing Malika's blood-drenched fist and hearing Sam's howl. In the dark of the wagon, he seemed to be having another nightmare, except there was no waking up from it, and going to sleep wouldn't provide an escape, either.

Zeus sat by the bed, eyebrows twitching as he rested his head on the mattress and, in a daze, Nicholas patted the dog.

"It's okay," he told him. "It's okay. It's okay."

Isabel sat in the corner, gently rocking with the motion of the wagon. She seemed lost in thought, a kind of stoic shock on her face, as if she was still trying to understand what she'd seen; what the day had turned into.

After a time, the rocking ceased, and the wagon came to a standstill. The door opened and Nale pushed his head inside.

"We're in Fratton," he said. "One on from Orville. Seems quiet."

"Yes." Isabel's voice was weightless. "You have done well, Benjamin."

The Hunter eyed her. He didn't appear to know what to say. After a second, he whistled and Zeus left Nicholas's side, hopping over to the door.

"We'll do a sweep." Nale seemed to be about to add something else, then changed his mind and stepped aside so the wolfhound could canter down the steps. The door shut, and silence settled over the wagon.

Nicholas wanted to get off the bed, run a wet cloth over his beaten face, but his body was heavier than a sack of bricks. It was an effort just to push himself upright so he could lean against the side of the wagon.

*Sam's gone.*

He remembered this feeling. He'd felt it the day Anita and Max died. A numb nothing. A raw kind of denial. Sam had been so kind that day. They'd sat in the lounge and he'd told Nicholas the news about his parents, sparing him the horrors of his imagination by telling him exactly what happened when the train crashed.

Nicholas squeezed his eyes shut and dropped his head back.

Sam was gone.

The words sounded wrong. They echoed inside his head, as if his brain thought that by repeating them, they might sound truer.

*All is lost*, the voice in his head whispered, and even though Nicholas knew it was the demon, it spoke in his voice, and he believed it.

*All is lost.*

*All is lost.*

On the other side of the wagon, Isabel got to her feet, and her sudden movement caused Nicholas to flinch. His nerves were shot. Isabel didn't seem to notice, filling the tin kettle with water and setting it on the portable stove.

Nicholas said nothing. The images he'd seen in Jessica's head kaleidoscoped before his eyes. Jessica birthing Malika. That was why Diltraa was the only one who could vanquish the red witch. The demon was her father, Jessica her mother. They were both part of her.

"I tried," he murmured, staring at his grubby hands, the cuts and grazes, thinking of Merlyn. He had no idea if he was alive, or if Malika had used the gauntlet against him, too. If Merlyn were here, he'd make everything better, but he was gone, too.

If Isabel had heard him speak, she showed no sign of it.

He had tried but he had failed. Sam and Jessica were dead and he had been too weak to stop it.

And Diltraa had prevented him from hurting Malika. Every time he'd tried, the pain had nearly knocked him unconscious. Sitting here now, Nicholas couldn't feel the demon anymore. It had sunk back into the pit of his mind, biding its time. Part of him wondered if the demon was there at all or if he was simply losing his mind, imagining the Skurk had implanted Diltraa when really it was Nicholas who wanted to taste blood and grind on sheep carcasses.

The bulbs dimmed and he drew patterns on the bedsheets. He was only vaguely aware of Isabel moving about the wagon. The kettle whistled and she clinked mugs together, then padded over to the bed.

"Here. Drink it."

He knew she wouldn't take no for an answer and as he cradled the tin mug, his mind drifted back to Aileen's garden, where Liberty had brewed something to help him sleep. The grief lingered behind his eyes. Its roots reached all the way into his chest.

Isabel perched on the bedside. She took his hand and raised the mug to his lips, tilting it gently.

"There," she breathed. "Strong tea cures all ailments. My old nanny always brewed it for twice as long when the winter nights started to outstay their welcome."

The tea warmed Nicholas's belly and he breathed in its peaty aroma, trying to will himself to stop shaking. The heaviness of the tea in his belly made him want to vomit.

"That was centuries ago," Isabel murmured. "When I first met Jessica, she was a baby. Her mother worked for me, tending to the house. When Jessica's mother died, her father was broken, lost himself in bottles, and Jessica saw to him without complaint. I knew she was special the moment I held her."

Nicholas had never pressed Isabel about her past. She was always so tight-lipped. He wondered why she was suddenly talking about those years and realised that, in her own way, Isabel was grieving.

"There was a light about her, that was unmistakable," she continued. "An innocence; she inherited her mother's strength. But evil always seeks to corrupt the innocent. That night in the Pentagon Room, the night I died… The demon sensed her power and, out of jealousy, it used it to birth the red witch. Jessica lived with that knowledge until her death. She spent five-hundred years seeking atonement, doing her best, hoping one day she could undo what happened that night."

"She fought Malika for me…" Nicholas murmured. Jessica had died so that he'd live. The thought filled him with shame. He should have saved her. Why couldn't he ever save anybody?

Isabel straightened. "We must not waste her efforts. We will defeat the red witch, one way or another..."

"It stopped me. I couldn't..."

"You will try again."

Nicholas pummelled the mattress with his fist. "You're not listening. I tried. I tried with everything I had." He wouldn't cry. "But it stopped me. The demon wouldn't let me."

"There will be a–"

"THERE WON'T."

Isabel glared at him and the crockery rattled on the shelves behind her. The lights in the room buzzed, almost blinding him.

"You must compose yourself," she said.

"Compose?! You didn't see what she did! Jessica… And Sam. And–"

"I saw well enough."

"She's dead! They both are! Don't you get it? They're gone and the only reason I'm not is because your fancy light show distracted everybody."

He was shaking uncontrollably. He'd been turned inside out so that all his nerves were exposed, and Isabel was being so cold. The old woman hadn't moved from her spot on the bed and although her eyes were bright, her expression was neutral.

"Are you finished?"

He had nothing. He sipped the tea and felt his strength slowly returning.

"They took him," he murmured.

"Your friend."

Nicholas swallowed the lump in his throat. "Both of them. Sam and Merlyn. We have to go after him. Merlyn's alive. I know it."

"We must consider our next move carefully." Isabel sipped her own tea. "Malika's stronger with Jessica gone. That much we can be certain of. She has tipped the balance. She is nursing the Prophets and she'll be seeking to consolidate her power."

"How can you talk about this so calmly?" Nicholas asked, heat bubbling through him.

"Would you prefer I scream and destroy the furniture?"

"I don't know."

He stared into the bottom of his mug. It was as empty as he felt. Was Merlyn at Hallow House? Or had Malika taken him somewhere else? He tried to sense him and when he couldn't, the weight of hopelessness became almost too much to bear.

"She already took Hallow House," he said. "What else is there for Malika to do?"

"That is what we must discover."

Nicholas attempted to think about anything other than Merlyn and Sam. The way Sam's eyes had burned white. His scream. His final breath. Merlyn's slumped form being carried off by a Harvester. The thought nearly brought the tea back up and Nicholas coughed, instead thinking about Malika. She wouldn't stop at taking Hallow House; her ambitions were greater than even that. The Prophets wouldn't settle for dominion over one small part of the country – they wanted the world.

"She's going to leave the house," he said. "If she wants to ensure she becomes the big boss of everything evil, she'll go from town to town, the way she did in Cambridge and Bury, turning everything and everyone as she goes."

"I'm afraid you may be right."

He placed the mug on the table by the bed and spotted something on the floor. Holding his breath, he picked it up, turning Sam's battered fedora over in his hands. Isabel or Nale must have found it in the clearing and salvaged it. Nicholas had never seen Sam without it.

He caught Isabel looking at the object and then their eyes met. There was nothing to say. She had liked him, too, and now he was gone. The best thing they could do for him was continue to fight.

*"Find a way lad."*

Sam's final words replayed in Nicholas's head and he chewed the inside of his cheek.

He placed the hat at the foot of the bed just as a knock came at the door. He and Isabel stared at it, not moving. Nicholas was too exhausted to push his mind outside and check who it was, so he went silently over and listened.

"Who is it?" he asked.

"Nicholas?" A woman's voice. "Nicholas Hallow?"

Frowning, he pushed the door open and found the faces of a girl and an elderly woman peering up at him. They were both dark-skinned and seemed oddly familiar, but Nicholas wasn't sure why.

"Ben Nale sent us," the woman said. She had salt-and-pepper curls and bulky jewellery about her neck and wrists. "I'm Gloria and this is my granddaughter, Francesca. We're with the others in the caravan. Might we come in?"

Nicholas had grown accustomed to being suspicious about strangers, but they didn't seem like Harvesters and nothing blipped on his radar. He nodded and moved back so the girl could clomp up the steps in her blue wellington boots. Her grandmother followed, taking them without any complaint.

"Wow." The girl's eyes shone at the interior of the wagon. Wearing a duffel coat, she couldn't be any older than six, but there was steel in her elfin features.

"Nale's a bit of a pack rat," Nicholas said. He gazed at the woman. "Sorry, but… I feel like we've met before."

Gloria smiled. "I feel the same way but mostly because Liberty never stopped talking about you."

Nicholas's heart thudded in his chest. "Liberty?"

"My daughter." Gloria rested a hand on the girl's shoulder. "And Francesca's mother."

Nicholas nearly kicked himself. The resemblance was uncanny, and he stared at the pair with fascination. It was so obvious they were Liberty's family; they possessed the same long limbs, high foreheads and inquisitive eyes.

"She talked about you, too," he said. "And her brothers."

Gloria's brow furrowed. "They're in the north somewhere. When Cambridge fell, they were sent to Liverpool, then Manchester. They could be anywhere now. We've not heard from them in a while."

Nicholas nodded. The Dark Prophets were tearing apart families all over the country. Francesca had lost her mother and she was only a kid. No wonder so many Sentinels had such tough exteriors. Their losses were unimaginable.

Isabel rose from the bed and crossed to the centre of the wagon. Gloria bowed her head.

"Miss Hallow, it's an honour."

"Miss Rayne."

"She's in my head, nan," Francesca said, tugging at her grandmother's sleeve.

Isabel smiled. "My, you've got something about you, little one. You're Sensitive, like your mother. Strong with it, too."

"I don't like people in my head," the girl said.

"We have that in common. Far too many secrets, I'm sure. Does your grandmother know about the books you read when she's fallen asleep by the fire?"

Francesca sheepishly pushed out her bottom lip.

Isabel winked. "The curious ones always grow to be the clever ones."

The girl eyed her and then wandered off to examine the puppets dangling by the window.

"Liberty was always so good with Francesca," Gloria said.

"Nan, I'm called Fran now."

"Yes, dear." Gloria's curls bounced as she shook her head. "I'm not blessed with the Sight. I'm afraid I don't really understand it the way I wish I could. She's difficult to keep track of sometimes."

"I'm sure you're doing the best you can," Isabel said, her kind tone surprising Nicholas. There was something about the Rayne family that was so endearing – even to crotchety five-hundred-year-old women like Isabel. The family were so warm and calm.

Nicholas went to the kettle. "Did you want some tea?"

"That would be very kind of you."

"Come, let us sit," Isabel said, going to the table. Gloria followed and the two women watched Francesca as she strained on her tip-toes to dab the puppets' legs. Nicholas wondered what it had been like for her, knowing about her abilities from birth and having a mother who nurtured them. Would Francesca grow to be a powerful Sensitive, perhaps more powerful than Liberty? Would she get herself into the same messes he had?

"You hail from Cambridge?" Isabel asked Gloria.

"Yes. The Raynes have lived in Cambridge for generations. Just after it fell, we were evacuated and brought to the camp at Hallow House. We were only just settling in when the house fell. Last time I saw anything like it was during the Blitz. Reminds me of those times like you wouldn't imagine. The bombed-out buildings, the refugees. Never thought I'd live to see it happen again, and definitely not here."

"This is the war to end all wars," Isabel said.

"I just worry about Francesca's future." Gloria's gaze went to the window. "If the Prophets come to power, what sort of a world would that be?"

"It won't come to that."

As the women talked, Nicholas made the tea and then set two chipped mugs in front of them. Gloria's smile was radiant, and her bracelets jangled as she took his hand, squeezing it tightly.

"Nicholas, she was so fond of you, my daughter. Even though you only met briefly. I think you reminded her of her when she was young. You have the same look about you. Oh, don't be offended. It's in the blood, that curiosity. It's innate. Can't be learnt. She had that look, too."

Though her touch made him uncomfortable, Nicholas smiled. "She helped me. I liked her. She was… she was really brave. And funny."

"Ha." Gloria's expression wavered between amused and sad. "Yes, she had a way with words, too. Drove her father up the wall." She sipped her tea and peered over at her granddaughter. "Francesc– I mean, Fran, come here a moment, there's a lamb."

Francesca strolled slowly over. "Nan, Uncle Sam was here. Will he be back soon?"

A lead weight dropped in Nicholas's stomach. Gloria and her granddaughter had distracted him from the memory of what had happened in the forest. He swallowed and fought the tide of gloom threatening to drag him under.

Gloria caught Nicholas's eye. "I don't think so, dear."

"I want his story. The one with the earthquake."

"I know that one," Nicholas said. "I can tell it to you."

"That's okay, I'll wait for Uncle Sam."

Gloria swept the girl's braids to one side affectionately. "Ben thought we might be of use," she said. Although she wasn't Sensitive, she could read the room as well as her daughter; she could tell talking about Sam was painful. "Well, not me, I'm only good for knitting and napping these days. But Fran…"

"She has quite a talent," Isabel observed. As the girl pouted, she added, "Don't worry, young lady, I won't poke about in your head again. Tell me, has she performed any rituals before?"

"Just simple things," Gloria said. "Nothing… dangerous."

"Mum always got me to find her keys," Francesca added.

Nicholas couldn't believe what he was hearing. Isabel seemed to be suggesting that, somehow, Francesca could help them fight Malika. She was Sensitive, but he knew what it was like when you opened your mind up to the universe. All sorts of things poured in.

"She can't…" he began. "I mean, you can't expect her to help us against Malika. She's five years old!"

"I'm six and a quarter!" Francesca declared, practically stomping her foot.

"She won't see anything," Isabel said. "If we are to discover Malika's next move, we're going to have to look for her, but she's more powerful than ever. You won't be able to part the smoke-screen alone. We need a little extra… what is it you say? Juice?"

"We can't," Nicholas argued. "What if something happens? She's just a kid."

"I'm not scared," Francesca said.

She resembled a tiny version of Liberty. Spirited and determined. But she wasn't her mother; Liberty was dead, and Nicholas wouldn't let Isabel put her child in harm's way.

"Let me try first," he reasoned. "That's what you wanted. You told me we'd try–"

"There's nothing to argue about," Isabel said. "The girl will be quite safe."

"Nicholas." Gloria took his hand again. "Please, if Francesca–"

"Fran!"

"If she can help, let her. I trust Miss Hallow, and Liberty trusted you."

Nicholas's gaze drifted between the three of them, finally settling on Isabel's rigid glare, and his defiance dimmed. She'd never led him astray before. Everything she'd ever done had been for the greater good; she wanted to stop Malika and the Dark Prophets as much as he did. Selfishly, he realised that this could help them find Merlyn, too.

"Fine," he said. "As long as she doesn't get hurt. Let's just get it over with quickly."

For the next five minutes, Isabel ordered him about retrieving candles, aromatic herbs and a rudimentary bowl from the cupboards. He dragged the table into the centre of the floor, setting down the objects and, together, the four of them crowded around the table.

Isabel lit the candles and dripped wax into the bowl, murmuring under her breath. Nicholas watched with interest. He'd never seen her in action before, at least not in human form, and his fingers and toes tingled with anticipation. He just hoped she knew what she was so doing. He concentrated on keeping Diltraa buried; the demon was a ticking bomb but, for now, it seemed to have retreated. Perhaps its energies were spent. Or perhaps being near Malika was what had drawn it out in the forest.

"Hold hands," Isabel instructed, and Nicholas took hold of hers in one and Francesca's in the other. The girl's expression was solemn, the candlelight winking in her dark eyes, and Nicholas resolved to do everything he could to protect her. The thought of Malika discovering them made his throat close.

"We call thee, spirits of the whispered planes," Isabel said, her eyes closed. "Guide us, peel back the cloak of darkness, reveal her to us."

"Malika," Nicholas said.

"Don't interrupt."

"I just thought we should be more specific."

"Just let me—"

Isabel's voice faded as Nicholas's consciousness drifted suddenly. He couldn't feel his body anymore. In panic, he blinked, seeing the wagon as if he was floating above the table. But this was different to when Diltraa had paralysed him. He felt calm and, below, he saw himself sitting hand-in-hand with Isabel and Francesca. Isabel's incantation was working.

He felt invisible hands at his shoulders. They drew him higher and he floated further, melting up through the wagon's roof and into the night air. Charred fields rushed by beneath him and the forest was no longer aflame. He felt the wind in his hair, although he half wondered if he was imagining it.

Nicholas was drawn over rooftops and then he saw Orville. The village huddled below him, filled with Harvesters, but he soared overhead without anybody seeing him. He came to a train station and rushed down to the track, flying above it as if he were on wheels, following the track out into the countryside.

He raced along the train track, faster and faster, until he felt like he was about to lose control and crash into the buildings on either side. Villages and towns zipped past and he sped faster still, and as he craned to look up, he glimpsed skyscrapers on the horizon.

It was the London skyline.

Nicholas gasped, and he was back in the wagon. His hands shook as he released Isabel and Francesca, marvelling at the fact that his body had been here the whole time. Even so, his stomach felt like it had been left three loop-the-loops behind on a rollercoaster. He fought to keep his tea down.

"My tummy feels funny," Francesca said as Gloria squeezed her hand.

"You're braver than Dorothy, darling," the old lady said, adding to Nicholas, "Oh, we've been reading *The Wonderful Wizard of Oz*."

Nicholas found Isabel staring at him. "Well?" she asked.

"They're leaving. Catching a train." He almost laughed at how ridiculous it sounded. Malika's army was going for a merry day out on the railway. "Her and the Prophets and her army. They're abandoning the house. But why would they do that? They fought so hard to get it."

"What is the train's destination?"

"London."

"Of course." Isabel made an expression like she'd sucked half a lemon. "If one wishes to conquer a kingdom, one must first conquer its capital. We were fools to think Hallow House would be the seat of Malika's power; that was merely a tactical move, a frivolous demonstration of her power. It is London she wants to make her own."

"We saw videos," said Nicholas, thinking about the news clips Dawn had found online. "London's already infested."

"Then Malika's work is already half done."

"We have to stop her leaving," he said. "Or at least stop her using the railway, slow her down."

Isabel's forehead crinkled at him and he could tell what she was thinking. The Sentinel numbers were dwindling by the day. They couldn't possibly take on Malika's army in their present state.

"We won't have to fight," he said. "We'll sneak into Orville's station and blow up the trains."

"And how do you suggest we do that?"

Nicholas peered around the wagon. "Pretty sure Nale will have some sticks of dynamite lying around here. And if not, one of his Hunter buddies will."

"You would risk killing everybody on board?"

"I suppose," he said, but he knew he couldn't do that; not if there was a chance he could save Merlyn. If he was alive and on that train… "Okay, so we sneak onto the train, find Merl and anybody else they've got locked up and get them to safety before the fireworks."

Isabel didn't appear convinced. "We could be caught or killed ourselves."

"You were never a gambler, were you?"

Francesca yawned loudly, and her grandmother got up from the table.

"It's time we got you to bed, little lamb."

"No, I want to blow up the train," Francesca complained sleepily, but she didn't resist as Gloria clasped her hand and helped her to her feet.

"She gets worn out when she's done something big," Gloria explained. "And we've not exactly been getting many full nights' sleep of late."

Isabel rose. "You have been invaluable; both of you. May the Trinity look kindly on you."

"It feels good to be useful at my age," Gloria said.

"I couldn't agree more."

Gloria cupped Nicholas's cheek and her hand was soft. "You should get some sleep, too. I could always tell when Liberty had been burning the candle at both ends. You need rest to recharge, like a battery."

"I'll try, thanks."

Gloria led Francesca to the door. The little girl stopped and then ran back to Nicholas, throwing her arms around him.

"Mummy liked you a lot," she whispered in his ear. Then she went back to her grandmother and they left the wagon.

Nicholas blinked, struggling to control the squall of emotions in his chest. He felt exhausted with loss. He wasn't sure how much he had left to give. Each death took a bite out of him and he felt chewed up, half pulped, rattling toward an inevitable ending.

"Use it."

He looked at Isabel, who was half in shadow by the door, her eyes twinkling. He had a feeling she knew what he was thinking.

"Every loss, every bruise, every rotten, stinking second of self-doubt. Use it."

"I don't know how."

"When I lived in Hallow House, I met a young woman whose life had been marked by tragedy since childhood. Nevertheless, she strove and fought and pushed her head above the roiling waves to fill her lungs with life's sweet air. Like you, she wanted more. Like you, she saw the good, and she wanted to nurture it, ensure its survival. And she succeeded because she found you."

Nicholas nodded, knowing Isabel was talking about Jessica.

*"You are my hope,"* she had said.

"Come, it is time we laid her to rest."

In a sweep of her purple kaftan, Isabel left the table and went to the door. Nicholas followed her, then paused and ran back to retrieve his backpack. He couldn't leave the collars unattended, even here. His mind still wasn't made up about Nale and he wasn't ready to test the Hunter's loyalty, even if he had rescued him from the forest.

Outside Nicholas listened to the quiet. In Cambridge, quiet meant things were watching you, but Fratton didn't seem to have fallen yet. The wagon was parked in a junkyard and, a little further off, Nicholas saw the caravan and minibus that made up the rest of their sorry troop. They could be part of the yard's collection. Any Harvester who stumbled across them wouldn't give them a second thought.

"There." Isabel sighed as she approached the back of the junkyard. Behind the empty shell of a car, they found somebody had dug a grave, which was edged with pale flowers. Beside the grave rested a body covered in a sheet.

A twang of shock went through Nicholas.

"She's just been out here like this…?" he murmured.

"She is gone," Isabel said simply.

*Yes*, Nicholas thought, sensing the body. It didn't feel cold or empty the way he had expected. It felt calm. Quiet. Ready.

But who had dug the grave? He sensed an echo of Nale and knew the Hunter had done this. Nicholas didn't know how he felt about that. He stood at Isabel's side, his thoughts filled with everything he had known about Jessica, feeling the space where she had once been, and knowing the world would never be the same without her.

"From the ground, we came," said Isabel. "And to the ground, we return." She gazed at Nicholas. "Help her."

He nodded and bent down to push his arms under Jessica's body, then he lifted her gently into the grave. She felt so light. He wondered if all worries evaporated with the end of life. Solemnly, he drew back and returned to his place beside Isabel.

"Jessica Bell. Kind souls are remembered kindly. We will remember you."

Isabel tapped her staff to the earth and the ground vibrated gently as the grave slowly filled itself in. Nicholas watched as it swallowed Jessica's body and he couldn't help thinking about Sam and Anita and Max. He clenched his teeth and heard Sam in his ear.

*"Find a way lad."*

When the ceremony was over, he and Isabel stood together, not speaking, lost in their own thoughts. Nicholas was just contemplating returning to the wagon when he stopped and listened, sensing somebody was near.

He heard the crunch of footsteps on gravel. He hugged the side of the hollow car and peered around it. Across the junkyard, the unmistakable shape of Benjamin Nale strode from the gate, and he wasn't alone. Squinting, Nicholas made out two figures, young women, and for a moment his suspicions returned. Had Nale returned with Harvesters?

Then the figures stepped into the light of an overhead lamp and Nicholas almost released a cry. He stepped from the cover of the car and, seeing him, one of the women broke away, hurrying for him. Her purple hair tangled with the wind.

"Guess who's back," said Dawn.

She grinned and hugged him and Nicholas crumbled.

# CHAPTER FOURTEEN
## GRIMMS & OTHER EVILS

IT SOUNDED LIKE DAWN AND RAE had been through the wars. Back in the dark-wood comfort of the wagon, Nicholas listened as Dawn revealed what had happened since she and Rae left Cambridge. Her descriptions of the countryside sounded like Hell itself. They'd found and lost her mother, battled all sorts of nightmares, then holed up here in Fratton, waiting.

"We couldn't make it to Orville," Dawn said. "We saw smoke and heard things in the forest."

Sitting at the table, Isabel by his side, Nicholas eyed Rae. Zeus had flopped by her side at the door and she seemed even more withdrawn than ever, staring back out into the junkyard. He wondered how she'd coped with Dawn. They had never spent time alone together before and he couldn't imagine how they'd handled each other.

"But…" He almost couldn't bring himself to ask. "What about your mum?"

Dawn's gaze dimmed and she contemplated the table before them. "She didn't make it."

"So it was all for nothing?"

"Nice," Rae said.

Nicholas glared at her. "Don't start."

"Rae, he doesn't mean it like that. And no, I don't think it was for nothing. Here…" Dawn grabbed her rucksack and rooted around in it, eventually taking out a book. Or, *half* a book. It looked like Zeus had used it as a chew toy.

"She gave me this. Mum. It's a first edition, which is why it's, well…"

She placed the half-book in Nicholas's hands. The title had been worn off the maroon cover and he gingerly turned it over in his hands. The pages were so ancient they threatened to disintegrate any moment.

"What is it?" he asked.

"A demonology. *Grimms & Other Evils* by Atticus Klove."

Isabel snorted. "There's a name not often spoken in civilised circles."

Nicholas stared at her in surprise. "You've heard of him?"

"Heard…? My dear, I *knew* the over-inflated baboon. He published that infernal tome during my first lifetime."

No wonder it looked so old.

"You sound like a fan," Nicholas said.

Isabel's eyebrows nearly reached her hairline. "Of that insufferable oaf? I have never met anybody so self-obsessed. He spent a decade scribbling that atrocity, curating every nasty hellbeast he encountered, and another defending its authenticity when it was published."

"He was a Sentinel," Dawn said.

"Not after he unleashed *that* upon the world. Esus exiled the swine. Not that Klove cared. By then he'd made his fortune and toured as if he was Nostradamus himself, spouting half-truths and nonsense like gospel."

Dawn fiddled with her bracelet and her eyes seemed double their normal size as she stared at Nicholas. "There's something in there that might help with… well, all of this."

"Pish!" Isabel sneered at the book. "It seems Klove's insidious power has dwindled little. I thought you had something about you, girl; I didn't take you for one to be so easily fooled."

Dawn stopped fiddling, glaring at Isabel. "Even if most of it's rubbish, there's something in there that could be exactly what we've been looking for."

"If that is so, I shall fly a broomstick around this wagon in my undergarments," Isabel said.

Brushing her purple hair behind her ears, Dawn took the book from Nicholas and flipped through it, stopping on a certain page and laying it on the table for them to see. Isabel ignored it, but Nicholas leaned forward.

"Impet—" he began. "Impetu-what?"

"*Impetuverta*," Dawn said.

"Completely unsubstantiated," Isabel scoffed.

"Except it isn't." Dawn returned the woman's scowl and Nicholas almost smiled. Where was the shy girl he'd met just a few months ago?

"You better explain," he said.

Dawn tapped the page, which bore a strange diagram that sort of resembled a man, and faint words Nicholas could barely read, let alone pronounce. "Remember the gauntlets? The ones Malika created? They kill Sentinels by opening a portal inside them and letting a demon in. That's *impetuverta* in action. It's a spell, or an enchantment. *Impetuverta* means 'energy transfer' and it's all about swapping one thing for another, like taking a shoe out of a box and replacing it with, I don't know, a bomb. Except the box is a person and the shoe is their soul."

Isabel pursed her lips. All eyes were on Dawn, including Rae's, and Nicholas tried to figure out how the incantation could work for them, why it might help them, as Dawn had claimed. This stuff always scrambled his brains.

"What are you saying?" he asked.

"You're going to raise the Trinity," Dawn said, "*inside* the Prophets." They all stared at her.

"Preposterous!" Isabel said. "Your head's in the clouds, girl."

"Listen." Dawn pointed at a diagram of a man on the page. "*Impetuverta* needs a host and if Nicholas and Rae are going to raise the Trinity, they'll need something to raise them *in*. We can use the incantation to kill two birds with one stone. Raise the Trinity *and* destroy the Prophets."

Her words rang through the wagon and then silence fell over the small gathering. Nicholas didn't know what to think. It was a radical idea and all he had to do was look at Isabel's sour expression to know what she made of it. Rae's face was less decipherable, and Nicholas purposefully avoided Nale's outline in the corner.

If Dawn believed the incantation could work, though, it had to be worth a shot.

"You're saying that if we raise the Trinity inside the Prophets..." he began.

"The Prophets are toast," Dawn said.

"I like the sound of that."

Isabel stood, leaning onto her staff. "I have heard quite enough. Girl, these are desperate times and I commend your desire to do right, but this won't stand. We will find another way – one that has a chance of succeeding."

"Except there isn't another way." Nicholas stood, too. "There isn't. I've looked everywhere."

Isabel faltered momentarily, shooting him and the half-book a wary glance, as if it might belch or belly flop off the table. For a second, Nicholas suspected she might be swayed, but then her usual stony demeanour returned, and her eyes shone at Dawn. "Child, who gave you that tome?"

"I already said, it was–"

"Your mother, yes." Isabel's voice was feather light, her eyebrows pinched together in a way that suggested both sadness and benevolence. Dawn suddenly seemed to grasp what the woman was implying. Her cheeks flooded hotly.

"No. Mum was an expert on this stuff. She studied rituals for years. I know she wasn't–"

"She was incarcerated," Isabel cut in softly. "I know you want to help but this isn't the way. Atticus Klove was a hack. Nothing he wrote held any water and he eventually drowned in the slime of his own creating. Namely that monstrous novel."

Dawn's forehead crinkled in surprise and, for a second, she appeared confused, but then her gaze hardened.

"This is it, I know it."

Isabel waved a hand, stepping away from the table. "You can't know that."

"Listen!" Dawn's voice was tight. "There's no other way."

Isabel slammed the floorboards with her staff and Nicholas could see she was trying to control her temper. He had to do something. Find a way to make them both happy. But Dawn wasn't backing down. She must really believe the incantation had a chance of working.

"You don't know what you're saying." Isabel's voice was little more than a whisper. "You've lost somebody, so I'll excuse this impertinence, but Jessica is dead, Esus is battling to retain ground, *I* am the Vaktarin, at least for the time being. My word is final." Her glare was unwavering. "Take some time to gather your wits. I will not be so kind again."

"Kind? We're talking about the end of the world!" Dawn appeared ready to erupt.

"We are talking about *gods*," Isabel snapped. "When was the last time you were in the presence of a god?"

Nicholas had never seen Dawn look so angry. He gritted his teeth. The room was shaking. No, it wasn't the room. It was him. The contents of his skull quivered like jelly in a bowl. He could feel everything. Isabel's temper, Dawn's irritation. Both red and pulsing. The claws latching onto his eye sockets. Diltraa wanted this. The demon was watching, soaking up the threat of violence.

"She gave this to me, she *knew*," Dawn insisted.

"She was not well."

"No–"

The air seemed to have gone out of the room. Nicholas felt sick as the demon moved around inside him, begging to be let loose.

"Stop, both of you." Rae had moved to Nicholas's side and she sounded worried.

Isabel and Dawn looked at him.

"Nick, are you okay?" Dawn asked.

"It's just… the fighting."

Isabel clasped her staff tightly. "Enough. We will commune with the others, see what other ideas are out there."

Wearily, Nicholas peered at her. "I've looked–" he began, and then he stopped. As the demon's grip slackened, Nicholas's head cleared and he spotted his backpack on the floor. How could he have forgotten? He grabbed it.

"Dawn's right," he said, certainty flooding through him as he drew the sack from his bag, his fingers tingling as they brushed what lay within. "And I'll show you why."

He set the sack on the table top. He snuck a wary glance at Nale, but the Hunter seemed to be caught up in his own thoughts, so Nicholas drew out the three collars, resting them on top of the sacking.

The interior of the wagon glowed with their silver light and the arguing ceased in an instant. The collars seemed to be lit from within, and Nicholas peered around the room at the faces they illuminated. Everybody could tell they were hallowed objects, even without the ability to hear the way the collars murmured and pulsed with divine energy.

"Where did you get these?" whispered Isabel, her hand hovering near the table, as if she wanted to touch the collars but didn't quite trust herself.

"From a well in Orville. They belonged to the Trinity. Jessica hid them years ago. I… I'm pretty sure they're the missing piece. Or pieces. They're what we need to raise the Trinity." He flicked a look at Dawn. "And Dawn's incantation is what we'll use to do it."

Nicholas snuck a glance at Nale. The Hunter had shrunk back into the corner of the room and he was brooding silently on what was happening. Isabel attempted to make a sound, but her voice failed her. The light of the collars glimmered in her jewellery and twinkled in her eyes.

"I sense them," she whispered hoarsely, her hand caressing the air above the collars. "The power. The strength. They are near. These trinkets... They are indeed hallowed."

"So we find a way to put the collars on the Prophets after they hatch," Nicholas said. "They'll act as a conduit for the incantation, right? And the Trinity will return inside the Prophets, killing them in the process."

He half-smiled at Dawn, knowing how much it meant to her that her mother was right. Isabel's hand trembled closer to the collars. It glowed with silvery light.

"Yes," she murmured. "Yes. That is what we shall do. The power in these collars may be enough if the incantation fails us."

"Is she here?" A fraught voice pushed in through the wagon door. "Where is she? Where is she?!"

A round shape waddled up into the wagon. Aileen spotted Rae and then Dawn. The former landlady clutched her breast and stumbled towards her granddaughter, crushing her into a hug.

"I never thought I'd see you again!"

"Hi Nan." Dawn squeezed her back.

"You're so brave. Let me look at you, let me… Oh, you're positively wasting away. When's the last time you ate?"

"It's been a while."

"You, too, dear?" Aileen said to Rae. "You all need a good meal in you."

Dawn took the older woman's hands. "Nan, I… Mum, she…"

Aileen's gaze softened and she pulled her granddaughter into another hug. "No, she's not with you… It'll be okay. We'll get by. We'll get by. You're such a brave girl."

When her grandmother released her, Dawn peered over at Nicholas. "Where are the others? Sam? Merlyn?"

He shuddered. The mention of their names was like a blade between his ribs and the grief punctured him as if for the first time.

"My turn to talk," he said.

★

So now everybody was on the same page. While Nale and Zeus patrolled again, Nicholas told Dawn and Rae about what had happened to Hallow House. He couldn't believe what he was saying. It had only happened hours ago, but it had already taken on the dream-like quality of all painful memories.

He missed out the fact that he'd absorbed Diltraa's energy, and when he reached the part where Sam was killed and Merlyn was taken, Dawn paled and began picking her nails. Rae stared at the floor, her dark eyes troubled. He wondered if she could sense his trauma. The connection between them might go both ways, but the only sign she'd showed that she knew how he felt was a few minutes ago here in the wagon.

Seated beside Dawn, Aileen sniffed into a tissue and Nicholas knew she was taking Sam's death as hard as anybody. She had Pyraemon in a stranglehold, and the cat looked like it was considering shredding her arm to escape, but maybe it knew it had found a sweet deal with the landlady.

"He died fighting," Aileen said. "Always knew he would."

Dawn put her arm around her and Aileen shook with sobs for a minute, and then let out a deep sigh.

"Food," she said, getting up suddenly and going to the kitchenette at the back of the wagon. Pyraemon shot back to his corner, his fur blending in with the darkness. "Food'll help. An army marches on its you-know-what…"

Nicholas watched her contend with the bread bin for a moment, then he turned back to Dawn and Rae.

"Malika's leaving," he said.

"Leaving? What do you mean?" Dawn asked.

"She's heading for London. They're commandeering a train, her and her army. Pretty sure they're leaving tonight."

He took bread from a plate Aileen was passing around. He wasn't hungry but chewing it made him feel more normal.

"There's a train station round here?" Dawn teased her bread into pieces. On the other side of the wagon, Isabel was resting in an armchair, though Nicholas couldn't tell if she was asleep – even in repose, her back was ramrod straight.

"A train depot, actually," he said. "We're at the end of the line out here. Malika has her pick."

"So what's the plan?"

"Blowing it up would be easier now Rae's here, but… they've got Merl." He couldn't entertain the thought that Merlyn might have already been turned, so he carried on thinking out loud. "And who knows if blowing up the train would do anything to stop the Prophets anyway? The impetu-thing still seems like our best chance. At least this way we've got half a shot." He followed Dawn's gaze to Isabel. "She didn't mean what she said. Or, she did, but she never was good at being polite."

"I liked her better when she was a cat," Dawn said.

Nicholas grinned. "Try petting her. She'll love it."

"Tempting." Her expression softened. "Nick… I'm sorry about Sam."

"Thanks. Me, too. Your mum… That must've been tough."

Rae got up suddenly and went outside.

"What's with that one?" Nicholas asked.

Dawn shrugged, crumbling her bread onto her plate. The apocalypse seemed to be killing everybody's appetite.

"Go easy on her," she said. "She's complicated."

"You don't have to tell me that."

"No, really. You think some Sentinels had it bad growing up? Rae had nothing. No family. Nobody who understood. And there's stuff she's done that she regrets."

"She said that?"

"She doesn't have to."

Nicholas peered at the door, remembering what he'd seen when he first connected with Rae. He'd glimpsed those hollow years when she lived on the streets, and he'd felt the hopelessness like it was a parasite in her chest. He considered going to talk to her, but then he remembered what Sam had said in the forest on the way to Orville earlier that day, and he knew Rae would have to wait.

"Sam said something about names," he said. "How they can have power. Do you think that's true?"

Dawn blinked as if in surprise. "Well, in lots of mythologies there's such a thing as a 'true name'. Deities and powerful beings often had secret names that they only trusted their most loyal advisers with. That's how Isis got her son Horus on the throne. She tricked Ra into revealing his true name, which gave her power over him."

"But... they're just stories, right? They don't apply to the real world?"

"You mean the Trinity?" Dawn's eye twitched the way it did when her mind was cycling through information and she was trying to order it all into something coherent. "You know, nobody's ever uncovered the names of the Dark Prophets. But that might just be because we can't pronounce them."

"But if we could learn them, it might give us some power over them?"

"Theoretically, yes. But *actually*, I have no idea. I still think the best shot is the impetuverta ritual." She considered Atticus Klove's book, drawing it closer so they could both see the page.

"So how does it work?" Nicholas asked. "The impetu-thing."

"It's all about energy. Summoning rituals always are, but this is doubly difficult because you're creating a portal inside a living creature. And you're not doing it just once, you're doing it with three separate entities. It's basically the Big Mac of incantations."

"Gee, great."

"You were born for this, literally. Just remember that."

He didn't fully believe it but just hearing Dawn say it made him feel better. He missed Merlyn telling him things like that. Attempting to focus, he peered closer at the half-book. They went over the incantation together and Nicholas attempted to memorise it.

*Vita gregaria hemlock ressa vie.*

Why were these things always so difficult? As he repeated the words over in his mind, Nicholas thought of the collars in his backpack. They had been buried for centuries and their power had dimmed but he could still feel them. Every second since he had taken them from the well, he sensed their presence like a constant source of warmth. They were practically urging him to return the Trinity. A thought struck him.

"Would it work without the Prophets?" he asked. "The collars, I mean."

"You know anybody willing to die?" asked Dawn. "Cos that's what the incantation will do to them. Anybody who puts those collars on will die so that the Trinity can take over their body."

Nicholas thought of the remaining Sentinels in their little junkyard commune. Isabel and Aileen would do anything to set the world to rights, but would they die for it? He didn't think Rae would, and he couldn't even think about Gloria or Francesca dying. Of them all, Nale had the most to prove, and he was the reason the Trinity were dead, but Nicholas doubted he'd sacrifice himself to set the world to rights.

"Right," he breathed. "Prophets it is."

*Soon*, he thought at the collars, sensing their impatience.

At that moment, Zeus came bounding inside, followed by Nale. Nicholas stood quickly, partly because he wanted to be on his feet if Nale tried anything, and partly because he wanted to know what they'd seen during their patrol of the area.

"Anything?"

Nale shook his head.

"Good. We might actually make it to the train depot in one piece."

Dawn slapped his arm. "Don't say that. Tempting fate."

"No such thing."

"You're living proof there is."

"Oh, yeah." He sighed. "I suppose we should make a move, then.

Dawn, you stay here with your nan. Me, Nale, Isabel, and Rae can handle this on our own."

Dawn shook her head. "If Malika's army's there, you'll need everybody you can get. We should all go."

"Stay here," Nicholas said firmly. He couldn't lose another friend to Malika. An image of the red witch plucking out Jessica's heart sent a hot wave of anxiety coursing through his chest.

"The girl is right."

Isabel stared at them from her seat. "If she wishes to fight, that is what she must do."

They had been here before, Nicholas realised. Back in Bury when Dawn had insisted on confronting Laurent with him. He couldn't tell her what to do any more than he could change the weather. Besides, she'd survived the wilderness without him.

"Fine," he said. "Aileen, are you coming too?"

The landlady nodded as she put her arm around Dawn's shoulders. "I'm not letting this one out of my sight again."

"Nale?"

The Hunter merely nodded.

"That's settled, then. Nale, go get the others, tell them the plan. We leave in ten minutes."

They spent the next few minutes gathering their things. Nicholas pulled on his armour and grabbed Sam's battered fedora from the bed. He grazed his fingers along the rim, and then put the hat on. It fit surprisingly well. He raided a trunk in the corner for weapons and felt the weight of a small axe. It wasn't as good as his old one but it would do. His hand ached for the Drujblade. He'd come so close. Next time he wouldn't fail. He tucked a dagger into his boot and reached into his backpack to check the collars, his fingers grazing something wooden.

He drew out a carving of a fox.

Merlyn's.

He must have stowed it in Nicholas's bag without telling him. Maybe Merlyn thought he could use the luck. Sorrow bubbled up from Nicholas's belly and he stroked the carving, gritting his teeth. He wouldn't stop until Merlyn was safe and Malika was dead.

"I'm coming," he told the carving. "Get ready."

Tucking away the fox in his bag, he went to the wagon's door and stuck his head out, seeing that the sky above the junkyard was still an inky grey that looked solid as a wall. He descended the steps to the ground, where the remaining Sentinels had assembled around the wagon. Their murmuring ceased when Isabel emerged. She stood on the steps surveying the troops and Nicholas counted twenty of them. Further back, Gloria and Fran stood by the minibus. Gloria had her arm around her granddaughter, who seemed desperate to run over and join them.

"Who's staying back with them?" he asked Aileen.

"Blake. She's one of the best." He noticed that Aileen had the cat stuffed into a satchel at her back. Pyraemon's head stuck out like a soft, very grisly toy's.

"They should get out of here. Head to safety."

At his side, Dawn leaned in. "If Malika's leaving, they should be safer here than on the road."

Nicholas eyed Liberty's family. "I hope so."

On the steps, Isabel cleared her throat and scrutinised the Sentinels. "The train station lies on the far side of Orville. We shall rely on the Sensitives among you to give us fair warning of anything in the vicinity. There is a chance you'll encounter the red witch... or the Prophets. If that happens, you have the Trinity's blessing."

If they were scared, the Sentinels didn't show it. Isabel explained that they would be attempting to rescue any Sentinel prisoners and prevent Malika's train from leaving. "Fight to kill. And keep the Trinity in your thoughts."

Nicholas couldn't help thinking the Trinity wouldn't be any help. They were dead, their spirits bound to whichever dimension gods passed into when they perished. The only help the Trinity would be was if he and Rae could bring them back.

"Go," Isabel said. "Be watchful, be safe."

The Sentinels turned and followed Nale across the junkyard. Isabel used her staff to clomp down the steps and joined Nicholas and the others.

They had to walk past Gloria and Fran to leave the yard, but Nicholas couldn't say goodbye to anybody else, so he simply nodded to them. Gloria dipped her head in response and Fran had a hand tangled up in her braids.

Nale led the party out into the countryside. Nicholas kept his eyes on the sky, hoping that Malika hadn't sent out any scouts. There were no shapes among the clouds, though, and the countryside was so dark it was like slipping between folds of velvet. They filed into the forest and walked along its fringes, just out of sight of the road but close enough that they could break for it if necessary. Nicholas had no idea how the fire had burned itself out, but he imagined the oppressive atmosphere had helped.

Ahead, Dawn and Aileen ambled hand in hand, and Isabel made her way to the front to lead with Nale. *Good,* Nicholas thought. If anybody could subdue the Hunter if he got out of hand, it was her.

Nicholas found himself walking beside Rae.

"You have fun out there?" he asked.

"More than you, by the sounds of it."

"True. Look…"

"It feels weird. Without the old man." Rae's gaze stayed ahead.

"Yeah. It does. Are you–"

"Will you just shut up for two seconds so somebody else can speak?"

Nicholas shot her a stunned stare. He was used to filling the silences with Rae. She never offered him more than a handful of words and he had to fill in the gaps for her.

"You always…" Rae wouldn't look at him, so he knew it was important. He squeezed his mouth shut and waited.

"Twig was my friend. We met in London and he was annoying and got things wrong all the time, but I let him tag along. And then in Bury, he died. Because of me."

Nicholas remembered Rae talking in her sleep, shouting about twigs. He'd made it into a joke, even though he knew she was in pain, but he had never imagined Twig might be a person. A mixture of guilt and surprise twisted through him and he couldn't help gazing at her in sympathy.

"I'm–" he started.

"I just wanted you to know. I don't need sorries. And stop looking at me like that."

"Sorry." He winced. It had slipped out before he could stop it.

"That's why this is important," she said. "Stopping the Prophets and all of it. I need to... I want to make it better. All of it."

"I want to make it better, too," he said.

"It's not easy."

"What?" He raised an eyebrow. "Life?"

"Being in my head. It's... it's like there's these voices always telling me things and I don't deserve anything. I never really had friends."

Nicholas thought of Diltraa and shuddered. He brushed the thought aside.

"Hey, we're good."

"You freaked me out. I always knew I was a weirdo and then I found out that was true… And then you were in my head and you saw things nobody ever saw."

"I wouldn't tell anybody about that."

"I know. That's why… That's why we're good. Because I say so. Not you."

Nicholas grinned and nodded.

They walked the rest of the way in silence and, despite everything that was happening, a weird sensation inflated his chest. Rae had talked to him. He'd thought he already knew her from what he'd seen in her head, but those images had been taken by force. Now Rae *wanted* to talk to him, maybe let him in, even just a bit and, somehow, it made the world seem less hopeless.

They found the other Sentinels congregated at the edge of the forest. Orville lay on the other side of the road, quiet as a graveyard. Nicholas sensed a few Harvesters concealed in the village. The Sentinels drew their weapons and Nale turned his dark brow on Nicholas in question.

"Ten," Nicholas said. "Max."

Nale blinked and Nicholas held his gaze. He was still so angry at the Hunter, and he felt Diltraa's will urging him to attack him, make Nale pay for what he did to the Trinity. But now wasn't the time. In fact, now would be the worst possible time to confront Nale.

The other Sentinels turned to Nale and the Hunter motioned with his hands. *Go*, the signal meant and, silently, the small army rippled across the road and entered Orville. Nicholas felt a hand on his arm and smelled Isabel's perfume.

"You boy, wait. They're going ahead," she said.

"What do you mean?"

"There's something we need to do in Orville first. Don't argue."

He couldn't think what she meant. Were they going back to the well? Was there something else hidden in the tomb? She ignored his quizzical glare and they stood watching the Sentinels filter into Orville. An older Sentinel approached Rae and she flicked Nicholas a wary glance before going along with him. Finally, Nicholas and Isabel were alone.

Anxiously, he waited, trying to sense what was happening in Orville but not wanting to exhaust himself. After what felt like hours, but was probably only minutes, the old woman motioned for him to follow her and, together, they left the shelter of the forest, crossing the road and coming to the village high street.

Nicholas glimpsed the other Sentinels hurrying down each side of the cobbled street. If he squinted, he could just make out Nale at the front, Zeus clipping along beside him.

Three houses away, a shape hurtled from an alley, crashing into one of the Sentinels. They became a muddled mass of thrashing limbs and then the figure – a Harvester – grunted and collapsed. The Sentinel extracted a blood-red blade from the Harvester's chest.

"We have to–" Nicholas began.

"Don't move," Isabel said.

A figure was walking towards them. Nicholas's head buzzed and he realised this wasn't a living person; it was a shade. One of the villagers who had been trapped here when Nicholas was born.

"It is time you released them," Isabel said.

"Release? What do you mean?"

"They have been bound here for sixteen years. They deserve peace as much as anybody else; perhaps more so. You alone can give that to them."

Nicholas swallowed. The villager, a woman in her fifties carrying shopping bags, was almost upon them. He'd only encountered the Orville phantoms a couple of times. On the first occasion, it had been a man who couldn't see him. Now Isabel wanted him to release them? He wasn't sure where to even begin but, before he could formulate a clear thought, the villager was upon him, so close he could touch her if he wanted to.

Drawing a breath, he reached out and took her shoulder. The woman stopped, appearing confused, and he attempted to calm her with his mind. He imagined tendrils of light leaving his fingertips and moving through her until they reached the place her thoughts lived, finding images of the people she had loved, the laughter that had spilled between them. He squeezed her shoulder, giving her permission to let go, and the woman sighed, then vanished.

A chill ran the length of Nicholas's spine.

"I did it," he murmured.

"There are many others."

Nicholas nodded and, as if in a dream, he approached the first house on the high street. Opening the front door, he went into a lounge. A family of four stared at the door in shock, unable to see him, and he slipped silently through the room, laying a hand on each of their heads. They each sighed, as if relieved, and faded into nothing.

He continued through the town in a kind of trance. With each house he entered and every person he touched, the sense of serenity inside him grew, seeping into his bones, as if they'd given him something. He felt their peace. They didn't hate him for what he'd done all those years ago. They were simply eager for rest.

In one house, he found a woman who looked a lot like Rae, and he wondered if this was her mother. He wished Rae could be here to see her, even though he knew deep down it would do nothing for her. The woman was an echo. When he touched her shoulder, he sensed her joy at having a daughter and he wanted to cry for Rae, for everything she had missed, but he channelled the emotion back into Orville, feeling everything. Every hurt. Every blush. Every sting and song and sulk.

Finally, he found himself outside Rumours, the shop his birth parents had lived above. Only three phantoms remained. He found them in the living room upstairs. Smiling, they turned to welcome him, and they seemed to understand why he had returned. Something in his chest fluttered, like a bird in a cage, and he wanted to take this moment in his hands and stretch it out forever.

First, he went to Judith, who was still reading her book and checking her watch. He grazed her arm with his fingers. The midwife who had brought him into the world. And he thought of Sam. He filled her with everything he had ever associated with Sam. Comfort. Pride. Bravery.

She looked up briefly, her cheeks tear-stained.

Then Judith was gone.

Nicholas hoped she was with Sam.

He resisted turning to the remaining two figures by the window. He couldn't do it. He wouldn't. When this was all over, he'd come back, find a way to speak to his parents, ask what they saw in him. Had the demon inside of him changed him forever? Could he ever be fully good?

His mother approached him, her narrow face so eerily similar to Anita's, and placed her hands on his shoulders.

Nicholas gasped. He felt a soft weight where her hands lay and tears pricked his eyes. He couldn't do it. He couldn't let her go. This wasn't just about freeing them from the shackles of Orville, it was about saying goodbye. To all of them. His parents. His sister. Max. Sam. After this, they'd all be gone.

His mother's eyes glistened in response to his and she nodded slowly, the look of understanding on her face stabbing at his chest.

At last, he extended a quivering hand and clasped hers.

She smiled and became nothing.

His father stepped forward and extended a hand. Choking through the tears, Nicholas shook it, feeling sudden warmth, feeling in that one shake a world of possibilities, of things never said or done, and he didn't want to ever let go. But then his father, too, was gone.

He took a moment alone in the room. They'd been trapped here for so long, now they had peace.

"Thank you," he said.

Then he left the place he'd been born, the ground zero of his life, and joined Isabel in the street.

"You have done a remarkable thing," she said softly.

Nicholas nodded, unable to speak.

They moved swiftly down the street and the veil of sadness that had settled over him evaporated when a series of shouts came from around a corner. They stopped by a newsagent and peered around it. At the other end of the street rested the train depot. Through a chain fence, he glimpsed rail tracks and a series of long, dark rectangles. In front of the old trains, Sentinels and Harvesters clashed. Blue light crackled from the Harvesters' gauntlets, and Nicholas watched as Dawn dodged a deadly blast of lightning. The air steamed around Rae and she hurled energy at their attackers, sending them spinning.

"Come," Isabel said, pacing forward quickly. Nicholas checked his knives were still fastened at his belt and clutched the small axe in his hand. The village had left him drained and the thought of fighting made his body ache, but the sight of Dawn and Rae willed him on.

*Merlyn*, he thought, tightening his grip on the axe.

At the fence, Isabel swept the air with her staff and the metal links burst apart in a spray of shrapnel. They flew into the crowd, only striking Harvesters, who toppled as if they'd been shot.

"Welcome back," huffed Dawn.

"Thought you might need a hand," said Nicholas, although all the Harvesters in this part of the depot were now on the ground, dead or unconscious.

"Where are the others?" he added.

Dawn nodded up the length of the nearest train and Nicholas saw Nale leading a band of Sentinels towards a crowd of Harvesters.

"So many of them," Isabel muttered.

"This way." Nicholas hopped over the tracks, making his way between the trains. One of these was Malika's, but lights were shining in most of the trains. Decoys. Of course Malika had thought of everything.

The deeper they went, the quieter it became, and the air grew thick somehow, as if somebody was stirring oil into it. Nicholas felt queasy.

"You feel that?" he whispered.

Isabel nodded but continued stepping over the tracks. Behind Nicholas, Rae stumbled.

"You alright?" he asked.

"Fine."

He tried to ignore the darkness under her eyes. She looked the way he felt after he'd used up too much energy sensing. The fight with the Harvesters had weakened her. She'd never admit to it, though, and at that moment, Nicholas spotted an old locomotive that couldn't have worked the tracks in a century.

"Stop," he hissed, holding the others back behind a carriage. He stared at the old train. Its red-painted carriages were rusted, the netting in the windows yellowing. It spoke of a past era of glitz and glamour, when train journeys were grand adventures.

"That's Malika's," he said.

"You sense her?" asked Isabel.

"No, I'm using the God-given power of my eyeballs. Trust me, that's hers."

"You sense anybody on board?" asked Dawn.

"Yeah. A dozen at least in the first few carriages."

"Hmmm." Isabel peered closer at the relic, as if attempting to see through its walls, and Nicholas realised that's exactly what she was doing. He sensed movement within the train, though something was blocking him from pushing his mind inside to see for himself. Either Malika or the Prophets had placed a protective barrier over it.

"Two guards," he said, eyeing a couple of Harvesters stationed outside the train's doors. A man and a woman.

Rae stepped in their direction, but Nicholas grabbed her arm.

"Let me," he said. She looked so exhausted.

Ignoring her annoyed glare, he turned his thoughts inward. He had been itching to try something new on the Harvesters ever since he had made the demon swarm turn on itself in Cambridge. Jessica had said that emotion was his power; it was time to see if that trick worked on something bigger.

"Nicholas–" Dawn began.

"Quiet," he hissed, reaching out with his thoughts. He imagined them as a cord and searched for a hook in the male Harvester's mind. Something he could use against them. He trembled with concentration and found what he was searching for.

"What you say?" the male Harvester asked. His partner sneered.

"Didn't say anything. Too much grog for breakfast?"

"Don't start that again."

"Need to learn to hold your liquor, princess."

He shoved her. She shoved him back. His fist squeezed into a bundle of knuckles and they began tussling.

Not wasting a moment, Nicholas used the distraction to pounce on the fighting Harvesters. They noticed him too late and Nicholas punched the man, knocking him unconscious. Before he could tackle the other Harvester, the woman threw herself at him and they scrabbled on the ground.

As the Harvester pinned him down, Nicholas felt a sudden blast of heat. The Harvester screamed, her flesh cooking in front of him. He freed his arm and buried his fist in her jaw, sending her flying.

"You shouldn't have done that," he said, turning on Rae as he got to his feet.

"It's fine."

He bit down the urge to argue. "Inside," he said. "Quickly."

Wrenching open the train door, he checked inside before letting Isabel, Dawn, and Rae up first. Then he stepped up into the carriage and shut the door.

"Did you do that? With the Harvesters?" asked Dawn.

"Mhmm."

Nicholas peered around the interior of the train. They had to be quick. Find Merlyn, hope that he hadn't been turned, then get off the train so Rae could blow it to smithereens.

He peered through a glass window into the first carriage. It was narrow and carpet-lined with bronze lamps set into the wall. It seemed deserted.

"Rae, are you–" Dawn said.

Nicholas heard a sound and Dawn exclaimed, "Rae!"

He turned and found Rae had collapsed. She was slumped against the far door, unconscious. The temperature in the carriage plummeted, as if a fire had been snuffed out.

"What happened?" he asked.

Dawn crouched over Rae, her eyes huge with worry. "I don't know. She just went down. I think… She's been killing demons for days. She refused to sleep…"

"She's out cold," Nicholas said, anxiety and guilt flooding through him. They needed Rae. She was literally their fire power. Without her they were a quarter less effective. Steeling himself, he knew what he had to do.

"Stay with her," he told Dawn.

"Where are you going?" she asked.

"To check the train. I'll be quick. If Merlyn's on here, or Malika, or both… This is our best chance at saving him and stopping her."

"Be quick."

Nicholas shared a look with Isabel and knew she was coming with him. Taking a breath, he slid open the door to the first carriage and then stopped. The floor was shuddering. Dust shook from the lamps.

"Wait… wait…"

For a second, he had no idea what was happening. Then he realised what the juddering meant.

They were moving.

# CHAPTER FIFTEEN
## PRISONERS

"No no no!"

Nicholas threw himself at the nearest window, not caring that any Harvesters still in the depot could see him. The train trundled along, slowly gathering speed, and he spotted Sentinels running alongside it, yelling to one another. A hundred thoughts darted through his mind. Should he, Isabel, Dawn, and Rae get off? Help the other Sentinels clamber onboard? Continue searching the train regardless?

"We have to help the others," he decided, dashing back to the door they had come through. Throwing it open, he leaned out, ignoring the ground as it blurred beneath him. Glancing back down the length of the track, he spotted four figures chasing behind the locomotive. He recognised them as Sentinels, though he didn't know them by name.

"Any sign of Nale? Aileen?" Isabel asked.

Nicholas shook his head and swivelled to look up to the front of the train. They were pulling up into Orville station, but the train was speeding up rather than slowing down. Soon they'd be out in the countryside, on their way to London.

The train's engine gathered momentum and the tracks clacked louder as they picked up speed. The station whizzed by and then they passed through the village before shooting out into open countryside. As the train sped faster and faster, Nicholas was forced to draw himself back inside and haul the door shut.

"What the hell?" said Dawn. At Nicholas's glare, she added, "Sorry, I don't have anything else."

"How's Rae?" he asked.

"Still out."

The train shuddered and Nicholas grabbed the wall to stop from falling over. The countryside zipped by in a queasy blur.

"It shouldn't be able to go this fast," he murmured.

"She's enchanted it," Isabel said.

Nicholas found Dawn's uneasy stare. "Looks like we're going to London…"

Isabel unleashed her most feline scowl and Nicholas tried to figure out how this had changed things. Rae was unconscious. Nale was nowhere to be seen. It was up to him and Isabel to find Merlyn and anybody else they had captive on the train, and then stop Malika. Maybe confront the Prophets. Raise the Trinity. End it all on this express train from Hell. And that was assuming they even made it past the first carriage. What was that expression? Snake pit? It sort of applied here. He'd been in snake pits before, though.

"I don't sense anybody in this carriage," he said. "Dawn, you okay to stay here with Rae? We'll sweep each carriage one at a time and then double back for you."

"You sure you don't need back-up?"

"Just keep an eye on Rae. The nap should do her good."

Dawn nodded, and Nicholas turned to Isabel.

"You and me are going for a walk," he said. "I'll scan. You keep an ear out for Harvesters."

"You realise I am no longer a feline."

"Shame. If you were, you could've snuck through this whole train like a ghost. You have any weapons?"

Isabel thumped the floor with her staff.

"Right. My guess is you've got about six lives left anyway."

"I require only one."

"Well, technically you're already on your third." After a nod at Dawn, they made their way into the narrow carriage. The windows on their right showed the countryside whooshing past in a murky streak. To their left were doors that led into old-fashioned compartments. The first was filled with objects draped with black sheets. No Harvesters, just the outlines of some sort of sinister cargo.

"What is all of this?" Nicholas thought out loud.

He tried to sense what the boxes held but they were magically protected. Typical. They didn't have time to stop and crack any of them open and, besides, they could be full of something that would atomise them on sight.

They continued past more box-crammed compartments before stopping at the border of the next carriage. Through the glass in the door, Nicholas saw Harvesters pacing, repeatedly turning to peer into the stalls. They were sneering and spitting, and although Nicholas couldn't hear what they were saying, he sensed what lay in the compartments.

"People," he hissed at Isabel. "They've got prisoners in there."

"If we attack, we must ensure nobody alerts the rest of the train."

"You got anymore tricks?"

Golden flecks sizzled briefly in Isabel's eyes and then she returned Nicholas's gaze. "I have just locked the door at the far end. There is no way for the Harvesters to move into the next carriage. We must move swiftly while they are trapped."

Nicholas grinned. This was the kind of magic he needed. He turned his attention to the carriage, steading himself against the door as the train rocked. The axe was too cumbersome in the cramped space, so he slipped it into a loop in his rucksack and drew the dagger from his boot. Flashing Isabel a 'get ready' stare, he slid the door open loudly enough to draw the Harvesters' attention.

It worked. All eyes snapped in their direction and Nicholas was glad he'd not had time to size up the competition. These were definitely Harvester heavies, not dissimilar in size and girth to the one that had attacked them in his old house on Midsummer Common. The first, a meatsack with enormous biceps, immediately charged at him, and Nicholas met him eagerly.

He slashed his blade, aiming for the Harvester's throat, but the man wasn't as clumsy as his size suggested. He dodged the blow and threw a fist in Nicholas's face. Every one of Nicholas's teeth rattled and he was surprised when he didn't spit any free. Momentarily disorientated, he found himself bludgeoned again, and then he was on the floor, the Harvester looming over him.

"Come, fiend," said Isabel.

"No, he's mine," Nicholas grunted, and the Harvester cackled.

"Oh, yes, I'm yours sweetheart. Gissa kiss."

Seizing his moment, Nicholas grabbed the Harvester's ankle, slipping his hand beneath his trouser leg and grazing the skin. Balking at the sensation of touching the creep, he focussed his mind, funnelling his thoughts through the connection, into the Harvester's skull.

"Agggghh!"

The Harvester emitted a horrified screech and the carriage trembled as he crashed into the wall. He began slapping his arms and chest as if he were trying to put out a fire.

"They're on me! They're all over me!"

The half a dozen other Harvesters, smaller than the first but equally as imposing, eyed Nicholas.

"Witchcraft," spat one of them. "Nothing better than skinning a witch."

"Come and get it," Nicholas said. In a single smooth motion, he leapt to his feet and buried his dagger under the jaw of the shrieking Harvester, who ceased flapping and clutched his neck. Nicholas tore the blade free and the man's throat sprayed red across the window.

Nicholas barely noticed the Harvester collapsing at his feet. He was drawn to the blood-spattered pane beside him. He couldn't stop staring at it. As he pressed his hand to it, something pulsed in Nicholas's ribcage. A dark yearning. The demon wanted more.

Snapping his head to glare at the Harvesters, Nicholas knew exactly where to get what Diltraa wanted. He launched himself at them and the next few moments passed in a bilious blur of screams and savaged flesh. Power coursed through him and Nicholas hurled psychic spears at his opponents, weakening them from the inside before he carved them open with the dagger.

In a flash, he'd made it to the other end of the carriage, leaving a trail of mutilated bodies in his wake.

Only one Harvester remained. The man turned tail and threw himself at the door leading to the next carriage. When he found it locked, the Harvester bellowed and wrenched at it, sweating, glancing anxiously over his shoulder as Nicholas approached. Isabel's incantation held, though. The door was locked tight.

"LET ME IN! LET ME IN!"

The Harvester's shrieks were like catnip to Diltraa and Nicholas felt the demon shuddering with pleasure. It was almost too easy. Nicholas grabbed the Harvester's arm and immediately the man released the door. He appeared confused for a moment as he felt Nicholas's mind needling inside, then Nicholas clocked his jaw with his fist and the Harvester went down, out cold.

Panting, he searched for more Harvesters to fight, but found there were none.

*More*, the voice in his head rasped. *More!*

Ignoring it, he turned and stared back down the corridor.

Isabel stood at the far end. Her face was white with shock and, for the briefest moment, she looked fearful that he might turn on her. Nicholas gritted his teeth and fought to suppress the red mist clouding his vision. His belly gurgled as Diltraa fought back but, finally, the demon's bloodlust abated. Diltraa fell silent, and Nicholas made his way back to Isabel.

"So now they fear you," the old woman murmured. "Though perhaps not for the right reasons."

Shrinking away from her horrified stare, Nicholas tried not to think about what he'd just done. The arcane pleasure he'd taken in killing the Harvesters.

No, not him. Diltraa. It didn't seem to matter that the Harvesters were technically Diltraa's allies. The demon took what it could, and it had revelled in the slaughter as much as Nicholas was nauseated by it.

Taking a settling breath, Nicholas focussed on the compartments the Harvesters had been guarding. He went to the first one and drew open the door.

The seats had been removed and it had been turned into a cell, the window painted black so there was no light. Three figures flinched back as he peered in, rattling chains, and Nicholas saw that they were shackled to the walls. One of them had a raven tattooed on the back of his neck.

"Sentinels," Nicholas murmured.

"I shall examine the others." Isabel vanished, and Nicholas stepped into the cell. A man, not Merlyn, and two women. One of the women returned his look without blinking. She had a busted nose and sharp cheekbones.

"Friend or foe?" she asked.

Without answering, Nicholas bent to inspect the chains. They were bolted to a strip of metal hammered to the wall. He drew his axe and swung, and the blade cut through the chains as if they were made of cardboard.

The Sentinel with the busted nose shook her restraints free. "I almost had it."

"Hey, you're welcome."

"Well, sure, if you've got an axe, that sort of takes the fun out of it."

"I can strap you back in if you'd like."

The woman broke into a grin. "Maybe another time."

Nicholas extended a hand and her fingers bit into his forearm as he helped her up. She was taller than him and broad-shouldered. Her hair was dirty blonde and her eyes were hawk-like and mischievous. He turned to unchain the others.

"How long you been in here?" he asked.

The other two prisoners were younger, perhaps early twenties, and practically slumped against one another. They seemed too exhausted to cough more than a "thanks" as they unfolded slowly from the floor, stretching their thin limbs.

"Going by the length of my fingernails, I'm going to say two days," the female Sentinel said. This time she extended her hand. "Kai."

"Nicholas." Her handshake was as unforgiving as her demeanour. He guessed she was in her thirties, though her jeans and hoody were so grubby that it really was a guess.

"Nice hat," she said, and Nicholas's hand flinched toward the brim of the fedora, but he didn't care if he looked stupid in it. It was Sam's and it felt good wearing it.

Kai gestured to the skinny duo. "Halle and Ryan have been in it for the long haul. Got caught in Brighton. Been shown the sights like royalty for weeks."

Nicholas eyed the pair, noting their emaciated faces, their matted black hair and red-rimmed eyes, and anger stirred in his chest. "Why'd they chain you up? Why not just kill you? This seems worse than death."

The woman, Halle, cleared her throat and he noticed the bruising where somebody had tried to throttle her.

"Didn't say," she croaked. "Our own fault for getting caught."

The man beside her, Ryan, touched her arm and Halle peered at him in a way that told Nicholas they were siblings. Peering closer, he noted they shared the same snub nose and chocolate brown eyes. Twins. He couldn't understand what Malika had to gain from taking prisoners. It made sense to eradicate the Sentinels, exterminate them like pests, but cart them across the country for weeks? Perhaps she was stocking up to create more Harvesters. He couldn't think what other purpose they might serve.

He considered his axe, then he handed it to Kai.

"We're taking the train," he explained. "One carriage at a time. Malika's onboard… and the Prophets, we think."

"Sick axe." Kai tested the feel of the weapon. "So where's this old rust bucket of a train going?"

"London."

"I've never seen London," said Ryan. "I've heard of you. You were in Bury, right? With Esus and the others."

"That's right." It seemed he was getting a reputation. He wondered what the Sentinels were saying about him and then decided he could live with not knowing.

"Out of the frying pan into the fire for you," Ryan said.

"You could say that. Here." Nicholas drew three daggers from his backpack and handed them out, keeping one for himself. "You all good with these?"

Halle and Ryan appeared nervous.

"We're Sensitives," Halle explained. "But… well, that doesn't work so well when you've not eaten for days."

"Do what you can," Nicholas told them. "And stay behind the others. First scrap of food we find is yours."

The twins nodded and Nicholas crossed the cell, poking his head into the corridor. Aside from the bodies of the Harvesters he'd killed, he found it deserted. Isabel was nowhere in sight.

Apprehensively, he moved out and motioned for the others to follow. "Boy. In here."

Isabel's voice came from the next compartment. There, Nicholas found another dingy cell with half a dozen more Sentinels chained to the walls. A couple of them were no longer shackled and rubbed their wrists, which were red and bleeding. Isabel had worked partway around the cell, releasing them one at a time, no doubt using her staff.

"Geeze, how many are there?" Nicholas breathed. These were only the first two compartments in the carriage. "Is this entire train filled with Sentinels?"

"I've seen what they can do." Against the wall, one of the Sentinels murmured almost to himself. "Turn a guy crazy, make him kill his own family."

"They warned us… The rumours." A young woman spoke up. "That couple in Cambridge… Nobody wanted to believe it."

Nicholas realised they were talking about Sam's friends, Richard and his wife. Richard had been the first Sentinel turned into a Harvester in Cambridge.

"She's making an army out of dead Sentinels," the woman continued. "She just hadn't got round to us yet."

Nicholas could tell she was on the verge of delirium, dehydrated and half-starved, but she seemed to be speaking sense. It was the same conclusion he'd come to. Malika was hoarding Sentinels to grow her army.

When Isabel had released the final prisoner, she stood observing them as they stumbled to their feet, grateful and eager but clearly exhausted. There were seven in this cell. Nicholas had freed three. Counting him and Isabel, they suddenly had their own small battalion of twelve.

"You are weary and you are scared," Isabel said, casting her gaze about the room. "But you are needed now more than ever. We must take this train. Will you help us?"

"Just tell us where the bugs are," one of the Sentinels said.

The female Sentinel bowed. "I will fight for you until my last breath, Ms Hallow."

Isabel almost smiled and Nicholas handed out the last of his weapons – a couple of arrows, an old steak knife, a penknife and a slingshot. He wanted the Drujblade back now more than ever. He hoped Malika really was aboard. This time he'd grab the blade and he wouldn't let go until it was his. She'd have to cut off his hand if she wanted to keep it.

As he left the compartment, he found Kai returning from another cell.

"Anything?" he asked.

"Just some dead guy one room on. The others are empty. Guess they're expecting more guests soon."

"Dead guy?" Nicholas asked. He stared down the corridor, seeing the twins guarding the door to the next carriage.

"On a table, but the room's weird. Ceremonial, almost. There are candles and stuff."

Nicholas's brow furrowed. What new madness was this? He focussed his mind as he approached the compartment Kai had just been in, and he knew what lay inside even before he laid eyes on it.

There, stretched out on a table, was Sam.

His skin was eggshell white, his eyes closed, arms limp at his sides. He looked so peaceful he could be sleeping.

A strange sensation flooded through Nicholas. Part of him wanted to touch Sam's cheek, but another wanted to turn and run the other way. He still couldn't believe Sam was gone.

Swallowing, he stepped inside, taking in the strange ornaments on shelves, the symbols painted on the walls, the totems dangling from the ceiling. What was all of this? It could almost be a shrine, but what was its purpose?

Curbing his curiosity, Nicholas approached the table Sam was laid on.

Something twanged in Nicholas's gut as he saw that Sam wasn't lying as motionless as he'd first thought. A second later he realised Sam wasn't dead. The old man's breathing was so shallow his chest barely moved, but as Nicholas brought his face closer to Sam's he heard the whisper of a breath.

"He's alive," Nicholas murmured.

Sam's head shifted in his direction. He'd heard him.

"Sam?"

The old man frowned and his lips quivered.

"Nicholas?"

His voice was a dry rasp.

"I'm here. I'm right here."

"I can't see you," Sam croaked.

"I'm standing beside you," Nicholas said. "Can you move?"

Then he choked. Sam's hand had jerked to life and clamped around Nicholas's throat. As Nicholas gagged, the old man's eyes snapped open, and although they were chalk white, they shifted to glare right at him.

"Ah, now I see you."

It wasn't Sam's voice. Or, it was, but Nicholas had never heard him sound so malicious, like he was gargling venom.

"Sam–" Nicholas gagged. He was an idiot. He'd seen with his own eyes as Malika used the gauntlet on Sam, but he'd been so relieved to find him alive that he'd forgotten. This wasn't Sam anymore. Sam was dead. This was the thing that had stolen his body.

The old man rose from the table like somebody emerging from the grave and Nicholas fought to free himself from Sam's vice-like grip, but Sam wouldn't let go. He threw his legs over the side of the table and dropped to the floor, sneering as he squeezed Nicholas's throat.

Nicholas realised he'd dropped the dagger in the confusion and wondered if he could have used it on Sam anyway. A vein throbbed in his temple as he fought for air and his eyes bulged at Sam's face, knowing the real Sam would never hurt him like this.

Screwing up a fist, he punched the Harvester. The old man's sneer widened, and Nicholas punched him again, dizziness sapping at his strength as his lungs began to burn.

"Think you'll find that's mine, old boy," Sam sneered, snatching the fedora off Nicholas's head and placing it on his own.

"Release him!"

Isabel's voice boomed in Nicholas's ears and suddenly he was free. Sam flew back, propelled by an invisible force, striking the wall and flopping to the floor.

Nicholas coughed and gulped for air, massaging his bruised throat.

"That is no longer your friend." Isabel came to his side, her cat-like features trained on Sam, who was already pulling himself up.

"Kind of got the impression," Nicholas wheezed, eyeing the thing that had once been Sam.

"Need mummy and daddy to kiss it better?" Sam drawled. "Ah, lad, I'm sorry, I forgot. Such a pity."

Nicholas knew what the Harvester was doing but it didn't stop his words stinging. The monster seemed to have found Sam's voice. It wasn't as rasping as it had been. Now he could almost believe this was his old friend.

"Don't talk to it," Isabel warned him. "Go and join the others. I shall deal with this."

"What are you going to do?" Nicholas asked.

"Yes, please, enlighten us," Sam snarled. "What fancy trick are you pulling out of your hat this time, witch?"

"You can't kill him." Nicholas could tell from Isabel's expression that was exactly what she was thinking.

"He is already dead."

"Oh, he's in here alright," Sam spat. "He's telling me every nasty little thing he knows about you, lad. Got a list here that'd make ten big, fat books. Whew, anybody would think you're working for us."

Isabel stepped forward, her features hardening as she jabbed her staff at the old man. His head snapped back momentarily as if he'd been punched, but he quickly recovered. He grinned red teeth at Nicholas.

"Gonna let the witch do the work for you, as always? Still a boy hiding behind her apron."

"Nicholas, leave now," Isabel ordered.

But he couldn't leave. He stared at the old woman, remembering how she'd stumbled in the carriage; how much of the slack she was picking up for him. Clenching his fists, he focussed on Sam and reached inside the man's head, feeling for whatever parasite had attached itself to his brain.

Sam appeared unsettled for a moment, one eye squeezing shut. Then he launched himself at Isabel, knocking her off her feet. As soon as Isabel's back struck the floor, the Harvester was on top of her, but before he could do anything more, Nicholas buried his boot in the man's ribcage. Sam toppled sideways, and Nicholas swept up his dagger from the floor.

He came up behind Sam, grabbing the old man's head and pressing the blade to his throat.

Sam choked. "Find a way, lad."

Nicholas froze. They were the last words Sam had uttered.

"I believe in you," the old man gulped.

"Sam?"

"I believe you'll die screaming for your dead parents."

Sam's cackle made the hairs on Nicholas's arms shiver.

The confusion boiled into anger and he delivered a blow to the back of the Harvester's head that knocked him unconscious. The old man went limp and Nicholas heaved himself up. He couldn't do it. He couldn't kill him, even if it wasn't really Sam. The thought of Sam's throat gushing blood made him sick. He swept the fedora from the floor and put it on. It wasn't Sam's anymore.

As he moved away from the body, he saw that Isabel was back on her feet. She bent by the fallen man and pressed her fingertips to his temples, closing her eyes, murmuring under her breath. After a few moments, she shook her head and released him.

"There is no saving him," she said softly.

Nicholas couldn't look at her or the body. "There's no time for this. We need to keep searching the train. Let's lock him in here and decide what to do with him when we reach London."

They joined the others in the corridor. Isabel closed the carriage door and tapped the lock. Nicholas heard it click and caught Kai giving him a hooded stare. She must have heard the whole thing.

"So we're taking the train, yeah?" she said.

Nicholas nodded. "All twelve of us."

"And here I was looking for a challenge."

"What's the plan?" one of the other Sentinels asked. They all seemed so exhausted and hungry, like underfed wolves. He hoped they had the energy for whatever came next.

"One carriage at a time," he said. "Nobody gets left behind. Kill anything that tries to kill you. Oh, and Malika's mine."

"You're welcome to her," said Kai. "She makes my balls shrivel."

Nicholas smiled. This was what Sam would want. The real Sam. They were still fighting, even though the odds were stacked so high against them that they could all do with climbing equipment. *Find a way, lad?* He'd find a way alright. Even if it killed him.

"Isabel, you take up the rear, along with anybody who's less confident with a blade," he said. "Kai, you're up front with me. Everybody else who can fight, be ready to."

"Yes, ma'am," said Kai.

Nicholas surveyed his army one last time, and then paced down the corridor to the next carriage. Trying not to think about leaving Sam behind, he sent his mind roving, sensing Harvesters in the next carriage, and the next, but no more Sentinels. He frowned. Malika must be cloaking herself because he couldn't sense her either. Refocussing his mind, he searched again, but he couldn't even sense a dark gathering of energy that might signal a cloaking enchantment.

They were at the next carriage before he could attempt to make sense of it.

Throwing open the door, he charged at the first Harvester, taking her down with a psychic grenade and then plunging his blade into her chest. Diltraa's shiver of delight travelled through his abdomen and Nicholas shook it off as Kai swept past him to tackle the others. The floor convulsed as Isabel slammed her staff, which knocked every Harvester off his or her feet.

Within two minutes, every Harvester was dead.

Ignoring the bodies, Nicholas beckoned the others to follow as he went to the next carriage. It was deserted, so he continued into the one after that. They must be halfway through the train and he still couldn't sense Malika.

He glanced over his shoulder at Isabel and saw she was frowning, too. She knew something wasn't right.

They fought five more Harvesters in the next carriage, and the unease in Nicholas's belly was growing. These Harvesters were old; far too old to be elite guards. They seemed, for lack of a better word, disposable. They barely put up a fight as the Sentinels took them down.

At the door to the next carriage, Nicholas sensed movement and saw shapes through the glass.

"More," he told Isabel and the others, bracing himself. He grabbed the handle and jerked the door open.

A huge shape bowled toward him and Nicholas thrust his dagger forward, stopping just in time to prevent it from plunging into Benjamin Nale's stomach. The Hunter looked as surprised as Nicholas felt, and he clenched the blade tighter, suspicion digging at his own abdomen.

"What the hell–" he began, and then Nicholas shook his head as another figure appeared from behind Nale.

"Nale got us aboard just before the thing started moving," said Aileen. "But there's nobody here."

"Here or at the other end," said Nicholas. "How did you…" He stopped as Zeus bounded over and licked Isabel's hand. To Nicholas's shock, Pyraemon was still secure in Aileen's bag and didn't seem particularly interested in what was going on around him.

"You know what," Nicholas said, "it doesn't matter how you got on. Have you searched the rest of the train?"

"Just this carriage and, well, there's nobody here, dear." Aileen sheathed her sword. "Where's Dawn? And Rae? And who are your friends?"

"We left them at the other end of the train," said Nicholas. He avoided Nale's gaze. Although he was glad for the back-up, Nicholas still didn't know if he trusted the Hunter and he'd rather not think about it with everything else going on. Instead, he gestured to Kai and the others. "More Sentinels. They were locked up back there."

"Always happy to meet fellow Sentinels," beamed Aileen.

Nicholas barely heard her. He had to continue searching the rest of the train. A nagging sense of unease distracted him, and he knew he'd only be able to quiet it by searching further.

"Stay here," he told Aileen and the others. "I'll be back soon."

"Be careful, dear."

The carriage after that was deserted. Isabel stirred the air with her staff but reported nothing out of the ordinary.

Finally, they stood in the last passenger carriage, staring at a door at the far end of the corridor. There was nowhere left to go. Malika must be in there.

Nicholas approached the door and listened. Hearing nothing, he felt through the wood with his mind, but he couldn't tell if Malika was inside.

"She has to be in there."

"I sense nothing," Isabel muttered.

Nicholas gripped the handle and threw open the door.

The driver's carriage was empty. Through the front windows, he saw the track stretching ahead. No Malika. No Prophets. No driver.

Finally, he understood why he hadn't been able to sense the red witch. This wasn't her train.

"It's a decoy," he murmured.

"Impossible."

He faced Isabel, not wanting to believe it but knowing he was right. "That's why Sam's in that carriage. He was the bait, and we took it. She's not anywhere on this train and neither are the Prophets."

White-faced, Isabel appraised the driver's carriage. "Yes," she whispered. "That is why there are so few prisoners, and so few of her cads guarding them. Nobody is expected to survive this journey."

With growing horror, Nicholas realised the train wasn't slowing down. They were still travelling preternaturally fast, towns zipping past the window so quickly he'd get whiplash if he tried to spot their names.

"We have to stop this thing."

He scanned the driver's dashboard, surveying the wheels and pullies without knowing what he was looking at. They didn't look right. One of the handles had been snapped off.

"We have to get off. Now." He peered back down the corridor at the Sentinels. "Find a way off!" he yelled. "This thing's not stopping."

The Sentinels gave each other horrified glances and then scrambled to search for an exit. Kai hurried up to the driver's carriage.

"Decoy?" she panted.

Nicholas nodded.

"Must be some way to stop it."

"You're welcome to try."

As she approached the dash, he went to a door at the side of the carriage and slid it open. The train was moving so fast he was almost sucked outside. Digging his nails into the frame, he eased himself back and slammed the door.

"We have to slow it down," he said, catching sight of something through the window. "That's the Shard ahead. And the Gherkin. We're almost in London."

"How unsightly," Isabel muttered, glaring at the skyscrapers. "What have they done?"

"Just wait 'til you see Leicester Square," Nicholas told her.

Kai kicked the control box and cursed. "It's enchanted or something."

Nicholas shared a hopeless look with her. The only way the train would stop was when it crashed into its final destination, wherever that was. From the view, he assumed it was Liverpool Street, but that was only a guess. If they jumped from the driver's door they'd be sucked under the train. The roof? Probably just as dangerous.

"The back," he said. "We jump off the back of the train."

"Seems like our best bet," said Kai.

The train rattled around them as they rejoined the others and explained their plan.

"Trinity spare us," breathed Aileen.

Hurriedly, they went from carriage to carriage, losing their footing as the train sped faster still. The tracks squealed, and Nicholas tried to ignore a sick feeling in the pit of his stomach. This was how Anita and Max had died. He'd imagined their final moments over and over in the weeks following their deaths. How they'd scrabbled to survive. On this train now, he felt like he was trapped in a nightmare version of their deaths, reliving their doomed attempts to escape, only this time it was him and a band of Sentinels trying to survive.

He wouldn't let their deaths be in vain. He wouldn't let Malika win.

He couldn't tell how many carriages they'd passed through. The old loco seemed to have turned into a carnival terror train that never ended. It was only when he saw the shredded door that he knew they were one carriage away from freedom.

"Go," he told the others, eyeing the door, which trembled under an attack from the inside.

"Mr Wilkins," Isabel murmured.

"Just get the others off," Nicholas said. "I'll hold him back."

"Sam?" murmured Aileen, but Nicholas didn't have time to explain.

"Go!" he urged.

Isabel appeared uncertain and then seemed to realise Nicholas wasn't going to back down. With Nale and Zeus charging ahead, she hurried the Sentinels along and, just as she disappeared into the last carriage, the shredded door buckled and a shape hurtled into the corridor.

Nicholas readied himself as, panting, Sam faced him. The old man's fingernails were torn and dripping blood. Diltraa shuddered with delight.

"Knew you couldn't stay away, lad."

"Where is she?" Nicholas demanded.

Sam's eyebrows went up. "She? I haven't the foggiest who you're talking about."

"You know exactly who I'm talking about. She set this whole thing up."

"Did she?" Sam's eyes became slits. "If you're clever enough to figure that out, you're clever enough to know she's miles away, lad. You'll never catch up."

What did he mean? Malika wasn't going to London? Nicholas eyed Sam, knowing that Harvesters lied. The truth was their plaything and he had no idea which lie was really the truth or the other way around.

"You're willing to die for her?" Nicholas said. "Cos this train's about to be in a bunch of pieces."

Sam beat his chest. "Made of tough stuff, this old codger. Take more'n a train wreck to break him."

Nicholas stumbled as the carriage jolted underfoot, and then righted itself. The track wasn't designed for this sort of speed. They were going to come off the rails before they reached Liverpool Street.

He couldn't worry about that now, though, because Sam had taken advantage of the lapse in his concentration, throwing himself at Nicholas. They crashed to the floor and Sam landed on top of him. Pain exploded in Nicholas's ribs as the old man dug his knuckles into them. He grabbed Sam's arms and flipped him over his head. Sam grunted as he hit the floor and Nicholas rolled over, bringing the dagger down, aiming for Sam's heart.

Liver-spotted hands stopped him at the last moment, catching the dagger just above Sam's chest.

"Can you do it lad?" Sam panted.

Nicholas gritted his teeth and bore down with all his strength, but Sam moved and the blade sank into his belly.

The old man gurgled with laughter and threw a fist. Nicholas dodged backwards and lost his balance. As he got to his feet, he watched as the Harvester drew the blade free and tossed it out of reach.

"First blood," Sam drooled.

Nicholas was mesmerised by the dark stain spreading across Sam's shirt. He'd stabbed him. He'd stabbed Sam.

*More,* Diltraa urged. *Moooooore.*

Sam flew at him again and Nicholas threw up his arms to fend off the blows. But one caught his jaw, pain exploding there and, as he reeled, Sam caught his arms and whirled Nicholas on the spot, slamming him against the wall. He shoved Nicholas's face into the window, wrenching one arm behind his back, and hissed in Nicholas's ear.

"She'll be so happy knowing I'm the one who did it. I'm the one who killed the Trinity's pup. Then I'll find the girl and end her, too."

Nicholas grunted and struggled to free himself, but Sam's grip on his arm was unyielding.

"Just healed, hasn't it?" Sam hissed. "The fracture. Easy enough to break again. Find the flaw and you find the man. What he's capable of. Think you can take me with only one arm?"

Nicholas screamed as Sam twisted.

The train bucked. Nicholas glimpsed sparks through the window. An awful piercing shriek filled his ears and he felt sick. The train jolted again and it was enough of a distraction for him to push himself away from the glass and crush Sam against the door behind him.

Seizing his chance, Nicholas smashed the Harvester in the face. Sam's head wobbled and he appeared dazed. Nicholas dealt another blow and the old man collapsed like a sack of cement.

His victory was short-lived, though, because at that moment the trained bucked again and Nicholas's feet left the floor. He landed so hard on his back that it winded him, and as he gasped for breath, his surroundings shuddered.

A sound like rupturing metal tore through the carriage and Nicholas was lifted into the air again, then tossed to one side. The front carriages must have smashed into something and the train had come off the tracks. He and Sam were sent spinning like a jumble of rag dolls.

Nicholas struck the wall, then the ceiling, then the floor. The windows smashed and all he could hear was screaming metal and his own caterwauling voice in his head.

*I'm dead, I'm dead, I'm dead.*

# CHAPTER SIXTEEN
## MINDSCAPE

NICHOLAS COUGHED AND ROLLED OVER.

Every inch of him felt bruised and, as he raised his head from the ground, he saw he was covered in ash and rubble. He retched again, almost enough to deposit a lung in front of him, and he wondered how long he had been unconscious. It felt like it could be seconds or hours, and the grimy light offered him no clues.

Grimacing, he shoved off a window frame. The carriage had crumpled around him and Nicholas remembered the time he'd been trapped in a bus with Malika. Pushing away that thought, he saw that he was lying on the carriage wall. Above his head, the other wall resembled a beaten-up paint tin and all around him were the remnants of doors, windows and the train's steel skeleton.

He pried himself up.

"Ahhh." He winced at the spike of pain in his healing arm. Clearly a train wreck wasn't the best idea when your bones were still repairing themselves. Hesitantly, Nicholas found his feet and crouched in the cramped space, taking shallow breaths and wondering how many of his ribs were broken.

He tried to sense his surroundings, but his brain felt like mush.

*The others.* He had no idea if they'd made it off the train before the crash. Had they seen the whole thing from the track or were they still onboard, cocooned inside somewhere?

A noise. Nicholas turned his head at a faint groan. It was coming from a little further into the wreckage. He shrugged out of his backpack and found that he'd handed out all his weapons and he'd lost his dagger in the crash. All that remained were the three collars humming softly at the bottom of the bag and Merlyn's good luck charm.

"Great lot of use you were."

Slipping the rucksack back on, he seized a warped metal strut from the floor and raised it before him like a baseball bat as he tramped through the wreckage. He realised he'd lost the fedora in the crash and searched for it as he went, but the groaning sound distracted him as it grew louder.

Nicholas reached down and flipped over a bench.

Sam lay pinned beneath a section of wall. Only his head and torso showed, and he was straining to lift the wall, but it was too heavy for him. The old man spotted Nicholas and his expression drew into a feeble entreaty.

"Lad, help me."

Nicholas grimaced. "Help yourself."

He turned his back on the Harvester, searching for a way out of the metal prison. Sam's voice raged pathetically behind him.

"You can't leave me here! What would your parents say!"

"They'd say you're the scum of the frickin' earth," Nicholas muttered, easing himself out of the train through a warped window. He found himself standing beside a five-foot cup of coffee. The sign had been severed from the shop's awning and it lay in a nest of bricks and mortar.

Gazing skyward, Nicholas glimpsed the cathedral-like iron ceiling of Liverpool Street Station. He'd been right; this was the train's final destination. The station had been destroyed when the locomotive ploughed into it. The floor had ruptured and, on the far side, the entrance to the underground had been blasted apart by the driver's carriage. Dust and smoke hung in the air.

"No bodies," Nicholas murmured. He couldn't see Isabel or any of the Sentinels lying amid the wreckage. Ignoring Sam's bitter screams, he staggered into the station, peering through the rents in the train's side but seeing nothing more than its broken innards.

"Where are they?" he whispered, before realising he was going the wrong way. He had left Dawn and Rae at the back of the train, not the front, and that was where Isabel and the others had been heading when he fought Sam. Cursing, Nicholas turned back on himself and stopped short when he spotted a figure easing itself over a pile of rubble.

It was Isabel. She was covered in ash and she no longer had her staff. Nicholas gasped as she faltered, nearly tumbling as she attempted to scale the debris, and he ran to help her.

"Boy," she uttered, taking his hand and stepping down to join him by the train.

"Are you okay?" he asked. "Where are the rest of–"

"What are you made of?" a voice asked. "Titanium?"

Kai appeared on top of the same mound Isabel had just scaled.

"You're alive," Nicholas said in surprise.

"You could sound happier about it."

Kai turned to help another figure over the rubble. One of the Sentinels they had freed stumbled as Kai helped him down and Nicholas caught him. He barely weighed anything. It seemed he'd used up the last of his strength escaping the train.

As Kai helped another Sentinel over the mound, Nicholas's heart began hammering anxiously.

"Where's Dawn? And Rae?" he asked.

He spotted a flicker of purple and Dawn appeared atop the mound. She was as grubby as everybody else, her face smeared with blood. She reached down to help somebody up, a crossbow slung over her back, and Nicholas watched as Aileen, her face white as chalk, heaved herself up. Something wasn't right with the way she moved.

"Here," Nicholas said, easing the young Sentinel over to Isabel. He scrabbled up to help Aileen and saw that her left leg was stiff with a makeshift splint.

"Broken, dear," the landlady winced, gripping his hand. "Could've been worse. Nale fitted the splint. Oh!" She slipped, and Nicholas caught her, helping her down into the station, finding that she was surprisingly light despite her doughy size. A dusty Pyraemon was still strapped to her back, appearing more disgruntled than ever.

"What about–" he began, but then Zeus bounded down to nuzzle his side, and the unmistakable shape of Nale bowled into view. The Hunter was bloodier than anybody else, his long hair lank with sweat and grease. He was carrying an unconscious Rae and, for a second,

Nicholas thought Nale had done something to her. Broken her neck, maybe. Then he remembered that she had passed out on the train and she was still out cold. It was a miracle she had survived the crash at all.

Dawn gave Nicholas a meaningful stare. "We couldn't have done it without him. He helped most of us jump off the back before the train crashed. We saw it happen."

"Trinity above, I can't believe you survived it," said Kai. Nicholas counted and realised five Sentinels hadn't made it, including the twins, Halle and Ryan. He wondered how long Kai had shared her cell with them. If she was cut up about losing them. He glanced at her, but Kai was busy taking in their surroundings.

"So I'm thinking we get the hell out of here ASAP," she said.

Nicholas nodded and squeezed Aileen. "Know of any safehouses around here?"

The ex-landlady's eyes were glassy with pain but she nodded, her forehead crinkling with the effort of concentrating on anything outside of how much her leg hurt. "Yes, dear. There's one not far," she said. Her voice was lighter than usual and Nicholas worried she'd pass out before they reached the safehouse. "I can get us there."

"Good. That's good."

He supported Aileen as Isabel led them through Liverpool Street Station. In a stroke of luck, the stairs leading to street level had survived the destruction. They climbed slowly. Nicholas glanced back to check Dawn was alright and saw that she was walking beside Nale, who was still carrying Rae. Though she seemed tired, her features were as fixed with determination as ever.

As they reached the street, three of the Sentinels went ahead to scout the area. Nicholas didn't know their names, but they looked less frail than the twins on the train had. Perhaps they hadn't been held captive for as long.

The street was quiet. It had been raining but the air remained thick with a rotten stench. Bins overflowed and the gutters were clogged. London was worse than Cambridge. Nicholas supposed the bigger the city, the quicker it fell apart when all the things that kept it going were removed. Half a dozen cranes saluted the churning sky. One had toppled over and crushed an entire street.

The three scouts returned.

"Clear," one of them gruffed; a middle-aged woman with startling yellow-green eyes.

The scouts fanned ahead again and they all followed, making their way down a narrow street.

"Never… never known it so quiet," huffed Aileen as they hobbled along. She was right. London was eerily desolate. Occasionally, Nicholas imagined he saw movement behind net curtains, but he couldn't be sure his mind wasn't playing tricks on him.

"Where's everybody gone?" he murmured. "Ten million people can't have just disappeared."

"Here," Aileen said suddenly. She pointed to a newsagent on a street corner and they all congregated before the corrugated barrier protecting the front door.

Nicholas knocked.

"It's abandoned," Dawn murmured unsurely, but then a rectangular window opened in the door and a pair of eyes blinked through at them.

"Yes?" a male voice asked.

Nicholas wasn't sure how you were supposed to gain entry to a newsagent safehouse. He was about to say something cryptic about ravens and the Trinity when Aileen hobbled forward, hissing through her teeth but not complaining.

"Did you hear the one about the vampire who walked into a bar?" she asked.

"No, why'd the vampire walk into a bar?"

"He thought it was the blood bank."

The eyes rolled and there came the clatter of locks being drawn back. A door opened in the corrugated barrier and Nicholas found himself staring up at a young man with enormous shoulders and a barrel chest.

"Quickly," the man urged, and Nicholas helped Aileen inside.

"That's how you get into a safehouse?" he murmured. The former landlady shrugged.

"The jokes get worse. Why'd you think my hair's white?" She let go of his hand and leaned against a shelf stacked with food. Although the newsagent had appeared abandoned on the outside, it was like any other inside. The newspapers had started to yellow but the fridges hummed and the condensation-speckled bottles made his mouth dry.

The door clanged shut and the man locked up. When he turned to greet them, Nicholas realised what a strange sight they must make. Eleven exhausted, mashed-up Sentinels, some delirious, at least one unconscious, many of them staring longingly at the shelves. And a three-legged dog and one-eyed cat.

"Hassan," the shopkeeper said, "but my friends call me Sunny."

"Sunny, I could kiss you," Kai said. "Figured all the safehouses round here were toast."

"Most are; the Harvesters got too good at sniffing them out. This place is only here because mum's good at glamours. Any Harvester wandering past sees a derelict building. Seems to work well enough."

"Almost too well," Nicholas said. "We thought it was abandoned, too."

Sunny chuckled and Nicholas realised he was handsome. His skin was walnut-coloured and he had a boyish face, his thick black hair messily styled in a quiff, his eyes surprisingly light and alert. His short-sleeved shirt and ironed jeans looked like they'd forgotten it was the apocalypse.

"We are most grateful for your hospitality," Isabel said.

Sunny nodded. "It is my honour, Miss Hallow."

"How'd you know...?" Dawn began.

The shopkeeper jangled his keys. "Well, I just figured..." He nodded at Nicholas. "Him and a woman giving off seriously old-school power vibes. Had to be the ones everybody's gabbing about. Just about every Sentinel to pass through here in the past month has talked about what happened in Bury. Some of them claim they were at the Abbey Gardens when it all went down with that witch. Said they saw this guy–" he gestured at Nicholas "–killing Harvesters with just a thought."

A chill skittered up Nicholas's spine. He'd never get used to being talked about. And he wished he really was as powerful as the Sentinels seemed to think. Killing Harvesters with a well-aimed thought was a trick he wished he had at his disposal.

Anxiously, he gestured at Rae, whose head rested on Nale's shoulder. "Is there somewhere she can rest?"

"Sure, sure, sorry. Been days since I saw anybody who wasn't my old mum. I love her but there's only so many times I can listen to her stories about meeting David Bowie. She swears he was a Sentinel but who knows?"

Sunny went to a vending machine in the corner. "Hey, help yourselves, too. No way I can get through the stock all by myself. Especially the Monster Munch. Never understood the appeal."

The Sentinels approached the shelves hesitantly at first, but their hunger quickly got the better of them and Nicholas saw one of them chewing on a chocolate bar with the wrapper still on.

Sunny punched a code into the vending machine, which rumbled momentarily before swinging open to reveal a narrow hallway. He beckoned for them to follow and Nale went first with Rae. Nicholas helped Aileen as Zeus clipped alongside them, and they came to a dazzling lounge dressed in purple and gold fabric. The bright smell of spice filled the air. Above the hearth hung a painting of two women and a man, who Nicholas realised were meant to be the Trinity, except their features looked Indian.

"Thank you, dear," sighed Aileen as she sank into the sofa. Her satchel emitted a strangled shriek and Pyraemon scrabbled out of it, shaking his head and then scratching his ear.

"No worries." Nicholas stretched, his backpack biting into his shoulders, but he wouldn't take it off until he needed the collars. He had to keep them safe. He watched as Pyraemon stretched and then squeezed himself onto the sofa beside Aileen.

"Neat," Kai said, coming into the lounge clutching a can and a packet of crisps. Isabel went to stand by the fireplace and Zeus circled the room, going from Dawn to Kai to Nale and back around again.

"Rooms are up here," Sunny said, pausing by a door.

"Lead the way," said Nicholas. He went to Aileen, who had been staring blankly at the painting of the Trinity. "Do you think you can make it upstairs?"

Dawn went to the woman's side. "Come on, Nan, I'll help you."

Guiding them up a flight of stairs after Sunny and Nale, Nicholas thought grimly of how much damage the train had actually caused. Rae was out cold, Aileen was half hobbled and, thanks to Diltraa and the run-in with Sam, Nicholas felt, at least mentally, a mess.

Determining to keep going no matter what, he helped Dawn get Aileen into one of the bedrooms. Together, they eased her into the pillows of a single bed and manoeuvred her injured leg under the blankets. Pyraemon jumped up and made himself comfortable at the foot of the bed.

"Thank you, my loves. I think I'll just catch my breath for a moment..." Aileen's eyes were already closed. Dawn stroked her arm and Nicholas was glad they had each other.

"Think she'll be alright?" he asked.

"I think she's down for the count." Dawn grabbed a couple of bottles of water from the bedside table and handed him one. "Whatever we do next, she's not coming with us. Which is sort of a good thing. She's too old for this sort of thing now."

"You can be the one to tell her that," Nicholas said.

"She already knows, she just wasn't ready to accept it."

Dawn leant down to kiss her grandmother's forehead, and then she and Nicholas stepped out onto the landing. "Are you okay? After..." She paused. "I mean, you know it wasn't Sam..."

The bottle made a noise as Nicholas's grip tightened around it. "I suppose so. I know it wasn't him, but the things he said, the way he talked..."

"That's how they get you."

"Yeah." He eased up on the bottle. "We have to find Merlyn. I can't... We can't lose anybody else."

Dawn brushed a lock of purple hair out of her face. "I know you don't want to hear this but what if he's already... you know?"

"No way of knowing that until we find him."

"Right."

He opened the bottle and downed the whole thing in one. Coolness flooded through him and he hadn't realised how dehydrated he was until he sucked every last drop of water out of the bottle.

"Where's Rae?" he asked. Nale had carried her up here but he didn't know which room she had been taken to.

"I think I saw–" Dawn began but Nicholas was filled with a sudden panic. In a second, he sensed Rae's energy and he chased her beacon to the end of the hall. Her usual crackling red sparks had simmered to a dull glow.

When he reached the door to her room, he froze. A figure was curled up on the bed and Nicholas knew it was Rae because he recognised her boots. Nale was towering over her, reaching down. Something in his hand caught the light.

Nicholas burst into the room. "What are you doing?"

The man cast bloodshot eyes at him and Nicholas saw red.

"Get away from her!" He threw himself at Nale, shoving him away from the bed.

"I– I–"

Nale protested but didn't resist, his voice a gravely cough, and Nicholas continued to shove him, driving him across the room until the Hunter's back was against the wall.

"What were you doing? What were you going to do to her?"

"I– I–"

Rage seared Nicholas from the inside out, as if a hot poker had been buried in his gut. He stared up at Nale, not seeing his size, only seeing the Trinity, their throats spraying blood, and then Nale looming over Rae, his hand outstretched.

"What are you still doing here? With us?" Nicholas's voice didn't sound like his own. "You don't belong here. You lost the right to that the night you killed them!"

Nale's mouth opened and closed without emitting any sound, and his drawn expression only made Nicholas madder. He wanted to pummel him. Break him. Tear him limb from limb.

"You're nothing!" Nicholas spat, and it felt so good to let it out, to spit venom the way he used to. "You're less than nothing! You are the viscus slime that feeds a young elkling!"

"Nicholas–"

Nale's voice inflamed the rage roiling inside and Nicholas gnashed his teeth, feeling every sinew in his muscles as if for the first time. He watched the vein in Nale's temple ticking and hunger twisted his gut at the thought of blood.

"I should end it here, end your misery," he hissed, and Nale's eyes were bulging now. Fear. It was intoxicating. It fluttered there, teasing him, and Nicholas wanted to eat the fear like a sticky pudding. Devour it whole.

"Your eyes," Nale gasped, but Nicholas didn't listen.

"Let meeee," he hissed, and he felt so hot. Hot with rage and desire. His hand was around Nale's throat and no matter how much the Hunter fought, Nicholas wouldn't release him. "Let me see what a traitor looks like from the inside."

"Nicholas!"

Dawn's voice snapped something in Nicholas's mind. He saw his fist at Nale's throat and the terror in the Hunter's face. The man felt suddenly heavy and Nicholas released him with a gasp, staggering backwards, finding a sink in the corner of the room and leaning against it.

"Nicholas, your eyes..." Dawn said. "Your eyes were *white*. What happened?"

He felt like he was going to throw up. He could still feel Diltraa moving around inside him. Slithering in the spaces between molecules, desperate to get hold of his body. The demon was so persuasive. It wanted so little. Just freedom.

"I don't know," Nicholas choked, and even now his voice didn't sound right. His eyes had been white? Like the demon's. Diltraa was taking advantage of his exhaustion. He peered into the mirror above the sink, searching his reflection, but his eyes were normal. Dark shadows were etched beneath them and he looked fit to drop, but there was no demon showing. No horns. No fangs.

No. It wasn't the demon who had forced his hand. Nale had been up to something. He'd seen it with his own eyes before the demon had taken hold. Unsteadily, Nicholas turned to point at the Hunter.

"He was doing something to Rae."

Dawn's bemused gaze passed between them.

"Nale?" she asked.

Shaking, Nale raised his hand. Silver caught the light and in Nicholas's mind he saw a weapon, something sharp and meant to draw blood, but then he squinted closer and the object came into focus.

Not a weapon, but a silver necklace.

A raven pendant winked in the space below Nale's hand.

"Thought it might help," the Hunter said.

"No, he was doing something, he was trying to hurt her!"

Nicholas cried out as pain tore through his chest. It felt like something was attempting to burrow out of him. His legs gave way and he grasped the carpet in his fists, unable to catch his breath.

"Nicholas!" Dawn was beside him. "What's happening? Let me help you!"

He couldn't see anymore. Blackness clouded his vision and a hot breath fell on his neck.

*"They're all afraid of you."*

Nicholas trembled. The voice had hissed in his ear so softly he almost thought he'd imagined it.

*"You'll never be able to do it. You'll kill everybody trying. Better to just let go."*

"Stop it," Nicholas grunted through gritted teeth.

In the blackness, a shape began to form. Clay-coloured skin stretched over sharp bones and a hairless head. Horns twisted up from a warped skull and in the crevices of a gaunt face, white eyes blazed like fire. Diltraa was there, in Nicholas's head, confronting him in the landscape of his mind.

*"Easier to slip into the abyss, young one,"* the demon rasped, its metallic teeth flashing. *"Relinquish control. It is too much for one human to bear. Release me and I shall spare the ones you love."*

Nicholas's hands were in his hair. His nails dug into his scalp and he beat his palm against his forehead.

"Stop it, stop it!"

*"You are harming only yourself–"*

"STOP IT!" Nicholas yelled.

*"SURRENDER!"*

Nicholas was cowering in the darkness and Diltraa reared up to stand over him.

"Nicholas." Dawn's voice sounded so far away. "Nicholas, what's happening?"

*"Surrender or I shall carve the flesh from your bones where you stand."*

"You can't have me," Nicholas grunted, but he felt so weak. The demon's hooves beat the floor before him.

*"I shall carve away your flesh and take possession of your rancid corpse!"*

Nicholas was clenching his jaw so hard he was sure it would split apart. Waves of nausea slapped him, and he fought to push Diltraa down the way he had done countless times, but something was different. He hadn't slept in days. He couldn't fight the demon. He was too weak.

Weak.

Weakness.

*"Feeling is your power,"* Jessica had said.

For so long, Nicholas had fought with emotion, both his own and the emotions of the people around him. At times it was overpowering.

Nicholas caught his breath, stifling a pained sob. Maybe that was it. He knew he couldn't fight the demon. He had to embrace it. Perhaps that was what Jessica had meant. He had to embrace the dark if he wanted to save the light.

Taking a deep breath, Nicholas lowered his arms and stared straight up into Diltraa's twisted face.

"You want me?" Nicholas said. "You can have me. All of me."

He opened his mind to everything he had ever felt, filling the black space with every pain, every joy, every disappointment. He saw them as bright colours that lashed onto Diltraa's limbs like chains, and the demon howled, struggling against the restraints but unable to break them.

As the demon thrashed and screamed, it became bathed in a white light that obliterated everything. Nicholas felt Diltraa's hold on him evaporating and the blinding light filled his vision.

*"The train has been destroyed, your eminence."*

*She stands by the carriage, her curls like viper-tongues of fire.*

*"Good."*

*And suddenly there.*

*There it is.*

*An image of her destination.*

*A bright, shining spire. A glass spear in the dark.*

Retching, Nicholas emerged from the vision. His face was squashed into the carpet. He'd collapsed. For a moment, he had no idea where he was or what he'd seen. As he heaved himself up, though, he found himself staring into Dawn's face.

He was back in Rae's room.

"Is it you?" Dawn asked.

At first, he didn't know. He checked his arms and his hair, and he felt like himself. He turned inward, scanning his mindscape. The demon wasn't gone. He felt grains of Diltraa's power lodged into every corner of him, but Nicholas had defeated it. He had absorbed Diltraa into his very being.

"It's me," he panted. As the confusion of what had just happened settled, he remembered what he'd seen when he overpowered Diltraa and he laughed incredulously.

"I know where she is," he breathed. "I know where Malika is."

# CHAPTER SEVENTEEN
## UNVISIBILITY

BACK IN THE LOUNGE, THEY FOUND Isabel pacing. Or at least attempting to. She hobbled back and forth over the rug, Zeus watching her as she went, and Nicholas winced at the sight. She must have injured something jumping from the train and, without her staff, she appeared as stiff as a newly awoken mummy.

"You're making me dizzy," Kai drawled from the sofa.

Isabel ignored her, but she stopped pacing when she saw that Nicholas and Dawn had returned.

"Malika may have been absent from our train," she said, "but that doesn't mean she is no longer relocating to London."

"You're right," Nicholas replied, catching Nale giving him a wary glance as he joined them in the lounge. As Zeus hopped to attention, going to Nale's side, Nicholas refocussed on Isabel. "In fact, I know exactly where she's going."

Isabel threw him a quizzical stare and as much as Nicholas wanted to enjoy forcing her to ask, he couldn't hold it in any longer.

"Turns out I have a direct line to her gutter-worm of a brain."

Isabel's frown hovered between annoyance and intrigue. "Boy, you know how I feel about riddles."

"The… The you-know-what in my head. It's a conduit. They're connected, which means *I'm* connected. And I've seen exactly where she's headed."

It was so obvious he should kick himself for not thinking it before.

"The Shard," he said breathlessly. "She's going to take over the Shard."

The old woman's expression was blank and Nicholas realised she wouldn't have any idea what the Shard was.

"It's a skyscraper… A—" he looked to Dawn for help.

"A big building, like a tower," she said.

"It is a spire?" Isabel asked. "One of some significance?"

"Yeah… but no. It's huge. You can see it from basically everywhere in London. It sort of looks like… I mean, it could've come out of a comic book or something. And it looks like a massive weapon."

He could tell Isabel was struggling to imagine such a thing, but her head dipped in agreement anyway.

Kai yawned loudly. "Sorry. It's great that we've uncovered Evil HQ and all but… long day. Train crash. Carb-y overload courtesy of our fine host…"

"Perhaps it is better we talk in private," Isabel said.

Nicholas's gaze moved from one tired face to another and finally settled on Sunny as the young shop owner came back down the stairs. "We could do with a few hours. Do you have enough room for everybody?"

Sunny laughed, then coughed. "Sorry. If you'd seen all the rooms upstairs you'd find that funny, too." He beckoned the Sentinels. "I'll show you where you can sleep."

"I for one could do with some zeds," Kai said, stretching like a cat as she got to her feet. "Can't remember the last time I slept in a bed. Night, Nick. Or is it morning? I can't remember."

"Night, but not for much longer." As Kai traipsed up the stairs, he turned to Dawn. "You should rest, too."

"Promise you'll do the same," she said.

"I promise I'll think about it."

"I'm serious."

"I can tell by the eyebrow. You only raise that thing when you want to argue. Actually, do you still have your laptop?"

Dawn nodded.

"Can I borrow it? Just for tonight? I need to look some stuff up, assuming I can get online."

By the time Dawn had brought him the computer and then gone to bed, Nale and Zeus had slipped out through a back exit to patrol.

Nicholas found himself alone in the colourful lounge with Isabel. He sank wearily into the sofa. Even though he was still wearing his backpack, the cushions were so comfortable they made him lightheaded, but he knew that if he fell asleep now he wouldn't wake up again for a month.

"So we're assuming Malika's still taking over London," he said. "Will you please stop pacing? You're going to wear out a hip."

Isabel stiffened but then relented. Perhaps she realised it was futile putting on a front with a Sensitive. She lowered herself into an armchair and closed her eyes.

"Yes," she said. "Malika will take London. It is the capital, the seat of power in the south, a mark of status. She will want it more than anywhere else, if only to prove her dominance."

"But we have no idea what she has planned. And how do the Prophets fit into all this? They've not been spotted anywhere."

Isabel's eyes drew open, hovering on the painting of the Trinity. "They have been mustering their strength. They were newborns not a month ago. This poison that has been spreading through the country is their doing, and as they grow in strength, so shall the world wither."

"Unless I can get the impetu-thing right."

*Impetuverta*, he reminded himself, repeating the name of the incantation. He tried to remember how it went. It was only short. He should be able to memorise it.

The old woman nodded. "Yes. I believe that may be our only option."

Nicholas's thoughts wheeled through what he knew about London, where Malika might strike. The Houses of Parliament? That was the most powerful place in London, or had been before it was abandoned. The Tower of London had a certain medieval poetry to it. Neither of those felt right, though.

As an HQ, the Shard would inspire terror, plus provide somewhere to lodge her army and incarcerate the Sentinels they'd taken captive. His gut twinged at the thought that Malika was keeping prisoners. She wasn't killing them all on sight, which meant Merlyn could still be alive. He clung to that thread of hope. It was the only thing keeping him going.

"Every time something happens, I think I must report it to Jessica," Isabel murmured.

Nicholas nodded slowly. That's how he felt about everybody he loved. In the months since Anita and Max died, the mornings were the worst. He'd enjoy a brief moment of not-remembering before he woke up enough for it to all come crashing back down again.

"It can seem so futile," Isabel continued, picking at her bracelets. "Five-hundred years she waited, and it took only a moment for her to be snuffed out."

"But we have a chance to make things better."

"We have held the Prophets at bay for so long. This could be the moment the chord snaps. Chaos is always just an angry word away."

"I think you need sleep more than any of us," Nicholas said.

"I am quite capable of deciding that for myself," Isabel snapped. Then she winced and put a hand to her side. Nicholas pried himself from the sofa and went to her.

"You're hurt."

"I'm—"

"Let me see."

He moved her hand out of the way and drew back a layer of fabric. The layer beneath it was stained red just below her ribs.

"Does it hurt?" he asked.

"No."

"That means yes."

Isabel sucked in her bottom lip.

"I'll see if I can find something to clean it up," he said, looking around the lounge.

"We have a first aid kit in the kitchen."

Nicholas straightened in surprise. A woman was sitting in the chair in the corner. He hadn't heard her come in, but somehow he knew she'd been sitting there ever since they had arrived. He just hadn't noticed her until now.

"I—" he began. "You weren't there before. Or, you were, but..."

"Sometimes the only way to convince people to leave you alone is to not exist for a bit," the woman said. She was in her sixties and painfully thin, although Nicholas could tell she had been beautiful once. Her resemblance to Sunny suggested this was his mother.

"Glamour," Isabel grunted.

"Neat. You can make yourself invisible."

"Not invisible," the woman corrected him. "*Un*visible."

"What's the difference?" he asked.

"You simply have to make yourself unremarkable in comparison to everything else in the room," the woman explained.

"A parlour trick," Isabel said with a hint of scorn, although Nicholas could tell she was impressed. She winced again and he remembered her wound.

"Sorry, did you say something about a first aid kit?"

"Kitchen. Through that door."

"Thanks." He found the kitchen quickly and checked under the sink, spotting the green first aid box. He grabbed it and went back into the lounge.

"Hey, where'd Sunny's mum go?" he asked, squinting at the chair in the corner. His attention kept getting drawn elsewhere. He couldn't tell if Sunny's mother was still with them.

"I believe she tired of my company." Isabel's face was more ashen than ever and Nicholas shook his head, forgetting Sunny's mum and hurrying over to Isabel.

"Here."

He knelt by her chair. He popped open the first aid kit, his hands trembling. He still couldn't believe he had an inside line on Malika. The advantage had finally swung into his court. If he could exploit Diltraa's link with her again, he should be able to get into the Shard undetected and stay one step ahead of Malika for once.

"It is only a shallow cut." Isabel hissed through her teeth as he dabbed the wound with antiseptic. "My, that smarts."

"I'm being as gentle as I can."

"I know. In my time, it would have been leeches. Not entirely unpleasant but they look rather stupid when they fall off fat and dozy."

He felt her eyes on him as he cleaned the wound and began going through the bandages, searching for the right size.

"This thing inside you, it is the reason you saw her plan," Isabel said.

"Mhmm."

"And it offered the information willingly?"

Nicholas fixed a bandage in place with medical tape. "Not exactly.

I sort of… It's hard to explain. I stopped fighting it, kind of accepted it as part of me, and that meant I could access everything it had on offer."

"This is dangerous ground. Perhaps unprecedented."

"Hey, I've always thought of myself as a pioneer. There, that should stop you leaking."

"I do not like it."

He shrugged. "Merlyn's better at bandages than me."

Isabel pressed her lips together. "You know that is not what I meant."

Nicholas rocked back on his heels and snapped shut the first aid box. He peered up into Isabel's face. He could swear it was changing by the day. Becoming less like the old headmistress and more like her old self.

"Whatever it takes, right?" he said. "It can't control me anymore. It's tried. It's weak, though. This is my body and I'm not giving it up, especially to the thing that tried to kill us all just a few months ago."

The woman's eyes sparkled at him and he went to draw her clothes back over the bandages, but Isabel caught his hand. She held on firmly and he met her gaze in surprise.

"We have so little time," she said softly. "The years pass so swiftly. You won't waste them, will you?"

He wasn't sure he liked the way she was talking.

"Course not. When we're on the other side of this, I'll introduce you to all the things you missed while you were dead."

"That would be agreeable."

"I'll schedule nap times and everything."

She squeezed his hand. "I'm your great, great, great great-grandmother twice removed and aye-aye-aye. Just don't forget that."

They stared at each other for a few seconds and then Nicholas heard footsteps behind him. He turned to see Sunny reentering the lounge.

"That's everybody set up for the night, or what's left of it," he said. He ran a hand through his black hair, which was starting to stick up at odd angles. He must have had the busiest night in months. "There are beds for you both, too, if you want them."

"Thank you, Hassan," Isabel said, fixing her clothing. "I am quite comfortable here."

"Me too," Nicholas said, slipping onto the sofa. "Nale's not back from patrol yet. I'll wait up for them. The back exit's secure, right?"

Sunny nodded. "No way in or out without a key. Which Nale has. I figured if you trust him I'd trust him."

Nicholas didn't say anything.

"I'll turn in for a few hours," added Sunny. "If there's anything I can get you first?"

Nicholas sat up. "Actually, do you have a map?"

"Uh, I think we have." Sunny went to a bookcase and took down a slim volume. "It's an *A-Z of London*. Does that work?"

"Perfect. Thanks."

Nicholas took the book from him and Sunny smiled, extending his hand, but not towards Nicholas.

"Come on, mum."

Nicholas stiffened with surprise as Sunny's mother got up from the sofa. She had been sitting right next to him and he hadn't noticed.

"Night all," Sunny said, putting his arm around his mother as they went through the door and up the stairs.

"How the hell does she do that?" Nicholas shook himself and glanced at Isabel. Her eyes were closed, her breathing shallow. He turned his attention to the *A-Z of London*, finding Liverpool Street Station and the road he was sure the safehouse was on. He traced a line down Gracechurch Street, past Monument, over the river and London Bridge to the Shard. It couldn't be much more than a mile. No wonder Malika had picked Liverpool Street.

His eyelids began to scratch, and Nicholas rubbed his face, the drowsiness weighing down his limbs. His weak arm twinged and he blinked at the map, then he got up and went into the kitchen. The fridge hummed and the light had been left on over the stove, no doubt for any Sentinel hunting for a midnight snack.

Standing by the sink, Nicholas took a few deep breaths and closed his eyes.

"*Esus,*" he whispered. With the last of his energy, he thrust his mind into the ether, searching for the Trinity's emissary, trusting that Esus would hear him.

The air in the kitchen quavered, as if a stone had been cast into a pool, and Nicholas opened his eyes. The stove light flickered and buzzed, and then reflected in a silver mask. Esus stood by the fridge, his black robe rippling about him like smoke.

"You are still alive."

"Don't sound too happy about it."

Esus hissed and Nicholas wasn't sure if that was the phantom's version of a laugh.

"The demon has yet to break you."

"We bonded. I sang it a few Kumbayas. Took it for dinner and a show. Putty in my hands."

The phantom's irritation lashed in a wave across the tiled floor but it no longer had any effect on Nicholas. He sighed.

"Look, it's been a long day, can we just talk?"

"You have news?"

Nicholas put his arms wide. "Can you tell where we are?"

The silver mask moved almost imperceptibly, though it could have been a trick of the light.

"London."

"Capital of England and Malika's new favourite holiday destination." Nicholas smiled. "She's going to take the Shard. Or try, at least. Tomorrow, we're going to stop her and the Prophets. For good."

"We?"

"So far, everybody in the safehouse. All twelve of the able-bodied ones, anyway. But we need help. We can't do it alone."

"I shall rouse allies in every quarter."

"I was hoping you'd say that."

The phantom stood so still it could be sleeping. Nicholas remembered glimpsing what lay under the mask and pushed the image from his mind.

"That is all?" Esus asked.

Nicholas shook his head, chewing the inside of his cheek as he tried to put into words something he'd been wondering ever since Hallow House fell.

"Did you know all along?" he asked. "What Jessica did to the Trinity? Who Malika is? Their connection?"

No reply.

"I'll take that as a yes." Nicholas's laugh was humourless. "I don't get it. Sentinels and secrets; they never learn, do they?"

"Knowledge can be used to ill ends by men hungry for power."

"And lack of it can create a great big mess like the one we're currently in."

"You believe you know everything–"

"I don't." Nicholas stared the phantom down. "That's the difference. I know there are things I don't know, and I'll admit it to anyone. Secrets are for people desperately clutching at power."

"Do not overstep your bounds, child," Esus growled.

"Oh, now I'm a child again? Funny, it seems like people only call me that when they want to make me feel stupid or insignificant." He straightened. "I'm discovering I'm neither."

Nothing. No movement from the phantom; not even a lash of angry energy. They stood glaring at each other and Nicholas realised he wasn't scared of Esus anymore. The Trinity's emissary had nothing on him. He wasn't the boy Esus had scoffed at just a few months ago. Esus had been twisted by the demon inside. Nicholas had overpowered the demon in him. He was stronger. He'd made the demon into an ally.

"Rouse the ranks," Nicholas said. "We're taking the Shard tomorrow at midday. If we're lucky, we'll survive. If not, well, you'll have an even bigger mess to clean up."

The phantom's head dipped and Nicholas realised Esus was bowing. He almost clapped with delight but instead he gritted his teeth and watched as the phantom decorporealised, becoming black smoke and then disappearing altogether. The stove light flickered and went out.

The sound of the back door creaking caused Nicholas to jump, but he composed himself when he saw it was just Nale returning from patrol. The Hunter stopped short at the sight of Nicholas in the dark kitchen and Zeus went to lap noisily from a bowl of water.

"Anything?" Nicholas asked.

Nale placed a chain of keys on the side.

"Demons everywhere."

Nicholas nodded. He considered Nale, sensing the man's thoughts as a black, nettling sprawl of branches. They were so confused and hardened, coated in shame and guilt. At first Nicholas was surprised he could sense anything from Nale, but then he realised Nale had lowered his defences. They weren't raised the way they had been for the past months and realising that intensified Nicholas's own guilt.

"I'm sorry," he said. "About what happened earlier. And for the way I've treated you since the well."

The shadowy crevices of the Hunter's face lifted in surprise.

"You don't have to apologise," Nale gruffed.

"I do. Because this thing you've been carrying around, it's not your fault. You did what you had to."

"Always a choice," said Nale, but Nicholas wasn't going to join the Hunter's pity party. Not this time.

"Normally I'd agree, but sometimes that's not true. You were asked to do something horrific by somebody you trusted. You couldn't say no. Sometimes terrible things happen and you have to make terrible choices. I get that."

Nale raised his eyes to meet Nicholas's and he saw that they were shining with emotion.

"We need you, Nale. What you did... what Jessica made you do. We can undo it. We can fix everything. But we need you."

Zeus nuzzled Nale's hand and yawned. The Hunter nodded and petted the dog.

"Now get some rest," Nicholas said. "It's a big day tomorrow."

Nale nodded again and went past him into the house. Nicholas released a slow breath and returned to the lounge, slumping into the sofa, the collars in his backpack digging into his spine. Isabel snored softly in her armchair and he watched her for a while, wondering if she was dreaming of Jessica, or perhaps of catching mice.

He opened Dawn's laptop and settled in to research mode. He searched for the words 'Dark Prophets' and 'true names', but half the pages didn't load. The internet had gone screwy since Ginnungap began. And the ones that did had nothing about the Dark Prophets or their possible names. Some crackpots had written blogs about demons and how their true names could be used to summon and control them, but there was nothing about the Prophets.

Frustrated, he dumped the laptop on the coffee table and took up the *A-Z* once more, slumping back on the sofa.

Flipping wearily through the pages, he attempted to memorise the names of the streets they'd use to get to the Shard. He found himself walking the lines, following a dotted path, imagining what the Monument looked like, and then seeing the River Thames, its surface solid with bodies, and although they were fish-pale, they weren't dead, but reaching for him, pinching his exhausted limbs as they dragged him underwater.

★

*Clack clack-a-clack. Clack clack-a-clack.*

"You always loved trains, you know that?"

Anita smiled at him, her brown hair tied back from her face, and surprise pinned Nicholas to his seat. His sister sat opposite him and, beside her, Max dealt cards onto the table. The rest of the train carriage was empty. It rocked around them as if trying to lull them to sleep.

"I don't think I like them as much anymore," Nicholas said, and Max snorted with laughter.

They were dressed the way they'd been that morning. He remembered Anita's lingering hug, and the way she'd stared at him out the cab's back window. Like she'd never see him again. But here she was, as if no time had passed.

"You've been on quite a journey," she said.

"You, too."

Outside the window, the sky was pink and orange, the countryside rippling with blue flowers.

"I wish we'd been able to tell you," Anita said. "That we're not your real parents."

"You are," he said. "You were."

"It was just too difficult, and you were so young. I spent so many years afraid." She bit her lip. "But look at you now. All grown up and so strong. I want so much to be with you."

He ran a hand over his hair, feeling velvet-y stubble instead of curls, and he was wearing his demon-hunting armour. He was himself now, not the Nicholas of a few months ago.

"You are with me," he said, and he wanted to say so much more, but he couldn't find the right words. Something caught the corner of his eye and he saw a black cat perched on the table over the aisle.

"You haven't met Isabel," he told Anita.

His sister reached across the table and clasped his hand, but it felt cold. Nicholas looked down and a spasm of horror shot up from the pit of his stomach.

He was gripping hold of skeletal fingers.

Not his sister's.

Something else's.

He looked up and found himself staring into a grinning skull. Purple fire blazed in hollow eye sockets and he knew instinctively who this was. *What* it was. A Dark Prophet. A thing of nightmare and fear made flesh. The sight turned his guts to jelly.

A rustling voice hissed in his head as, outside the window, the countryside blazed with vermillion fire.

***"Nicholassssss…"***

An overpowering urge to run stole through him and the more he stared at the grinning skull the less he could remember about life and hope. Then the train was spinning, hurling him at the ceiling, and Anita was screaming, Max's deck of cards fluttering in the air—

"Nicholas!"

He sat up with a start, still seeing bones and purple eyes. He barely registered that he was still in Sunny's lounge. He'd felt the Prophets and their presence lingered like a foul smell. They were so strong. It was as if they'd turned him inside out and smeared his innards across a wall.

"They're close," he panted.

"Still having funky dreams."

Through the grogginess, he realised somebody was leaning over him, gripping his arm. "Rae," he exclaimed, and her mouth twisted into her version of a smile. Without thinking, he hugged her. She smelled of soot and oil, but she seemed to be in one piece and her energy was spitting red sparks again.

"Good sleep?" he asked when she squirmed free.

"Weird dreams. Fire and bones and stuff."

Nicholas ran a hand through his bristly hair. "Yeah, me too. They're getting stronger. The Prophets. I can feel them." It was true. The oppressive air of the streets now seemed to be everywhere, even in this room, somehow in him, seeking out fissures to wriggle into. Currents of dread wove around him and he knew it was more than his own anxiety about what was to come. The Prophets were infecting everything with foreboding. They must be about ready to hatch.

Peering past Rae, Nicholas saw that Zeus had flopped by Isabel's feet. Nale and Dawn were standing by the stairs and, through a door, he saw Sunny in the kitchen loading up a tray with mugs. Sombre light was poking through the curtains. He wasn't sure how long he'd slept, but he didn't feel any better for it. Quite the opposite, because today was the day the world would change, one way or another. He winced at the straps of his backpack gnawing at his shoulders. He fought the urge to shrug it off. If the collars were digging into him, at least he knew they were safe.

"So what's the plan?" Dawn asked.

Nicholas pulled himself together, massaging his arm. "We should wake the others first. Get everybody on the same page."

"I'll go," Nale said, catching Nicholas's eye before he went for the stairs. Nicholas felt a small sense of satisfaction that, even during Ginnungap, he'd done some good. His chat with Nale had already had an impact on the Hunter, whose posture seemed less hunched than usual as he disappeared up the stairs.

Sunny handed out tea and toast and although nobody seemed to have much of an appetite, Nicholas forced them all to eat something.

"An army marches on its stomach," he said, and Dawn groaned at the cliché.

"Sounds painful."

As she nibbled a piece of toast and Rae fed hers to Zeus, Nicholas checked Isabel's wound.

"Stop fussing," she said, but he could tell she appreciated his concern.

"Looks okay, as far as I can tell," he said.

"It shall not prevent me from battling the hell-witch."

Nicholas pressed his lips together to prevent himself from arguing. Isabel would never agree to sit out the battle of the century. Besides, she was handy with enchantments. Hopefully she could avoid any physical combat by relying on her nimbleness with magic.

He turned at the sound of footsteps on the stairs. Nale led a bleary-eyed trail of Sentinels into the lounge. Kai's hair resembled a bird's nest and she yawned loudly as she stretched and then propped herself up against the wall. Nicholas noticed Aileen was missing. She must still be recuperating in bed.

Sunny sat next to Dawn on the sofa and Nicholas couldn't tell if his mum was with them. He supposed it didn't really matter and so he got to his feet, going to stand in front of the painting of the Hindu Trinity. Nale loomed at the back and Nicholas could swear the Hunter appeared less haggard. Perhaps he had slept.

"I suppose that's everyone," Nicholas said, surveying the makeshift army. "So, this is where we're at. Malika and her forces are taking over the Shard, which means that's where we're taking them down, Prophets and all."

"How do you know that?" Rae asked.

Nicholas tapped his temple. "I see bad people."

"Whoop-de-doo for you," said Kai.

"Esus is summoning every Sentinel he can, but we can't count on them arriving in time. Basically, it's on us to do this." He glanced from face to face. "At midday, we're breaking into the Shard."

"Why midday?" Dawn asked.

"Same reason we never went out at night in Cambridge. The really bad nasties seem to snooze through the daytime. Safer for us."

"What are her numbers like?" asked a Sentinel Nicholas recognised from the train.

"Your guess is as good as mine, but I'll say lots," he replied. "At least fifty times the people in this room; more, in all likelihood. And she has the Prophets and a pack of cross-dimensional demons at her disposal."

"I'm liking these odds," Kai deadpanned.

"I know," Nicholas said earnestly. "Look, this is nuts. I get that; you all get that. It's nuts but it's all we've got. If Malika takes the Shard and consolidates a base, who knows what she'll do next. She could tear open the whole universe. Chaos is sort of her thing. All I know is that this is the last chance we'll get before the Prophets come into their full power."

Every face was solemn. Nicholas knew he was asking them to risk everything; their lives, their futures. They were Sentinels, though. That sort of came with the P60.

"You think you can stop them? The Prophets?" one of the Sentinels asked.

Nicholas met the speaker's eye and knew he had to be honest. "There's a chance I can, but there's also a chance I can't. I won't know until I'm in a room with them."

Nobody moved. Over a dozen eyes blinked at him and he waited for somebody to challenge him. To throw a fit. To remind him how ridiculous this all was. Nobody spoke, though, so he continued.

"Sunny's mum got me thinking. She can glamour, make herself unvisible."

"Invisible?" Kai asked. "Is she here now?"

"She's resting," Sunny said, though Nicholas had a feeling even he wasn't entirely sure of that.

"She has this gift and it's pretty impressive. She can redirect your attention away from her, essentially making herself invisible. That's what we'll have to do if we want to get into the Shard."

"A glamour?" Dawn asked. "Can anybody else here do that?"

Everybody shook their heads, including, begrudgingly, Isabel.

"I don't mean a literal glamour," Nicholas said. "What I mean is that for me and Rae to get into the Shard, we'll have to ensure Malika's army is looking elsewhere."

"Decoys," Dawn said.

"Exactly. We split into pairs and force Malika's army to scatter around the Shard. While they're busy, we'll sneak in."

Nobody said anything for a moment. Isabel had remained oddly silent throughout and Nicholas wondered if she was still thinking about Jessica.

"Why are only you and Rae breaking into the Shard?" Dawn asked.

"Because we're the ones who are meant to go up against the Prophets," Nicholas said.

"According to who?" Dawn asked. "Some fusty old prophecy? Since when do you–"

"Since the apocalypse."

Dawn shook her head. "You'll need help. I have Atticus Klove's book for the ceremony. Isabel's got her own sort of fire power."

"Isabel's going to lead one of the decoys," Nicholas said. Even if she wanted to fight Malika, he couldn't let her.

"Nonsense!" Isabel rose from the armchair.

"You can't take another hit," Nicholas told her. "This way you can help without getting caught up in the eye of the storm."

"Do not forget your place, boy. I will not take orders."

"If Miss Hallow wants to fight at the Shard, let her," one of the Sentinels said.

"No."

"I'm coming to the Shard," Dawn said, also standing.

"I say we take a vote," Kai suggested.

A number of voices rose, striving to talk over the next, and the room began to hum with tension. The air around Nicholas thickened and he felt woozy attempting to keep the Sentinels' emotions from flooding into every corner of his mind.

"Okay okay OKAY!"

His shout silenced the room. Or, more specifically, the fact that the floor had started to shake did. He gave Rae a grateful look and could have sworn her lip had tugged into a half-smile.

"What was that?" one of the Sentinels asked.

"That's about one millionth of what Rae's capable of," Nicholas said. He drew a breath. "Okay, look, it's great that everybody wants to hit ground zero, but this won't work without the decoys."

"I'll lead one." Nale's voice reverberated between the Sentinels.

Nicholas nodded gratefully. "Thanks."

"I'll lead another," Kai offered, crossing her arms. "I've got this itch that only killing Harvesters can scratch."

"Brutal, but good. Thanks."

"And when I'm done scratching," Kai added, "I'll come to the Shard for the big finish. There'll be fireworks, right?"

Nicholas grinned. "It'll make the fourth of July look like a ladybird's tea party."

"I'll lead another," said one of the Sentinels from the train.

"Thanks."

"So I'll be decoy four," Sunny said and Nicholas smiled, then glanced away because he could feel a blush creeping up his neck at Sunny's intense stare.

"That's four teams of two. Good," Nicholas said, going to the coffee table, upon which the map of London still rested. Zeus went over to sniff the map, and for a second it looked like the wolfhound was studying it for tips.

"This is the Shard," Nicholas said, bending down to mark it with the teapot. He slid a teacup to one side of the map. "That's London Bridge, Decoy One."

"Aw, come on," Kai drawled. "There's got to be a better name than that. I vote Team Hellraiser."

"Fine. Hellraiser. Decoy One. You're London Bridge." He moved another cup to one side. Zeus's wet snout followed it interestedly. "That's St Thomas's Hospital. Decoy Two."

"Mary Poppins!" Kai yelled.

"Fine, Mary Poppins. Decoy Two."

He distributed another cup and a teaspoon. Zeus barked. "They're Borough Market and Monument. Decoys Three and Four." Before Kai could say anything, he quickly added: "So that's the four spots. Kai, you can be Hellraiser. Nale takes Mary Poppins. Sunny gets Monument and, sorry, what's your name?" he asked the Sentinel from the train.

"Meg."

"Right. Meg, you're Borough Market." He peered around the room. "You divvy up team members amongst yourself, but for now, is everybody clear on which Decoy is which?"

"Affirmative," said one of the Sentinels, while the others nodded.

"Good." Nicholas stood. He felt like he should deliver some stirring words, but he wasn't sure he had any left, nor what the Sentinels needed to hear to get them in the fighting frame of mind.

Rae saved him the embarrassment.

"Let's just do this," she grunted.

"Right," he said. "So me, Rae, Dawn and Isabel will go first. We'll need a fifteen-minute head start or we'll never get past the decoy points once they're crawling with Harvesters, so give us a chance to clear them first."

"You got it boss," Sunny said.

"Next…" Nicholas murmured.

"Weapons?" Dawn suggested.

"Yeah. Sunny, you have any lying around?"

Sunny broke into a ridiculously handsome grin.

They spent the next hour in the basement sorting through the safehouse's impressive stock.

"Some are mine, some got left behind by Sentinels who had to leave in a hurry," Sunny explained, revealing rows of shelves stacked with weaponry. "Take whatever you need."

"Siiiiick!" Kai raised a sickle and ran a finger along the curved blade. "I'm going to look so badass with this."

"Yes," Nicholas said, "that's the goal."

"You know it, sister."

He caught Dawn giving Kai a guarded look and smiled as she went back to inspecting a modest dagger. Rae surveyed the stock with only passing interest. He supposed weapons weren't that exciting when you were a walking atomic bomb.

Towards the back of the basement, he heard a clomping sound and Isabel emerged from behind a shelf. She clasped a walking stick engraved with runes.

"That was my grandad's," Sunny said. "Hasn't been touched in years."

"Yet it possesses some of his power still." Isabel struck the floor and the runes glowed gold.

"I've never seen it do that," Sunny breathed.

Isabel raised an eyebrow and appeared pleased with herself. She seemed to have regained some of her old spark, but Nicholas hadn't liked the look of her wound. He wished he could find a way to convince her to hang back and tend to any survivors after the battle, but even imagining her reaction to such a suggestion made him wince.

Isabel left the basement and Nicholas continued to help the other Sentinels load up on weapons. Then he went to check on Aileen. The former landlady was in bed, clutching Dawn's hand. She dabbed her eyes.

"You have my crossbow, don't you dear?"

Dawn nodded. "Yes, Nan. Thanks."

"You take care of each other, you hear?"

"We will."

"And come back to me."

Dawn smiled sadly.

"We will," said Nicholas. "Just concentrate on resting up. Sunny's mum is around here somewhere. I'm sure she'll come if you yell."

"Never thought I'd miss a battle, especially one like this," murmured Aileen. "Perhaps if I just–" She heaved herself up off the pillows but gasped in pain when she tried to move her splinted leg. Pyraemon glared at her.

"Nan, please. Just... hold things together this end." Dawn helped Aileen get comfortable again. "Try not to worry."

Aileen touched Dawn's cheek. "Ask anything of me, dear, but don't ask that."

Dawn kissed her palm and stood. "Let's go."

"Trinity bless you all," said Aileen as they left.

It was mid-morning by the time they gathered in the unlit newsagent, loaded up with knives and bows and armour. Zeus skipped between the Sentinels excitedly, sniffing and wagging his tail.

Rae stood impatiently by the door. Having strapped on his and Dawn's battle armour, Nicholas trudged over to Rae, Dawn at his side. He turned to find Isabel right behind him. She seemed to be daring him to say something, so he simply gave her a blank look and addressed the shop.

"Everybody got their teams?"

Heads nodded and Nicholas felt their eagerness and anxiety. It beat in his chest, a dozen heartbeats all thudding alongside his.

"Good luck," he said. "Don't forget to give us fifteen minutes. And try not to... you know." He sniffed, unable to say the word 'die'. "Sunny, will you do the honours?" He stepped back to let Sunny unlock the door. Only a sheet of corrugated iron stood between them and the hell that had become London.

"Ready?" Sunny asked, gripping the side of the barrier.

"Ready."

Sunny drew the safety barrier back and Rae led the way out into the city.

# CHAPTER EIGHTEEN
## SPLINTER OF GLASS

THE STREETS WERE THICK WITH A worming humidity. The sky threatened a storm that would never break, and Nicholas's mouth dried up instantly. It was as if he'd sucked in a mouthful of sand. Soon, nothing would be able to survive the Prophets' poison.

He remembered the way the Faceless Man had infected Bury St Edmunds and shuddered. The same fate awaited London. It was being swallowed up by the Prophets, gestating in a hellish limbo that bred death. Where Bury had burned, though, the capital was simply crumbling. As he, Isabel, Rae, and Dawn made their way down Dukes Place, they were almost crushed by falling debris as high-rise buildings began to come apart.

"What's doing that?" Rae asked.

"The heat, maybe," Dawn offered. "The mortar's melting so nothing's holding the bricks together."

"It's hot?" Rae asked.

"You're joking, right?" Nicholas said. Rae gave him a blank look and he realised he'd never seen Rae break a sweat. She always looked cool as a cucumber. It must have something to do with her abilities.

"You get all the good stuff," he muttered, which she either didn't hear or chose to ignore.

Isabel appraised their surroundings, scrutinising the tall buildings with interest. "This city is a living thing and the Prophets are a virus. They're squirming into its every pore, undoing everything that can be undone."

"If they're doing that to buildings, what are they gonna do to us?" Rae said.

"Nothing," Nicholas said bluntly. "Don't think about it."

"Sort of hard not to."

"Think about how good it'll feel when we have their heads on pikes," he suggested.

"That helps."

They made their way down Vine Street, sticking to the pavement, even though there was no traffic and no people. Nicholas thought about pictures of Pompeii and middle-American towns that dried up with the oil. He never thought he'd be in a real-life version of the end of the world.

"Last I was in London, it was as a child," Isabel murmured, craning her neck to peer at the buildings around them. They passed a few abandoned construction sites and Nicholas stuck close by her, worried she was frailer than she was letting on.

"Which was, what? The 1500s."

"Actually, yes. It was my aunt's wedding. I never liked her; she was a silly heart, giggly and tiresome, and she never liked me because I wasn't. I spoiled her cake with salt and although I never admitted to it, she knew I was the culprit. I was glad she knew, old trout."

Nicholas smiled inwardly but he searched Isabel's face for any sign of delirium. She seemed as sharp as ever, if weary.

"Battle," Isabel said, as if she'd read his mind. He couldn't be entirely certain that she hadn't.

"What?"

"The onset of battle stirs things in the brain. I suppose the closer we are to death, the more we remember about our lives."

"Nobody's dying," Nicholas said.

"Of course they are. In all likelihood, I shall number among them. That's reality for you; you would do well to accept it."

"I propose a ban on talking until we're at the Shard," Nicholas said.

"Yes." Dawn threw him a dark look. "I want to hear the things that are going to kill us before they do it."

They fell into silence. Rae edged further ahead to ensure their path was clear. At one point, Isabel hefted her walking stick at the sky and a winged monster crashed to the ground. Nicholas hadn't sensed its presence. He had to focus. The air was so full of strange signals, though, he was having trouble separating them. He kept getting distracted by the dark energy pulsing through the streets. The Prophets were already here. He clenched his fist. What good was a Sensitive who couldn't sense anything?

As they approached Tower Bridge, the rest of the city melted away, because there it was. Across the River Thames, striking up from the ground like a great splinter of glass, was the Shard. All that lay between him and it was the bridge, a ribbon of water, and a few little streets.

The Shard mirrored the churning sky and green fire burned at its topmost point. Malika was already home.

"It's bigger than I remembered," Dawn murmured.

"Now I understand the witch's desire for this edifice," added Isabel, a mixture of admiration and unease etched into her face.

Rae's expression was vacant. Nicholas wondered if she'd ever seen the Shard before. There was still so little he knew about her. His gaze shifted from his bodyguard to Tower Bridge and the water below it. The Thames wasn't crammed with bodies the way he'd dreamed it, but it looked tortured enough without them. Mist hung over its surface and firefly-like sparks flashed in its depths. An acrid smell seared his nostrils and he realised Malika or the Prophets had done something to the water. Polluted it.

"The bridge looks clear," Rae said, her gaze set on the blue-and-white palatial structure that bridged the Thames. It almost resembled a country house in the middle of the bridge, complete with led-plated windows, its twin crown-like rooftops speaking of great wealth and opulence.

"Doesn't mean it is, though," Dawn added.

"Let's assume it isn't," Nicholas decided. "Stay close. Rae, try to keep the blasts contained. We don't want to spoil the surprise."

She nodded.

*And keep an eye on Isabel,* he thought at her.

Rae didn't show any sign that she'd heard him but, as they made their way down the road to the bridge, she moved closer to the old woman. Nicholas paced backwards, making sure nothing was following them, and then they were on the bridge, the towers high above them.

A hundred memories swirled in his mind. His parents bringing him here as a kid. And through the fog of memory, Nicholas sensed something. His gaze flew up at the tower windows.

"Rae—" he began but she'd seen it, too. A figure behind the glass. She gestured with a hand and he heard a yelp; then a shape toppled out of the window and plummeted to the bridge below. It crunched into the tarmac a few feet from them.

Clutching his dagger, Nicholas edged forward. The shape coughed and attempted to pry itself from the ground. It was a Harvester in a jacket bearing the Prophets' three-pointed insignia. The horn he'd been about to blow when Nicholas spotted him was still clutched in his hand and Nicholas stamped on the Harvesters fingers, kicking the horn out of reach.

Before he could set his dagger to work, though, the Harvester burst up from the ground and hurtled at him.

"Had to make it difficult," Nicholas grunted, attempting to seize the man's arms. The Harvester ducked and landed a blow to Nicholas's ribs, but the fall had broken him and he sagged against the side of the bridge, hacking up blood.

Nicholas grabbed the Harvester by the shoulder and prepared to strike, but something fiery barrelled into the Harvester's chest and he made a winded sound like he'd been punched. Rae had beat him to it.

The Harvester tumbled back over the side of the bridge and silently fell. Nicholas heard the splash and grimaced as he watched the Thames hiss and bubble around the Harvester, the putrified water eating him up until nothing remained.

"Not a pretty way to go," Dawn said, appearing at Nicholas's side.

"Uh, people…"

Rae's voice drew Nicholas's attention away from the water and he swore. They weren't alone on the bridge anymore. A wall of bodies blocked the way they'd come and more still spilled towards them from the other side, barring their way across. They had stopped the Harvester sounding his horn but that didn't seem to have made a bit of difference. The Prophets' army was made up of men and women and strange, ugly creatures with claws and luminous eyes.

"How many, you think?" he asked as he regrouped with Dawn, Rae, and Isabel at the centre of the road.

"Harvesters?" Dawn murmured. "Fifteen maybe. I don't know what that thing with six legs is, and there's maybe two monsters with spiky tails. I think they're called–"

"Spikpiggs," Isabel said.

The Harvesters Nicholas could handle, but the creatures always made the meagre contents of his stomach curdle. Half a dozen of them lumbered between the Harvesters, some little more than bone and saliva, others bristling with razor quills.

"Rae?" he said, eyeing Malika's forces as they closed in on either side.

"Do I still have to keep the blasts contained?" She gave him a pointed glare and, not waiting for an answer, strode purposefully back the way they'd come, rubbing her palms together so that the air shimmered with heat.

"Try, maybe," Nicholas yelled after her. Under his breath he added, "Or just try not to die."

Knowing she could handle herself, he stood between Isabel and Dawn, facing the remaining forces. He couldn't help scanning their faces for Merlyn, desperately hoping he wasn't among them. The fact that he wasn't provided little comfort.

"Do your worst," he said through gritted teeth and, as one, they charged. Isabel swept her stick in an arc and the Harvesters were all blasted off their feet. Nicholas fell on them and quickly slashed with the dagger, hearing a faint blast as Rae tackled the forces at their backs. Dawn grunted as she tussled with one of the Harvesters and Nicholas hurled a psychic grenade at her attacker, knocking him back, but something barrelled into Nicholas before he could make sure Dawn was alright.

His forehead cracked against the road and Nicholas rolled over as a shrieking creature threw its full weight on top of him. Unable to draw breath, he dodged the monster's elongated maw as it snapped at him and drove his dagger between what he hoped were its ribs.

Hot liquid gushed over his torso and the monster trembled and gibbered before going limp.

"Here." Isabel extended a hand and helped him up just as a scaly shape launched itself at them. The old woman caught the creature's skull with her walking stick and it crumpled as if the air had been sucked out of it.

"So much for quietly sneaking in," Nicholas muttered.

"Quickly," Isabel urged, "before more arrive."

Wiping his dagger on his trousers, Nicholas searched around for Rae and caught her strolling casually towards them, a steaming pile of bodies at her back. She still hadn't broken a sweat. He just hoped she didn't burn out the way she had on the train.

Picking their way hurriedly between the corpses, they crossed the bridge. Nicholas scanned the area with his mind and sensed more multi-legged things prowling along the waterside. For once, he was thankful for the sickly fog filling the streets; it gave them a tiny advantage.

"This way," he whispered, leading Isabel, Rae, and Dawn down a side street, away from the skulking creatures. If they took the path along the river, they would be at the Shard within minutes, but they had to conserve their energy for the fights they couldn't avoid.

"You feeling okay?" he asked Rae.

"Better than ever," she said, and he couldn't help noticing the way her eyes shone. She was enjoying being able to use her power, test its limits, see what sort of damage she could really do. But there was no anger there anymore. She wasn't destroying out of regret or resentment; she was doing it to protect her own.

"Dawn?" he asked.

"Fine," she said, pulling her hoodie up to cover her mouth and nose. The air really was disgusting.

Isabel merely nodded at him and he boomeranged his mind around the next corner, searching. Nothing came back so they turned and followed a cobbled street, hurrying past a row of ruined buildings.

Behind the rooftops above them, the Shard dipped in and out of view, looming larger with every passing moment. Nicholas had never been inside and he had no idea what to expect. He assumed Malika and the Prophets would be in the uppermost levels; all the better to survey their realm. But where would Merlyn and the other kidnapped Sentinels be?

Finally, they came to Weston Street. From here, they could see the street escalator that led into the Shard. As Nicholas had expected, it was heavily guarded by both Harvesters and scaly, red-eyed creatures that skulked on all fours. Their black talons clacked the pavement and their metallic fangs were grimy with blood.

"I've got this," said Rae, but Nicholas put out a hand.

"Wait," he said. "We wait for them to clear off."

"Clear off? They going for tea and scones sometime soon?"

"More like they're going to call on Mary Poppins and the Hellraisers."

"The decoys," said Dawn.

Rae looked unsure but she hung back with them as they hid out of sight in an archway that led to an overgrown mews. Nicholas had never met anybody so ready for a fight, except perhaps Merlyn. Fighting had never appealed to him, even before the apocalypse – he supposed that was why he was the Sensitive and Rae was the brawler. She paced the mews, while Isabel sank into a low doorstep, whispering into her walking stick and conserving her energy.

"Talk me through the impetu thing," Nicholas said to Dawn. Anything to keep his mind busy. The decoys would attack soon. Until then, all they could do was wait.

"Impetuverta," she said. "At least get the name right before you attempt to use it."

"Words were never my strong suit."

Dawn produced a piece of paper, which she unfolded to show him. She had copied the page from Atticus Klove's book.

"Tell me what I'm looking at," he said. "Rae, keep an eye on those guards."

"Yes, master."

"You know it's not like–" he began, but then he saw the amused glint in her eye and sighed, returning to the diagram.

"First you bless the ground, then the air–" said Dawn.

"Then do the Funky Chicken Dance?"

Dawn didn't laugh.

"Sorry. Just trying to make myself feel less like the idiot who's got to get this right."

When she seemed satisfied he was taking her seriously, Dawn returned to the paper. "So first you recite the blessings, then you take the objects belonging to the Trinity – the collars – and you call on them while reciting these words. Have you got them memorised yet?"

"*Vita gregaria* something-something. Wait, don't tell me." He pinched his forehead, annoyed. He was sure he had it down. "*Vita gregaria hemlock ressa vie.*"

Dawn nodded. "Then their names."

"Thekla. Athania. Norlath."

"In that order, too, presumably. That's how they appear in most books."

"And then?"

"If it's going to work, I assume the collars will glow or give some sign that they've been charged…" Dawn looked him dead in the eye. "Then we put them on the Prophets."

Nicholas released a breath. "Easy. Don't know why everybody's making such a big deal out of this."

"I believe—"

Dawn was cut off by the sound of an explosion. Nicholas felt it in his bones and the scent of burning wood filled the air. It was close.

"Borough Market," he said, rushing to Rae's side to peer through the archway. The street was full of smoke and it was thickest at the far end near the market.

*Look,* Rae said in his head and he turned to see armed figures spilling out of the Shard. He heard another explosion, this one further away.

*Kai,* he thought at Rae. *Or Nale. Or both.*

They shrank back as the Harvesters raced past their hiding place, some heading for the market, others fanning further afield. When the street had fallen quiet again, Nicholas turned to Isabel and Dawn.

"Now or never."

"Let us see how sturdy this glass tower really is," said Isabel, hefting the walking stick.

Returning to the archway, Nicholas scanned the area with his mind, sensing only the two Harvesters guarding the entrance to the Shard. He waved the others out and together they swept down the smoky road, Rae at his side. Funny how he felt safer when she was around.

*Me first,* Rae thought. *I'll keep it quiet.*

He nodded, and she paced toward the guards. The second they spotted her, they raised their weapons.

"Bye guys," said Rae. She slammed her fist to the ground, and the cement exploded beneath the Harvesters' feet. They flipped through the air and Rae threw a fiery blast of energy at them. Their charred bodies flopped lifelessly to the ground.

"Just… don't burn out," Nicholas told her, and she nodded before racing up the motionless escalator that led to the Shard's lobby.

As soon as she disappeared over the top, Nicholas heard muffled cries and heat blasted his face, even down here, but Rae kept her word. If he'd sneezed it would have been louder than her attack.

After a few seconds, she beckoned from the top of the escalator for them to join her. Nicholas sent Dawn and Isabel up first, keeping an eye on the street, then hurrying after them. When he reached the top of the escalator, he peered through the Shard's doors at the lobby, which was overgrown and filthy. Once, it must have gleamed, tended to meticulously by people who wanted to impress businessmen and touring royalty, but since the days of Ginnungap it had fallen into disrepair just like everything else.

And, just like everywhere else, the lobby was heavily guarded. Nicholas glimpsed Harvesters and creatures beyond, but Rae was undeterred. She took the double doors in her hands and looked at him and the others, making sure they were ready. Then she threw them open and hurtled inside, flicking her hands at anything that moved, hacking with living blades of fire and burning her attackers to a crisp.

Nicholas slammed the doors behind them and wound rope around the handles to slow down any returning Harvesters. He saw Dawn skid across the polished floor and loose a stream of arrows at the guards, while Isabel used her walking stick to pluck Harvesters from their feet and toss them against the walls.

Closing his eyes, Nicholas felt around for Diltraa's connection to Malika. In a flash, he saw her.

*Malika purrs as she caresses three glass coffins.*

*Inside each of them, something twitches and spasms in waking.*

Nicholas severed the connection, afraid she might sense him, and only just ducked in time to avoid a blade decapitating him. A bloodied Harvester lunged for him and Nicholas seized the figure's hand, searching with his mind for the Harvester's weakness. He snagged it like a thread, blinked, focussed, and the Harvester started screaming.

"Oh God! It burns! Make it stop!"

The Harvester staggered away, rolling on the ground as if attempting to quench invisible flames.

Nicholas surveyed the lobby. The floor was littered with dead things. His gaze snapped up just in time to see a shadow scuttle across the ceiling right above–

"RAE!"

The monster launched at her, flipping through the air and latching onto Rae's shoulders. Her legs went from under her. The creature resembled an enormous spider, except it was scaly and covered in barbs. It thrashed its slavering jaw at Rae's ear. She wrestled with it, managing to evade its fangs but grunting from the exertion.

Brandishing a curved dagger, Dawn raced forward, ready to plunge it into the beast's back but, at the same time, Rae thrust her hands into the creature's abdomen and the air rippled with heat. The monster exploded in a blast of fire and guts.

Caught in the discharge, Dawn flew sideways and collapsed in a heap. Grimacing, Nicholas smelled singed hair and, his heart pounding, he raced over to her, rolling Dawn onto her back. She was conscious but looked stunned, her eyes struggling to focus.

"Dawn. Dawn, can you hear me?"

She blinked, nodding, and then winced. Her right hand was black and the skin had peeled in red-raw patches.

Rae appeared beside them. "I'm– Oh shit, are you okay? I'm sorry."

"It's okay."

Nicholas helped her sit up and Dawn examined her hand.

"My backpack," he said, turning so Rae could rifle through it. As she pulled out bandages, he watched Isabel subdue a final Harvester by striking him with her stick. Rae bent down to carefully wrap up Dawn's injured hand. She winced again but remained silent.

"We must move," said Isabel, sniffing the air.

"Dawn, can you–?" Nicholas began.

"I'm fine." She got to her feet, ashen-faced and clearly in pain but her focus had returned. Together, the four of them crossed the ravaged lobby, the marble floor littered with bodies. At the far side, Nicholas hesitated by the elevators.

"Quicker than the stairs," he reasoned.

"And easier to detect," Dawn said.

"Or smash to pieces with us inside," added Rae.

The counter above the central elevator began to count down from forty. Back-up was on its way. They didn't have much time.

"It is a conveyor of some sort?" murmured Isabel, frowning at the row of elevators, and Nicholas rolled his eyes.

"Stairs it is," he said, leading them to a door beside the last elevator and pushing it open.

*Hang on, Merl*, he thought. *We're here. We're coming.*

Still helping Dawn, Nicholas, Rae, and Isabel bundled into the cool stairwell. As the door clanged shut behind them, Isabel touched her stick to it. *Click*. They were locked in. Even if a Harvester happened to have a key, the door wouldn't open any time soon.

Nicholas craned to look up. The grey breeze blocks seemed to pile on top of each other in a never-ending wall.

"We're inside," he panted.

The others looked at him, and he knew they were all thinking the same thing as him. *The easy part's over with.* Now that they were inside, they had to keep moving. Stay ahead of the enemy. Every part of him felt alive. Charged with adrenaline.

"How many floors to the top, you think?" asked Dawn.

"Probably better if we don't know," he grunted. "Let's count along the way."

They began to climb. Rae went first, her jaw set, and he could tell she was beating herself up about Dawn. Each time they passed a door, Nicholas felt for a presence. The first few floors were deserted save for food supplies and a few Harvesters, but they weren't worth taking on.

They continued up. Dawn released her hold on Nicholas, adamant that she was okay. Rae glanced back at them.

*It wasn't your fault,* he thought at her.

*Don't.*

*You don't.*

*You you don't.*

She was impossible sometimes.

At the sixth floor, Isabel had slowed down and her breath rasped in her throat. Rae hung back in a way that suggested she was watching their backs, and Nicholas was grateful she was still keeping an eye out for their eldest member. If she noticed, Isabel made no show of it.

The tenth floor felt different.

Hovering outside the door to the level, Nicholas surfed the vibrations of energy, sensing spikes of pain and misery. The emotions were dull colours; browns and greys that had forgotten that they could be purples and greens.

"What is it?" asked Dawn.

He frowned. "Something… I think we should check in here."

Isabel and Rae caught up with them.

"In here," Nicholas said. "Hostiles and… others."

"Sentinels?" Rae asked, and he nodded.

He flashed them all a look, checking they were ready for the next wave, and although they appeared exhausted, he knew they'd fight tooth and claw. Literally.

Shoving open the door, he crashed straight into a Harvester, but he'd already sensed the woman was there and he kicked her legs from under her. She hit the floor and he plunged the dagger into her chest.

A second guard cracked a whip at them, but Dawn caught the whip and Rae blasted the Harvester into the stairwell, slamming the door.

Breathlessly, Nicholas scanned the tenth floor.

It was an open-plan office. There were desks and computers and, beyond them, huge windows that stared out over the Thames. Harvesters hopped onto the desks, trampling stationery and screens as they charged.

"Guard the door," Nicholas told Dawn and she stationed herself at their backs as he, Rae and Isabel tackled the Harvesters. Isabel incapacitated a handful using an incantation that temporarily stole the Harvesters' sight, and Rae set one on fire, seemingly by accident. The man's screams were awful. Rae put him out of his misery with the blunt end of a fire extinguisher.

"There'll be more," panted Isabel when they had subdued every Harvester that had come at them. She looked exhausted and Nicholas felt the tiredness as a weight attempting to drag her down. She resisted with her trademark stubbornness.

"There." Nicholas pointed to a couple of narrow corridors that seemed to lead to meeting rooms. "In there."

"We'll go," Dawn said.

Nicholas nodded and went to the elevators. "I'll keep an eye out here."

The three women divided into the corridors and he peered out of the window at the city. Flashes of fire lit the streets nearby. Explosions at London Bridge, Monument, and Borough Market. The others were doing their worst. He hoped they were okay. Further afield, buildings crumbled spontaneously, as if they were as exhausted as the Sentinels fighting amid them. He watched in awe as chunks fell out of a tower block, which then caved in completely, blasting ash and debris through the streets.

"Nicholas."

The tightness in Dawn's voice caused a lump to constrict his throat. She'd returned from the corridor, her eyes huge.

"In here," she said, gesturing back the way she'd come, and something about her expression rendered him silent. Leaving the elevators, he followed her.

And then he felt it. Weak but unmistakable, a trickle of warmth like syrup, close enough that it was torture, and he crossed the space in a dream, knowing what that feeling meant and finding that he could barely breathe.

"Merlyn."

The door was already half ajar from Dawn entering, and Nicholas hurried into a dark cell.

It had been a conference room at some point. He could tell from the blinds, the whiteboard in the corner and the desk with the weird phone. They all added to the surreal quality of a world gone mad; one that had forgotten what an office was used for before it was a place to shackle prisoners.

All Nicholas cared about was the figure in the chair, his legs and wrists bound in place, his chin to his chest.

# CHAPTER NINETEEN
## ROOM 23

FOR THE FIRST TIME IN A long time, Nicholas's mind was blank; free from the froth and foam of other people's emotions. He forgot about Isabel and Dawn standing by the door. Or Rae, who he sensed further down the corridor. All he saw was Merlyn. Alive. His heart beat a slow patter that filled Nicholas's ears.

He was by Merlyn's side in a flash, touching his hair, tentative at first, unsure, but when he felt it was really Merlyn, he ran his fingers over the teenager's face. The contours were both familiar and strange because Merlyn had been beaten, the swelling altering the terrain of his features.

"Merl, can you hear me?"

Nothing. Then a flutter somewhere in the depths of his mind, like a butterfly in a cage.

"Merlyn. It's me. I'm here."

Another internal twinge and then Merlyn physically twitched in the chair. His chest heaved, and Nicholas helped lift his head, grimacing at the bruises and dried blood. His blond hair was snarled and still full of ash from the forest. Merlyn's eyelids creased and finally flickered open.

Fear spiked in Nicholas's gut again. Would Merlyn's eyes be cold and hard like Sam's were after he'd been taken? As Merlyn blinked at him, though, his green eyes struggling to focus, all fear melted away.

"It's you," Nicholas breathed.

"You… you know anybody else this handsome?"

His voice was brittle as eggshells but, in Merlyn's bruised face, a glimmer of his cheeky smile danced, and Nicholas felt tears constricting his throat.

"Here." He struggled out of his backpack, which was suddenly uncooperative in his haste, and retrieved a bottle of water, pushing it to Merlyn's mouth. Merlyn gulped, his sore lips making Nicholas suddenly angry. The relief that Merlyn hadn't been turned snapped into rage at how he'd been treated. Malika had left him to suffer as an insult to Nicholas.

When Merlyn couldn't drink any more, Nicholas began to untie his wrists. Merlyn gasped as Nicholas peeled the rope away, exposing deep, raw grooves in his flesh.

"I'm sorry. I'm sorry. Oh God, I'm sorry."

His ankles were easier to release, although they were equally sore, and Nicholas kept apologising, over and over, not just for the ropes but also for allowing this to happen. Allowing Merlyn to be captured and tied up and used as a punching bag.

Free from his restraints, Merlyn slid from the chair and sank to his knees and Nicholas went to the floor with him, kneeling before him and wrapping his arms around him.

"I thought…" He couldn't say it.

"Tough cookie, me. No crumbling…" Merlyn sounded a little more like his old self and the weight of his head on Nicholas's shoulder made him feel intact again, somehow, like something vital had been missing.

He wanted to know everything. What they'd done to Merlyn. What they'd told him. The lies. Had they tried to break him? Find out everything he knew about Nicholas and the others? But he couldn't bring himself to ask, not with Merlyn in his current state. Maybe not ever. All that mattered was Merlyn was alive.

"I have to tell you something," said Merlyn.

"What?"

"About Malika."

Nicholas frowned. "What about her?"

"She's going… to the Shard," croaked Merlyn.

Nicholas smiled, choking and laughing and squeezing him tighter.

"Easy," said Merlyn.

"Sorry."

"I didn't tell you to stop."

Nicholas wiped the grime from Merlyn's forehead, studying his face, forgetting everything. Nothing outside of this room mattered anywhere near as much as this.

"Been busy saving the world?" asked Merlyn.

"Trying to," said Nicholas, and he remembered he was being selfish. Even beaten and bruised, Merlyn had a way of reminding him what was important. "We're on the tenth floor. Office or something. We're heading up to the top. To the Prophets."

"Gonna kick some supernatural booty." Merlyn sounded so tired.

"Basically."

"Big booty, the Prophets."

"I know."

"You can do it."

"Guys." Dawn's voice came from the door. "They're trying to get in through the stairs. And the elevators won't stay jammed for long. We can't stay here."

Nicholas nodded and pushed Merlyn back so he could gaze into the bruised landscape of his face. As if understanding that he had to move, Merlyn nodded and Nicholas helped him to his feet, but Merlyn's legs shook uncontrollably and he sank to his knees again, sweating through a grimace.

"Not so fast," he wheezed. He couldn't have been given any food or water since he was captured and his body was a trembling wreck. Nicholas bit down the anger, knowing he'd get his chance at revenge soon.

"We have to," he insisted, hoping that by being stern he could fire Merlyn up, get him moving even if it was the last thing he felt like doing.

They tried again, but Merlyn couldn't get up. They were back on the carpet in seconds.

A walking stick struck the floor beside them and Nicholas looked up at Isabel, her expression steely. He'd forgotten she was there, still by the door with Dawn.

"Help him," she said.

"I'm trying."

"Not like that. Trinity's sake, are you a Sensitive or not?"

"I… what can I do?"

She slammed her staff again and huffed. "Lend him a portion of your energy."

Nicholas frowned. "I can do that?"

"Of course. You are an empath, boy, innately graced with the ability to manipulate energy. Give him some of yours. Help him."

All he had to do was look at Merlyn to know it was worth a try; there was no way Merlyn would get out of here as he was now. Besides, Nicholas was the reason for his sorry condition. If he could help redress that imbalance, it was the least Nicholas could do.

He didn't know where to start. The kiss of life seemed too cheesy to be a real thing, so he drew Merlyn close, wrapping his arms around him and pressing his palms against his back. He felt the steady beat in his ribcage. Heard his breath in his ear. Clearing his mind, he twinned their breathing, imagining that every exhalation poured white light into the air around them. He imagined it encircling Merlyn, following the rivers of his veins, sinking into his skin. Warmth. Life.

Merlyn gasped.

"Wow, who needs caffeine?"

Blinking, Nicholas came out of the daze and found Merlyn beaming at him, his bruises partially healed, the whites of his eyes shining.

"It… worked."

"Not too much, I hope," Merlyn said. "You okay?"

"Actually, yeah." Nicholas didn't feel weakened by the transaction; quite the opposite. He stared down at his hands in disbelief, the creases in his palms glimmering with red and white light. He clenched them into fists and breathed into his belly, sensing an awakening. A swell of confidence. It took him a second to realise that what he was feeling was Merlyn. Whatever it was that existed between them, they had both been nourished by it.

"Okay," Dawn said from the door. "Merlyn, welcome back, really glad you're alright, but we really should move like ten minutes ago."

"Glad Dawn's still calling the shots around here," Merlyn said, getting steadily to his feet and giving Nicholas a hand up. He saw that the grooves in Merlyn's wrists where the ropes had bound him had now faded to silvery lines. Soon there would be no sign he'd been tied up at all.

Shrugging back into his rucksack, feeling the weight of the collars within, Nicholas caught Isabel half-smiling at him. In an instant it was gone and with a swish of her purple kaftan she swept from the cell. Nicholas went after her, Merlyn just ahead of him. They went back into the main office by the elevators and Nicholas saw that around a dozen more Sentinels had been freed from their cells. They congregated around Rae, gratitude etched into their exhausted faces.

At the door to the stairwell, Nicholas heard grunting and sensed Harvesters preparing to batter their way inside, but then a sharp lasso of pain seared through his mind. His gaze flew to the elevators and he saw that the counter above the central elevator was counting down from forty.

"It's her," he said, sensing Malika. The others flanked him quickly, Rae and Dawn on one side, Isabel and Merlyn on the other. The newly released Sentinels gathered at their back, some brandishing office equipment as weapons – computer chords and splinters of desk wood. Together, they watched the numbers count down to ten. Then stop.

The elevator dinged.

The doors parted and Nicholas saw red, but the figure who stepped forward wasn't Malika.

It was Sam. He was wearing a dark red suit and a reptilian smile, his beaten fedora on his head. He must have salvaged it from the train wreck, but it looked wrong on him now. He wasn't the Sam that Nicholas had loved. He was like his evil twin. A twisted version of Sam Wilkins.

The old man surveyed them. Behind him, at least a dozen Harvesters were crowded into the elevator.

"Sam," Merlyn said.

"No." Nicholas raised an arm in front of him. "It's not him anymore."

"Wouldn't you love to think so?" Sam's voice was lazy and drawling. "That'd make it easier for you. To believe the old man's dead?" The serpentine grin spread uncomfortably, as if Sam was dislocating his jaw in preparation for a meal. "He's in here watching everything. And he's screaming. Ah, such sweet music."

"The others," Dawn said, and Nicholas's gaze flicked to the other two elevators. More were descending. Unease slithered through his belly. He'd sensed Malika, so where was she? On her way down now? Or were his powers out of whack? He didn't have time to figure out the answer, though, because then the other elevators dinged and their doors opened. Two dozen more Harvesters jostled forward, pouring through the doors. A cat-like demon pounced ahead of them, launching itself at Rae and, just like that, chaos erupted.

Harvesters charged at Sentinels, and all around Nicholas, he sensed the sharp ending of life, like earth being piled onto a campfire. Blades severed veins and punctured hearts and Harvesters and Sentinels alike became casualties, their bloodied corpses collapsing.

At the centre of it all, Sam advanced slowly on Nicholas, fitting a gauntlet to one hand.

"What happened to him?" asked Merlyn, slipping his hand into Nicholas's.

"Malika."

"Can we–"

"Always wondered what one of these felt like," uttered Sam, raising his hand so that blue lightning crackled between the fingers of the gauntlet.

"Don't engage," Nicholas told Merlyn.

"Come, come, boys, let's not be impolite." Sam sneered and, just in time, Nicholas sensed the Harvesters charging at his back.

"Merl!" he yelled, spinning to punch the Harvester. Merlyn drop-kicked another and Nicholas caught sight of a group of Sentinels rush at the cat-like demon, skewering it and forcing it against the window. The glass shattered under the demon's weight and it screeched as it toppled out of the building, dragging a Sentinel with it. The wind ate their screams.

A polished shoe swung at him and Nicholas caught it before it could crack any of his ribs. He panted, staring up at Sam, and then dragged Sam's leg out from under him.

*It's not him*, he thought to himself. *It's not Sam. It's not Sam.*

He whipped a dagger from his belt but then something barrelled into him and he found himself somersaulting. In the confusion, he lost sight of both Merlyn and Sam, staring up at a bare-chested Harvester whose torso was carved with symbols, including a three-headed monster.

He hurled a psychic grenade at the Harvester, whose eyes went bloodshot. The man screamed and covered his face and then Nicholas spotted a prowling, reptilian creature about to pounce at him.

Rolling out of the way, he found himself outside one of the elevators. The doors pinged open once more, but the car was empty. A rush of adrenaline flooded him and Nicholas felt an irresistible urge to roll into the elevator and go higher. Scale the Shard.

It took him a moment to realise it wasn't an urge, it was his senses telling him where he had to go. He was being drawn up and, just like a few days ago when he succumbed to the call of his old house on Midsummer Common, he couldn't ignore the pull.

"No," he murmured, spotting Isabel facing off against Sam. He couldn't leave them.

As Nicholas clambered to his feet, Isabel caught Sam across the face with her stick and shot Nicholas a commanding stare.

"Go," she urged him. "Just go. Now!"

"Merlyn," he said, but Merlyn was on the other side of the office, wrestling a Harvester with a tattooed skull. He still couldn't believe how much Merlyn had recovered. And he'd done that. It was Nicholas's energy that now coursed through Merlyn, and Merlyn's through him.

Nicholas hesitated a moment longer and then hopped into the elevator. The last thing he saw as the doors closed was Sam backhanding Isabel across the face and Nicholas had to bite down the impulse to seize the doors before they closed and go to help her.

His panting filled the quiet of the elevator. His hand moved forward and he found himself pressing the button marked '35', the highest this elevator would go, even though he had no idea what lay in wait on that floor. His body was responding to something beyond himself and he hoped it was the Trinity guiding him, maybe even the collars, and not Malika. Silently, the lift began to climb, and Nicholas tried not to imagine it as a coffin.

"The Prophets. The incantation. The Trinity."

He whispered to the elevator, attempting to reassure himself that he was doing the right thing. He didn't have a choice. This was the end of the world and only he could save it. The burden was his to bear and, as much as his friends were in danger on the tenth floor, they would face certain annihilation if they ended up in a room with the Prophets. They'd already lost so much.

Merlyn was okay. Merlyn was alive. Nicholas had to focus. Let Merlyn do his thing and trust that he'd make it out of this in one piece.

*Upstairs,* he told Rae using their special connection.

*Upstairs?* Her voice echoed in his head.

*I'm going up, follow me when you can.*

She didn't reply and Nicholas assumed she was busy fighting. He attempted to sense Kai and the others but the space between them was too confusing, polluted with the Prophets' dark energy, so he tapped into Malika instead.

*She stands staring up at the Shard.*

*The street is soaked in blood.*

*And she is vibrating with the chaos around her.*

Malika had joined the fray outside. She never could resist the battlefield. All that stood between him and the Prophets were a few more floors.

33... 34... 35...

The doors opened and Nicholas crept out into a plush hotel lobby. The Shangria-La Hotel was only halfway up the Shard. He had to find a way to keep going upwards.

*Up, up,* the voice inside urged, and Nicholas swept through the lobby, finding another set of elevators and getting in. There were more numbers in here, counting up to 95, the very top of the Shard. He didn't need to hit any of them, though, as '46' lit up the second he stepped inside. As the elevator climbed, Nicholas shrugged out of his backpack in preparation, feeling the collars through the waterproof fabric, repeating the incantation in his mind.

*Vita gregaria hemlock ressa vie.*

*Vita gregaria hemlock ressa vie.*

The elevator slowed. The number '46' shone at him and Nicholas balled his hands into fists, his nerves nearly fraying, thinking of Merlyn and how close they were to being free from all the insanity.

The doors opened.

Nicholas found himself staring at a soft-lit corridor. The wallpaper was cream with curling gold designs that resembled deep-sea creatures.

No Harvesters charged him. No demons. He edged into the corridor, the hush unnerving. Doors lined the walls, more than he could count. The hotel was bigger than he had imagined, and Nicholas moved as if in a dream to the door marked 23.

It was already ajar.

He stepped into the room and found a lounge that resembled something straight out of the 1920s. Everything was white or gold. Bronze statues nursed orbs of light and the sofa formed a perfect C around a low glass table. Above it, a chandelier twinkled, and a huge window offered a view of London.

And sitting watching him was Malika.

Nicholas froze. She shouldn't be here. She was outside killing Sentinels. He'd seen it only moments before, using Diltraa's connection.

"Welcome." That prickly purr always made his skin tighten around his flesh. She didn't get up from the sofa. Dressed all in black, she sat cross-legged, her skirts pleating petal-like around her legs. Nicholas thought of old movie stars and smoky jazz cafes. Malika had always looked out of place everywhere he'd seen her. In the upturned bus; the Moyses Hall Museum; Hallow House. Not here, though. Here she made sense. Time had coughed her up and she had finally found her place.

"You… You're—"

"Not meant to be here?" Her teeth flashed. "You're surprised?"

"I—"

"You were expecting me to be fighting in the streets with the dogs? Is that it?"

He pressed his lips together. His blood was already boiling. He squeezed the strap of his backpack, his free hand going to the dagger at his hip.

She'd tricked him. Somehow. Perhaps she'd sensed him tapping into the connection, but did she know about Diltraa, too? Or did she simply believe Nicholas was using his powers as a Sensitive?

In a ripple of black, Malika rose from the sofa. She swept to a drinks cabinet by the window – through the floor-to-ceiling glass panels, the city festered in gloom. "My, but we got cocky." Malika poured herself a glass of something honey-coloured and dropped a needle onto a record. A trumpet trilled through the lounge. A woman with a husky voice began to sing about summertime and easy-living.

"You thought you could outwit the hand of the Prophets. Charming, really." Malika's laughter threatened to shatter the chandelier and all he could think about now was the Prophets. He eyed two doors across the room. Could Malika's masters be in there?

"Where are they?" he demanded.

"Now, now. Patience isn't just a first name."

She was enjoying this. As Nicholas circled the sofa, he noticed a couple seated at the far end. An elderly woman and a man. Neither had eyes and their bodies were stiff with rigour mortis.

"Did you enjoy the train ride?" Malika asked, swaying to the music.

"No worse than any other I've been on."

She observed him over the rim of the whiskey glass. "You are so determined. Few your age possess such tenacity. It is a formidable quality; I should know. I thought you might enjoy the train. And now look at you. Split in half with a gooey demon centre. The lengths to which you're willing to go are admirable."

So she knew. Of course she knew. Diltraa was her father. She must have smelled it on him the second she saw him in the woods the night she killed Jessica. She'd tricked him; used Diltraa against him, drawn him to the Shard for this final meeting.

"Daddy always had a temper." Malika's cat-like eyes gleamed. "I've always been more placid. Must have inherited it from *her*."

"Don't talk about her." The thought of Jessica and Malika being in some way linked still made him feel like he was losing his mind. They couldn't be more different.

"Mother? It upsets you to think of her with her heart torn out? Her suffering is over. Yours is only just beginning."

Malika turned her back to peer down at the city and Nicholas's shoulders tensed. The drujblade was slung between her shoulder blades, nestled in a leather holster. He could tell she wanted him to see it. All he had to do was cross the lounge and finish this, drive the blade into her heart, but his feet refused to move.

"You like the place? I wanted to spruce it up before the Trinity's puppy arrived."

He ordered his legs to step forward but they wouldn't obey. Why couldn't he move?

"Londinium, they called this settlement once. Perhaps we shall reclaim that name, if They take a shine to it. I was always a fan. *Londinium.* It's grand, no? Inspires memories of empires and blood. We shall fashion a new empire of chaos and glory."

"You can try." He could still speak. His body was refusing to cooperate, but he still had that.

She twirled and nudged her hips from side to side, her eyes shining at him. He realised she had drained the couple on the sofa and she glowed with vitality.

The record changed. A whiskey-smooth voice sang about being in heaven.

"Oh, let's dance. What is it they say? Deny a lady a dance and deny her the world."

Malika swept toward him and although his muscles howled at him to run, he couldn't. Then she was upon him and her hand was in his, the rucksack on the floor, her black fingernails entwining with his. His legs jerked to life and although he resisted with everything he had, he couldn't prevent himself from stepping into the rhythm. They tiptoed forward and then back, and then they swept in an arc through the lounge.

Nicholas's skin crawled. She smelled of metal and liquor. Her face was so close he could smash their skulls together, clamp his teeth around her nose, but his body wasn't his anymore. He had never danced like this before, but his body was moving as if he had trained for years.

"Isn't this wonderful?"

Malika sighed, as if they were enjoying a moonlit evening out.

Nicholas struggled to stem the bubbling panic. For now, she wanted to dance, but what if she commanded him to plunge the Drujblade into his throat? There had to be a way to break the enchantment. He pressed his mind towards hers, feeling for the threads of her consciousness, but they were slippery and he couldn't grasp them the way he could the Harvesters'.

There must be another way.

"She made you," Nicholas said, seizing onto the one thing he really knew about Malika. "Not on purpose, but Jessica still made you. You're part of her."

"I was. No longer. I have outgrown anything she ever was."

"There's some of her in you. There has to be. You wouldn't exist without her."

"Perhaps, but look who remains." She rested her head on his shoulder and her red curls almost smothered him. The Drujblade was so close. If he could just unlatch one hand and slip it across her back, he'd have it. He could end her right here.

But she had complete control over him. He was her marionette, subject to her every whim, and he realised this was his fault. He'd absorbed Diltraa's energy, twinned himself with the demon, and Malika was exploiting that.

"He is in there." Malika whispered. "Daddy. He wants to come out and play." She pressed her ear to his chest and Nicholas's insides shuddered. Diltraa spasmed and attempted to claw its way out.

"No." Nicholas's voice came out strangled. His ribs were contorting outwards, the thing inside him threatening to crack them in two.

Malika raised her head and the pain vanished. Nicholas was caught in her cat-like eyes and he saw red flecks in them that he'd never been close enough before to observe.

"He was a nuisance, a necessary evil," Malika purred. "I'll not be the one to release him. I allowed him to perish in Hallow House. He fell under this very blade, bested in battle by Esus. I have a feeling he won't be in a forgiving vein for some time."

She was right. He could feel Diltraa's rage.

"Come, let us visit the nursery."

As suddenly as it had begun, the dance ended. Malika released him. Nicholas tested his feet and found they were under his control once more. As Malika turned, he went to seize the knife from her back, but his hand refused to cooperate.

"Play nice," the witch said as she sauntered away.

Cursing under his breath, Nicholas followed her. Hopelessly, he spotted his rucksack on the carpet, the collars whining at him from within it, and he tried to bend down to pick it up, but his body wouldn't comply. Malika had eased her grip, but she hadn't let go of him entirely. All he could do was go after her.

The Drujblade taunted him from her back and he curled his fingers into a fist, trying to figure out a way to get his hands on it. There had to be one. The Skurkwife wouldn't have imbued him with Diltraa's essence if it was all for nothing. Then again, the Skurkwife had been a Chaos Priest. Perhaps Merlyn had been right. The Skurkwife couldn't be trusted. Perhaps the priest was in league with the Prophets after all.

He tried to remain calm, but in the confusion, he'd failed to fully digest what Malika had said. The nursery. That could only mean one thing. She was taking him to the Dark Prophets.

Swallowing the stone in his throat, he tried not to imagine how they'd kill him. He was utterly defenceless. The collars were in the backpack and he had no weapons. He felt like he was bound for the gallows.

They left the apartment and went down a corridor lined with Harvesters. They reached a set of stairs and climbed. Nicholas tried to pay attention to where they were going, but his mind was getting foggier with every step he took.

Now they were in a spa reception, the old holistic aromas mixing with something sharper. A pair of Harvesters stood on either side of a set of double doors and, when they saw Malika approaching, they pushed them open to reveal the pool area. Nicholas followed her inside.

"It is as if they built it knowing, one day, it would serve this very purpose," Malika said as she paced around the pool. Water reflected onto an elaborate ceiling that resembled the curled pages of a book, and the room resembled something out of the past. A Greek bath with marble floors and dark wood stalls.

Nausea spasmed Nicholas's stomach. He couldn't tear his eyes from the objects in the pool.

No, not in the pool, but *on* it. The glass coffins rested on the surface of the water as if they weighed nothing. Inside, things twitched as if in response to the spasms in his gut, and bile seared the back of Nicholas's throat. Already, he felt their fingers scraping at his skull, looking for ways inside, and they were so gentle, it was all he could do not to permit them.

"They're hungry," Malika purred. "And who better to serve up as the first meal of the Dark Prophets than the child of the Trinity?"

He recognised the coffins; he'd seen them before at Hallow House. Jessica said they had once contained the Trinity, the divine waters preserving them. Malika had put something new in the coffins. She had brought them all the way here so the Dark Prophets could rise from the ashes of London.

"It is time," said Malika, beaming as her gaze caressed the glass coffins.

Unable to look anywhere else, Nicholas found himself following her gaze. Something within the central coffin trembled. A dark shape. It jerked and twitched and then a bone-white hand slipped over the edge of the coffin and the first monster gave birth to itself.

# CHAPTER TWENTY
## Chaos

THE THING THAT ROSE FROM THE coffin was unlike anything Nicholas had ever seen. His chest cramped painfully, his heart convulsing, and he forgot everything that had happened to bring him here. Every moment. Every demon. Every cross word or smile or choking tear. It all shrivelled into nothing. The world faded to grey around the naked thing that had emerged dripping from its slumber.

It resembled a man, but a demon's idea of what a man might look like. Two arms, two legs, a hairless head, rope-like muscles. But its skin was see-through, laying bare a yellowish skeleton that nestled in the transparent jelly of its muscles. No organs. Just sickly half-flesh and bones. A mockery of a man. The nightmare Nicholas had been having.

The Prophet stood in the coffin with its back to him, perhaps bewitched by the windows and their view of London. Nicholas prayed it wouldn't ever turn around. If he looked into the thing's face he'd go mad.

The creatures inside the remaining coffins slid away their lids and meticulously eased themselves up. They were identical in every way. They didn't move like newborns but beings in full control of their every motion, first sitting, then standing. Together, the three Prophets appraised the city. All Nicholas could hear was the ripple of water and a high-pitched whining that must be panic.

**The world.**
**It darkens.**
**It wails.**

306

Their voices vibrated through the air, making the pool water shudder. Every hair on Nicholas's arms prickled. He wanted to crawl out of his skin.

"Londinium," Malika purred at Nicholas's side. "It is ours."

The central Prophet turned.

And Nicholas thought his head had exploded.

Pain like nothing he had ever experienced seized his skull. It was as if the Prophet had peeled open his cranium, exposing its shivering contents, and he couldn't prevent the images clawing their way in, flashing before his eyes, each one a shard between his ribs.

*Decay and dead things. Foxes with their innards mashed into tarmac. Maggots and carrion crows and oozing fluids.*

*Anita and Max. Their corpses mangled in the remains of the water-logged train.*

Screaming. A wretched screaming echoed around the pool and Nicholas realised it was coming from his own throat. His palms were clamped over his ears and he prayed for death, anything to stem the torrent of images.

*Liberty. Dead. Her eyes sightless, her body stiff. Sam howling as Malika destroys his mind. Merlyn's face crumpling under fists. The taste of blood.*

*Rae and Dawn dead twenty floors below.*

When he thought it might never end, he found himself staring at the floor. He was on his hands and knees, choking sobs, sweating into his armour. His mind reeled with what he'd seen. His sister's dead body. And his friends. They couldn't be dead. He'd have felt it.

There was movement in the pool. Nicholas tried to resist looking, but his head snapped up and he cringed under the penetrating gaze of all three Prophets.

They had no eyes, just gaping sockets in which pricks of purple light glowed, but he knew they could see him. Their gaze raked through him, seeing everything, knowing his darkest thoughts and deepest shame.

**The child.**

**He lives.**

**He bows.**

"Your first offering." Malika didn't bow. She stood proud, her gaze unflinching, and Nicholas jerked up from the floor, dragged to his feet either by the will of the witch or the Prophets, and he grunted fearfully as he was shuffled closer to the pool edge, his attempts to resist thwarted.

**Yesssssss.**

Their hiss echoed through every bone in his body, from his toes to his temples. Terror sank fangs into him. He was barely two metres from the Prophets, their grinning skulls trembling with pleasure, and he kept seeing Rae and Dawn's dead faces and Anita and Max smashed inside the train.

**We have so much to show you.**

**So much.**

**So much.**

"No," Nicholas grunted through gritted teeth. "Stop."

**He is weak.**

**He feels.**

**He dies.**

"He is stronger than he appears," said Malika and Nicholas wondered if there was pride in her tone. "He remains while so many of his comrades have been slain."

**Yes.**

**This offering.**

**It is fitting.**

"Do it, then," Nicholas spat. "If you're going to kill me, just get it over with."

The Prophets regarded him, and he sensed their amusement. They were all-seeing, all-knowing, older than time, and he was nothing. Less than the smallest bug under the biggest boot.

**Let us show you.**

**What will happen.**

**Our glorious reign.**

"No," Nicholas whimpered but he knew he couldn't stop them.

Frozen in place, he watched helplessly as the central Prophet stepped over the rim of the coffin and into the pool. It moved through the water effortlessly and then rose before Nicholas, its rigour-mortis grin unchanging as it stepped up and out of the pool. It raised a skeletal hand and clamped long fingers around Nicholas's head.

*Fire. Blood. Erupting volcanoes. Plagues. Ash.*

*Armies of demons.*

*Monuments fashioned from the corpses of men and women.*

Nicholas lost all sense of time. The images whirled before him and he felt their truth. This would happen. The Prophets were going to destroy everything.

*Portals opening. Realities collapsing.*

*This world falling, and the next, and the next.*

*Until the universe is plunged into chaos.*

The fingers unlatched from his skull and Nicholas vomited at the Prophet's feet. The other two Prophets had joined the first. All three of them stood dripping in a line.

**He sees.**

**He knows.**

**He cannot stop it.**

"Why?" Nicholas panted. "Why do you want that? What can it possibly accomplish?"

**Chaossssss.**

Their blissful hiss travelled straight through him, along with their thirst for carnage. He couldn't remember any feeling other than rage.

If Rae and Dawn were dead, Merlyn and Isabel might be, too. He couldn't bear to think it. He was on his own. There must be a way to defeat the Prophets. He had been chosen by the Trinity. He could do it.

The incantation. Perhaps it would work without the collars.

*"Vita gregaria—"*

**Silence.**

His voice caught in his throat.

**They will never return.**

**The Trinity.**

**We are all.**

Nicholas tried to speak again but it was as if a golf ball had lodged in his throat. His mouth flapped uselessly, no sound coming out. *Don't freak out*, he told himself, fighting the tide of panic. The Prophets wouldn't break him. He was the Trinity's emissary. There was a way, there had to be a way.

Perhaps just thinking the words. He could project them the way he projected his mind. If he just concentrated hard enough, he might be able to give the words shape without the use of his voice.

*Vita gregaria hemlock ressa vie.*

*Vita gregaria hemlock ressa vie.*

"There are others," he heard Malika say to the Prophets. "Sacrifices to help you gain in strength."

**Summon them.**

The Prophets spoke as one and their spitting voices broke Nicholas's concentration. As Malika swept from the room, he watched as the Prophets turned as one and paced slowly to the windows. They gazed out at their domain.

**So ripe.**

**So ready.**

**Such chaos exists already.**

Nicholas tried to move but he was still frozen on the floor by the pool of his own vomit. He attempted to speak but nothing came out. Though they appeared distracted, the Dark Prophets hadn't relinquished control over him. His mind was still his own, though.

*Vita gregaria hemlock ressa vie.*

*VITA GREGARIA HEMLOCK RESSA VIE.*

He screamed the words in his head, imagining them as fireballs hurtling at the Prophets, but they were as ineffectual as cinders. The Prophets seemed unaware he was doing anything whatsoever.

Nicholas felt weak from the exertion, but he refused to give in.

*Rae?* he asked. Their connection was all he had left now. Perhaps she was nearby; on her way up through the Shard, coming to help him.

*Rae? Can you hear me?*

Nothing. No response.

Either she was too far away to hear him, or she was caught up fighting.

Or she really was dead.

He wouldn't believe that. *Demons lie.* That was the number one rule. Demons will do anything to convince you that the darkest possibility is a reality. He wouldn't buy into the things the Prophets had showed him.

Their prophecies clung to him, though, and he found it difficult to think. His head was full of fog and fear. There had to be something he could do. There had to be something…

The collars.

They were still in Malika's room. Perhaps the incantation wouldn't work without them. He had to get away from the Prophets, retrace his steps back to Malika's room and retrieve his rucksack. That was the only way anybody would survive this.

He heard shuffling footsteps and his eyes swivelled to the side. A couple of armed Harvesters entered, shoving a weary line of Sentinels into the pool area. Their eyes darted about them, first seeing Nicholas, then the coffins, before finally they fell on the Prophets. Soft wails came. A young man's knees buckled at the sight of them and a Harvester kicked him in the ribs before dragging him to his feet.

Nicholas's eyes bulged at the Sentinels as they were lined up against the wall. Twenty of them at least. He wanted to say something. Reassure them or demand they fight. And then he remembered what Malika had said. Sacrifices. This was why she had been taking Sentinels alive. This was why the train had been full of them.

They were going to be fed to the Prophets.

The witch swept down the line, skipping over the tiles before the Sentinels.

"Where are your Trinity now?" she sang. "Where are your saviours? Behold! Welcome the true gods; the all-powerful Prophets, and tremble in their divine presence!"

The translucent figures by the window paced slowly towards the Sentinels. The intended sacrifices cringed away from the old gods, pressing their backs to the wall.

"They're inside," one of the Sentinels whimpered. "They're in my head. Trinity spare us…"

Nicholas wondered if they were seeing what he'd seen. The world burning. Chaos reigning. The looks of fear and devastation on their faces suggested they were.

The Prophets left the Sentinels and returned their attention to Nicholas.

**Let them see.**
**Let them watch.**
**Their saviour falling.**

Nicholas gasped. An invisible hook was wrenching his insides upwards. His body lurched up from the floor and he hung suspended in the air before the Dark Prophets, whose voices rustled as they approached. They were talking to one another in a strange, guttural whisper and he sensed their hunger. It overwhelmed him and for a moment it felt like *his* hunger. He wanted to devour and consume and destroy.

**A delicacy.**
**So fresh.**
**Such power.**

He fought an insane impulse to laugh. Perhaps this was what happened when death – true death – stared you in the face. You lost your mind. Forgot your name. Your loved ones. All you could do was laugh.

**Yesssssssss.**

Although they stood motionless, their talons raked his mind, not searching for ways in but carving their own path. Penetrating his skull effortlessly, as if it was made of nothing but smoke.

Impulsively, he threw up every barrier he could; everything Liberty had taught him and everything he'd learned on his own in the bleak months since Ginnungap corrupted the world.

Instead of protecting him, though, the barrier seemed to nourish the Prophets. The pits of their eyes glowed mauve and he sensed their strength growing as his limbs grew heavy. He was still hanging in the air, pinned there by their will, and he'd never felt so tired, not even after a battle. It was an unnatural weariness rooted in his soul. He was being hollowed out second by second.

The trio of gods raised their see-through hands and twisted their fingers into claws, their grinning visages causing agonising spasms to cramp Nicholas's stomach.

Through the pain, something flickered in the depths of his consciousness. He tried to focus, though the effort exhausted him further, and then he caught hold of the thought struggling to the surface.

Demons.

The Dark Prophets weren't gods. They were demons. All this talk of them being glorious and divine and above everybody... it was nonsense. They were demons just like every other demon he had ever encountered.

*How do you fight a demon? With another demon.*

With Diltraa.

Nicholas's head felt like it was being shredded from the inside. He struggled to separate everything that was cramming into his skull. The Sentinels' fear. Malika's delight. The Prophets' hunger. His own thoughts were scrambled, lost in the white noise of emotion. He couldn't do anything with this din weighing him down.

Steeling himself, he focussed on blocking out everything. First, he dimmed the light on the Sentinels. Then he turned the volume down on Malika. Finally, he threw a wall up around himself; one strong enough that it'd take longer for the Prophets to break through.

Then he called for Diltraa. In an instant, the demon's hot essence flared and Nicholas grabbed it, nursing it within the palms of his mind.

*There*, he thought. *There you are.*

Diltraa couldn't reply. The demon had been absorbed into Nicholas's DNA. Nicholas had won. It wasn't separate from him anymore but part of him. Everything the demon had been was now at Nicholas's disposal.

Breathing deep into his stomach, Nicholas summoned every scrap of power available to him, gritted his teeth and strained against the Prophets' control.

"SSSSSTOOOOOOOOOOP!"

His bellow reverberated around him and silence fell like a guillotine.

The Prophets withdrew, and Nicholas gulped a grateful breath, able to think again, no longer crippled by their hunger.

He remained suspended in mid-air, but by his own will now, not the Prophets'. Focussing on the floor, he lowered himself, aware that all eyes were on him. He sensed the Sentinels' uncertainty and Malika's venom.

Most of all, he felt the Prophets' rage.

The central figure raised a hand and slashed the air. Pain sliced his chest and a livid red wound opened, but it was just a flesh wound, nothing he hadn't dealt with before.

"My turn," he said, and he summoned Diltraa's energy, hurling it in an arc at the trio of demons.

The Dark Prophets took an unsteady step back but remained where they stood.

"Okay, it's a start," Nicholas grunted, preparing to launch another assault, but already he felt the Prophets reaching for his mind again. This time they weren't just hungry; they were determined to crush him. Force him to his knees and blow him apart.

Their will wasn't as strong as before, though. Diltraa's energy was shielding him, and even when he felt Malika striving to exert her control over him, Nicholas brushed her away like a spider.

**What has he done.**

**He is not pure.**

**He is corrupted.**

Nicholas scoffed. "Says you." He turned to address the Sentinels. "Fight it. Don't look at them. Don't let them in–"

Before he could finish, Malika dealt a stinging blow to his cheek and he tasted blood. His lip throbbed.

"Silence," she spat.

Nicholas wiped his mouth and smiled, staring at his hand, which was now back in his control. "You don't get to tell me what to do anymore."

"I tire of your–"

He punched her. Malika reeled backwards. As she prepared to retaliate, a number of the Sentinels seized her from behind, grunting with the effort of restraining her.

As Malika shrieked and hissed, Nicholas spun to face the Dark Prophets. He gasped as the central Prophet swept upon him. It seized his face and every terrible thing it had ever seen crashed before Nicholas's eyes.

"No," he grunted. "No."

**Yessssssssss.**

**See.**

**See it all.**

Struggling to free himself, Nicholas balled his fists and pounded the Prophet. It barely registered the attack, but he felt its irritation and then his feet left the floor once more. He hurtled across the atrium and plunged headfirst into the pool.

The water closed over him, flooding his nostrils, and Nicholas somersaulted, unable to tell up from down. Floundering, he thrashed with his arms and legs and glimpsed the ceiling. He kicked up, breaking the pool surface and choking down a watery breath.

Across the room, he saw Malika, doused in arterial spray. The Sentinels who had jumped her lay dead-eyed at her feet. Nicholas sensed something beside him and he choked as a body bobbed beside him, its head torn free. It was another of the Sentinels who had apprehended Malika. The pool was turning red.

Worse, the Prophets had rounded on the remaining Sentinels. They reached out for them, and the Sentinels cringed back into the wall, frozen in terror.

**Now.**

**Yes.**

**Nowwwwww.**

"Cowards!" Nicholas bellowed.

The central Prophet turned its head, peering at Nicholas out of the corner of its eye.

"They're defenceless, and you're just going to kill them!" he continued. "That makes you cowards."

**They'll die.**

**Even with weapons.**

**They cannot prevent it.**

"And here I thought you only had eyes for me."

Malika was flexing and curling her fingers into fists. "Just kill him! He's nothing to you! Kill him and we'll dance on his corpse!"

They regarded her for a moment, perhaps weighing whether or not her outburst counted as insubordination. Then the Prophets moved for the pool once more.

A sound stopped them in their tracks. Nicholas frowned, unsure what had made it. It sounded like somebody tapping on glass, but he couldn't tell where it was coming again.

*Tap. Tap. THUMP.*

His gaze spun to the windows and his eyes widened.

Tiny black things were smashing the glass. Hurling themselves in waves.

At first, he had no idea what was going on; he'd almost forgotten what birds looked like. Then he saw them, hundreds of darting shapes, different colours and sizes, all of them swooping in a current before crunching into the panes.

"What the—"

Blood smeared the glass, but the birds hammered on, becoming a seething mass that obscured the city, and then the cracks appeared, spidering out.

"It's him," said Malika. "The half-breed."

Nicholas couldn't think what she meant and then the first pane shattered. The sound of wings filled the room as the birds poured inside, their chaotic jumble buzzing in the air. They ignored Nicholas and the cowering Sentinels, surrounding the Prophets. Pecking. Gouging. Shredding.

The air was alive with them and Nicholas whooped, although he still had no idea where the birds had come from nor why they were so ferociously attacking the Prophets.

Then he spotted the raven and his heart leapt.

Esus.

Finally.

The raven landed by the pool and in a burst of black light became the shrouded figure of Esus. The Trinity's emissary wasted no time, seizing Malika and hurling her into one of the marble statues. Nicholas heard the crack of her skull against stone and, as she reeled, Esus swept toward the seething mass of feathery shapes surrounding the Prophets.

An awful, ear-piercing sound made Nicholas's vision blur. The Prophets were screaming; not with fear but unbridled fury. The floor trembled and the pool water vibrated around him.

He watched as birds dropped lifelessly around the three figures, stiff with death, and then Esus was upon them. Nicholas tore his gaze from them to check on the captive Sentinels, and his temples began to pound when he saw an object lying on the tiled floor.

The Drujblade. It must have come loose when Esus struck Malika. Not daring to breathe, he swam to the pool edge and dragged himself out. Malika was rising from the floor, her forehead bloody, and the dagger lay between them, taunting him.

Ignoring the weight of his waterlogged armour, he launched himself across the floor.

Before he could reach the dagger, though, Malika was in front of him. She seized his hand, wrenching it upwards and pressing her face close to his.

"How's the arm?" she spat.

"Better." Nicholas rammed his forehead against hers and she released him. "Thanks for asking." He kicked her in the stomach and Malika tumbled backwards. Bending down, Nicholas swept up the Drujblade. His fingers tingled at the contact and, as he summoned Diltraa's energy, the blade spat and sizzled with green fire.

"Now this is more like it!"

He cast a look over his shoulder at Esus. The Trinity's emissary had raised a gloved hand at the Prophets and they seemed unable to move, their transparent flesh pecked to pieces by Esus's army. Whatever Esus was doing, it was working.

The phantom's mask shone at Nicholas.

"Finish it," he growled.

Nicholas nodded and squeezed the Drujblade, facing Malika, whose beautiful features were blood-smeared and twisted with anger. This wasn't going the way she had hoped, and she clawed at her dress in agitation.

"You want the dagger back?" Nicholas asked.

Her gimlet gaze reflected the green fire and he couldn't tell if she was worried. He remembered all the times he'd fought her before; the way she'd used his own mind against him; the barriers she'd created around herself so that his attacks became ineffectual. He'd grown since then. His powers were greater. More his and more in his control.

*"That is how you will fight,"* Esus had said in the woods all those months ago, when Nicholas had first used his power to get into somebody's head.

Now was Nicholas's chance to show Esus how far he'd come. Clenching his teeth, he wiped the water from his face and trained his vision on Malika, striking her with the serrated blade of his mind, feeling for the cracks in her defences. There had to be some way in.

Malika snarled, and they flew at each other. Nicholas parried with the Drujblade while continuing his mental assault, but Malika was always there, one move ahead, mirroring his every turn. She'd had five-hundred years to practice. He was an infant by comparison.

Then he found it. The piece of her that was a twin to Diltraa. The demon part of her; an ugly swelling like a molten hunk of rock. He clenched a psychic fist around it and Malika shrieked, her fingers snaking into her hair.

Finally, he had the upper hand. Mentally squeezing the demon stone, he landed a blow to her jaw and she staggered away, stunned. Seizing his moment, he knocked her to the floor and threw himself on top of her, the Drujblade poised in mid-air.

"No," Malika whimpered.

All he had to do was plunge the dagger. But then he felt the tremor. Not the floor but a psychic shudder of unease. He'd recognise that primal energy anywhere.

Esus.

Something was wrong.

Still shoving Malika down, he turned to see that the Prophets had healed. Their transparent skin gleamed, free from the bird's gouges, and the pits of their eyes shone with a sickly purple luminescence.

Esus crouched before them, shuddering, and Nicholas knew the Prophets were in his head, tearing at chunks of the phantom's mind like carrions, leaving nothing but shining bone.

"Esus," Nicholas murmured. He prepared to plunge the Drujblade into Malika's chest, but Esus's pain blasted through him like a freezing wind and Malika seized upon his distraction, striking Nicholas's jaw. The blow sent him tumbling across the wet tiles and Esus's pain was too much to bear. He could feel every molecule of agony the phantom endured as the Prophets burned their way through him.

Struggling to his feet, Nicholas shoved Malika aside and, roaring, he charged for the Prophets.

But he was too late.

The central monstrosity laid a hand on Esus's cowled head and the phantom emitted a howl that chilled Nicholas's soul. White and orange fire erupted around the Trinity's emissary, consuming Esus, and the stench of sizzling flesh and feathers singed Nicholas's nostrils.

Then the figure that had been Esus blasted apart in a torrent of smoke and ash.

The detonation reverberated through Nicholas and he collapsed to his knees.

Esus's mask clanged to the floor, spinning for a second and then lying still. Embers danced where he had crouched, and they flurried around the Prophets before drifting out through the shattered windows.

Something bludgeoned Nicholas in the back of the head and he fell onto his front. The Drujblade was wrenched from his fingers and he felt Malika on him, her hot breath in his ear.

"See now, the power of the Prophets. Nothing can stand in their way. Not the raven. Not the Trinity. Not *you*."

His face was pressed to the cold tiles and he could barely breathe. Choking and gasping at the reality that Esus was gone. One of the oldest creature he'd ever encountered had been obliterated in the blink of an eye. Exhaustion whittled at his strength and he still felt Esus's pain; his howl had been awful.

*Merlyn. Dawn.* He couldn't let that happen to them. He had to fight. But he was so cold now, bound in his wet clothes and squashed against the floor. It would be so easy to give in.

Then he heard the sounds.

Cries and shouts. An explosion.

*Hang on.*

Not his voice in his head but Rae's. She was close. But his grip was slipping.

*I can't stop them. They're too powerful.*

*Just hang on.*

*My bag, the collars*, he thought at her, but she didn't reply, and he feared the Harvesters had got her, but then the doors across the room burst open in a blaze of cinders, and Rae charged inside.

Instinctively, Nicholas threw a shield up around her to protect her from the Prophets and, as Rae lobbed volleys of flaming missiles at the Prophets, Nicholas glimpsed Merlyn, Isabel, and Dawn. They helped the remaining Sentinels out through the door and, somehow, Nicholas found the strength to reach into Malika's mind again, locating the Diltraa twin and crushing it.

The witch shrieked and he was free. Grabbing the Drujblade from her fingers, he prepared to bury it in her chest, but then he sensed Rae weakening, the shield around her depleting.

*You can't stop them,* Nicholas thought at her. *We have to fall back.*

Rae's face was set with determination as she pushed the Prophets back. An invisible barrier seemed to be protecting them, and although the barrier was aflame, the Prophets remained untouched.

**She is the Trinity's second.**

**Such power.**

**We must have it.**

"Nick, come on!"

Merlyn beckoned from the door and Nicholas hesitated. Then he saw that Malika had dragged herself to the other side of the room and he knew this wasn't his moment.

"I'm thinking of giving the place a makeover," Rae said through gritted teeth. "Better move."

Clenching the Drujblade, Nicholas hurried to Merlyn's side. He looked as exhausted as Nicholas felt, and they wrapped their arms around each other as they went into the hall and raced to join Isabel and the others.

Behind them, the room exploded.

# CHAPTER TWENTY-ONE
## THE PRICE

"WAIT, WAIT, WAIT."

Nicholas wasn't sure if he'd said the words or thought them. His ears rang with the sound of the explosion and his bones were still rattling. The hallway was choked with smoke and debris and half the floor had caved in, but he stopped abruptly as he and Merlyn reached the entrance to the stairwell.

"We can't stop," breathed Merlyn, squeezing Nicholas's hand.

"Just a moment." Nicholas squinted back the way they'd come, waiting, attempting to see through the charred air, praying that Rae was still alive. She'd survived before. The time she levelled a building in Bury, the whole thing had collapsed but she'd emerged unscathed.

*Rae*, he thought.

Nothing.

Nothing.

Nothing.

"Nick," urged Merlyn.

"We can't leave without her."

A spark lit up on his radar and Nicholas's heart leapt as a figure plunged through the smoke, running straight for them.

"Go!" Rae yelled. She was covered in ash but otherwise appeared to be in one piece. Nicholas's relief soured as he spotted shadows shifting behind her. He couldn't tell if it was the Prophets or Malika or Harvesters. They didn't stick around to find out. As Rae caught up with them, she, Nicholas, and Merlyn tumbled into the stairwell, taking the steps two at a time.

The air boiled at their backs and Nicholas waited for the stairs to give way beneath his feet, but the Shard held, despite what Rae had done.

"That was sort of extreme," he panted at her.

"Had to get you out of there." She shrugged. "Only way I could think of."

"Thanks."

"They were pretty gross."

"Demons generally are."

Nicholas could still feel them. Rae had slowed the Prophets down, but she hadn't destroyed them. He sensed their burning anger, feeling their movements in the wreckage above their heads, and he knew they didn't have long.

"Here." Rae held something out to him.

Esus's mask.

"Thought it might be important."

Gingerly, Nicholas took it from her and gasped, nearly tripping.

"What is it?" Merlyn asked.

"I can see it all." Images flickered across the surface of his mind, like light on water.

*Esus as a child. Growing up. His family. The marauding demons. Esus's terrible choice. His pact with the demon. His time with the Trinity. His determination that Nicholas win. His fiery death.*

It was all imprinted here in Esus's mask. Nicholas held on to it tightly and tried to refocus on his surroundings, bounding down the steps. Over the edge of the stairwell, he caught sight of Isabel and Dawn going ahead, helping the injured Sentinels who had been held captive.

"I need my bag," said Nicholas. "The collars."

"Where are they?" asked Merlyn.

"Room 23. Hurry."

Above them, he heard sounds of something smashing through brick and metal. The Prophets were punching their way through the building, seeking him out. Nicholas forced himself to breathe, focus on getting the collars. The memory of those purple lights burning in bony eye sockets would paralyse him if he didn't keep moving.

They caught up with Isabel and Dawn and Nicholas followed the beacon the collars were sending out to him. They were calling, their high-pitched hum filling his head. They wanted to be used. The Trinity were desperate to return. At the forty-sixth floor, he guided everybody into a hallway and then into Malika's '20s-style apartment.

It was full of battle-wearied Sentinels. He had no idea how they'd known to gather there. Perhaps the collars were already working. Uniting the Sentinels even as the Trinity waited. The floor above them shook and Nicholas scanned the floor desperately for his bag, but it wasn't where he'd dropped it.

"Lose something?"

He found Kai smirking at him, his backpack slung over her shoulder.

"Steal something?" he deadpanned as she handed it over, relief flooding through him. He felt inside, and the instant his fingers grazed one of the collars, he knew what he had to do. The knowledge hit him between the eyes like a yellow dart and he felt sick with it, but also relieved. Because now he knew. He knew the choice he had to make.

"This door," he told Kai. "Barricade it the best you can."

She nodded as the floor trembled and Nicholas felt the Prophets closing in.

"Man, I've never seen anything like this," Kai breathed, wincing at the booms of destruction that seemed to be coming from all sides.

"Yeah, big-time apocalypse," said Dawn.

"I was talking about the apartment. It's freakin' ridiculous. I mean, gold-plated lamps? Who needs that in their lives?"

"Only people who can't afford platinum," said Merlyn.

"Oh," Nicholas said. "This is—"

"Introduce us when we've survived Ginnungap," Kai interrupted.

She was right. No point wasting time on pleasantries when the world was crashing down around them.

"The doors," he reminded Kai.

"It's been an honour," she said. Before he could reply, she grabbed the nearest Sentinels and set them to work. As they went about breaking up furniture and hammering it across the doorway, Nicholas turned to Merlyn, Rae, Dawn, and Isabel.

"We need to talk," he said.

In the bedroom, he closed the door. Dawn and Merlyn stood by the bed, talking to each other under their breath, while Isabel inspected her walking stick by the window. Rae prowled beside him, her energy spitting like a Catherine wheel. She unleashed the entirety of her power so rarely; she'd had a taste fighting the Prophets and he could tell she was desperate to try again.

"Did you see them?" asked Dawn. He didn't have to ask who she was referring to. Grimly, he nodded, though he found it difficult to meet her gaze.

"That bad?"

"Worse."

Dawn and Merlyn shared a worried glance. What had they been talking about just now? He sensed their worry, but he couldn't read their minds; he didn't want to. He reached into his bag and drew out the collars.

"Time to wake up these bad boys," he said softly, fighting the nausea. "Rae, guard the—"

"On it."

"Thanks. Isabel, watch the windows." Even as he said it, she was drawing the curtains, closing them off from the outside world.

Ignoring Merlyn's concerned look, Nicholas sat cross-legged on the carpet, setting Esus's mask beside him. The collars felt prickly in his hands and their humming was louder than ever, creating a rhythm that thrummed through him. And he knew now. After all this time, he knew what they wanted.

He placed the collars in a row before him. He held his palm over each in turn and sensed their power. He smelled long grass and felt the sun on the back of his neck. They were close.

"*Vita gregaria hemlock ressa vie.*"

The collars trembled.

"*Vita gregaria hemlock ressa vie.*"

The engravings burned white gold. The light was blinding. He squinted and tried to focus but it was too much. Before he knew what he was doing, his fingers had found Esus's mask. He tugged it over his face, the charred scent of ash making him lightheaded, but it dimmed the radiance and he continued.

"Thekla! Athania! Norlath!"

The collars pulsed with light and he felt the Trinity's energy in them. A warmth like nothing he'd ever felt. It nourished his soul, soothing his aches and pains.

Screams and shouts came from the main apartment. The sound of splitting wood and people being torn apart. Filled with the light of the Trinity, Nicholas turned to look at the bedroom door. The wood creaked, and he blinked at it, watching as the wood fused tighter in the doorframe, sending out roots that forked into the wall around it, reinforcing the door.

He returned to the collars.

"Nicholas—" Dawn's voice was snatched up by an unnatural wind that had stirred in the bedroom. Waxen petals drifted around him, spinning in his gravity.

"Nicholas, you're doing it," said Dawn.

"I know."

But he couldn't look at her. He sensed what they wanted. Not the Prophets. That wouldn't work. They wanted what *he* wanted. It was the reason his power was feeling. The Trinity could only be awakened by compassion. By love. He had to sacrifice the things he loved.

"What are you doing?" Merlyn asked, but Nicholas didn't answer. As he glanced over at Merlyn and Dawn by the bed, he was overpowered by love. It was all he could feel, spreading through his veins like gold, filling him with hope.

There was a price for everything.

This was the price.

The world for the ones he loved.

He could only gain by losing.

He had his own terrible choice to make and he wouldn't flinch away from it.

Tentatively, he got to his feet and he sent his thoughts out, calling Merlyn, Dawn, and Rae to him.

"What's happening?" asked Dawn, her face hollow with fear.

They lined up before him.

"It's the only way," he said, and he made them kneel before him. Their eyes were wide, but they didn't know; they couldn't understand the way he did. This was the only way. He sensed them struggling but he was stronger.

"Boy," said Isabel, but he made her stop talking. Kept her by the window.

Of all the things he thought he'd have to do, this was never one of them.

*"Find a way, lad,"* Sam had said, and he had found a way, and it was terrible and beautiful, and he understood now. Why he'd had to embrace Diltraa. Why Nale had used his blade on the Trinity. The choices were limited, but there was always a choice until there wasn't. He couldn't let the Prophets kill his friends. If they did that, there was no point in going on. The world would burn and millions of innocent lives would crumble to ash.

"It's the only way," he said again. Dawn's eyes were glassy with tears. She knew what was going to happen.

"I'm scared," she said.

"Don't be." He found her fear and soothed it. "This is it. This is what we have to do. I'm sorry."

Merlyn and Rae were staring at him, tears in their eyes. They stared past him at the door, hearing their comrades being slaughtered, and they knew, too.

"Do it," Merlyn said.

Rae nodded and there was nothing left to say. It was on him now.

Pushing aside the uncertainty and pain, Nicholas reached down and the first collar floated up to his fingertips. He bent forward and placed the collar around Rae's throat.

"Norlath," he murmured.

The collar erupted in gold and white fire. Rae became a blazing pillar of light.

He attached the second collar to Dawn.

"Athenia," he murmured, and she too became lost in divine luminescence.

As he fitted the final collar, he tugged off Esus's mask and pressed his lips to Merlyn's.

"Thekla," he whispered, tasting tears before the blinding explosion of light.

He was knocked from his feet. His back slammed into the wall. Disorientated, he lay there for a moment, Esus's mask on the floor beside him. Then the fog began to clear, and he knew he'd done something terrible, but he couldn't remember what.

A light flickered before him, brighter than the sun, and he blinked at it, unable to focus. Gradually, the light faded, and from it emerged three figures. Their hair was whiter than the purest sands, their eyes as blue as sapphires. Their collars glimmered with gold and they smiled benevolently at him.

His friends. But not his friends.

"Nicholas," said the being that had been Merlyn. It looked just like the boy he loved, but also different.

Where the Trinity stood, the floor pulsed with a golden radiance and the wooden furniture had exploded with life. The chest of drawers by the wall had erupted with pink flowers and blossom flurried through the air, caught on a current that smelled of beginnings.

"What did I do?" Nicholas choked.

*"You did what you were born to do,"* said Not-Merlyn.

*"You have been brave,"* added Not-Rae, her expression calm and motherly.

*"You have given hope to the world,"* said Not-Dawn.

Nicholas shook his head. They looked like his friends, but their voices were different. Lighter and filled with the wisdom of millennia. His gaze went from one to the next, finally lingering on Merlyn. Something wrenched at his heart.

"You're Them."

*"We are."*

The words reverberated through him and he couldn't believe he'd done it. He'd finally accomplished what he'd been born to do, and the cost had been worse than he could have imagined. He'd chosen the world over his friends.

"My Gods," whispered Isabel. She went to the floor, bending her forehead to the carpet.

*"Isabel Constance Hallow,"* said Not-Rae. *"You have pledged your life to the plight of the world. You have sacrificed much and done so gladly. Come. Let us thank you."*

The old woman raised her head and Not-Rae cupped her chin. As Nicholas watched, Isabel's appearance changed. Her hair sprang into black curls and her cheekbones sharpened. Her purple kaftan became an emerald gown and gold rings sparked across her knuckles.

The breath caught in his throat as he recognised the woman now kneeling before the Trinity. She looked like the painting he'd seen in Hallow House; the true Isabel Hallow, who had lived five-hundred years ago. Except she was younger, more vital. Lightning flashed in her eyes and he sensed her power swelling.

Not-Rae released her, and Isabel got to her feet, clasping her walking stick, which had become a sceptre, to her breast.

"I lived only to serve the Trinity," she uttered, her voice clear and steady.

*"So now we serve you,"* said Not-Rae.

*"For the good of the world,"* added Not-Dawn.

Not-Merlyn's eyes sparkled at Nicholas and he sensed Thekla's energy, so different from Merlyn's. He wanted to weep but he couldn't. Around them, the room had burst into colour and life. The carpet eddied with blades of grass and the wardrobe had grown into the wall, its roots burrowing deep into the building.

*"Nicholas,"* said Not-Merlyn, and Nicholas found himself getting to his feet.

*"Let us look upon the world."*

The room flickered and then they weren't inside anymore. Nicholas stood beside the Trinity atop the Shard, between the three glass triangles that pointed up to the sky. Isabel lingered a little across the way, peering over a low barrier that was all the only thing between them and thin air.

"How did we get up here?" Nicholas asked.

Not-Merlyn offered him a wry smile. *"We are the Trinity."*

A stinking wind wrenched at his armour and Nicholas compelled to stare over the edge at the city. Below, demonic specks prowled the streets. He watched as buildings collapsed on the horizon, razed to the ground by nothing more than the Prophets' insidious will. They were destroying everything, piece by piece. Undoing mankind and all it had achieved.

Not-Rae's troubled gaze swept the city.

*"The Prophets' grip on the world is tightening."*

Nicholas followed her line of vision. From here, he could see the darkness spreading out beyond the reaches of London. A porous mould consuming everything in its path.

"You can fix it, though, right?" Nicholas stared into their faces, seeing a strange combination of his friends and the gods that had overtaken them.

*"We can try."*

"Try?

*"Everything is fallible,"* said Not-Dawn.

*"Even the strong,"* said Not-Rae.

*"Especially the strong,"* said Not-Merlyn.

Nicholas shook his head. "But… you're the reason we did all of this. You're the reason we fought. You have to fix it. You have to." Tears stung his eyes. "Otherwise it was all for nothing."

His parents. Anita and Max. Liberty. Sam. His friends.

They couldn't have died for nothing.

*"You demand certainty where there is none. It is understandable."*

Not-Rae placed a hand on his arm and he sensed her nurturing spirit. She was Norlath, the mother. The world was her playground.

*"We are all children in this world. Uncertain. Confused. But the more we attempt to exert control, so it becomes all the more chaotic. That is the dark wisdom of the Prophets. They endure because Man will always seek to control that which is uncontrollable."*

He didn't understand. How could they talk like there was still any doubt? The Trinity were the only things that could restore the world to the way it had been.

The ground trembled and Nicholas heard splintering glass. The Shard groaned, as if an enormous weight had come to bear upon it.

*"It is time,"* said Not-Merlyn.

Nicholas squinted at a hatch that led up into the platform. A dozen nightmare creatures prowled into view, rippling with the darkness, baring fangs. Another figure appeared, and Nicholas's throat constricted. Sam. The old man's face was bruised, and Nicholas couldn't remember what he'd looked like when he wasn't this monstrous thing.

Sam's gaze glimmered at Nicholas before turning to the Trinity. At first, he seemed confused, but then he noted the collars and his mouth puckered into a leer.

"Oh my, this is quite the twist, lad."

More Harvesters emerged behind him, brandishing weapons. Some threw nervous glances at the Trinity, while others licked their broken teeth and seemed more determined than ever to prove that good would never stand in the way of evil.

Another hatch popped open on the other side of the platform and Nicholas watched as Kai emerged, followed by a stream of Sentinels. In an instant, the fighting erupted, but Nicholas couldn't concentrate. He felt the Prophets rising through the Shard, pulverising everything in their path.

The clash of steel rang, and Nicholas sealed his mind off from the dying thoughts ricocheting around him. He couldn't handle that on top of everything else. He searched the battlefield, sensing her before he saw her.

Malika tore out a Sentinel's throat and emitted an ululating cry. Her breast heaved and then she noticed Nicholas watching her and her blood-speckled expression darkened with amusement.

"How many is that now?" she asked him, inspecting her fingernails. "I lose count. They're all so forgettable. You, on the other hand. You're full of surprises."

"It's over," he told her, although he was still filled with doubt. "This is the end."

She grinned and her teeth were red. "I'm looking forward to getting my fingers around that beautiful brain."

"And this is why you don't have any friends."

He hurled a psychic spear at her and brandished the Drujblade, which erupted with green fire. Undeterred, Malika swung her fists, cuffing his temple, and he ducked, swinging, missing. She was fast. The battle was as much in their minds as their fists. He threw everything he had at her and Malika returned in kind. He felt her cracking Jessica's ribs as she punched a hole in her chest. Smelled the tang of blood and saw Jessica's sightless corpse; the still-shuddering heart being plucked free.

"She was delicious, did I tell you that?"

He blasted the image apart and it was replaced with Merlyn in his cell. His screams shredded Nicholas's nerves and Nicholas dug into Malika's memories as he swung the Drujblade at her. There. The Pentagon Room. The site of Malika's birth. Her despicable entry into the world. Jessica splitting down the middle. Forging a hybrid monstrosity.

"You're not real," he yelled, using Esus's mask as a shield. "You're nothing. You shouldn't exist."

Malika snarled as she dealt a blow to his jaw. "Chaos is my father, ambition my mother. You'll never know the delicious sweet nothings that have whispered in my ear since birth."

He heard a shout and saw Zeus streaking through the Harvesters, knocking them over and lunging for their extremities. Nearby, Nale hefted an enormous sledgehammer, dealing blows that took Harvesters out like bowling pins. The decoys had all arrived to help fight the Prophets' forces.

He spotted Isabel throwing sparks at Sam. Her green eyes gleamed with enchantments.

"Do not force me to harm you, old man!"

"Did you love him?" crowed Sam. "Did you dream of cosy nights by the fire?"

Isabel cracked him over the head with her sceptre and the Harvester went down on one knee, blood trickling between his eyebrows. Isabel dealt another blow and Sam's eyes rolled back in his head. The Harvester collapsed before her, whether unconscious or dead, Nicholas couldn't tell.

Then everybody froze. The floor trembled and Nicholas sensed the poisonous thoughts of the Prophets. They all heard them. The Prophets were smashing their way up through the floor. Bang. Bang. *Bang*. A pale fist burst into the air and Nicholas shuddered at the see-through flesh and the skeletal hand it contained. The Dark Prophets clawed their way up through the hole in the floor.

Silence fell over the battlefield as the Prophets rose, finding purchase and assessing their surroundings.

Horror crashed around Nicholas. Sentinels and Harvesters alike trembled in the presence of the Dark Prophets.

The purple sparks in the Prophets' eyes burned into every one of them, and then their rictus grins spread wider.

They had spotted the Trinity.

A whistling screech poured from their throats, full of joy and fury.

**It is now.**

**At last.**

**The final battle.**

Around them, Sentinels howled, throwing their hands to their ears and collapsing. Nicholas felt the Prophets polluting the air with parasitic energy, attacking the Sentinels from the inside out.

**Watch them.**

**See them squirm.**

**Watch them die.**

"*Enough!*" roared Not-Merlyn. He reached behind his back and drew a blade of golden light from the air. Not-Dawn rubbed her palms together and flexed to create a golden bow, while Not-Rae summoned spells that flickered and spat in her hands.

Nicholas sensed another presence and saw Isabel was whispering into her sceptre, which pulsed with light. As she worked her magic, the Sentinels lowered their hands and rose from the ground. She was shielding them from the Prophets.

He had to do something. But he'd failed to uncover the Prophets' names and he'd absorbed Diltraa, rendering the demon useless. There had to be something.

As one, the Trinity charged at the Prophets. Not-Dawn set loose a series of flaming arrows and Not-Rae pummelled them with crackling spells. Not-Merlyn swung his fiery blade at one of the skeletal figures, but the Prophets raised a protective barrier and the Trinity were cast backwards. They tumbled, their weapons extinguishing, and they only just prevented themselves from toppling over the edge of the Shard.

The Prophets turned their simmering eyes on the battlefield and hissed.

*DIE.*

They spoke as one, raising a skeletal hand each and pointing to the Sentinels. Lightning blasted from their fingers and three Sentinels blasted apart in clouds of ash. They didn't have time to scream.

"Stop!" Nicholas bellowed, attempting to feel his way into their heads once more, but Malika seized him and shoved him face down.

**DIE.**

Three more Sentinels exploded into ash.

A figure bowled forward hollering at the top of his lungs.

Nicholas strained to see and caught sight of Nale.

"Nale," he grunted. "What are you doing?"

The Hunter hefted his sledgehammer and charged at the Prophets, bellowing as he went. As he swung the hammer, it looked as if he might succeed in mulching one of the figures, but at the last second, the Prophet caught the hammer in its fist. One of the others seized Nale by the throat and lifted the enormous man from his feet as if he weighed no more than a scarecrow.

**The traitor.**

**So willing to die.**

**He desires to prove himself.**

Nale pounded at the Prophet's arm but it wouldn't release him.

**Then die.**

Nale roared and before Zeus could reach his master, the Prophet snapped Nale's neck. The Hunter dropped to the floor.

"Nale!" Nicholas yelled, but it was no good. Nale's head lolled lifelessly to one side. Zeus whimpered as he licked the dead man's face and for a second it seemed the wolfhound was considering charging the Prophets, but the dog resisted, lying down beside Nale, nudging the man's hand.

Nicholas's gaze roved between the Prophets and the Trinity.

They were too evenly matched. The Trinity wouldn't be able to defeat them. There had to be something he could do. He had raised the Trinity, but there must be more. This wasn't it. It couldn't be.

He stared at the unconscious body that used to be Sam, remembering what the real Sam had said to him.

*"The names of things, they're not just names."*

"Names," Nicholas whispered. His gaze slid to the Prophets. Could he get into their heads and uncover their true names? There must be a way. But as he snaked his thoughts forward, he felt Malika and the Prophets blocking him. There *must* be a way.

"Malika," he uttered.

If anybody knew, it was her.

Struggling in her grip, Nicholas hit her with everything he had, thrashing with his limbs and his mind, and Malika stumbled backward. As Nicholas drew himself up, clutching the flaming Drujblade, she growled at him, baring her teeth.

"You know their names," he said, and he could tell from her reaction he'd struck a nerve. Her brow furrowed and she snarled once more. "You know them, and you're going to tell me, one way or another."

"Just make me."

"I was hoping you'd say that."

He pounced, plunging the Drujblade towards her throat. She caught his hand and strained to prevent the blade from finding its target. Grunting with effort, Nicholas forced down with all his strength, the muscles in his arms screaming with the effort, but Malika slipped to one side, dodging his blow, and the dagger bit only the air.

"Tired?" the witch drawled, dealing another blow to his jaw, landing it in exactly the same spot she had struck him when they fought by the pool.

Nicholas lashed out with his mind, hurling psychic darts at her, and Malika stumbled. He found the misshapen stone deep within her that was Diltraa's twin, the core of her being, and wrapped his mind's fist around it. Malika gasped.

He took his moment, leaping at her. She caught the chest plate of his armour, but she was dizzy, confused by the ferocity of his inner and outer attack, and he wrestled her to the ground. Determination ticked in his temples. He felt the dead with him. Her every victim. He saw the train through her eyes. His sister's dying moments. The innocents she'd killed, and their strength filled him, flooding him with urgency.

"You can't," she hissed, "you're nothing. You can't." And her eyes wheeled about the battlefield, searching for blood, the one thing that would give her strength. But he had her pinned to the ground.

He heard the Trinity attacking the Prophets once more. The floor trembled and the sound of smashing glass echoed around them as the Shard cracked and splintered under the weight of the assault.

Malika spat and clawed at him, but Nicholas was more driven than he'd ever been. Malika had the one thing he needed to end the Prophets once and for all. He reached into himself, summoning Diltraa's dark energy. He sensed her next move as her talons went for his throat, and he swatted away her blow as if they were playing a game.

The Drujblade blazed green fire.

And this was it.

His moment at last.

Releasing a triumphant cry, he plunged the Drujblade into her chest.

Her cat-like eyes bulged up at him.

She choked. Spat blood.

He sensed her confusion. Her rage. And, beneath it all, a sickly admiration.

"Tell me," he ordered, and she cackled as black blood speckled her lips.

"You did it," she gurgled.

"Tell me!"

He scanned the corridors of her mind, which were already dimming, searching for those three words that would free the world.

"I saw this moment," Malika said. "The night you were born. I saw you. Here."

He ignored her, tearing aside the barriers of her mind. Then he found it. A dark room where a purple light flickered. She attempted to slam the door on it, but she was too weak. Nicholas hurtled into the room and seized the light.

And he had them.

He knew the true names of the Prophets.

He went to leap up, but Malika lurched from the floor, seizing his wrist and slapping a dirty hand over his mouth. She was whiter than the moon, her eyes big and searching.

"They'll write stories about me," she gurgled. "The Prophets' queen. I'll live forever."

Nicholas wrenched her hand from his mouth. "They'll forget. People always do." He held on to her, the woman who had killed Anita, Max, Jessica and Sam, the one responsible for all this chaos, and he realised he'd beaten her, but he didn't feel any differently.

Malika convulsed with a strangled sort of laughter. "Hell hath no fury..."

Then her gaze went blank and she was gone.

Nicholas let her collapse to the floor, whirling away from her. The Trinity and the Prophets fought in a storm of sparks and blinding light. Where the Trinity moved, the floor erupted in tongues of greenery. Tree roots burst through the floor, twisting around the Prophets' feet. The Prophets wheezed and hurled dark energy in every direction, withering the roots and sending rivers of lava oozing across the floor.

Taking a deep breath, Nicholas screamed at the top of his lungs. "Odium! Chao! Vilkria!"

Silence fell over the battlefield.

The Prophets stood motionless.

Around Nicholas, Sentinels and Harvesters alike froze, perhaps sensing exactly what he did. The heaviness in the air lifted and Nicholas filled his lungs with air that tasted less noxious by the minute.

The Trinity met Nicholas's gaze.

The Prophets looked unchanged, but Nicholas could feel that something was different. He paced slowly toward them, unafraid, seeing them for what they were.

"Odium, Chao, Vilkria," he said. "Now we can name you. You aren't the Prophets. There's nothing supreme about you. You're demons. A disease. You don't belong here."

The Prophets hissed at him and one of them raised a skeletal hand. Nicholas's feet left the floor and he hung in the air.

"Stop," he said, and he lobbed a psychic grenade at the Prophet, whose grip slackened. Nicholas dropped to his knees and then got up, throwing a barrier around the Prophets, containing them. His entire body tensed with the effort of keeping it in place, and the veins in his temples throbbed, but he had them now.

"You won't harm another living thing. Your time is over." He sensed their weakness and before he was conscious of what he was doing, he had gathered up every scrap of pain he'd ever felt. The grief. His parents. Sam. His friends. He took every painful emotion that had ever made him weak or tired or hopeless and he fed them into the Prophets, whose whistling shrieks were music to his ears.

**Humanity is weak.**

**It will fall.**

**It is inevitable.**

"No," Nicholas said. "We're done with you."

He nodded at Not-Merlyn, who hefted his sword and plunged it into the chest of the central Prophet. The creature's screech nearly deafened Nicholas, and one of the three sheets of glass that formed the Shard's highest point shattered, raining glittering shrapnel on the battlefield. A smile played on Nicholas's lips as he watched the Prophet burn from the inside out, drinking in its pain as its bones blackened and its see-through flesh fell away in chunks.

Seeing that the Prophets could be hurt, Not-Rae and Not-Dawn threw themselves at the remaining two. The Prophets fought with everything they had left, but they were beaten. They were mortal now. They were nothing more than demons playing dress-up.

As their Harvester army froze, aghast, around the Shard's summit, the Trinity tore at the Dark Prophets with their bare hands, easily overpowering them, peeling the flesh from the bones. Not-Merlyn buried his fist in one of the Prophets' faces, his hand bursting through the back of its skull.

The skeletal monsters crumpled.

The purple glow in their eye sockets dimmed and went out.

Triumphant, the Trinity stood peering down at the steaming remains at their feet.

Not-Rae, Not-Dawn, and Not-Merlyn surveyed their work and then gazed at the weary faces of the fighters.

Moments trickled by as the survivors digested the enormity of what had happened. Then a roar filled Nicholas's ears. The Sentinels thrust their weapons skyward and the remaining Harvesters, confused and broken, were easily apprehended. They went to their knees and their hands were fastened behind their backs. They were dragged away, pushed through the hatches that led down into the Shard.

The Trinity smiled, their skin speckled with black blood, their expressions bright and benevolent. They were radiant, their purity unmarred by the filthy remnants of their foes. As one, they moved across the battlefield, touching the fallen Sentinels and Harvesters alike.

The skin of the dead fighters glowed faintly and they looked as if they were sleeping.

When Not-Merlyn approached Sam's unconscious form, Nicholas hurried over.

"Is there any way of saving him?" he asked.

Not-Merlyn shook his head sadly and pressed a hand to the old man's chest. He released a slow breath and then became still.

*"He is at peace,"* he said, standing.

Blearily, Nicholas realised he couldn't sense anything from Sam anymore. No man. No demon. He wasn't a Harvester anymore. He had found peace.

Grief shuddered through him and Nicholas stood beside Isabel before the Trinity. The remaining Sentinels bowed and then made their way back into the building, no doubt to hunt down any remaining agents of the Prophets and spread the good news.

Nicholas realised he was still clasping Esus's mask.

"So that's it," he said.

*"The Prophets will never return,"* said Not-Dawn. *"Thanks to you."*

"What about my friends?"

Not-Merlyn's brow furrowed. *"They died; drifted beyond the veil the instant we entered them."*

Nicholas chewed the inside of his cheek. His eyes stung and he felt numb, the victory dimming in the face of what he'd lost.

He flinched as Not-Rae reached for him, stroking his cheek.

*"So much loss for such a young soul."*

He wouldn't cry. He couldn't. He couldn't imagine life without Dawn and Rae and Merlyn; especially when they were still standing before him. Themselves but not themselves.

"What'll we do now?" he asked, his voice tight.

*"We? Perhaps it is time to think about you."* Not-Rae smiled. *"You have earned a little selfishness. What do you want?"*

His friends back. That's all he wanted now. Without them, he was nothing.

"I don't know."

Not-Rae dropped her hand and shared a secretive look with her siblings. Not-Merlyn sheathed his sword between his shoulder blades.

*"We are not for this world any longer,"* he said.

"You're leaving?" asked Isabel. "But there is so much more to do. The world–"

*"Will rebuild itself even in our absence."* Not-Merlyn sounded tired, as if he had made a difficult decision. *"Our time was back then, when the waking cries of the world rang still. Now it is Man's time. You must find a way. Without us."*

Nicholas didn't know what to think. He'd spent so long trying to bring the Trinity back, it didn't seem fair that they could leave so soon – and with his friends.

*"Be kind and be brave,"* said Not-Merlyn.

The Trinity took each other's hands and their eyes shone gold.

Their legs went out from under them and their bodies flopped lifelessly to the ground. Nicholas lurched forward, unable to stop them, and landed beside Merlyn.

"No, that can't be it. It can't be."

He cradled Merlyn's head in his lap and now the tears ran freely. He glanced up at Isabel and found she, too, was crying.

"We have to do something," he said. "There has to be a way."

"Such is the price," Isabel murmured, the regret in her voice causing his insides to fold in on themselves.

He rocked Merlyn and searched for any sign of life, but there was nothing. Just a blackness.

He paused.

No. It wasn't total blackness. There was a tiny something.

A speck of light. Nicholas probed it and shook as the light grew.

Not daring to believe it, Nicholas peered down at Merlyn and gasped. His eyes were open. Merlyn blinked and yawned as if emerging from an afternoon nap.

"What… What happened? I–"

Nicholas had crushed him in his arms and Merlyn's confused muffles were caught in his armour.

"Mm-hhh-grr-haaa."

"Sorry," Nicholas said as he released him and stared into his face. The face he thought he'd never look into again without a pit of grief opening in his abdomen.

Merlyn ran a hand through his hair. "Uh, you know I love your hugs but I'm suffering a serious case of the Jason Bournes here."

"Me too."

Dawn sat up, closely followed by Rae.

Isabel's face split into a slow grin. "The Trinity are indeed merciful."

Laughing, Nicholas helped Merlyn to his feet. Then he took Dawn's hand, while Rae pulled herself up. Nicholas threw his arms around all three of them, choking on laughter, and when he finally released them, their bemused expressions only made him laugh harder.

"You'll never guess what happened. Not in a million years."

Merlyn dragged the collar from his neck. "I found fame as a jewellery model?"

"We were Them." Rae's forehead crinkled with confusion, as if she was recalling a strange dream.

"You remember?" asked Nicholas.

"Some of it."

Merlyn screwed up his face. "Why does she get to remember?"

"Perk of being chosen, I guess."

"Hey, who are you?" Merlyn asked Isabel. He hadn't seen the Trinity work their magic on her, transforming her, and he was looking at her in a daze.

"I am myself," Isabel said, her eyes twinkling. "At last."

"Guys, look."

Dawn had wandered to the rail at the edge of the platform. The others joined her and stared out across London. The clouds began to peel away and the sun's rays lit up the Shard for the first time in months. The city seemed to sigh and grow still. The buildings had stopped crumbling and, in the warm light, London already looked better. Smiling, Nicholas covered his eyes and leaned in to Merlyn.

# CHAPTER TWENTY-TWO
## Together

IN THE DAYS THAT FOLLOWED, NOTHING and everything seemed to happen at once. The Sentinels who had survived the Shard bore down the bodies of those who hadn't. Nicholas couldn't believe how many there were. Sam and Nale among them.

A special ceremony was held on the banks of the Thames and Nicholas watched silently as the bodies were burned. His vision became blurry as Sam's fedora went up in flame, and he knew the old Sentinel would be glad that he was being laid to rest alongside his comrades. Sam hadn't made it to the final battle, but he had helped Nicholas defeat the Prophets anyway. If Sam hadn't told him to look for the Prophets' names, and thereby rendered them mortal, Nicholas wasn't sure the Trinity would have been able to defeat them.

The smoke roved up into a clear sky and the sun caressed Nicholas's weary face. He found himself thinking about the bedroom in Room 23 that had bloomed in the Trinity's presence, and imagined the Trinity all around them now, their golden energy trickling into every street, reviving, scrubbing away every evil thing the Prophets had wrought.

Isabel and a delegation of Hunters oversaw the destruction of the remains of the Prophets and their kin. Malika's carcass was heaped by theirs and they were taken down to the modest beach by London Bridge. From the street above, Nicholas watched Isabel consecrate the remains before they, too, were burned.

They returned to Sunny's safehouse and Nicholas was glad to find the landlord alive, although he was missing an ear.

"Thrall demon," he said cheerfully, his smile as dazzling as ever. "Nearly got me. Luckily I had a dagger hidden up my sleeve."

Sunny showed Dawn to Aileen's room, and then Rae to hers. Zeus hopped inside after her, quieter than Nicholas had ever seen him, his head slung low to the ground, and he kept thinking about Nale. The Hunter's life had been marked by remorse and tragedy, but he had died a hero's death. Nicholas wished he was here to share in their victory.

Nicholas and Merlyn took the bedroom next-door. Isabel went to the room at the end of the hall, saying nothing as she shut the door, although Nicholas could sense her exhaustion. He felt numb to all that had happened. He was both alive with a frantic kind of energy and heavy with a tiredness that ran through to his marrow. It was mid-morning; they had spent all night cleaning up the mess of the Shard.

"I'll do breakfast later," said Sunny. "Or dinner. Or whatever the hell it's called when you have a meal at a weird time."

"I'm gonna sleep for a month," said Merlyn, collapsing onto one of the two single beds.

"I'll set an alarm." Sunny winked at him and Nicholas smiled wearily.

"Are you waiting up? For the others?"

Sunny nodded.

"I can stay up with—"

"Thanks, but I can manage." The landlord winked at Nicholas again, his gaze going to Merlyn and then back. "You rest."

When the door had closed, Nicholas fumbled with his armour. His fingers felt swollen and wouldn't co-operate.

"Here." Merlyn got up and helped him undo the protective gear, tossing it to the floor. Nicholas dragged off his boots and flexed his toes appreciatively as Merlyn led him to the bed and they crawled under the sheets.

"Can we sleep forever?" asked Merlyn, his face so close Nicholas felt his breath on his cheek.

"Mmmhmm."

There was so much he wanted to say but the words got lost on their way out and he pushed his head into Merlyn's neck, smelling sweat and smoke. Underneath that was the unmistakable Merlyn scent that made Nicholas feel calm.

The nightmares lasted a couple of nights. He kept seeing the Prophets, their grinning skulls and their grasping fingers. They got in his head and, in the hazy purple dreams, they won. He watched his friends blasted to ash and he awoke hot and exhausted, caught up in Merlyn's reassuring arms.

Two days later, the aches and pains hadn't lessened much but Nicholas was almost too busy to notice. The safehouse became the base of operations as Sentinels sought advice on how to begin reparations. They all wanted Nicholas. Word had travelled quickly that the Trinity's empath had defeated the Prophets, and nobody seemed to care that the truth was more complicated and far less valiant. Like the Trinity, he was becoming a figure of myth and rumour, and Sentinels would bow when they approached him, offering him lodgings and trinkets and anything else they could think of.

"We must receive them all," said Isabel, and a room was set up for them to host Sentinels. She did most of the talking, advising the Sentinels on how to tackle the remaining demons and re-establish their communities. Aileen helped oversee the rebuilding of safehouses, hobbling around on crutches, scrutinising blueprints and constantly refilling the increasing number of teapots. She'd given Pyraemon a trim, too, combing out his matted fur, and he looked like a different cat as he followed her around, glaring at every Sentinel with an air of superiority.

All Nicholas wanted was to be with his friends. Whenever he wasn't in counsel, he had Merlyn by his side, Dawn and Rae close by, and knowing they were there made him feel safe. He'd thought he had lost them, and for the briefest moment, he really had. He'd been willing to sacrifice them to save the world, and that knowledge weighed heavier than anything else. It was a choice he shouldn't have been forced to make and it didn't matter that they had agreed to it. The burden was his to bear.

The closest they came to talking about it was the third morning, when he and Merlyn were brushing their teeth and Merlyn refused to change his T-shirt. He made a joke about being divine, and divine beings didn't have dirty laundry, and then he caught Nicholas's guilty expression.

"What's that look?" Merlyn asked, his toothbrush still in his mouth, which was foaming with toothpaste so he appeared rabid.

"Nothing." Nicholas spat in the sink.

"It's because of what we did, isn't it?"

Nicholas rinsed out his mouth and ignored their reflections in the mirror about the sink.

"Hey. It's okay."

Merlyn stopped him from turning away. The air felt thick between them and Nicholas could sense Merlyn's worry, his need to make it okay, his feelings for Nicholas, and they were so warm and simple that they melted away the guilt as if it was nothing more than morning mist.

"Kiss me." Merlyn puckered up his toothpaste-foamed mouth and Nicholas laughed, pressing his lips to Merlyn's, and then he spat and laughed some more, and that was that.

Word came from all over the country. The smarter demons had retreated, creeping underground and getting lost in the sewers. Hunters were dispatched to take them out. Nests were torched, entire buildings purged of swarms and, slowly, civilians emerged from their holes, encouraged by the daylight.

But Nicholas felt restless.

Five days after the Prophets' defeat, he went to Isabel's door. When she answered, she appeared tired and Nicholas felt a familiar pang. He kept expecting her to vanish the way the Trinity had. She was the oldest person alive, but she seemed to have picked up the life she'd been forced to leave behind five centuries ago.

"Yes?" she asked. She was dressed in a collared mauve Anarkali gown that Sunny's mum must have loaned her, her black hair in a bun. The pleated skirts and intricate patterns suited her.

"I'm going home."

"Home?"

"Cambridge."

He'd been thinking about it for the past few days. The safehouse was too small and more Sentinels were arriving every day, cramming into every available room to ask for guidance that he wasn't equipped to give.

"They have things covered around here," Nicholas said. "Dawn and Merlyn and Rae are getting antsy. Zeus, too. They need somewhere that's theirs, at least for a while."

"And there is somewhere in Cambridge?"

"My house is still there. I'm taking them with me."

Isabel studied him for a few seconds and he had no idea what she was thinking.

"Then I shall come, too," she said at last.

"You want to?" He'd assumed Isabel would stay and continue to address the Sentinels. She had been the Vaktarin, the Guardian before Jessica took that title. She had been chosen by Esus to guard and advise the Sentinel community; but that had been five-hundred years ago. Things were different now. There was no Vaktarin. Nothing for a Guardian to guard except for humanity itself, and that was everywhere.

"I should like to see your home," said Isabel, and Nicholas wondered at the sentimentality in her tone. Perhaps, finally, she was ready for retirement. He remembered the first civil conversation they'd had, back when Isabel was a cat. She had talked about their bloodline, how they were linked through the ages. As far as he knew, they were both each other's last living relative.

He realised he was relieved. He'd been expecting her to forbid him from leaving and he'd come up with at least five arguments to convince her. The last thing he'd expected was that she'd want to go with him.

"Good," he said.

The next morning, Dawn said goodbye to a tearful Aileen, who had decided to stay in London for another week to help Sentinels set up the safehouses.

They found a Land Rover in the street and Isabel unlocked it with her sceptre, then got the engine running. Nicholas sat up front with Merlyn, who drove them north through London, out into the countryside and all the way to Cambridgeshire. Dawn, Rae, and Isabel sat in the back, while Zeus had squeezed into the boot.

After pacing forlornly for a few days, the wolfhound had taken a shine to Rae and now followed her everywhere. He slept on the floor by her bed at night and Rae took him out for walks, where he brought her demon trophies. Nicholas had no doubt that Zeus would become as loyal to Rae as he had been to Nale.

When they arrived at Midsummer Common, Nicholas felt his lungs clearing, the tension in his shoulders lessening. Church bells rang somewhere in town and they had passed people in the street, sweeping and clearing the debris as if there had been a parade or a marching band rather than a demonic infestation, and he marvelled at humanity's ability to bounce back.

"So this is your place?" asked Merlyn as they approached the house on the common.

"Was. Is." Nicholas just wanted to get inside. The last time he had been here, he had felt certain he would never return. Now it was just ten steps away and his insides fizzed at the thought of reclaiming Anita and Max's house.

The front door creaked and caught stubbornly as he pushed it in. The house was a mess, but it wouldn't take long to clear it up. At the moment, all they had was time. And each other.

He gave Dawn his parents' bedroom.

"Are you sure?" she asked, tugging at her hair, an old habit he'd not seen her do in a while.

Nicholas only nodded. It made sense for her to have it; this was the only room with easy access to all the books in the hidden alcove.

Rae, Zeus, and Isabel took the spare rooms down the hall. Nicholas and Merlyn settled in Nicholas's old attic bedroom and Merlyn spent an hour going through his comic books and films.

"Yes!" he yelled, holding a DVD aloft. "You have *Evil Dead II*. I was afraid I'd never get to see it again after the whole apocalypse thing."

"More afraid than getting turned inside out by the Prophets?"

"Nicholas, this is a classic."

They fell asleep reading *Hellboy* and Nicholas slept the best he had in months. Diltraa never resurfaced, not even in his dreams; the demon had been absorbed entirely into his DNA and Nicholas knew he'd be able to keep control of it.

The next day, they threw open the windows and doors and got the house back in order. Zeus bounded around, excitedly knocking over black bags. Everybody was so happy to see him not moping that they didn't mind.

"This'd be a lot easier if we had electricity," grumbled Merlyn, leaning against a broom and rubbing his lower back.

"Tuh!" exclaimed Isabel. "A lifetime without it never bothered me."

"We can't all be a thousand years old."

The next day, the fridge began to hum.

"Grid's back," panted Dawn, racing around the house like it was Christmas. She plugged in Nicholas's old laptop and nearly wept when it powered on. In the living room, they all gathered around her and waited patiently as she hacked a Wi-Fi connection and scanned the news.

"The government's reconvening in a secret location," she said. "Blaming terrorists for an 'outbreak of mutated wildlife'. Ha! And they say something about 'chemical air-strikes' that polluted the skies and turned creatures into monstrous versions of themselves."

"Poor, deluded fools," muttered Merlyn.

"Anything about Sentinels?" asked Nicholas.

"Yeah, we deserve some credit."

Dawn shook her head. "Wait, there's something here about 'brave vigilantes' saving a pregnant woman, but that could be anybody."

"Definitely a Sentinel," said Nicholas.

"Yeah, credit where it's due," said Merlyn.

Isabel shook her head. "It is better this way. Sentinels are not glory hunters. We fight because we must."

"Sing it, sister." Merlyn flapped his hands dramatically and Isabel glared at him in a way that reminded Nicholas of when she had been a cat.

Having the internet made it easier to communicate. Dawn set up a group in something called the Dark Net where Sentinels with access were able to connect. She oversaw the setting up of teams of Sentinels in each city to eradicate the remaining demons. She held seminars teaching younger Sentinels about the different types of demon, and Nicholas loved seeing her poring over books in the living room. Research was her friend and he was sure that her tactical ideas on demon hunting were saving lives all over the country.

Life was ebbing and flowing in a way Nicholas had forgotten it could.

One day, he visited Anita and Max's graves. He went alone and sat cross-legged telling them about everything that had happened. Emotion shuddered through him and more than once he struggled to get the words out, his eyes filling with tears, but he kept going. He skipped nothing, and he was sure that somehow, somewhere, they were listening.

When he got home, he set about making dinner.

Zeus lay by the back door, snoring softly, his three paws twitching. Nicholas wondered if he was dreaming about Nale.

Merlyn leaned back in his chair, balancing on its back legs, and Nicholas shoved him upright as he went by.

"Hey!"

"You'll thank me when your brain isn't all over the floor."

"Who says I don't want my brain all over the floor?"

Nicholas stirred the pot and dipped a finger into the pasta, tasting the sauce. "You're right, it'll probably be better there than in your head."

"Fine by me."

"What's fine by you?" Dawn came into the kitchen and Nicholas nearly dropped the salt shaker into the pan. He stared at her in amazement.

"What did you do?"

Dawn ran a hand over her head. She'd cropped her hair so short it resembled Nicholas's buzz cut. It made her eyes appear larger, her cheekbones more pronounced. She looked nothing like the girl he'd met in Bury all those months ago.

"You inspired me," she deadpanned.

"Huh."

"Badass," said Merlyn, swinging back on his chair again. "I always liked a chick with short hair."

Although she tried to hide it, Nicholas could tell Dawn was pleased with the attention.

"What's cooking?" she asked, attempting to peer over Nicholas's shoulder.

"Pasta. Found it in the back of the cupboard. It's probably carbon dated by now, but it seems edible."

"Is that cheese sauce?" asked Dawn in disbelief.

Nicholas grinned. "The cows came back." It had been months since the Red Polls grazed on Midsummer Common and Nicholas had thought they were gone for good, but that morning he'd drawn his curtains to find a handful of them had returned. Isabel had helped him milk one and make cheese.

Merlyn drummed his hands on the table. "Man, I'm starving."

"You're always starving," said Rae, strolling into the kitchen with Isabel behind her. There was a lightness to Rae that Nicholas had observed growing over the past few weeks. The past no longer seemed to weigh her down. He supposed this was the longest she'd stayed in one place without having to fight to survive. She seemed settled. At peace.

"Any new cases?" he asked her.

"A few."

She had been helping get people off the streets. Finding them homes.

"That is a most pleasing aroma," said Isabel, easing herself into a seat at the table.

Merlyn's eyes rolled up at the ceiling and he shot her a mischievous stare. "'Most pleasing aroma'? Remind me to teach you some proper English."

"I am quite happy with the way I speak."

"Sure, if you want to sound like a walking stiff."

"Insolent child."

"See!" Merlyn banged the table jubilantly. "That's a rubbish way to insult somebody! You want to throw some four-letter words in there. Add a little spice. Chuck some chilli at it."

Isabel pursed her lips. "A few four-letter words have come to mind presently."

"Here we are," interrupted Nicholas, heaving the saucepan onto the table. "Help yourself."

"Ah man!" Merlyn seized a spoon and began shovelling pasta onto his plate. He noticed Isabel squinting at him and paused, then muttered something under his breath as he passed her the plate. Isabel's eyebrows went up appreciatively and Merlyn served everybody else before finally plonking a steaming plate in front of himself. He peered around the table as if waiting for permission.

"Eat it while it's hot," said Nicholas, and that was all the encouragement Merlyn needed. He attacked his pasta like he'd not eaten in weeks. Nicholas supposed none of them had seen a proper meal in a while, and definitely not something homemade.

"Did you hear?" asked Dawn. "A Harvester den was raided in Norfolk. They were planning a takeover of Aldeburgh, had this crazy idea of setting up a stronghold on the coast."

"Who took them out?" asked Nicholas.

"Actually, Kai. She has her own pack now."

"Hunters," shrugged Merlyn through a mouthful of food. "They've got a nose for that short of thing."

"We shall help." Isabel gave Nicholas a meaningful look. Every day since arriving at the house, they had shut themselves away in Max and Anita's study for a couple of hours. Together, they scanned the country for Harvesters and demons and any other nasty thing that might still be wriggling around. They fed the intel to Hunter packs around the country, who dealt with them in ways that Nicholas could only assume were deadly.

"Tomorrow," he said. "Today is just us."

Rae had sat quietly beside Merlyn as they ate. He'd promised not to interfere with anybody's emotions anymore, but Nicholas could sense her stronger than ever. They were still linked. She didn't seem to mind.

"I was thinking about going for a walk," she said. "Zeus needs the exercise."

Merlyn's cutlery clattered against his empty plate and he leaned back, rubbing his swollen belly. Nicholas was only halfway through eating his.

"I could do with some fresh air," said Merlyn.

"Now that the air is fresh again," added Dawn.

"Hey, remember that time we almost destroyed the Shard?"

Everybody looked at him.

"Well, we did!"

"Egad!" Isabel exclaimed.

Merlyn gave her a blank stare. "What the hell does that mean?"

"Is that not a four-letter word?" Isabel looked pleased with herself. "It appears there are some things you might learn, too, youngling."

Nicholas laughed and rubbed Merlyn's arm, then he got up and began to clear away. They dumped the dirty crockery in the sink and then went out onto Midsummer Common. A misty rain fell in fine sheets and Isabel strolled off to greet the Red Polls. Merlyn kissed Nicholas on the cheek before running off to play tag with Dawn, Zeus hopping excitedly between them.

Nicholas found himself strolling with Rae, whose gaze flickered from the budding trees to the river to the sky before settling on him.

"It's nice here," she said. "I like it."

"What say we stay a while?"

Just a few weeks ago, he couldn't have imagined ever returning to Cambridge. The city had been a toxic wasteland teeming with demons and crumbling buildings. But as soon as the Prophets had been defeated and the dead had been buried, he'd thought of nothing but Midsummer Common and his sister's house. He couldn't think of anywhere else he'd rather be, though he knew they wouldn't stay here forever.

The country was rebuilding itself and with Jessica and the Trinity gone, it was up to the five of them to unite the Sentinels and ensure this never happened again. To provide a solid foundation upon which to build.

When the time came, though, he wouldn't mind leaving the house behind. He glanced from Isabel to Rae and then Dawn, smiling as Merlyn tripped and stumbled, styling his fall into a crooked cartwheel that sent Zeus into a tailspin. And Nicholas knew that no matter where he was, if he was with them, he'd be home.

# ACKNOWLEDGEMENTS

HERE IT IS. THE END OF the trilogy. At times it felt like I'd never make it, and it's thanks to a number of brilliant people that I have. Firstly, my editor Jonathan Barnes at Peridot Press. You took a risk on a newbie author who just wanted to write about talking cats, and you've been amazing every step of the way. I'm forever grateful that you taught me the difference between 'kerb' and 'curb'. (And massive thanks to Nev for introducing us in the first place.) Thanks also to Scott for the seriously cool covers. I'll never get tired of staring at them.

When it's not the best job in the world, writing can be an isolating slog, so thank you to all the friends who kept my sanity (mostly) intact. Christina, John, Barbara, Lois, Kirsty, Ben, Heather, Jez, Rob, Jonny, Bobby, Rosie, Rich, Lydia, Thom and anybody else I've forgotten. You were (are) cheerleaders, idiot-detectors, (dare I say it) fans, and drinking buddies long before anybody else and I love you forever.

To the bloggers who reviewed, offered outstanding criticisms where necessary, and helped this writer grow up: thank you. In particular, Mieneke at A Fantastical Librarian and Paul at The Eloquent Page. Special thanks to my team of beta readers, including Kyra Halland and David Estes, but especially Troy H. Gardner, whose creativity is equal to none and whose hawk-like proof-reading abilities make him a writer's dream reader.

Thank you to everybody who has ever left a review on Amazon or Goodreads – you're the superstars of bookdom and without your support, books like this would get swallowed up by the machine. And to the readers who loved this trilogy from the start and who I kept writing for – Lynn Worton, Steven Coyne, Emily Ip, Jamie Barber, Simon Vandereecken, Sarah McMullan, Steve Barnes, Mark, Tom, Joe, and Anna Treherne. Without you there would be no books.

And finally, my family. Dad, you encouraged me to write, write, write, and then ask how what I've written can be better. Jess, you're wiser than you know. Meggie, you've always been there with the best advice and hugs. And Mum. You're missed, you're remembered, and you're in every page. Thank you.

# HELP US CAST A SPELL!

THANK YOU SO MUCH FOR READING The Sentinel Trilogy! If you enjoyed the series, it would mean a lot if you would consider leaving a star rating and a short review (or a long review!) for Sentinel, Ruins, and Splinter on Amazon and/or Goodreads. Books live and die by word of mouth, and your support is hugely appreciated. Oh, and if you tweet about the book (you legend), please do @JoshWinning so I can retweet and follow back. Thanks for coming on this journey with me! JW